"Best mystery/thriller that I have read in many years. The easy to follow plot thrills and builds from page one with characters who I became so attached to that I grew more and more concerned about how they could survive such an overwhelming worldwide conspiracy. I loved the ending that left only a slight hint that I might look forward to reading a follow-up novel." **Alice Cunningham**

"This thriller is riveting. Impossible to put down. Its complex plot takes all of the strong characters working together to follow their leader to death's door as they back O'Sheen's keen sense of Country, loyalty, and perception in solving an international crime. There are enough plot twists to keep the reader quite surprised. What a great read. I'm impatiently waiting for more." **Barbara McClary --- Published biographer, award winning children's author**

Online book club

Ed Sheehan's book, *Hologram Conspiracy*, is an explosive action thriller with the ability to keep the reader glued to his seat from start to finish. The story is about a one–time covert agent for the CIA – Pat O'Sheen. Told in the first person narrative, Pat O'Sheen is portrayed as a talented, selfless, and fearless warrior with no thought for himself. Blessed with a wife and 3 children, Pat O'Sheen comes upon a top government secret that sets him up for several dangerous voyages throughout the book. With an audio – graphic memory, the lives of his children, friends, and former colleagues come together to give an enchanting storyline that keeps the reader asking for more.

The book was divided into 3 parts. Each part narrated an aspect of the story that will introduce the next part. This was well done and built up the story in a realistic manner that one could easily identify with. Also, the author's choice of words was simple enough to encourage an easy flow of the story from start to finish. The story had several themes, e.g., resolution of religious conflicts which was emphasized in the story. The numerous action and confrontational scenes were vividly described leaving the reader with no doubt as to what happened. I saw myself in the scenes severally.

This contributed to the appeal of this book as a future award winning movie.

The plots were captivating, thought – provoking, and intense. You have to be on the edge of your seat to read this book. The character development was so well done that I had to pause severally and applaud the author. Male and female roles in a relationship were clearly defined without making any of the roles less than the other. This contributed to making this book an unprejudiced read, especially as pertains to the female gender. Also, Pat O'Sheen exhibited a wholesome personality that was not deficient in any area. This was commendable on the part of the author since he was the protagonist in the story. The story also had emotional moments, intrigue, suspense, romance, and humor. What I enjoyed most about the story was Dale's southern speech and accent when she was responding to the Director of the CIA's condescending attitude. Addressing a member of the team, these were her words: "Mr Kramer, somehow you have captured my man's heart as if you were one of his offspring. But the recent goings-on by your compatriots in the CIA have put my family in unheralded peril. The master of the house is not currently available, but he would want me to greet your unwarranted intrusion with utmost kindness. But I dare say, your present accompaniment disillusions me to the probability of successfully completing his wishes." This was one amongst so many of her responses with the southern accent. I saw Pat O'Sheen's strength in her and understood why she was his wife. My reason is that I didn't like how the Director of the CIA underestimated her.   **OnlineBookClub Review**

Hologram Conspiracy

By

Ed Sheehan

Cotsdale Publishing Birmingham, Alabama

This is a work of fiction. The events and characters portrayed are all created by the imagination of the author. Their resemblance, if any, to real-life counterparts is entirely coincidental.

Copyright – Ed Sheehan 2018
All rights reserved: This book, or any parts thereof, may not be reproduced or transmitted by any means.

ISBN-13: 978-0-9888596-1-6

Library of Congress Control Number: 2018909261

Cotsdale Publishing, 1176 Bristol Way, Birmingham, Alabama 35242

Dedication

To Dale, my high school sweetheart, my wife, my first editor, and the mother of our three kids and dearly loved by our three grandkids. She has always shared my love of God and our country.

Chapter One
Paris, France

I scanned everyone's face while walking through the crowded Charles de Galle Airport in Paris. Based on my expertise at spotting a tail, I was sure that no one followed me to the airport. I had been in Paris for three days investigating several threats against the American singer our business was contracted to protect. The threats against our new client made no sense, but I had to check them out. In my past careers, I had worked two undercover operations in France, and I spoke French like a local. I uncovered no threats against our client.

After arriving at the security screening area in Terminal 2A, I moved off to the side where arriving passengers would funnel through to the escalator that descended to the baggage claim area and customs. I had arrived early and had time to call my wife at home in Birmingham, Alabama where it was 9:00 a.m.

"Hello, Hon."

"Hey. Where are you?"

"I'm at the airport in Paris waiting on our son's flight to arrive with our client."

"What about the threats?" Dale's tone reflected her concern.

"Nothing. The threats against Keisha must have been bogus."

"That's great. I was worried."

Dale had begged me for years to stop accepting dangerous Army and CIA assignments. She was also opposed to our youngest son working for the CIA. So a year ago, at the age of fifty-one, I finally agreed to abandon my covert career and formed the protection agency with my youngest son.

"I knew you would be relieved.

"Dale, there are bunch of people coming from the gate area. I'll call you tonight. I love you."

"I love you."

No one else was milling around awaiting arriving passengers. I was looking forward to seeing our client, Keisha Steele. She was a nineteen-year-old new singing sensation whose lyrics depicted a struggling lower class; lyrics that reflected her life before her manager, Jonny Wright, discovered her talent. All of her songs encouraged hope. Her musical compositions were ingenious, and her crystal-clear, perfectly-pitched voice was cultured way beyond her nineteen years.

I was feeling great until a grabbing pain hit my gut. It was a familiar pain that I hadn't felt since my last undercover mission for the CIA over a year ago. Life-threatening danger almost always followed the pain in my gut. I had always considered the pain as a warning from my guardian angel, an opinion that I was too embarrassed to share with anyone, not even my wife of over thirty years. The pain made no sense in this setting. *Where was the threat? What was I missing?*

I changed my focus and started studying the faces of the people who were in the lines to be screened before entering the restricted gate area, paying particular attention to people who didn't have carry-on luggage.

Coming toward me from the gate area was my friend and former Army Special Forces comrade-in-arms, Brendan Clary. It was hard to miss his six-feet-six inch broad frame. He was leading our client and her manager as they walked behind a large group of people who probably deplaned with them. My son, Jody, followed ten feet behind Keisha and Jonny. Jody was about my size but he was better looking than me. When Keisha Steel saw me, she ran past Brendan and jumped into my outstretched arms.

There was a dark-haired man in the security screening area moving from near the front of one of the screening lines to the back of the longest of the three lines. *He did not have any carryon luggage.* I pretended not to notice and focused my attention back to Keisha "Was your flight okay?" I knew Keisha didn't like to fly.

"It would have been much better if you were on the plane with me." Keisha had a crush on me.

I advised, "We can talk in the hotel room where we are not out in the open. Go with Jody and Brendan to the baggage claim and through customs while I get my rental car to follow y'all to the hotel."

Brendan picked up on my concern. We had worked together for almost twenty years and sometimes he seemed to understand my psyche better than I did. His extremely high IQ could be intimidating at times. I shook my head almost imperceptibly to ease his concern.

As I walked away from the screening area, I stopped at the nearest set of TV screens showing arriving flights, glanced up at the screens, and then at the dark-haired man. He had already left the screening area and was walking away in the opposite direction. I was relieved that he didn't followed Keisha down the escalator.

I followed the Limo at a distance in the rental car. No one else was following the Limo, but I still had the heebie-jeebies. When we approached the hotel, the ache in my stomach intensified for no apparent reason.

I still had a dull ache in my stomach when we were getting Keisha and her manager, Jonny Wright, settled into their hotel suite on the third floor.

Brendan Clary saw my concern again and pulled me into the second bedroom and asked me what was wrong. I told him about the man at the airport and said that I was going outside to check for surveillance. When Brendan objected, we agreed to conduct an electronics sweep of Keisha's hotel suite.

The sweep discovered a listening bug under the coffee table in the common area of the two-bedroom suite. When Brendan reached to remove the bug, I stopped him. I did not want to expose that we had discovered the bug. My youngest son, Jody, distracted Keisha and Jonny as Brendan and I retreated back to the bedroom.

Brendan apologized, "How did you pick up on surveillance that escaped me?"

"I was at the airport longer than you."

Jody entered the room and closed the door behind him. "I told Keisha and Jonny that we found a listening device under the coffee table. I told them that it was probably placed there by independent photo hounds—the invasive European paparazzi."

I nodded, "Good idea, Jody. Maybe that's all it is. But I am going to check outside."

I explained my plan for moving Keisha to another room in the hotel if a threat arose and gave Jody the key. Jody liked my plan.

When I opened the door to enter the common area of the suite, Keisha jumped back from the door knowing that she had been caught eavesdropping. She approached me with Jonny on her heels. Her manager was a small man with large, dark-brown eyes, and a wrinkle-free, tanned skin that disguised his age. My trained eye could see his Cherokee Indian ancestry. He was very capable and diligent in guiding Keisha's career. Keisha was going to make him rich and famous: she was a talent manager's dream. But I believed that Jonny was more concerned about Keisha's wellbeing than he was about fame and fortune. Perhaps I was Jonny's biggest fan.

Keisha reached out both hands to me. I grabbed them in my two hands and looked into her expressive and beautiful brown eyes.

She asked, "Did I hear you say that you are going to leave the hotel?"

I nodded, "I won't be gone long."

"Jonny isn't comfortable with you leaving." *Meaning, Keisha wasn't comfortable with me leaving.*

I looked into her eyes and smiled, "I'll miss you, too. You will be safe with Jody and Brendan while I'm gone. I have to do the job you're paying me for."

"Send Brendan or Jody out." Keisha had natural beauty. Her creamy chocolate skin was flawless. She wasn't a diva, but when a photographer caught her with the right expression, her face radiated beauty.

I released her hands and saw the disappointment as her beautiful eyes suddenly lost their luster. Placing a finger under her lowering chin, I asked her for a smile. She gave me a beautiful smile, the white teeth contrasting her dark skin, but the smile lacked enthusiasm. I said,

"Keisha, my job is to cover every possible threat against you, imagined or not. I should be back in less than thirty minutes." I kissed her forehead. The pain in my gut was almost gone, but I wasn't about to ignore its earlier warning.

Turning to Jonny I instructed, "If you hear Jody's cell phone ring, be ready to help Brendan and Jody move Keisha to another room that I've prearranged in case of a threat."

I turned back to Keisha, "If you have anything that you would refuse to leave in the room temporarily, put it near the door. If we decide to move you, Jody will not allow a delay to retrieve personal items.

Jonny Wright said, "You are scaring Keisha." *Meaning, I was scaring him.*

Jonny was right. I was overreacting. At that thought, the ache in my gut intensified. "Don't worry, Jonny. I'm just being overly cautious. That is my job."

I knew that I might have raised a false alarm as I retreated to my hotel room directly across the third-floor hallway from Keisha's. I should know if my paranoia was accurate in the next thirty minutes. If I were wrong, Keisha and Jonny would be relieved and would accept my apology.

I thought about disguising myself. But when the ache in my stomach intensified, I decided to wear something that would attract attention rather than disguise my appearance. It was weird how the ache would sometimes retreat or increase depending on how my plans changed. I should have been killed many times over the many years of my perilous career. My body was riddled with bullet holes, but by the grace of God, I am still alive.

I donned a lightweight, black trench coat that came to my knees, checked my Glock 22 pistol tucked in the holster under the back of my belt, and grabbed a hat. I walked down the six-feet wide, lushly carpeted hallway to the stairs. I ran down the stairs two at a time, slowly passed through the lobby while observing every occupant, and stopped inside the swinging glass doors to scan the sidewalk.

In this nice spring weather in Paris my trench coat would attract immediate attention. My slacks and turtleneck sweater underneath were normal wear for Paris at this time of year. I wanted the predators—*if there were any*—to recognize me when I walked out of the hotel door. But if it became necessary, shedding the coat and hat would allow me to blend into a crowd.

Pushing open the right side of the glass doors, I entered the cool, refreshing Parisian air and scanned the sidewalk to my right. While putting on the black wide-brimmed hat, I scanned the right side of the park located across the four-lane boulevard from the hotel. The park occupied a full city block with streets on all four sides. It was busy with people enjoying spring in Paris. One man's attention seemed to be focused on me for too long. The man had a full black beard and wore a NY baseball cap.

I turned left and sauntered slowly along the sidewalk as cars sped by in both directions on the four-lane boulevard. I kept my head down while scanning the park from under the wide brim of my hat. After several steps, I spotted *him* on the far side of the park. He was more professional than the first man that spotted me. He was Middle Eastern and clean-shaven with short black hair. *More importantly, he was the same man I had seen in the screening lines in the airport terminal.*

In just the split second that I scanned him, I decided that he was a hired mercenary. I had encountered too many like him in my past career. This was definitely about me. *The death threats against Keisha were bait to make sure I came to Paris with her.*

I walked past a few stores while scanning the rest of the park. A third man seemed to be watching me. Another Arab who wasn't just in the park to enjoy the pleasant Parisian spring. I turned left and entered a store.

The store looked very much like an American convenience store. Three rows of shelves containing all sorts of packaged convenience items stood to my left, and a checkout counter stacked with last-minute enticements was on my right. A young, skinny, redheaded male clerk was ringing up a paying customer at a cash register. Straight ahead there was a short hallway with two bathroom doors on the left. There were also two doors on the right: the first one contained the words "Employees Only" written in English and in French. There was another door on the wall at the end of the short hallway. It was probably an exit to an alley.

My scope of the store was completed in the few seconds it took me to walk three steps into the store and turn back toward the store's glass front. I stood eight feet inside the store's plate glass windows and looked across the street toward the park. By standing that far inside the windows, I knew the sunlight outside would reflect the park's image off the glass and not reveal my observation from inside the store. The Arab from the airport was talking on his cell phone and was looking toward the guy on his left. The guy with the NY baseball cap was replying on his mobile.

I pulled my secure phone from my pants pocket and called Jody. As I waited impatiently for him to answer the phone, I noticed the clean-shaven Arab getting into a sedan across the park.

Jody answered, "Yes?"

I warned, "Jody, there are at least three adversaries in the park across the street . . . probably more. They are on the move. I think they are coming for me, **but you need to move Keisha to the other room now**."

I moved behind the first row of shelves to hide from the street when the customer finished paying for his purchase and was exiting through the front door.

After a long hesitation, Jody finally responded with a loud, worried tone, "**Dad, where are you**?"

"I'm at a convenience store three doors to the left of the hotel exit."

After another hesitation, Jody warned, "**Dad, three guys are coming for you**. Don't go out the front or back door. Go up the stairs and turn down the hallway to the left and go out to the front balcony. I'm in control here. **Move now.**" The phone went dead.

The urgency in Jody's voice alarmed me. The specifics of his instructions were confusing. I knew that Jody's five years of CIA training taught him to use Google Earth and various CIA programs to learn about every nook and cranny, balcony or staircase, in any area where his services were required. I managed to survive with quick observation for decades without computers or smart phones.

***

Jody had walked to the window when his phone rang and was peeking through the curtains while he was talking to his dad. He saw a sedan speed up to the corner to his dad's left. Three bad-looking dudes got out and were hurrying toward his dad's location. The car accelerated toward the back of the buildings.

Jody had also seen four bad-asses enter the hotel: two while he was talking to his dad, and two others less than a minute behind the first two. That was why he disconnected from his dad so quickly. He and Brendan moved Keisha and Jonny to the other hotel room according to his dad's plan.

In the new hotel room Jody suddenly gasped and ran from the unregistered room declaring, "We left the folder containing Keisha's itinerary on the coffee table." He left so quickly that he didn't hear Brendan's protest.

A minute later, Jody entered Keisha's first suite. As he reached for Keisha's folder, he heard a gunshot echo down the hallway. Whoever organized this attack knew what room Keisha was supposed to occupy. *Of course: the microphone bug.* His dad had been right. It wasn't the paparazzi.

But why would such a force come against Keisha? Jody realized that this attack had nothing to do with Keisha.

It was too late to retreat. Jody grabbed the heavy oak coffee table sitting in front of the couch, turned it on its side, and dragged it to the front of the open larger bedroom door. Seeing the listening bug still attached to the bottom of the table and he declared loudly, "Your target is no longer in the room. You will confront lethal force if you enter."

Seconds later, he heard a key enter the doorknob to the suite. *A key! The shot in the hallway must have been a maid.*

He pulled his Sig Sauer P-226 from his shoulder holster and knelt behind the heavy, overturned coffee table. Although his dad's preparations should assure Keisha's safety, he knew he would be lucky to survive a big assault from four hired killers. Brendan couldn't leave Keisha to help. Jody was trapped. If he had expected anything like this, he would have brought more people. *What was happening?*

Chapter Two
The Mystery

I ran toward the back of the store, opened the second door on the right, entered a narrow staircase, and closed the door behind me. I waited and listened.

I heard boots enter the front door and heard the redheaded clerk say in French, "What is this?" I could hear the fear in his voice. I heard the clerk yell, **"He ran that way."**

The gunshot that followed sickened my soul. Many innocents had died in my previous careers, and too many times I had to accept the term "collateral damage". I helped my son start a celebrity protection business to abandon such madness. Innocents were no longer supposed to die. I thought about exiting the door to avenge the clerk's death when I heard the crash of the back door caving in as if hit by a car. I knew that I had to move . . . *now.*

I climbed the old, squeaky, wooden stairs, turned right on a landing halfway up, and continued up. There was an arched opening at the top of the stairs, a hallway, and across the hallway a large, majestic, mahogany door. The hallway crossed to the right and left. Jody had advised me to go to the left, so after looking right to make sure the hallway was clear, I stepped to the left, backed up to the wall next to the top of the stairway, and pulled my Glock 22 from the crook of my back. My position at the top of the narrow stairway was easily defendable.

I heard the door open at the bottom of the stairs and heard footsteps ascending the squeaky stairs toward the landing. I waited long enough for them to ascend up from the landing, took a silent deep breath, spun partly into the arched opening, and aimed my Glock 22 at two men. I squeezed off two rounds in less than two seconds and the front man fell forward onto the steps—*too gracefully*. I fired two more quick shots at the second man, apparently missing him again and again.

I spun out of the doorway, went to one knee, and spun back. I fired three more shots at the motionless man. The man did not adjust his aim toward my new position. I had missed him again—*three more times! Impossible from ten feet.*

I spun out of the doorway expecting a barrage of bullets from the man. No barrage came. The whole scene didn't tally, and for reasons I could not explain to Parisian authorities later, I ran down the hallway abandoning my defendable position. Over the years, I had learned not to second-guess my impulsive decisions during dangerous encounters. I had never attempted to explain to my priest and confessor that a divine guidance seemed to lead me through my violent career. Violence and divine guidance seemed oxymoronic.

I ran down the hallway noticing that none of the magnificent mahogany doors to rooms on both sides of the five-foot wide hallway had key locks. Footsteps again squeaked as they ascended the wooden stairs behind me. I picked a door to enter on the right but slowed enough to slightly open a door closer to the stairway to act as a decoy. I went through the next door and closed it quietly behind me.

***

A key was being used to open Keisha's hotel door. Jody's heart pounded as the door slowly opened. He saw a hand holding an S&W 1911, 45-caliber pistol enter the room first. Suddenly, the door burst wide open. From behind the overturned coffee table, Jody fired off a barrage from his P-226, successfully shooting the first man coming through the door in the head and the next man near his left shoulder. But heavy fire from automatic weapons forced him to roll back into the bedroom. He slammed the bedroom door, released the mostly used magazine clip in his P226, pulled another one from his pocket, and slammed the clip into the butt of his pistol as he crawled on his knees behind the far side of the king-sized bed. He put the partially used clip in his pocket. Jody's five years of CIA training had kicked-in automatically.

Jody was shocked when the bedroom door collapsed from the top down. The man must have jumped over the coffee table hitting the top of the door with his shoulder; the top hinge broke, and a large man fell into the room on top of the collapsing door.

Dad, help!

***

The room that I entered had a large conference table surrounded by heavy, leather chairs. More chairs were positioned against the wall between two large windows that were three-foot wide by eight-feet tall. The windows were not designed to open.

I heard my adversaries enter the adjoining room that I had decoyed. I picked up one of the chairs and drove it through the large, bottom pane of a window knowing that the crash would give away my location. I was an expert with a pistol and still mystified that I could miss from such close quarters on the stairs.

I climbed through the broken window and onto a narrow balcony. The balcony resembled the French Quarter balconies in New Orleans . . . or more likely, the French Quarter architects copied one like this. It had a thin wrought iron railing and lovely designed wrought-iron risers that ascended from the top of the metal railing to support the overhung roof.

Looking to the right I saw the end of the balcony blocked off by the high-rise hotel building. The only doorway off the balcony to the right was two rooms down, and it was most likely locked. *No escape there.*

Looking to my left, the balcony was blocked by another solid wall of an adjacent building, but that building had a slightly sloping roof only eight feet above the balcony that I occupied. The last ten feet of my balcony was opened to the sky. *Getting up on that roof would have been easy for me 10 years ago.*

I considered jumping to the sidewalk below until a bullet ricocheted off the wall next to my head. I had not heard a gun's report from the street, and I didn't see a shooter. *The gunman must have used a silencer.* I knew for sure that my adversaries were professionals.

I removed my overcoat as I ran toward the end of the balcony and threw it on the railing as a decoy. I leaped up and successfully landed my right foot on top of the three-foot-high metal railing. In the same motion, I dove upward off the railing and landed on my stomach on the edge of the roof. My knees and toes slammed against the side of the brick building. ***Ouch***.

I scrambled onto the roof and rolled to my left, out of the line-of-site from the balcony, and withdrew my nine-millimeter pistol again.

Still unable to locate the threat from the street, I peeked around the eave and saw a man exiting the window I broke out. The man seemed to hesitate when he saw the overcoat that I placed on the railing for a distraction. I pulled the trigger when my aim would put the bullet through the man's left ear.

I wanted to confirm my kill, but another bullet from a silent gun ricocheted off the roof beside me forcing me to abandon my second-best defendable position. I ran in a direction away from the street, angling up the sixty-foot long, slightly tilted metal roof.

As I passed over the peak, a barrage of bullets hit the tin roof behind me. Seeing the top of what might be a fire escape to my left, I carefully approached that edge of the roof and looked down at the fire escape. I heard footsteps climbing the tin roof behind me. I knew at least one, probably more, were in pursuit.

Déjà vu! Twenty years ago, I escaped by scaling down the outside of a fire escape from the roof above a fifth floor in . . . somewhere. Too much abuse to my body over too many years made that option seem ridiculous now. *I am now fifty-one; not thirty-one.* This time, I had to turn and fight. In the last few seconds of indecision, I heard multiple footsteps climbing the long slope on the other side of the roof. The thought of missing the man from ten feet away on the stairway flashed through my mind. I put my 9 mm back in the crook of my back, turned, and dropped down eight feet to the outside railing of the fire escape that served the occupants of the top floor. My right foot made it through the vertical wrought iron rails and both hands grabbed the railing.

Secured to the outside of the railing, I lowered my feet, and released my grip to drop to the railing below. My hands grabbed the railing, but both feet hit vertical bars and didn't offer enough help to sufficiently counter the pull of gravity. My grip was not secure enough to allow another slow drop. When I dropped, I landed awkwardly on the concrete below. The severe pain in my right ankle did not distract me from my perilous predicament. I dove to my left underneath the ironworks of the fire escape just before a barrage of bullets hit the pavement in the area I had just abandoned.

I drew the Glock 22 again and moved slightly out from under the fire escape and fired. My aim was accurate and a man fell back onto the roof. *I noticed that the man fell backward too gracefully—just like the man on the staircase.*

I heard multiple sirens approaching and heard the screech of car tires behind me. I spun on my knees toward the back of the building and saw the clean-shaven Arab from the airport rounding the corner on foot with his gun-hand extended. I squeezed the trigger just before I felt a sharp pain on top of my head. *I saw stars before everything went black.*

***

Jody recovered quickly from the shock of the bedroom door collapsing. He shot the head of the next man who ran through the door firing an AK-47 on full automatic. The man who crashed through the top of the door rose to his knees and shot. The bullet hit Jody in his trapezoid muscle under his left arm at the same time Jody squeezed the trigger of his pistol. Jody's bullet hit the man in the center of his chest. Jody fell backwards to the floor, but into a position that allowed him to see if anyone else was coming through the master bedroom door. He lay there momentarily trying to recover from the pain.

Suddenly, he realized the strike of the bullet to the man's chest didn't sound right. *He was wearing a bulletproof vest.*

Struggling with his pain, Jody rose to his knees and looked over the corner of the bed as the man was retrieving his gun and turning it towards him. Jody shot him between the eyes. He heard sirens approaching the hotel. He knelt by the bed for several dizzy minutes; ready for another assault from the man he shot near the shoulder. When the assault didn't come, he collapsed to the floor into a puddle of his own blood.

Chapter Three
Pierre

Jody awoke with two men leaning over him. They were inflicting severe pain to the bullet wound under his left arm. As they started coming into focus, he saw the IV bag and realized that they were helping him. He saw a couple of uniformed Parisian policemen crossing the room. Apparently they had put him on the bed.

A wiry man in a white, long-sleeved shirt with the cuffs folded up twice and a tie loosened at his unbuttoned collar approached the bed. He asked accusingly, "**What happened here**?"

He looked like the man in a picture in his parent's family room. The familiar scar over the left ear encouraged him to ask, "Are you Inspector Boudreaux?"

The inspector suddenly mellowed and his eyes squinted, "Yes. Are you are an O'Sheen?"

"Yessir, I'm Jody O'Sheen, Pat's youngest son."

Jody expressed his major concern, "Do you know my dad's status?"

"He is on his way to the hospital. He was shot, but he will survive."

"And Keisha Steele?" The reason Jody was in Paris.

"She and a large man named Brendan Clary are with Parisian security. She and her entourage will soon be on a plane back to the States. They are cancelling the concert."

Jody's heart slumped at his failure. His whole purpose in Paris was to assure Keisha's access to success.

Pierre Boudreaux noticed the disappointment but started his questioning anyway; "I have multiple homicides here; one dead maid on this floor, three dead in this suite, and several hospital cases including you and your dad, Jody. I need some answers. You seem up to it."

Jody reflected on their mission in Paris and proclaimed, "The only way you could have found Brendan and Keisha is with prior knowledge from Dad. He doesn't trust many people. He doesn't even share the whole scenario with me. Dad must have told you why we are here."

Pierre chuckled, "Yes. Pat had me clear this operation for him. Surely you don't think the Prefecture de Police normally lets foreigners into our city carrying guns?

"But Jody, I didn't find Brendan. He found me."

Jody reflected on the comment and said, "I'll answer all your questions in a moment, Inspector Boudreaux. But I need to call my mother at home."

Pierre handed Jody the cell phone that the police took from Jody.

Jody entered the prearranged code warning and then called his mother on his secure phone.

When Dale saw the Code 2 warning from Jody and answered the call, her first question was, "**Are you and your dad okay**?"

"Dad is hurt and on his way to hospital. But in the next couple hours he will be a real pain in the ass trying to get back to you."

Dale panicked, "**Tell me what is going on? Don't tell me this is top secret. You don't work for the government anymore.**"

Despite her panic, Jody answered calmly, "Mom, Dad was attacked outside the hotel. The police say he will be okay. I have too many ears listening. You need to go to Code 2. I'll keep you informed."

Dale understood, "You are sure your dad is covered?"

"Yes, he will be worried about you."

"Are you okay? Were you hurt?"

"Mom, I'm okay. **Go to Code 2 now.**" He wasn't about to tell her that he had been shot—or *that he had killed three people.*

***

Damn, Dale thought. *Code 2.* She hated Code 2 mostly because she was rarely told what the circumstances were or the severity of the situation. She was particularly concerned now because, for the first time, her son called in the code. Pat normally called her, explained the situation as much as his covert job would allow, and told her that everything would be okay.

Dale snapped back to reality. She looked around and saw Shadow, their black cocker spaniel, sitting near the back door watching her intently. When she said, "Shadow, Code 2," he jumped to his feet so quickly that his back paws slid on the tile floor almost sending him sprawling. But he quickly recovered and ran to the hall closet door. Dale opened the cabinet door under the sink and hit the blue button on the monitor: one of four monitors that Pat had installed throughout the house during the last ten years—part of a security system that her paranoid husband had updated probably 40 times. After punching the Code 2 button, she followed the route Shadow had taken to the closet. She opened the two side-by-side slatted, folding wooden doors and pushed coats to one side. She pushed a button that caused an imperceptible panel in the back of the closet to slide open. Shadow led her through the opening to a small landing and hurried down a long staircase. Dale closed the folding doors behind her and slid the coats back into place. She stopped on the landing and pushed the blue button on the keyboard to her right that closed the panel behind her. She followed Shadow down the long staircase to another landing where a large metal door blocked further advance. The metal door had no doorknob, and the hinges were not exposed on her side.

Dale reached to the keyboard on the right side of the door, punched a code in, and the heavy metal door swung into a room. She followed Shadow through the door and pressed the blue button on the other side to close the door. Shadow gave out a quiet but tense "woof". Dale sat on the floor with her legs spread. She was wearing blue jeans and a T-shirt. Her heart was racing. *Why?* Code 2 was not that uncommon during her marriage to her covert agent husband. Sometimes she suspected that her husband was just running "fire drills" when he called the code. After all, he had spent a lot of time and money excavating the bunker below the house and installing all the elaborate electronics. But too many times when she suspected that it was just a drill, he came home with another bullet wound.

Dale had never argued with him during the installation of the bunkers beneath their house or the training process of how to respond to the codes. The effort seemed to make him happy. He felt better with his family secure. Dale had worried about the expense until she learned that the CIA had covered the expense. Their house was designated as one of the locations the CIA might choose as an alternate headquarters in case of a nuclear threat against the United States. *Whoopee!*

Shadow slowly turned away from the metal door and dropped his tense, high-alert attitude. He sauntered slowly up to Dale with his tail slowly wagging, walked between her spread legs, stepped up on her right thigh, and started licking her neck.

Dale's heart stopped racing. She realized that this Code 2 had reached down into her inner core and grabbed hold of some raw nerve that had become insensitive years ago. *This code 2 was different because this time, she knew her husband had been shot? She didn't know how bad he was.*

Shadow licked her face. The dog smelled the enzymes her body produced in her anxiety and responded with a loving animal instinct to calm her. It worked. She grabbed his head and shook it, rubbed him behind both ears as his tail began wagging happily. She could see the smile in Shadow's face that only a dog owner could recognize. Life came back into focus. Dale slowly got up off the floor and methodically finished her preparations for Code 2.

***

I awoke in an ambulance and managed to say, "I have to get to the Fontainebleau Hotel."

The paramedic's responded in French with a Parisian accent, "The only place you are going, mister, is to the hospital. You have a serious gunshot wound to your head. But you should live."

Although I realized that I was drugged and saw the IV connected to me, I felt that I had to act. **"I have to get to the hotel now."**

"Mister, even if you were not hurt, you could not get any-where near that hotel. There was a mass murder there. The whole area is cordoned off."

I panicked and attempted to reach up and grab the man, only to realize that my chest and arms were restrained. I saw the man adjust a valve on my IV. Darkness enveloped me again.

Somehow that image of being involuntarily controlled remained with me as I regained consciousness again. My years of experience told me to keep my eyes closed and listen before letting anyone present know that I was awake. *I might be in the custody of my attackers.*

I heard a deep voice softly asking someone a question. The deep voice was familiar, and I heard a calm answer come from my son, Jody. I slowly opened my eyes. My drug-blurred vision cleared enough for me to start a slow scan of the room. At the foot of my bed sat Inspector Pierre Boudreaux, and as I scanned further left, I saw Jody lying in a hospital bed. When I tried to raise my head, the pain and dizziness almost made me pass out. I lowered my head back to the pillow and turned my head and eyes toward Jody, noticed the IV in his arm, and croaked, "Are you okay?"

Jody answered "Yessir, and so are you. We are safe."

I asked, "Keisha? Brendan?"

"On the way back to America, thanks to Inspector Boudreaux. Keisha wanted to come here, but Jonny insisted that they leave."

"What precautions have . . . ?"

Jody interrupted, "Mom and the family are on Code 2."

I started to breathe easier until someone came through the door dressed like a doctor. I looked at Inspector Pierre Boudreaux who watched the doctor enter. Pierre's demeanor showed no alarm. The doctor first looked toward Jody, who gave him a thumbs up, and he approached my bed with a hypodermic needle in his hand. He checked my eyes with a penlight and spoke in French "Mister O'Sheen, you still have some brain trauma. I am going to induce another temporary coma and order another CT scan to make sure there is no swelling in your brain." He raised the needle toward my IV.

Alarmed, I said, "**Stop.**" and looked at Pierre questioningly, "Don't nurses in Paris usually administer drugs?"

Pierre replied, "I asked my cousin to handle you personally. He is the doctor who stitched up your head."

"**Time out**," I ordered the doctor. My mind was replaying the shooting scene. "Doc, was I shot from the front or from behind?"

The doctor was perplexed by my question and responded, "How would I know?"

I reached up and felt the bandage on top of my head. "Was the wound on my scalp wider on the front or back?"

"It was thinner on the right and wider to the left side."

I corrected him, "You meant wider on the right side?" *That would be a shot from the roof while I was aiming at the clean-shaven Arab at the back of the building.*

"No, I meant wider on the left side." The doctor replied.

I said, "I need to talk to the inspector alone before you inject my IV."

Pierre interrupted, "Pat, I'll be back in the morning. Jody has given me enough information to keep me up for most of the night. You two need to get your rest or you won't be of any help tomorrow. Don't get paranoid, Pat. I've got the two of you covered. No one is getting in here tonight."

My head felt like it was about to explode, but I said, "I have one more question. You said, 'Most of the night'. What time is it? How long was I out?"

Pierre chided, "That was two questions. It is a few minutes past midnight. The doc put you out for about five hours. Get some rest, and I will see you in the morning." Pierre turned and left the room.

The doctor started injecting my IV while I was turning to ask Jody a question. Suddenly I forgot the question and slipped into darkness again.

Chapter Four
More Mystery

When I awoke in the hospital room, I heard a voice say, "Hey there."

I scanned the room. *Where was I?* Looking to my left, I saw Jody in a hospital bed next to mine. My mind started clearing, "What time is it?"

"It's 9:00 a.m. Paris time. You realize that we are in Paris don't you?"

I was beginning to remember, but my mouth was so dry and my brain so foggy that I just closed my eyes to let memories roll in at their own pace. I apparently nodded off, because I awakened later with a start and had to resurvey the room. Pierre was quietly talking to Jody. The doctor, Pierre's cousin who had injected my IV the previous night, was checking my vital signs.

I croaked again, "I'm thirsty. What time is it?"

Pierre stood up and answered, "Ten-fifteen," as he walked over to my bed with a plastic cup of water. Somewhere in my groggy memory I knew that Pierre was returning a favor. After I took a couple of sips of water, I tried to sit up. Pierre took the cup of water, raised the back of my hospital bed, readjusted my pillow, and returned the cup of water to my hand.

My head was throbbing, but I was regaining control. I asked, "Jody, how did you know they were coming for me?"

"When you called to warn me, I looked down from Keisha's window and saw a sedan pull up at the corner and drop off three hard-asses who started hurrying toward your location. The sedan sped toward the back of the building you were in.

"I also saw two hostile-looking men entering our hotel and then two more followed about twenty seconds later. They obviously weren't the leaders who were coming for you. They sent the "B" team after me."

Inspector Pierre Boudreaux protested, "Jody, they were not a "B" team. Those four were some of the best mercenaries in France. They are so quick when they act that we never arrive in time to apprehend them. All we ever see is their results . . . and they never leave witnesses. I have been able to gather enough information on them to recognize their M.O., but not enough for an arrest. Thanks to you, we don't have to worry about them anymore. I'm amazed that you got all four of them, and that you are still alive. You can be on my "A" team anytime."

Pierre deflected, "Pat, tell me your story."

I felt a deep surge of pride at Pierre's praise for my son. The short explanation of Jody's plight was surreal. *Had he actually fought off a bigger threat than I was exposed to?*

I relayed my whole story to Pierre and Jody.

Pierre looked quizzically at Jody for a plausible explanation. Receiving none, he relayed the facts to me. "The clerk at the desk was killed. The window on the second floor was broken out to the balcony as you said. But Pat, there were no other bodies, no blood on the stairway to the second floor, or on the balcony, and no blood on the roof. There was a small amount of blood at the back corner of the building, and a large amount of your blood where the paramedics picked you up."

Astonished, I said, "No bodies? No blood?" My memory of the shot to the ear of the man entering the balcony from the window is vivid, as was the man on the roof's reaction to my shot onto his chest. I couldn't be sure that I had hit the man behind the building. I read the confused look in Inspector Pierre's face and asked, "Am I a suspect in the murder of the clerk?"

Pierre answered, "I don't consider you a suspect, but we have procedures that we must follow. Your gun is in forensics to check against the bullet from the clerks head."

I looked at Jody and saw the same doubt that I saw in Pierre's eyes. "Pierre, when can we get out of here?"

Pierre answered, "I'm not sure. I'm going to my office now. I'll keep you informed."

I insisted, "Pierre, we need to get home. Our family at home may be in danger. They attacked Jody knowing that I wasn't in the hotel."

He replied, "The hospital won't release you for at least two days. I need to talk . . ."

"Screw the doctors, Pierre. Get me out of here."

Pierre knew that Pat was uncontrollable. "I understand, Pat. I'll do all I can." He looked at Jody. "Thank you for your help."

Jody nodded.

After Pierre left the room, I asked Jody; "What's your take?"

"Well, Inspector Boudreaux sees a lack of evidence to support your story. I think Inspector Boudreaux believes your concussion has affected your memory. There are two possibilities."

I looked at him expectantly.

"Either Pierre's assumption of the effects of your concussion are correct, or we have a major riddle to solve. Dad, your scenario of what happened makes no sense at all."

Chapter Five
The Adversary

Abdul Faisad, the leader of the project to assassinate the O'Sheens in Paris, had his hair cut western style and was clean-shaven for the operation. Faisad knew that he had the element of surprise and assumed they could easily accomplish the objective. There was no way O'Sheen could anticipate a large assault. Abdul was very pleased to see the small protection detail that O'Sheen greeted at the airport. He had hurried back to his position in the park across from the hotel to conduct surveillance. Then he saw O'Sheen leave the hotel, which allowed him to initiate the attack.

However, the attack had not gone according to plan. He had to admit that he had underestimated Pat and Jody O'Sheen. His instructions were that Jody O'Sheen was his main target to kill, and if possible, he was to leave Pat O'Sheen injured but alive. Abdul's uncle wanted Pat O'Sheen to suffer the pain of losing a son. The fact that he succeeded in the secondary goal was irrelevant after his team's failure to kill Jody O'Sheen.

Abdul clutched the bandage on his left wrist where O'Sheen had luckily shot him, and he was uncharacteristically nervous as his younger cousin, Mohammed, dialed the number on the phone and spoke a few words in Farsi (the primary dialect of the Persians in Iran). Abdul could report that the weapon-belt experiment was successful and that Pat O'Sheen was wounded, but the fact that O'Sheen's son was still alive would not be well received. Mohammed Faisad handed the phone to Abdul.

Abdul acknowledged that he was listening.

"I hear that Jody O'Sheen is still alive." Abdul could hear the acid in the words of the sheik.

Abdul reported honestly, "The son has nine lives like his father. We underestimated his capabilities. We succeeded in putting both O'Sheens in the hospital, but Jody O'Sheen survived his bullet."

Abdul explained in detail what happened and concluded; "The new weapon worked perfectly. Parisian officials are totally baffled. O'Sheen's explanation of the events lacks credibility according to the woman I placed inside the Prefecture de Police. The authorities believe O'Sheen's concussion has him too confused to give a logical explanation."

The sheik said, "Pat O'Sheen must be eliminated immediately. He is too dangerous. Particularly now that he realizes that his family is in jeopardy. Do you understand?"

"I understand. He and his son should be in the hospital for at least one more day where they are too well guarded. But plans are being made to deal with O'Sheen when he leaves the hospital, as well as plans to eliminate his son."

Another voice came across from the speaker phone. "Abdul, we want Jody to live. Pat O'Sheen doesn't know that his son was the primary target." The man spoke English with an American accent. "If you have trouble killing Pat O'Sheen, his son may become useful, and . . ."

Abdul interrupted, "His son killed three of my best mercenaries: my friends. And the fourth one is in the hospital under Parisian police guard."

The commanding voice continued in English, "Your mercenary in the hospital has to join his friends with Allah in paradise. Abdul, can you handle that?"

The American's voice was low pitched, with a tone of command that Abdul had learned to recognize at a young age. He was apparently the man in control. Abdul realized that he was no longer working for his uncle, the sheik.

Abdul was very angry at this new development, but his survival instincts kicked in. He answered in perfect English, "Yes. Your request will be handled. But Jody O'Sheen will die with him."

The voice calmly said; "O'Sheen's son will return to America alive, or you will join him in paradise."

Abdul was too angry to respond.

After a long pause, the sheik voiced, "Allahu Akbar."

"Allahu Akbar, God is great." Abdul responded as the line went dead.

Abdul Faisad was six-feet tall, muscular, and was an experienced killer who was well connected and well paid. He had contracted many lucrative jobs with the Saudi Princes and their extended families. He was also an educated man.

Abdul grew up in a poor community in Iran that inadequately subsisted on farms. His family's small farm was located next to a desert area of southern Iran twenty miles from the Iraq border. Only Allah could make those arid soils produce food. When it seemed that the community strayed from Allah's will, the little rain that granted their survival failed to arrive. A century ago, they would have nomadically moved to a better area. But after World War I, the **western world,** and more specifically Great Britain, put restrictions on their nomadic way of life. Abdul's parents' generation never learned the nomadic survival instincts. The result: people starved and people died.

His father explained his frustration to Abdul before he left for Jerusalem where he blew himself up to Allah along with fifteen Jews at the Wailing Wall (which is all that is left the of the second Jewish Temple).

Abdul was nine years old at the time of his father's death. After his father's sacrificial deed of martyrdom, Abdul's family had all their basic needs supplied for the first time in his life.

Abdul's early education was by the mullahs in the local madrasas that his father had enrolled him in near the impoverished area that was his home. There were no other schools in the area despite all of the Shah of Iran's promises to educate the masses. Abdul's unusual academic achievements, his servitude to the mullah schoolmasters, and his father's martyrdom provided him the opportunity to go to college in America.

He had been warned of the satanic lure that he would encounter in America. But even though he was taught about western culture, his rural upbringing in his community, and his devotion to Islamic law made it impossible for the video presentations to prepare him for what he was to behold in the secular world.

When he changed planes in Madrid at the age of nineteen and had to walk through the airport concourse to his next plane, beautiful women with exposed skin, bulging breast cleavage, and beautiful, long-flowing hair were everywhere. He had to stop and kneel next to a wall in an attempt to control his arousal. He had not seen so much female skin or hair during all of his nineteen years of life.

His arrival at Reagan National Airport in Washington was equally shocking. Nothing could have prepared him for the female attire at the airport, or the luxurious homes, shopping malls, multiple lane highways, and fast-moving, flashy, new cars that he saw on his cab ride from the airport to George Washington University (GWU).

His madrasas handlers had given Abdul the names of sixteen Muslim students at GWU: three of whom he was to contact immediately, and five more that he should eventually meet. The three initial contacts would train him on the surveillance techniques used to monitor the other eight who were being swayed by America's satanic lifestyle.

Abdul soon realized that he had seen only a small part of the satanic "American dream" on the way from the airport. On almost every major street in America were shopping strips or malls that were packed with shoppers buying unnecessary nick-knacks, immoral clothing, and ungodly music and videos.

He later learned from CNN that many of the obese men and women that he saw in the shopping malls were the American poor. The poor people where he grew up had wrinkled yellow skin, skinny skeletal frames, extended stomachs, and would never have the strength or a reason to walk through a shopping mall.

Abdul almost starved to death as a child more than once before his dad blew himself up at the Wailing Wall in Jerusalem. He had experienced being truly poor. He understood the agony of his neighbor when her breast milk ran dry because she lacked nourishment. He remembered hearing her wails at night knowing that her infant would die without her milk.

Abdul soon realized why he was sent to GWU. Many of the American students were sons and daughters of anti-Vietnam War demonstrators, and many of them were sons and daughters of Congressmen. Many of their parents fit into both categories.

Without a cause to demonstrate against, the students were getting more and more dependent on their alcohol and drugs. Abdul had the solution to their needs and was anxious to proselytize his Muslim faith to save the lost souls. His Muslim peers had to reign in his enthusiasm in fear of being "too noticed".

Meanwhile, he and his fellow jihadists at the university reported on their fellow Muslims who were being swayed away from their Islamic roots. One of them died in a mysterious accident. Abdul took that as a warning. While he spied on his fellow Muslims, he started to understand their attraction to the American way of life.

During his next four collegiate years, he realized that many of his professors, many who had doctorate degrees, were not big fans of the "Founding Fathers" who made so many Americans proud. The professors recognized that the individual freedom that the "Constitution" protected led America into debauchery and drunkenness. Many of his professors taught that "Capitalism" leads to greed, the constitutional political system leads to corruption, and that America's strong military encouraged war. He learned that former President Eisenhower warned that a coalition between the military and industry, a coalition that the retiring president had called the "Military-Industrial Complex", was a scenario that the government must prevent at all cost. America seemed to have forgotten President Eisenhower's warning.

Chapter Six
Currently

Inspector Boudreaux was present, but quiet, when I was being taken into custody at St. Bernadette Hospital in Paris. I was surprised that Jody only mildly protested my detainment.

Jody said, "Dad, are you safe? Are you sure you want me to go home?"

I glanced at Pierre who was standing in the background and saw him nod in response.

"I believe you and the family might be safer without me around. I'll be okay. But be cautious while getting out of France.

"Oh, and once you clear European air space, put your mother down to Code 3." Code 3 allowed Dale access to the whole interior of the house.

Jody agreed.

Pierre winked at me and followed Jody out of my room.

Jody left the hospital with a phone to his ear. "Robby, what is the status of the queen?" Robby Clark was in charge of protecting the family in Alabama when the codes were put into effect.

"She's secure in the bunker. What is the status of the king?" Robby asked. His tone betrayed his concern.

"Recovering, but detained in Paris by the police. I'm about to head home. Tell the queen that she will be moved to Code 3 once I'm airborne." Jody sympathized with Robby, "She must be really pissed by now."

"You got that right."

Several policemen accompanied a nurse as she pushed a wheelchair out the front door of the hospital to an awaiting ambulance. The man in the wheelchair had his head and face covered with a towel.

Three police cruisers escorted the ambulance to the Prefecture de Police, and five officers escorted the man in the wheelchair through a back door of the station with the towel over his head again.

Mohammed punched a speed dial number into his cell phone and handed it to his cousin, Abdul, to report O'Sheen's status.

Meanwhile, I left the hospital by a rarely used service door in the underground garage. Pierre's unmarked sedan was waiting by the door. I jumped in the back seat and slumped to the floor.

Thirty minutes later, I looked gratefully into Inspector Pierre Boudreaux's bemused eyes. Pierre had a conspirator's grin on his face as I hugged him and climbed up the stairs into the chartered jet. I turned at the top of the steps, "Pierre, please keep me informed of anything your investigation uncovers. I'll be back in three days to make a full report to your superiors. I hope to have a plausible explanation by then."

I walked into the plane, greeted the familiar crew, and buckled myself into the front passenger seat with the expectation of planning my strategy. But I quickly fell asleep when the plane went airborne.

When my plane arrived at the small private terminal at the Birmingham airport, Brendan Clary was waiting for me. Only Brendan knew that I was returning home.

Brendan stood 6'6" and had a head larger than Hoss Cartwright on the old TV series "Bonanza". Even though he scored highest on all the Army written tests and finished at the top of his sniper class, he was never fully accepted by his peers. His high IQ sometimes even intimidated me.

I had met Brendan in the rugged mountainous terrain in Columbia near Bogotá. Brendan credits me for saving his life on that mission. I blame myself for the death of five men in Brendan's Special Forces unit.

When I was cleared by customs, Brendan grabbed me in a bear hug. He loosened his grip when he felt me wince. He gave one of those "oh shucks" embarrassed looks that only a big man can pull off properly.

Brendan grabbed my luggage and led me out to the Land Rover. He drove around the city in circles for about ten minutes—making sure we weren't being followed—as I gave him my version of the events in Paris. Brendan couldn't offer a theory to relieve my concerns.

We stopped at the Golden Rule restaurant in Irondale and ate barbeque pork sandwiches. Mine was covered with Tabasco sauce. We circled back toward the airport making sure we got there before Jody's commercial flight landed. We watched as Robby Clark pulled up outside the baggage claim area and saw Jody come out of the airport door and throw his bag into the back seat. Robby and Jody had a short conversation standing on the sidewalk, and somewhat surprisingly, Jody jumped in the driver's seat as Robby took the shotgun seat. Jody sped off. Brendan followed him at a distance with his and my combined skills of observation in high gear.

Jody didn't take the turn onto I-59 South as expected but stayed straight on Airport Highway and slowly headed downtown. He turned left off the Airport Highway onto 42nd street, and then right onto 1st Avenue North. He drove at exactly the speed limit over the bridge next to the historic Sloss Furnace. Suddenly he accelerated at the end of the bridge, recklessly took a hard right, and disappeared into the city.

I said calmly to Brendan, "You lost him. He spotted your tail. I thought you were good at this?"

Brendan shrugged, "I guess Jody is better. At least we know that no one else is trailing him."

I proudly agreed, "Yep, let's head to the house. I do need to stop and pick up a few things on the way."

***

Jody drove up to the street leading to his parent's home. The house was the only one on a very short side street with an empty cul-de-sac. A gravel driveway angled from the cul-de-sac to what seemed like an ordinary, unmanned gate located twenty feet off the asphalt. Instead of turning left toward the house, Jody turned right, circled a block, and paused for several minutes at a stop sign where the route had taken him back to the main road in the middle-class neighborhood. Jody's house was directly across the street from where he stopped, and it was dark inside as expected. Robby Clark's house was on his left and Brendan's house was further down on the left. When he was sure that there was no stakeout, he drove to his parent's home.

He asked Robby to check the outside perimeter—not wanting him to witness the impending confrontation. Jody entered the house with the dread of a teenager who was dropped off at the house by the police after skipping school. He entered a complicated security code into his cell phone, a code that identified him and also turned off the alarm on the front door. His mom would recognize his code immediately. He entered the house, turned into the living room, opened the entertainment cabinet, and punched a button to reestablish the Code 3 security.

He wasn't surprised when his mother ran down the hallway with fire in her eyes.

Dale screeched, **"You abandoned your father?"**

"Mother, he is safe. He insisted that I come home to make sure you are safe. Dad will be okay."

Some of the fire retreated from Dale's eyes. "Don't bullshit me, Jody. You don't have to be here to protect me when the codes are called. Why aren't you in Paris with your dad?"

Jody took a deep thoughtful breath and replied honestly, "Mom, Dad was unable to logically explain his encounter in Paris. He was shot on the top of his head and had a concussion. Several people were killed. He was taken into police custody when the hospital released him. I need Brendan's help to do some serious research on Dad's observations. We can do the research securely from the computers in the bunker here."

As much as she wanted answers, the urgency in her son's voice made her back off. "Jody, what kind of trouble has your dad gotten into this time?"

"Mom, I don't know. He didn't handle the attack against him very well. His explanation to Inspector Boudreaux didn't make sense. I'm confused. The Paris police are confused, and . . ."

Dale interrupted, "Pierre Boudreaux is involved?"

"Yes." Jody walked over to the picture of a younger Pierre Boudreaux standing next to Jody's parents and picked it up off the mantel. "Dad seems to trust him."

"Yes. I trust him. Your dad is in good hands."

She threw her arms around her son, holding him tightly. When she felt the large bandage under his left armpit, she stepped back. "What happened to you?"

Jody lied, "A slight mishap." Jody took his mother back in his arms and softly said reassuringly, "Dad and I are both okay. I just realized how tough you are—how tough you have had to be all these years." Jody's tension that built over the past few days started to release in his mother's embrace.

Dale knew from the hug that Jody wasn't telling the whole story. She also knew that he would offer no more—like father, like son. She would have to wait until Pat got home to find out what really went wrong in Paris. She expected that Pat might not disclose much more than Jody. "What happened to Keisha's concert?"

"Jonny cancelled it."

Dale saw the defeat in her son's face. "It seems that the threat was against you and your dad. Not Keisha?"

Jody wasn't surprised that his mother connected the dots. "I think someone from dad's past caught up with him. My protection business has lost all credibility".

Dale put her hand lovingly on Jody's cheek. "Don't be too despondent. Your dad will come up with a solution."

Mandy O'Sheen was waiting in the kitchen following instructions from her mom to allow time to deal with Jody and her emotions. Robby had brought Mandy to the house into lockdown with her mother when Jody called the Code 2. She was about to walk out to hug her brother when the intercom light came on with an accompanying beep. Jody released from his mom's hug, walked across the room to the cabinet door on the entertainment center, and seeing the code on the LED punched a button. Brendan asked over the speaker, "Can I come in?"

Jody picked up the handset, pushed a speaker button, and asked; "Have the leaves started to fall?"

"They started falling 13 days ago."

"Yes, Brendan. Welcome." Jody punched a button on the console to release the front door security.

***

There is no way to adequately describe the shocked looks on Jody and Dale's faces when they saw me follow Brendan through the door. Dale gasped, ran around Brendan, and jumped into my arms. I embraced her more emotionally than normal. She drew back and took a better look at me. She reached up and gently touched the bandage on top of my head. I said "Ouch," in a soft, high-pitched tone with feigned pain. When she smiled, I knew she was okay. I was expecting more angry recoil from her, but apparently she was saving up her fury for later. I never understood how she could love me so much, or how she endured all the anxiety I had put her through during our thirty-plus years of marriage.

Mandy ran out of kitchen and hugged me and then hugged Jody. Mandy was a pretty lady. She was inches shorter than Dale, barely over five feet. We spent a good family hour together before Robby came through the front door. Mandy announced that she had to go home to get ready for work the next day.

I watched Mandy approach the front door to leave. Robby had reset the security and approached the front door before Mandy was able to grab the doorknob. He punched a code into the panel to clear the security. The way I saw Robby look at Mandy was very revealing.

Robby reminded Mandy that he had brought her here—that she didn't have her vehicle—and that he would have to drive her home. I realized that I didn't need to encourage Robby to make sure that Mandy was safe. When the two of them left the house together, I smiled.

Dale looked up into my eyes with a questioning look.

Jody and Brendan retreated to the computer bunker below the house.

Dale put her hand on my chest and slanted her head toward our bedroom, and I didn't hesitate to follow her.

When we were both satiated and lying calmly in each other's naked arms, Dale asked, "What was that peculiar look in your eyes when Mandy left?"

I sat up, placed my warm hand on her naked thigh, and declared, "Robby is in love with Mandy."

Dale abruptly sat up. "**Did he tell you that**?"

"No, I saw it in his eyes before they left tonight."

"You're wrong. She would have told me."

"I am not sure that she realizes it."

Dale got a sly smile on her face.

I squeezed her thigh, "I see that you approve. Don't start playing Cupid."

Dale giggled, "I won't make it obvious. But Robby may need help. He may never get her to understand."

I squeezed her thigh again and sighed, knowing that I had set the wheels of her mind in motion. I did not regret it. "Don't underestimate Mandy. She didn't recoil at Robby's look. I think that she understands." I smiled, got out of bed, and retreated to the bathroom.

Dale considered Pat's insight. He had a gift: a scary ability to read people and use their emotions to get into their heads. His ability scared her when they first met in high school. But he was never judgmental of her. The vulnerability that his talent imposed on her somehow made life easier. They rarely attempted the mental control games that put so many marriages in jeopardy.

***

The computer room that Jody and Brendan entered was in a bunker below ground next to the Code 2 bunker, but normally entered by a separate staircase. It was a large room, thirty feet long by twenty feet wide. The two bunkers were connected by a steel door that was concealed by wall to wall bookshelves filled from top to bottom with books. The books were organized systematically into groups of Civil War, WW1, WW2, "The Rise and Fall of the Third Reich", "War and Peace", classics, religious, and fiction classics that included Dickens, Daphne du Maurier, and Mark Twain; and also, the modern thrillers of Koontz, Flynn, King, and Ludlum. Jody assumed that his dad had read the books during the long hours of the boring, lonely surveillance of his career.

Jody and Brendan exchanged their thoughts of the events in Paris as they booted two of the four computers. Jody went to his email first, looking for any emails from his girlfriend, Lacy. Finding none, he sent her a quick email, "I'm back, and I love you. I'm at my parents' house. Call me when you get this."

Brendan started his research.

***

Later, when I entered the computer complex, Jody was alone. When he stood up, I knew what he was going to say.

Jody asked, "How in the hell did you get out of Paris so quickly."

I ignored the curse word and told Jody about the diversion that Pierre and I had arranged.

Jody was offended, "You could have shared the plan with me and let me fly home with you."

"That would probably have resulted in our enemy discovering the ruse." I asked, "Do we have other business to discuss before I rejoin your mother?"

"Yes," Jody answered somewhat frustrated. "Do you remember the job proposal we made for Keisha's concert in Melbourne (Australia)?" Without waiting for an answer he said, "I got an email that we have the job. I have to leave for Melbourne in two days to do a preliminary work-up."

I saw the file on the table, retrieved reading glasses from the desk drawer, scanned the file, and asked; "What do I need to do?"

"Dad," Jody responded reluctantly, "The email put a condition on contracting with us."

"What condition?"

"Keisha's manager, Jonny Wright, is concerned about what happened in Paris. I had to agree to keep you away from this Australia job."

He added, "Jonny doesn't want you associated with his client until Paris is cleared up and explained."

Jody had rehearsed many ways to present this condition to his dad. The look on his dad's face was proof of his inability to manipulate the words to achieve the desired result.

Before his dad could respond, Jody offered, "Jonny believes that you were the target in Paris, not Keisha. I think we can all agree on that. Let us go to Australia without you. It may act as a decoy for your enemies. You can spend the time trying to figure out **what in the hell is happening**." The last words were almost yelled.

I ignored the loud outburst, "Who are you taking to Melbourne with you?"

"Keisha asked for me and Brendan. I would also like to hire Claude and his people."

I knew that Claude was an excellent choice. We contracted with him for his Australian military background, and for all of his contacts in the Far East. But I had to demand, "I need Brendan with me, take Robby."

"Okay." Jody wasn't surprised. His dad's problems were obviously worrying him. "But can you give me your thoughts on what happened in Paris? Will it affect our trip to Australia?"

He continued before allowing me to answer, "You left us alone with our client in Paris even though you sensed that trouble was imminent. **Why**?"

I was surprised by such an unusual assault from my son. I replied, "I felt that I had to find out if we were under surveillance, and if so, to assess the magnitude of the threat and decoy it away from Keisha. The attack was bigger and faster than I could have anticipated. I miscalculated."

I added, "I might be dead now without your computer preparation that familiarized you with the area and recommend my means of escape."

Jody appreciated the compliment. "Do you have any idea who was behind this, and why they came for you?"

I answered, "I'm more concerned why they attacked you when they had me alone outside. I've made many adversaries over the years who would like to even the score. The most recent and functional ones are protected by the oil money in the Middle East."

Jody probed, "Why would they put a contract on you and **me** now? We withdrew from government service? Should I turn down the contract in Melbourne and help you work through this threat to our family?"

"**No**." I answered forcefully. "I agree that they are foremost after me. The fact that you and some of our best people are in Australia may encourage them to try to attack me again."

Jody recoiled, "If that comment was intended to comfort me, it failed."

I felt my past covert life unraveling, "Jody, you are learning that this has been my life. I can take care of myself. I have to solve this quickly . . . and hopefully quietly. That's why I need Brendan with me."

I saw a reaction in Jody that I had never seen before. Typically, Jody was not good at verbalizing his concern, so I probed, "Are you finally realizing why I didn't want you close to my previous careers?"

Jody shocked me by asking, "Are you the legendary covert operative, 'Coyote'?"

I chuckled, "Where did you get that idea?"

Jody knew that his dad wouldn't answer the question any more than Jody would disclose to him that Brendan had ratted on him years ago.

"Dad," Jody totally changed the focus of the conversation, "I killed four people this week. They had family, friends, and probably kids."

I replied, "Three, not four." By Jody's reaction I realized how cold my response must have sounded.

Jody countered, "I called to check on the status of the survivor. Pierre told me that he was killed in his hospital bed after we left. He was suffocated. I thought you knew."

"Well then, you didn't kill him." I realized by Jody's grimace that my cold acceptance of casualties was not shared by my son. My self-esteem took a deep drop. I was thankful that my son's heart had not grown as cold as mine and silently prayed that it never would.

I could tell that Jody was experiencing emotional trauma and wondered when in my own long career I had learned to put the injured and dead perpetrators, and even worse, the "collateral damage" and the pain of the family and friends out of my mind so quickly. Had my career, the service to my country, all of my sacrifice away from family, friends, and church made me lose my way? I remembered experiencing Jody's remorse when I was young.

I was not going to let this moment pass. I was going to encourage Jody to vent. *But how was I to start*? "Jody, you've been in firefights before where people were killed."

"Dad, I only participated in one fire-fight and bullets were flying everywhere. Maybe it wasn't my bullets that put men down, but this time there is no doubt that I erased the lives of human beings."

I argued, "It was kill or be killed." I added the rationalization that had worked for me throughout my violent career. "Jody, we are all going to die. It's how we live that defines and measures our value in this life and before God. There are a lot of wealthy Americans who jump on seemingly good causes in an effort to make their lives meaningful. It is rare to find someone who is willing to take the ultimate step and put their life on the line to protect an individual, a family, a community, or their country."

I added, "And very few people have the talents to make a real difference in defending their country and the innocent."

Jody nodded reflectively, "I accept your logic, but it still hurts." He changed the subject again, "When will you leave for Paris?"

I was surprised at his perception, "Tomorrow. I have to expose myself to discover where the threat is coming from."

"Mom's not going to like that. Will she be okay . . . safe?"

"She and you will be safe when I'm seen again in Paris."

I saw the concern again in Jody's eyes. I could tell that he didn't like the idea of me putting myself out there as bait.

I said, "Trust me. It's the best and only course of action. You were right in saying that the Paris mystery has to be solved before we can move on."

Jody left for his house. Lacy, would be there soon, and he needed her tender loving care.

Chapter Seven
Moment of Truth

When I rejoined Dale, she was in the kitchen. To a casual observer her smile would seem genuine, but I saw the tightness and the redness in her normally beautiful eyes. She took a bottle of chardonnay from an ice bucket, half-filled our glasses, and walked to the living room. We sat on the couch facing each other.

Dale started, "Pat, what went wrong?" (Dale rarely called me Pat like the army did after my first birthday in Vietnam on Saint Patrick's Day.) "We agreed that you and Jody would pull back from your careers with the CIA to make our lives safer. **What is happening**?" The further she got into her question, the higher and more intense her voice became.

I had to be honest. "Jody used my name, reputation and picture to advertise the new protection company. I should have had more oversight and not allowed that. Someone from my past must have recognized me, and it appears that someone from my past wants revenge. Did Jody tell you that he also got shot?"

"I was afraid of that when I felt the bandage under his arm. But no. He didn't tell me. He said he had a slight mishap and that you were alone outside the hotel when you were shot. If you were outside the hotel . . ."

I waited, regretting that she was starting to put it together.

She continued, ". . . then they didn't just want to just kill you, they wanted to kill Jody too." Dale's nature was not the type that panicked, "If they came for Jody, are they coming for all our family? **Will they come for Mandy, Scott, and me**?"

I answered honestly, "Dale, I'm sorry. I don't know the answer to that question yet. That's why I have to go back to Paris tomorrow."

She said, "So in my effort to protect our family by urging you to change careers, I may have put my whole family in real danger? What are you going to do?"

"Dale, don't blame yourself for this. Life is full of unpredictability. Although Jody put my picture on internet advertisements, I got it off a few days later. My name will be hard to trace to any family members except for Jody. The CIA lays out false trails for the families of all of its agents. I have to find out who is after me and why. And I have to stop them."

Dale admitted, "I've always been afraid of losing you. I have had nightmares after you come home with a new wound from another bullet. I managed to live with that through our whole life together. You usually have a comforting explanation. You are not offering much comfort tonight." A tear rolled from her right eye, "I thought your new business would put us past the danger. Now we are in more danger than ever before." Her voice trembled, "How do you expect me to handle this?"

I tried to reach out and hold my frightened lover. She pushed me away.

"Dale, live your normal life: go shopping, go to the movies, go to Bunko and Mahjong with your friends. I will figure out who is after me and eliminate the danger." I winced at my bad choice of words.

"**Eliminate the danger**?" She almost screamed, as she sensed death and destruction in my voice.

In all the happy years of our marriage, I was able to hide the "rough" parts of my job. Sure, this was different. For the first time my family was in real danger. But I wasn't sure how much to reveal to Dale. Jody and Inspector Boudreaux were concerned about my performance in Paris. I was too. How could I have missed the many shots on a man coming up the staircase only ten feet away? *Maybe I was losing it.* I needed Dale's support.

"Dale, I was totally ineffective against the attack on me in Paris. All of my military training abandoned me. I shot at a man many times from only ten feet away and missed him. I shot three other men but Pierre said that there was no evidence of that. I scaled off the roof of a building and got shot resulting in this." I touched the bandage on top of my head.

I saw the bewilderment in Dale's eyes; *this conversation wasn't going any better than it had with Pierre in Paris.* I would never explain to her the adrenalin rush that came in a fire fight, the extraordinary fast progression of events that moved unnaturally in slow motion during the action, and how my senses of sight and sound were so enhanced by the danger.

Maybe I was losing it. As hard as it was for someone else to believe, I knew the bullet should have entered the pursuer's left ear, even though no blood was found on the balcony. But how could I explain the lack of evidence. There was something bigger at play than just an attack on me. There had to be something that I was missing? *But what?*

***

Dale had rarely seen self-doubt in her husband's eyes. The only time she did remember seeing it was when her water broke at home late at night before the birth of their first child. Back then she had to calm his near panic before she would let him drive her to the hospital.

She agonized at seeing him engulfed in self-doubt now.

***

Dale slid over next to me on the couch and put her arms around me. "Eddie, you have to admit that we are getting older. Despite the fact that you are in incredible shape for your age, your eyes, ears, and knees are deteriorating. But your mind is as sharp as ever. You **will** figure this out."

I hugged her. "Pierre helped me arrange this short visit, but I promised to return to Paris to report to his superiors as soon as you were apprised of the situation, and after I verified that you were safe. I have to honor my promise to return to Paris."

I explained what precautions I wanted her to take until I solved the problem.

I kissed her politely, stood, and headed for the bedroom knowing that she would stay up for a while to contemplate my self-doubt disclosures.

The next morning I took a shower, dressed, and sat on the bed next to Dale. I put my hand on her shoulder to wake her. I reminded her that I had to leave for Paris. She stiffly climbed out of bed, grabbed my hand, and pulled me to her. I tried to cut the hug short to indicate that I was in a hurry. I didn't want to get into another long conversation. She hugged me harder and would not let go. I eventually leaned out of the embrace and looked into her eyes with an expression of concern. She smiled and affectionately gave me a pecking kiss on my lips.

***

Dale saw the tension in Eddie's face. When she kissed him, his face relaxed and broke out into that killer smile. *Well, maybe she wouldn't call it a killer smile anymore.* She slanted her head toward the bed. Pat nodded as the killer smile turned into a loving smile.

They knelt down together at the edge of the bed. She asked God to keep her husband and family safe. As usual, her husband asked Jesus to help him do His Father's will.

***

I had a brainstorm while praying next to Dale. I didn't share it with her because it was top-secret. It was while praying next to her that I finally found a logical course to follow: something that might explain my ineffectiveness in Paris.

Chapter Eight
CIA

Brendan was waiting for me in the Land Rover when I left the house. After I got in, he pulled away. I told Brendan that we were going to Langley, Virginia before returning to Paris.

Brendan looked at me questioningly, but he didn't ask for an explanation: Pat would tell him if it wasn't classified above his security level.

I called the pilots to change our flight plan.

Then I called Gene Tanner, my handler when I was on assignment with the CIA. I told him enough about the events in Paris for him to agree to arrange a meeting.

When we arrived at the massive gates of the facility in Langley, the guard, Schmitty, recognized me immediately, and he asked us to exit the car. He smiled as we shook hands while the other guard watched with concern as Brendan peeled his big frame out of the passenger door on the small rent-a-car. We surrendered our weapons while guards and their dogs searched the car and us. After Schmitty called ahead, he told us to proceed.

We were escorted to an outer meeting room due to Brendan's lower clearance level. Brendan and I were seated at a ten-person conference table. Brendan started to ask me a question, but I shook my head at him, indicated that we should remain silent. I knew that other eyes were watching and other ears were listening. Ten minutes later, Gene Tanner entered the room.

I knew I had to walk through this preliminary scenario to achieve my objective, so I partially explained my Paris experience to Gene and eventually focused on my failure to shoot the man coming up the stairs from ten feet away.

I dropped the bomb, "Is the Hologram Project now operative?"

Gene glared at me incredulously. He pressed a button on the table phone, stood up, and asked Brendan to leave the room. When Brendan hesitated, I slanted my head toward the door.

When Brendan left, Gene asked me to repeat the Paris story again.

I responded: "Gene, I've already told enough of that story in this room. I know it was recorded. If you want to know more of what I think is happening, we will have to go to a more secure area. Your reaction has already confirmed my suspicions."

Gene left the room to arrange a higher level meeting.

I sat alone for half an hour in the conference room. I knew I was being watched, so periodically I stood up, walk around the room to stretch my legs, and then sat down in the same chair facing the mirror where the camera should be focused on me.

They were looking for erratic, paranoid behavior. It was not uncommon for some of the best operatives to "lose it" after they were forced to retire. Ex-agents with my capabilities made the bureaucrats nervous. My mention of the top-secret "Hologram Project" in a semi-secure room put up a red flag that would rise to the highest levels.

Finally, Gene Tanner reentered the room. He approached me and whispered, "You have opened up a can of worms." He said at normal volume, "Follow me."

We went through two security checks that I was familiar with, and passed through a door that I had been through before. We went down a long stairway and into a room that I knew was the most secure room in the building from outside electronic surveillance.

Gene and I sat silently alone in the bunker without speaking. Ten minutes later the Director of Central Intelligence entered the room. I had not met the new DCI.

My suspicions were now fully confirmed. I wasn't losing my mind. I was shooting at hologram images projected by deflection ray technology, not at real people: hence, no blood on the steps, balcony, or roof in Paris where I thought I had shot my pursuers.

The insight that was fed to me on my knees next to the bed while praying with Dale was confirmed by the CIA's concern.

All covert operatives knew not to breach the security line that puts them in front of the CIA Director, but I was not intimidated: I had no other option. The CIA or the military had a major security breach that was putting my family in jeopardy. The previous director personally called me many times to get my opinion or to tell me that the President requested my services—services that usually put my life in danger.

The new DCI entered the secure conference room. Director Mary Collins was about 5'8" tall, with short auburn hair that curled inward about two inches below her earlobes. She had high cheekbones, a freckled contoured nose, and large green eyes, which was normally a beautiful combination—but her mouth was tiny and her lips were too thin to compliment the rest of her face. She had the figure and gait of an athlete.

She took the chair directly across the table from me, looked straight into my eyes and said, "Mr. O'Sheen, we haven't met, but I have reviewed your impressive service record, and I've heard what you have disclosed on your encounter in Paris. I want you to repeat it to me again. Don't hesitate to offer any additional speculation on your part."

I was impressed. I knew that Mary Collins worked her way up from Harvard Law School to become the District Attorney of New York City. That achievement alone would be considered the ultimate for most Harvard Law School graduates.

The CIA Director was a presidential appointment position. Like too many former presidential appointees, this CIA director had very little knowledge of covert field operations. But she seemed different from the political appointees that I had dealt with in the past, and I was comfortable reciting the complete details of my Paris story to her, including the conclusions that I had reached since entering the CIA headquarters.

Collins asked me, "How did you hear about the deflective ray technology project?"

I sighed to buy time to decide what to disclose. "I heard about it while I was working on a top-secret project for President Clinton."

"What project? That is not in your file."

"Director Collins, I am sure that most of the missions that I have performed for the past or the present presidents are not in any files on me."

The Director glared into my eyes. "Mister O'Sheen, I need to know who told you about the hologram project."

"President Clinton might be willing to tell you. I won't. And how I learned about it doesn't help us solve the current crisis. The technology has been compromised."

"Why do believe it has been compromised?"

"Director Collins, I was attacked by Arab mercenaries in Paris. I fired seven shots at a man pressuring me up a narrow staircase from only ten feet away and missed with every shot."

A fat man in the meeting spoke up. "O'Sheen, because of your age perhaps your eyesight is failing and your marksmanship has deteriorated."

For the first time, Pat released his eye contact from Director Collins to look at the fat man who sat eight feet away. "Sir, you have five wild gray hairs on your eyebrows that should be plucked and the nail on your left pinky finger needs to be trimmed properly." When the fat man looked at his finger nail, Pat said, "My eyesight is not failing nor has my marksmanship deteriorated."

Director Collins chuckled involuntarily, partly because she was released from the tension inflicted by O'Sheen's unblinking eyes staring into hers. She only saw four eyebrow hairs on Deputy Director Hill that needed to be plucked. She was convinced that the deflective ray technology had leaked. "So to summarize, Mister O'Sheen, you think that we have a mole who leaked our deflective ray technology?"

I responded, "Yes, Ma'am. And I have a plan to help expose the conspirators in Paris, but it must be implemented quickly. I gave my word to the Prefecture de Police to surrender to them tomorrow. That promise was necessary for them to let me come home to protect my family and to meet with the CIA to formulate a plan. My friends in France know that I honor my commitments. Most of my friends in the CIA have retired."

I explained, "My adversaries think I have been in the Prefecture de Police custody for the last two days. I won't have any problem sneaking into the prefecture. I plan for my attackers to see me leaving there, and I expect them to attack me with a large mercenary force. Their leader needs to recover his credibility by successfully fulfilling his contract to kill me. He won't take me as lightly this time. I will need CIA help to execute a sting operation."

The director stared at me, "You are willing to expose yourself to another attack?"

I nodded and explained, "I don't need the culprits looking for me around my family in America. My question is, can I get security clearance for an update on the deflective ray technology. I am in a unique position to help expose the security leak. If you want me to investigate in Paris, I need to be briefed. They will probably use the technology against me again."

Director Collins leaned back in her chair. She had never met a field operative in the CIA with legendary status equivalent to "Coyote", the codename of the man sitting across the table from her. Most agents were intimated by her title. O'Sheen wasn't even a slight bit nervous, and he seemed to admire her. She looked at her fingers while she considered how to proceed and realized that she was overdue for her nail appointment.

She raised her vision and looked back into Coyote's eyes. His eyes were multicolored, mostly brown and green. His graying eyebrows complimented his tanned face, and his short, salt-and-pepper hair showed no signs of balding. Her ex-husband had Pat's confident demeanor when she first met him. He had turned out to be an asshole. Face-to-face, O'Sheen was more enticing than his impressive file. She sensed his loyalty to the country, and his passion to protect his family was obvious.

She decided to trust O'Sheen and said to Gene Tanner as she continued to look deeply and steadily into Pat's eyes that never attempted to release contact with hers, "Gene, raise Pat's clearance to "Need-to-Know". Follow Mr. O'Sheen's lead. I trust his instincts."

I blinked my appreciation to Director Mary Collins and expressed my appreciation in my eyes without showing it on my face.

A clerk came up to me as the meeting was breaking up informing me that Mister Clary needed to talk to me. She led me to where Brendan was anxiously pacing in the lobby. His demeanor was alarmingly out of character.

Brendan hurried up to me, "Jimmy Sue and the kids have been in a car accident."

Before I could ask, he added, "The kids are fine. Jimmy Sue is in stable condition in the hospital. I haven't yet told you that Jimmy Sue is pregnant. I know how much that you were counting on my support in Paris. But, Pat, I need to get back to my family. I am so sorry."

I said. "Brendan, don't worry about me. What can I do to help?"

"I have a cab waiting out front and a plane reservation at the Dulles Airport."

Brendan restated his concern, "I know that you can't delay your return to Paris. I'm sorry that I can't be there to support you."

In my mind I cursed this new development. I was counting on Brendan's backup in the next attack against me. But Brendan's priorities were correct. I offered, "Take our jet back to Birmingham. I am going to be in meetings here for the rest of the day and probably most of the night. I hope to get support from the CIA in Paris, so your backup is less needed."

When Brendan hesitated, I ordered, "Go. I'll call the pilot."

As I watched Brendan run out the door, I knew my survival odds were just cut in half.

I worked into the night being briefed on the technical aspects of the hologram technology and formulating a plan with the CIA for my return to Paris. In the morning, I called Dale on her mobile phone. She was at the hospital with Jimmy Sue, Brendan, and Jimmy Sue's father, Shelby County Sheriff Bo Hannon. I told her where I was.

"You are supposed to be through dealing with the CIA," She realized that she had hissed the words.

I said, "Dale, I need their help on this one." I couldn't tell her about the top-secret information that explained my failure in Paris.

Dale had rarely seen her husband out-of-sorts like he was when he returned from Paris with the bandage on top of his head. He sounded like he had the situation under control now. His voice exuded confidence. She said, "Okay. I'm sorry I hissed at you."

I thought, *what an incredible woman.* We talked for another five minutes. She expressed her anxiety about Brendan not accompanying me to Paris. I downplayed her concern.

Chapter Nine
Paris

I had no trouble sneaking into the Prefecture de Police building in Paris. *They* were watching for me to sneak out, *not in*. I had to enter unarmed and was expecting to leave the same way.

I met with Pierre Boudreaux in a small interrogation room. Pierre informed me that forensics proved that my gun had not killed the young, red-headed clerk at the convenience store, and that Pierre's boss accepted my written report on the incident, but that I couldn't leave until his boss talked to me. He warned me that the interview would be recorded.

Pierre's supervisor asked Pierre to leave the room. His French accent had a hint of Peninsular Spanish: more specifically Basque. He started interrogating me in broken English. I told him in his Basque dialect in Spanish that he could interview me in French, or if he preferred, in Spanish. He smiled and continued in French for the sake of the French officials that would want to listen to the interview.

Twenty minutes later, I was alone with Pierre in his office. I told him very quietly and in confidence what I had planned with the CIA.

Pierre pushed his chair back from his small desk with a concerned look. "You should have consulted with me first. We can't allow an operation by the CIA in our city unless it is under our control."

I grimaced, knowing the answer before I asked, "How long will it take to get my operation approved?"

Pierre acknowledged in frustration, "Too long."

Pierre disclosed, "An American agent requested pictures of your pursuers from our office. My superiors cooperated with him."

"When?"

"Yesterday."

"Do you have a picture of the agent and his name?"

Pierre stood up and opened the top drawer in a vertically stacked four drawer metal cabinet. He pulled a poor quality security camera photograph of Agent Gene Kamper from the folder and handed it to me. He showed me a copy of the pictures they had shared with Kamper.

I handed the pictures back, thanked Pierre, and asked skeptically, "Can you give my gun back to me?"

Pierre handed me two forms, "Your license to carry a firearm in France has been revoked. Fill out this form to renew your carry permit, or this form for us to ship the pistol to your home in America."

I filled out the form to renew my carry permit in France and handed the completed form to Pierre. "Where do I retrieve my Glock?"

Pierre chuckled, "It will be shipped to your home in America. It didn't matter which form you filled out."

I laughed. All government bureaucracies worked the same.

Pierre laughed for a second. Then concern reentered his eyes.

I said, "Can you provide me with a car and backup when I leave?"

"Pat . . ." Pierre hesitated, considering his lack of options due to Pat's disclosure of an unsanctioned CIA operation. He and his wife, Kathie, loved Pat and Dale, ". . . my hands are tied. I can't help you. But you are free to leave."

I stood up. Pierre extended his left hand toward me containing a set of keys to his car and he said, "Good luck, my friend." He implored me in a whispered voice, "I have a good life, a lovely wife, and two great kids. Please don't ruin it all. There is a revolver under the driver's seat." He described the car.

I took the keys and nodded in appreciation. I knew without Brendan's backup that I may never see Pierre or my family again. Pierre's car and gun gave me a fighting chance.

Chapter 10
The chase

Abdul Faisad, the mercenary awaiting Pat O'Sheen, finally heard from his contact inside the Prefecture de Police office confirming that O'Sheen was inside. His inside contact indicated that O'Sheen was about to leave.

The large exodus of the police leaving the building during the regular shift change didn't surprise Abdul. He had watched the same shift change in the days before, only to be disappointed that O'Sheen wasn't among them. But this time he saw O'Sheen through his binoculars. His prey was wearing a Parisian police uniform jacket and walked with a casual demeanor as he left the building with the others. Abdul announced on his radio that the prey was on the move and to prepare for pursuit.

Through the binoculars, Abdul watched O'Sheen walk off to the left, away from the police officers walking to the police cruisers, and watched as he removed his uniform jacket and wrapped it around his left arm. O'Sheen looked around in all directions and suddenly focused on Abdul and his group on the hill.

Damn it. Abdul knew that O'Sheen had discovered them.

Abdul watched O'Sheen approach a government issued sedan, shatter the driver's window with his left elbow that was wrapped in the jacket, reach in to unlocked the door, and quickly enter the vehicle.

Abdul transmitted, "Team two. Move to intercept." He transmitted the make, model, and color of the vehicle. He assumed that it would take O'Sheen at least a minute or two to hot wire a French-made, government car. Abdul ran to his pursuit vehicle. When he resurveyed O'Sheen's location as his car sped forward, he saw that O'Sheen was already backing out of the parking space. *O'Sheen had hot-wired a Parisian tamperproof car in about fifteen seconds. Unbelievable.*

***

I knew that opening the door with Pierre's key would have disclosed that Pierre assisted me and may cause retribution against him. I hoped the prefecture wouldn't make Pierre pay for the window. I saw the clean-shaven Arab watching me through binoculars before breaking the window. If today turned out badly, I didn't want my pursuers to connect me to Pierre and his family.

I leaned under the dash as if I was hot wiring the vehicle for almost fifteen seconds before inserting the key in the ignition and starting the car. After pulling out of the parking lot, I headed toward the bridge over the Seine River. I reached under the front seat and was grateful to feel the handgun. Minutes later, I saw a Hummer pursuing me. *The chase was on.*

Pierre's government sedan wasn't a James Bond super-vehicle designed for a daring chase. I worried that they might capture or kill me before I could get to the safe house where I had planned the CIA ambush. As I sped south on the Boulevard Du Palais, I noticed a large Hummer closing from behind. After crossing the bridge over the Seine River, I turned a hard right at the next intersection, scaring myself when both right wheels lifted off the ground. After gaining control, I looked in the rearview mirror and saw that the Hummer had more problems taking the corner than I did. It slammed into parked cars on the side of the street.

I pressed the accelerator and glanced in the side mirror. The Hummer had already recovered and was in pursuit. I needed them to follow, but I could not allow them to catch me. I slid around the next hard turn to my left.

I started looking for an advantage that some might call "luck". I found it in a narrow street with cars lining both sides of the road. I was sure that residents owning larger vehicles regularly complained about the parking arrangement. I squeezed Pierre's sedan through the parked cars hoping that the Hummer would pursue and get wedged between vehicles. After I carefully maneuvered through a very tight spot, I looked in the mirror and saw that the Hummer had continued forward without turning down the narrow street. *Smart!*

I sped forward and looked in the mirror again and noticed a sedan pursuing me through the narrow opening between the cars at a much faster speed than I had managed.

The next cross street that I approached was wider. I slowed enough to evaluate both ways. The cars parked on both sides of the street were all aiming to the left. *One Way.*

I saw a side street a hundred feet from the intersection if I turned right, the wrong way up the one-way street. I turned right and saw the Hummer coming down the street toward me, approaching at high speed. My adversaries knew the streets of Paris better than I did.

I put the accelerator to the floor hoping that I could beat the Hummer to the street on the left. The sedan's response was poor and I realized that it was going to be a draw at the intersection. I kept my accelerator to the floor despite the fact that my small sedan was sure to lose in a collision. I had lost my fear of death in Vietnam decades earlier. If I was killed, my family would be safe. I hoped the driver of the Hummer didn't share my lack of fear in this game of "chicken".

***

The Hummer's driver, Mohammed, knew that his larger vehicle had the advantage and accelerated toward O'Sheen. Suddenly, he realized that O'Sheen was insane. He was accelerating directly at him with full intentions of a serious head on collision.

Instinctively, Mohammed slammed on the breaks to reduce the impact. He was glad that O'Sheen did the same. But then O'Sheen suddenly made a sharp left turn down a side street that Mohammed hadn't noticed through his fear. When his heavier vehicle finally stopped twenty feet past the intersection, he threw it into reverse and backed up. Abdul Faisad's sedan skirted around the corner in front of the Hummer as it was backing up. *Damn you, O'Sheen.*

***

Two turns later, I sped down the three blocks remaining toward the safe house. I noticed a man's head on the roof across from the safe house observing my approach. I hadn't had the opportunity to train this team, and I hoped that the sniper, who I assumed was CIA, would recognize that I was the man he was there to protect.

But something wasn't right. The CIA would not use a sniper that was too incompetent to avoid detection. I slowed as I approached the house on the right side of the street. In my rearview mirror, I saw the sedan speeding toward me from two blocks back, followed by the Hummer. I noticed an empty parking space in front of the safe house on the right. I fully accelerated the sedan toward the parking space, locked the brakes, and turned the steering wheel full left. The sedan careened too much for my comfort, but it cooperatively performed a 180-degree skid into the empty space in front of the house and slammed into the car parked beyond the empty space. *Sorry again, Pierre.*

The stairs to the house were only slightly behind and to my left. I grabbed the handgun that Pierre had left under the seat, opened the driver's door, and dove to the sidewalk while leaving the door open for cover from the pursuing vehicles. I quickly rolled to my left, rose up on my left knee, rotated the pistol over the trunk of the sedan inches behind the back window, and focused my aim at the sniper's location on the rooftop across from the safe house. The sniper was no longer visible. *Good. He understood.*

I turned my attention to the approaching pursuit. The sedan slowed and turned left at the closest intersection. The Hummer followed the sedan. *Damn. They must have seen the sniper, too.*

I ran a zigzag pattern to the left of the stairway and crouched behind a large shrub. I got a slight glimpse of the sniper on the roof across the street, but no other threat. I heard a door open above me and an unfamiliar voice say, "O'Sheen, come in."

I stood slowly while watching the roof across the street, straightened my right arm to hide my handgun behind my right buttocks, and peered up the stairs at the smiling face of the CIA man whose picture Pierre had just shown me: Agent Gene Kamper.

***

Abdul was impressed by O'Sheen's 180 degree maneuver, realizing that the move made it possible for him to exit the vehicle away from the pursuit, and away from the black-hooded sniper observing

O'Sheen from the roof across the street. Abdul immediately turned down the street to his left. Once he was out of sight, he stopped, grabbed his pistol, and jumped out. He waved Mohammed's Hummer over to the side of the road behind his sedan, and ran back to the intersection in time to see O'Sheen enter the house.

He ran back to the open widow on the Hummer and told Mohammed to assemble the pursuit team at Area 2, where he had more forces already assembled. Mohammed's nephew, Kareem, had already exited from the passenger side of the Hummer wearing two ammunition belts crisscrossing his chest and had an Uzi clearly displayed in his right hand.

Abdul's man emerged from the back seat of his sedan wearing a long trench coat that concealed his sniper rifle.

Abdul, despite his anger at Kareem, calmly said to him, "I want you to ride with me to Area 2. Get in my car."

When Kareem hesitated and look to Mohammed for approval, Abdul yelled, "**Now.**"

Abdul explained to the sniper that exited his sedan, knowing that he had a sniper on the roof across from the house to cover the front. "Get in position in the alley to cover the back of the house. Set up in a position of advantage, but out of sight: we don't want nosy neighbors calling the authorities. Maintain your position unless I call you off."

He grimaced as he watched Kareem enter his vehicle. He continued his instructions to his sniper, "Report immediately on any significant changes, and kill O'Sheen if he leaves the back of the house. We want to question him, but we can't let him escape. So kill him without hesitation and report afterwards."

On the way to Area 2, Abdul explained to Mohammed's nephew, "Kareem, you can't jump out of a car in a neighborhood looking like a commando. You may have drawn attention to us from neighbors by getting out of the Hummer in that outfit. Hopefully, they saw us leave and won't alert the police."

Training of zealous subordinates was a constant necessity.

***

I ascended the stairs while watching for the sniper on the roof across the street and warily walked through the opened front door. *Something didn't make sense about this whole scenario.*

I raised my pistol. The CIA operative was standing calmly, five feet inside the room, facing the front door. But I noticed that he was not standing in view of the sniper across the street. I moved away from the door, canvassed the room, and saw no threats.

The incredibly handsome young man seemed pleased and asked me to follow him into an adjoining room. I closed and locked the front door and followed the man into a small dining room.

Kamper pulled a chair out from the close end of the table, but he sat down facing the kitchen with his left side toward my chair. He gestured for me to sit in the chair, an action to show that he wanted to be in control. The young man didn't seem the least bit surprised when I rejected the offered chair, walked past him, and slowly sat in a chair with a better view of the interior of the house and the kitchen.

The man said, "You were briefed that my code name for this operation is 'Shadow: not the name I would have chosen. I'd prefer that you call me Gene."

I said, "I like the name Shadow. It is the name of my Cocker Spaniel." Not only did the man across from me look like Sean Connery from the early James Bond flicks, but he exuded that 007 confidence. He was slightly over 6' 2", broad shouldered, had a sculptured face with an attractive cleft on his chin, and penetrating blue-gray eyes. His hair was shiny black and combed back.

I jumped to the issue at hand; "Give me the details of the preparations."

Gene deflected, "I offered to help you get here. I know the people pursuing you. I told the agency that without my help, your chances of getting here safely were less than ten percent. I'm impressed that you made it, but why did you reject my help?"

I surmised that this young stud had not been in the covert community long enough to be wary of the double cross. *Or had he?* My mistrust level was raised, and I felt the pain again in my gut. I told him, "I was never informed of your offer."

I studied his reaction to my response and said, "If you knew the plan, and particularly if you have knowledge of the people pursuing me, then you would know that they would not have followed me if they thought they might be headed into an ambush. Our sting operation here would be doomed to failure."

When Gene shrugged his shoulders, I started out in a calm tone of voice, "They must have seen your careless sniper on the roof across the street, and if they still decide to attack, they will be more prepared. **Gene, you have jeopardized this whole mission."**

***

Gene was impressed. When he reviewed O'Sheen's CIA file, he came across a redacted codename. Though the name was covered with black ink, he thought he could make out the name "Coyote". Could this man be the legendary "Coyote"? He knew that the man sitting across from him was about the right age.

Up close O'Sheen's age made him look *over the hill*. His graying hair and his outdoor, weather-lined face showed his age. But from twenty feet away, if you ignored the hair and noticed how gracefully he moved, you could recognize a formidable foe. And somehow he managed to get to the safe house alive on his own. O'Sheen never lowered his pistol. But it was aimed at the kitchen doorway, not at him.

Gene disclosed, "That isn't my sniper on the roof across the street."

Before he could explain, another man entered the room. He had the demeanor of an Army sergeant. Gene noticed that O'Sheen never flinched, nor did he raise his pistol. His pistol was already aimed at the man when he turned the corner into the room.

The big man volunteered, "I apologize for the screw up by my sniper."

Gene introduced him, "O'Sheen, this is Brent Spellman. This is his operation, not mine. He can brief you on the preparations. My assignment is only to report that you made it here safely."

***

I knew the man had been eavesdropping. I had smelled him in the kitchen.

I stood up somewhat cautiously as Spellman approached. This whole scenario stunk. Spellman extended his large hand as I stepped forward. I grasped the extended hand and studied the big man's eyes while making sure I didn't lose sight of Kamper in my peripheral vision. The handshake was hard but not crushing, and it was offered without the slightest smile.

Spellman explained that he was with Special Forces, and that he and his men were on temporary assignment. By his demeanor, I surmised that he wasn't pleased with this assignment.

I took charge, "I need to see the armaments room. I feel like I'm standing here naked with a troupe of girl scouts about to enter the room."

Spellman smiled and led me down a hallway, reached under the chair rail, and pushed a button causing a hidden door panel to slide open.

I was very impressed when I entered the 8' x 10' room, lined on three sides with an arsenal of weapons and ammunition. Kamper and Spellman followed me into the small room.

I turned toward the arsenal but kept them in view as I set Pierre's revolver on a counter. I retrieved a weapons belt and put it on a counter next to Pierre's loaded pistol. I opened a box and retrieved two grenades, put one into the designed slot in the belt, and tossed the other a few feet in the air while I turned toward the two men watching me. The tension in Spellman's face at my move was obvious. On the other hand, Kamper was smiling. I caught the airborne grenade and returned the smile.

***

Gene watched in fascination as O'Sheen searched the room, found a silencer and screwed it into the end of the barrel of the Glock pistol he had retrieved. He unbuttoned and removed his shirt. Gene noticed three bullet wounds on his back; one near his left kidney, one behind his right armpit, and the other crossing the top of his left shoulder near the neck. He had previously noticed the long scab and stitches on the top of his head despite an obvious attempt to cover it with hair. This man was obviously a warrior. He watched him put on a Kevlar vest, replaced his shirt over it, and fasten the weapons belt over his shirt and around his waist.

***

I pulled a Glock 19 off a rack. I would have preferred my Glock 22. I pushed the lever that released the clip and let it fall into my left hand, pulled back the slide, and looked through the barrel while never losing sight of Kamper and Spellman. I found a silencer and screwed it into the end of the Glock 19 barrel. I pulled a box of 9 mm ammunition off the shelves, opened it, and had the 15-cartridge magazine of the Glock loaded in under two minutes. I chambered a bullet and turned toward the two men, with the barrel aimed slightly toward the ceiling. Spellman flinched. Gene smiled again.

I asked Spellman, "Shouldn't someone be watching for the attack?"

Spellman answered, "My men have it covered. I'll be warned." He pointed to the pager on his belt.

After removing my shirt, I put on a Kevlar vest and replaced my shirt. I grabbed an AK-47 and the long munitions clip next to it, grabbed another ammo box, and loaded the magazine. I attached the sling, and swung the weapon into the rest position behind my right shoulder, the barrel aimed toward the ceiling. I loaded two extra clips for the AK-47, and put them on my weapons belt. I picked up a stiletto knife off a shelf and put it into a sheath on my belt and grabbed some plastic handcuffs.

Chapter 11
Safe house?

Spellman gave me a tour of the safe house. I was impressed with the way the front door was steel reinforced including two steel studs on both sides of the door. Brent Spellman demonstrated the crank handle that opened the metal shutters over the front windows and explained that the same design was used throughout the house.

After climbing the stairs to the second floor, I was facing a solid-metal door that contained three slide bolts; all were in the locked position. A shuttered window was on the right side of the door.

I walked to the window and raised the bottom half of the double-hung window to its full height and slowly cranked the shutters slightly open, enough to reveal a very small, grassed backyard surrounded by a six-foot privacy fence that featured a gate to an alley. A narrow wooden stairway descended straight down from the door to the grassed yard, which offered a good means of escape from a fire for residents on the second floor . . . *or for me.*

I left the window and shutters open and followed Spellman down a hallway to a doorway that opened into small bedroom on the left. Another door next to it opened into a bathroom. Further down the hallway another door entered another small bedroom on the left. There was one large bedroom on the right. I noticed that it had its own bathroom. *Nice.*

We retraced our steps to the top of the stairway. I heard a quiet sigh of relief from Brent as we descended.

I followed Spellman down the hallway toward the kitchen and noticed a wooden panel that seemed out of place on the right. It was directly across from the weapons room. I asked, "Where does this panel lead?"

Sergeant Spellman seemed perturbed that I noticed the secret passageway. But he complied and reached under the decorative wainscot chair-rail that ran horizontally down both sides of the hallway and hit a button. The panel opened in the wall exposing a three-foot square area with a metal floor that had a chain attached at the rear. The chain rose to a pulley above and then passed back down through the floor in a groove on the back wall. The small butler-style lift could accommodate two people if necessary. Spellman showed me the button on the inside and explained the button would lower the lift to an underground bunker and to a passageway that led to a lift four houses down that would lift me to the first floor of the other safe house. I pressed the button and backed into the hallway. The panel closed as the lift started down.

I reached under the wainscot and felt three buttons. I pressed the first and the panel opened back up. I hit the second button and nothing happened. When I hit the third, the lift reversed direction and started up toward our level.

I was relieved at the revelation: *A much better means of escape than the back alley.* Spellman's disclosure encouraged me to start trusting him.

Chapter 12
Survival

Mohammed Faisad, under direction of his cousin, Abdul Faisad, had just positioned his four men under the staircase in the back yard when he noticed the shutter on the window opening above him. He pressed himself and his men against the wall of the house: hopefully out of sight. He wondered why O'Sheen would open the shutters as he listened to O'Sheen and Spellman's conversation on his ear-piece through Spellman's wired microphone. Spellman was effectively occupying O'Sheen while final preparations were being made for the assault on the house.

The assault team needed a few more minutes. He had three men on the second floor of the adjoining house. Six men were preparing to move on the front, while his five man team was now prepared in the back. Mohammed had told Abdul that the size of the force was overkill. But based on the first attack, Abdul disagreed, explaining that he had learned that O'Sheen had excellent survival skills. They were not going to fail this time.

***

A more relaxed Spellman sat down across from me at the dinette table in the kitchen and asked, "What can you tell me about the impending threat? How many men do you expect to attack? Who exactly are they, and why are they after you?"

I quickly explained the first attack in Paris without disclosing my inaccuracy with my pistol. Brent asked me if I had any hypotheses on who might be behind the attack.

I was giving an evasive answer when Kamper walked into the room equipped with weaponry like "Rambo".

Agent Kamper pulled a chair out from the end of the table, turned it backward, and managed to maneuver into the seat with his arms resting on the back of the chair. His first question to me was, "When do you think they will start their assault." *A question that Spellman should have asked*

Instead of answering the question, I asked Spellman, "Why are you and Kamper the only protection in the house?"

Spellman answered. "I have five men in the back yard. Didn't you see them when you opened the shutters?"

When I shook my head he said, "They must have noticed the shutters opening and hid. I plan to bring three of them inside when you are comfortable with the arrangements."

A very logical reply. I said; "We have walls on both sides that adjoin the neighboring houses. You didn't mention any precautions taken on those walls."

Brent's back stiffened. Then his face relaxed as his mind came up with a plausible answer, "The safe-house owns the houses on both sides. I was disappointed that you didn't ask about that sooner."

I nodded thoughtfully, disguising the fact that I knew he was lying.

I heard the pager vibrate on Brent's belt.

He continued talking, "If you agree, I'll go get my men now?"

He reached down to turn off the pager and started to stand while looking nervously into my eyes. His nervousness made me realize his intent. He reached for the revolver on his hip.

I dropped to the floor under the table and shot Spellman in his right knee with my silenced Glock and rose up as a gunshot echoed loudly off the kitchen walls.

From my knees I aimed my Glock at Gene Kamper's head since he was the only target visible. Kamper calmly laid his gun on the corner of the kitchen table and backed away from it. I stood and put the gun barrel of my Glock into his left ear, and walked around the table, and I saw Brent Spellman's bloody body lying on the floor behind the table with a bullet-hole through his left eye. The bullet blew off the back of his head.

I looked back at Gene who wore a bemused smile on his handsome face.

Abdul listened to the whole dialogue exchange on his earpiece and wasn't surprised when the lame-brained idea of allowing O'Sheen to enter the house in the hope of gaining information failed to offer anything of value. They hadn't planned on Agent Kamper's arrival. The conversation after the gunshot that he heard through his earpiece didn't include Spellman, so Spellman was the one shot. He ordered the attackers to get in position.

Gene sensed that O'Sheen was in a fire-tense mode that required him to explain, "I was asked to preview the preparations for your arrival . . ."

I raised my hand to stop him, approached Spellman, ripped open his shirt throwing buttons in all directions, tore the microphone wire off him, and stomped it with my heel.

Gene nodded his approval and continued, "I was told by the agency that they had used Spellman in the past. I can't explain why, but I was uneasy when Spellman welcomed me into the house, and my first attempt to leave the house was diverted in a guise to seek my expertise. Spellman probably sensed that I mistrusted him, and he wasn't going to let me leave to warn you of a possible double-cross."

Gene continued. "A half hour ago, I pressed my 'panic button'". I have had no response. It's possible that Spellman and his men have installed an electronic jamming device.

"I played the same 'show me your preparation' ploy, while I tried to figure a way out. I didn't expect you to arrive safely, but when you did, I revised my escape plan." Gene let out a deep sigh after his hurried monologue.

With his voice rising to a higher crescendo, he asked, "Why didn't a man of your experience immediately recognize that the lack of internal security in the house exposed a threat?"

I answered, "Quite frankly, I thought you were the bad guy. I played along to learn as much as I could about you."

I lowered my pistol. I was starting to be impressed with this young man. Gene approached the kitchen table with the lethal arsenal still surrounding his body while retrieving a manila folder from under his shirt in the crook of his back. He said, "Well, you learned that they know more about this place than we do."

I approached as he opened the file and spread pictures across the table. I warned, "Do we have time for this now? Spellman's pager going off was a signal for the assault to begin."

"I may not get another chance." Gene explained. "If you survive this attack, you will need this intel."

This young man brought back many memories of my younger years. Even though death was knocking at the door, he was going to fulfill his mission and deliver his message. I watched as Gene pointed at the first picture and asked, "Do you recognize this man?"

I answered "I spotted him as the leader of the attack against me and my son in Paris days ago. Who is he?"

"His name is Abdul Hussein Faisad, a mercenary who primarily works for Middle Eastern oil money."

He pointed to the next picture on the table. "This is Mohammed Kareem Faisad. Abdul's cousin."

Gene pointed to a man in the third picture of two men standing next to each other. "This is the Sheik Mohammed Abdul Faisad, Mohammed's grandfather. We haven't yet identified the man standing next to him, but we think he might have provided the hologram belts."

By the intonation in his voice, I knew Gene had nothing more to offer. I started toward the front of the house sensing the attack was imminent.

I slightly opened the metal shutters on one of the front windows. Gene moved up beside me and looked out.

I declared, "Nothing yet."

We heard an explosion on the second floor.

I looked at Gene, "I'm sorry, pal. I guess it's just you and me. Thanks for saving my ass from Spellman in the kitchen. I'll take the second floor and the back yard."

My sting operation had backfired. My own CIA had betrayed me. I knew that it was unlikely that I could survive this large organized attack. I regretted that the young Agent Kamper would die with me . . .

or maybe Gene was a rogue agent who had betrayed me: not the CIA. He was polished.

I started running toward the stairs and maneuvered the AK-47 into firing position as I ran up the stairs two at a time. I took a quick glance around the railing at the top of the stairs into a vacant hallway. I pulled my head back from exposure and pictured the second floor layout in my mind and heard the chopping of an axe. Apparently the explosives had not been placed expertly enough to sever enough of the 2 by 4's in the wall to allow the mercenaries to enter. My guardian angel was still covering me.

I started down the hallway and pulled out my Glock with my free left hand. The chopping had stopped by the time I could see through the last open door on the left. I opened fire with my AK-47 at a man carrying an Uzi crossing toward the room's right front corner. I kept firing a pattern to the left as another man came into view who was climbing through the opening in the wall. With two men down, I dropped on the floor to my right knee outside the doorway while raising my Glock pistol in my left hand up and over the extended AK-47 barrel that was still aimed at the opening in the wall. I slid forward slowly exposing more of the rifle barrel. If there was another man, he was probably in the front right hand corner of the room. The aim of my rifle barrel should convince him that he had the advantage. Sure enough, he came into view aiming his Uzi at me. I shot him between his eyes with the Glock 19.

I put a new magazine in my AK-47 while heading back toward the stairs. *I had a full magazine and a half left as backup for the AK-47 and thirteen rounds left in my Glock.*

***

Mohammed knew that Spellman had failed to complete his mission when he heard the pistol report through his earpiece and the sound of Spellman's microphone being removed and crushed. Fortunately, there were only two adversaries. He had a 14-man assault team. He got his men into position in the back yard expecting that the door at the top of the stairs would open. He heard the explosives detonate and two minutes later heard a barrage of gunfire on the second floor.

Minutes later the back door opened slightly and a voice yelled in Farsi, "The second floor is clear."

Mohammed led his men to the bottom of the stairs and proceeded upward in a fast, but controlled motion. He paused halfway up, when he heard the explosion from the RPG hitting the front of the house. He was expecting the explosion, but the sound of it made him pause. He opened the door partway and was peering through when everything went black.

***

I looked out the open back window and through the shutters and saw five men spread out across the back yard in an organized firing position. All were watching the back door. I recognized the bearded man closest to the bottom of the stairs and realized that Mohammed was waiting for one of their team to open the door.

I moved to the door, pulled back the three sliding bolt locks, and took a deep breath realizing the risk of my invitation to myself and Agent Kamper. I grabbed the knob on the left side of the door and moved to my right as I pulled the door slightly open toward me. I yelled in Farsi, **"The second floor is clear."** I returned to the partially open shutters at the open window.

I watched three men approach the stairs while two men remained kneeling in the firing position on the grass. *Well trained.* I aimed my silenced Glock through the shutter and shot both of the kneeling guards in their foreheads. I timed the hiss from my silenced shots with the rhythm of Mohammed's footsteps on the wooden staircase.

I had to pull slightly back to aim through a different louver to shoot the third trailing man ascending the stairs. I was hoping that the man's fall would not be too audible as he fell down the stairs. The sound of his fall was covered by an explosion at the front of the house. It sounded like they used a rocket-propelled grenade to breach the front wall.

The distraction of the explosion had cost me at least one more kill. I stepped left toward the door, knowing my failure to get one more man could cost me my life.

As the metal back door slowly opened, I saw the gap widen over the middle door hinge and shot the last man that was following

Mohammed through the opening. Almost simultaneously, I reached out with my left hand to slam the door before Mohammed could crash through.

The door rebounded back toward me violently. I switched the Glock to my left hand and jerked the door open without exposing myself. The body of the Mohammed Faisad fell into the hallway. His head was bleeding where it had been smashed between the metal door and the metal door frame.

I cautiously surveyed the damage I had inflicted in the back yard. Satisfied that there was no immediate threat, I reached down and dragged Mohammed inside, closed the back door, and engaged the middle bolt. I removed a set of plastic slip-lock handcuffs from my weapons belt, put it around Mohammed's left wrist, around the large top banister post at the top of the stairs, and secured the cuff to Mohammed's right wrist.

I was pulling another handcuff from my belt when I heard a machine gun barrage from below. The barrage came from an AK-47, not an Uzi. *It must be Kamper firing.* I heard two pistol reports as I cuffed Mohammed's ankles together. After the pistol reports, it was eerily quiet below.

Apparently, Kamper hadn't survived for very long. It wasn't the first time that I was forced to overcome overwhelming odds on my own. I considered retreating through the back door to the alley, but there was probably another sniper covering that exit. My best escape was down the butler-style lift located on the floor below.

Chapter 13
Unfathomable

Abdul Faisad had joined the sniper on the flat roof across from the safe house. He watched a Hummer approach the house and four men exit the Hummer in all directions to take up tactical positions facing the house. He could hear automatic fire from the safe house as Kareem jumped out of a second Hummer and sent a rocket propelled grenade into wall next to the widow on the right side of the front door. Two men pulled ladders from the top of the Hummer and approached the hole in the house to the right of the stairs. Both of them wore wide yellow belts. When the ladders were positioned to climb up to the opening, they suddenly disappeared at the foot of the ladders and their images reappeared near the tops of the ladders. Abdul's clean-shaven face broke into a broad smile.

***

After Gene Kamper watched O'Sheen bounding up the stairs like a teenager, he looked outside and saw a Hummer pull up to the front of the house. He heard a barrage of gunfire on the second floor. Several men exited the Hummer and spread out as a second Hummer approached. A man jump out and aimed a rocket propelled grenade launcher toward his window. Gene ran from the window and dove over the couch before the loud explosion temporarily deafened him. He was stunned but not hurt. He peered around the edge of the couch and saw two men coming through the gaping hole in the front of the house where the window used to be. He waited for them to be fully exposed and rose to his feet firing his AK-47 in a crossing pattern that should have torn the two men apart. Astonishingly, his rapid fire had no effect on them. *The ammunition from the safe room must be filled with blanks.*

He felt a sharp pain in his chest, quickly followed by another. Top-secret hologram belts occupied his last thought before he passed out and fell to the floor.

*****

I prostrated myself on the floor as I approached the top of the stairs. I saw Agent Kamper lying on his back on the floor below. One man was approaching Gene with his pistol aimed at his head. Another man had his gun aimed toward the kitchen and slowly headed that way. I could probably escape down the back stairs, but Agent Kamper might still be alive. I couldn't abandon him: that was not in my DNA. *Death be damned.*

I crawfished away from the top of the stairs, and once out of sight I stood and positioned my AK-47 in a firing position and rushed down the stairs. I fired my AK-47 at the man approaching Gene with no effect. I continued firing across the empty room to the man's right assuming that he was wearing a hologram belt. I noticed that all the bullets didn't hit off the tile floor or the wall, and I heard the thud of a body hitting the floor.

A sharp impact hit my right side at the same time that a gunshot reported loudly from the right side of the room. With the breath almost knocked from my lungs, I dove down the last five steps to the floor below. Nine-millimeter gunfire followed me all the way down. The man's hologram image was near the kitchen door.

I rolled to my left and emptied the rest of the second magazine of my AK-47 across the empty room. I heard another body hit the floor. I rolled to my right side and quickly slammed my last-full AK-47 magazine into place. I heard a noise from the front of the house and rolled to my left as a bullet hit the position I had fortunately just abandoned, and I fired at the man shooting at me from a gaping hole in the front of the house. I was relieved to see that three bullets found their target propelling the man backward away from the opening. I fired a short burst splintering the top of the two ladders to discourage another advance.

I looked to my left and saw a man in an awkward lump on the floor wearing a strange yellow belt. The belt suddenly went into a smoky meltdown akin to an audiotape from the television episodes of "Mission Impossible." *We will disavow any knowledge of your mission.*

I rotated up to a sitting position scanning the room as another man, with a wide yellow belt, slowly materialized from invisibility in the room to my right. He was squirming painfully on the floor. I realized that the man was not an immediate threat and rose from the floor and approached him with my Glock ready. I looked into the man's agonized eyes and noticed his right hand approaching the five multicolored buttons on his yellow belt. When the man smiled, I dove behind the sofa next to Gene as a small explosion deafened the room.

I instinctively rolled back toward the opening in front of the house in time to eliminate another attacker at the top of the ladder with my Glock. I pulled a grenade off my belt, pulled the pin, and threw it through the hole in the front wall. The exploding grenade should end the assault.

***

Abdul heard multiple sirens approaching. He couldn't believe what he had just witnessed. He broke radio silence to call off the assault. He tried to contact his cousin Mohammed several times.

***

I heard Mohammed's name barked on one of the dead men's radios. I picked it up and said in Farsi, "Mohammed is my captive. Abdul, you can run and try to hide, but I will eventually find you. I now know that you are a coward . . . afraid to join your men during the assault."

Abdul recognized O'Sheens voice from Spellman's earlier wiretap. He wanted to confront the man, but with the sirens approaching he was forced to flee the area. Mohammed had insisted on being the one to kill O'Sheen. Abdul should not have agreed to let him go in without his backup.

Chapter 14
Kamper

Gene woke up to what his subconscious registered as another explosion. He tried to sit up, but the pain forced him back down until his mind let his eyes come back into focus. He surveyed the room. He looked left and saw O'Sheen kneeling on the floor, firing his AK-47 toward what he remembered should be the front of the house. He saw that Pat noticed his movement. He watched the old man jump to his feet, jump over his prostrate body, and skid to his knees next to a body crumpled on the floor. Pat spoke in Farsi into a radio as he unbuckled a yellow belt and flipped the lifeless body off the belt. He turned and threw the wide yellow belt down the hallway.

Gene painfully sat up. His sudden movement caused Pat to look back in his direction. Gene had never seen such frightful redness in anyone's eyes. He watched Pat jump to his feet like a young man and run to the big hole in the front of the house. Multiple sirens were approaching from a distance. Pat turned back toward him again. Gene was frightened as the wild man approached him. But suddenly the stress in Pat's eyes merged into amusement. Maybe Gene's ego even imagined a hint of admiration.

Pat said, "I'm glad that you put on a bullet-proof vest."

Then Pat stepped past him and hurried toward the stairs saying, "I could use your help upstairs if you're able."

Gene didn't feel able. He unsuccessfully tried to jump to his feet. The pain in his chest made him fall back and roll over onto his stomach while wondering if the Kevlar vest was really a blessing. He pushed up onto his knees like the old man that just ran up the stairs two-at-a-time should have done. He struggled to his feet, picked up his AK-47, ejected the used magazine, and crammed a full magazine into place. He approached the opening in the front of the house. Two bodies lay at the bottom of the two ladders that leaned up to the hole made by the RPG explosion. Seeing no threat, he turned toward the stairs and saw the remains of another man surrounded by fragments of another yellow belt. He walked toward the stairs wondering why O'Sheen wanted him on the second floor.

At the top of the stairs, he saw Pat securing a set up plastic handcuffs to the wrists of the unconscious body of Mohammed Faisad. He noticed another pair of severed plastic cuffs on the man's wrists that had probably secured him to the top post on the railing.

Pat said, "Help me get him down the stairs."

Gene didn't answer and walked to the open window next to the back door. He saw a body lying halfway down the stairs, another at the bottom, and two on each side of the bottom of the stairs. *Incredible!*

While he was mesmerized by the scene out the window, he noticed that Pat had grabbed the large man under the arms, backed toward the stairs, held the man's head up, and dragged him down the stairs with trailing feet and butt bouncing up and down off the stairs. Gene ran down the hallway and saw the two men riddled with bullets from O'Sheen's AK-47. A third man had a 9 mm hole slightly above the center of his eyes.

Gene overcame his amazement and ran after Pat down the stairs, but he was unable to move fast enough to catch up.

Dragging Mohammed down the hallway, Pat asked him sarcastically, "Gene, can you at least open the lift panel?"

Obediently, Gene ran ahead and manipulated the switch under the chair rail. Pat had already arrived with the body in tow by the time the panel slid fully open. Gene watched the old man bend down, grab what might be a corpse, lift the large man off the floor and throw him onto the small metal floor of the lift.

Pat looked at Gene and asked, "Can you explain your presence here to the Parisian authorities?" Without waiting for an answer he ordered, "Handle him until I can join you."

Pat forced Gene to step into the small lift. He had to stand on top of the body. O'Sheen handed him his Glock pistol with the silencer still attached, reached over and punched a button that started Gene and his captive downward. Seconds later, a big yellow belt flew into the small space before the wall panel fully closed. While Gene was trying to formulate some logic to this bizarre scene, he blurted out; "Don't let them find my file on the kitchen table."

Chapter 15
Police

I ran to the weapons room while removing my weapons belt. I saw that Gene had made a total mess of the room. It reminded me of my children's rooms when they had been left alone for too long to play with their toys.

I discarded all my weapons to the floor of the room, closed the weapons panel, and ran to the front door. I unlocked it and opened it a few inches. I ran to the kitchen as the sirens stopped on the street in front of the house. I opened Gene's file and perused the part I hadn't seen. I tucked the file deeply into the back of my pants under my shirt as I heard the advance police team coming through the front door. I sat on the chair facing the kitchen door and placed my hands palms up on the table far out in front of me. When the police entered the room, I knew not to move a muscle as three policemen's weapons bore down on me.

The lead officer grabbed the upper arm of a subordinate standing next to him and waved the others on to secure the lower rooms. I heard another part of the team ascending the stairs to secure the upper rooms.

The officer in charge had fierce eyes and demanded that I raise my hands and stand up slowly. I recognized the dialect from the Burgundy region of France. I was tempted feign a misunderstanding of the command with an English reply. Instead, I raised my hands and slowly stood up. The officer circled the table and noticed the bloody body of Brent Spellman behind it.

The other officer approached and physically spun me around, forced my head forward over a kitchen counter, aggressively kicked my legs apart, and patted down my body searching for weapons without considering American sensitivities. I was told to return to my seat, with hands in front, palms down on the table. The man had either not felt the file tucked into the back of my pants or didn't consider it a threat.

I sat for several minutes as I heard reports broadcast through the officer-in-charge's radio describing the carnage in different areas of the house and back yard.

The officer-in-charge, his nametag identified him as Sabadeaux, his stripes identified him as a lieutenant, politely asked me, "Are you Pat O'Sheen?" I hoped he received my name over his earpiece from Inspector Boudreaux.

After I nodded, he said, "I need you to come with me to identify the dead on your team."

I knew that my answer would not be believable, but I answered truthfully; "I didn't have a team. All of the dead men are my attackers."

The lieutenant glared at me in disbelief. He was suddenly fearful and distrustful. "Stand up and slowly put your hands behind your back." He ordered the other officer, "Cuff him."

I was complying with the order when I heard a familiar voice say, "Lieutenant Sabadeaux, I'll take over here."

I turned my head slightly and saw Pierre Boudreaux entering the kitchen.

All of the guns in the room were still aimed at me.

"Cuff him with his hands in front." Pierre ordered.

I was glad that my hands were cuffed in front and not behind me. "O'Sheen, we want to know what happened here." I noticed the admiration on the lieutenant's face and his relief that Pierre was taking control of this bazaar killing-field.

Pierre didn't hesitate long enough for me to respond and continued his monolog, "You were being held at the Prefecture for another bloody battle that occurred only a few days ago. Due to lack of evidence, we had to release you. That was about an hour ago. Multiple calls entered our phone banks describing a war on Rue Deus. I ran to where I had parked my sedan and it was gone. I commandeered a black and white to get here and there was my severely damaged car in front of this house. And here you are again surrounded by mass homicidal mayhem. You will not convince me that this isn't related to the first incident."

I started to respond but was cut off again before I began.

Pierre gruffly commanded, "Get Orleon in here with her camcorder."

No words were exchanged for two minutes while we waited. I realized that Pierre was avoiding eye contact. My heartbeat increased and my head warmed around the stitches on its crown. My gut hadn't yet raised a red flag.

I was shocked at the beauty of the woman who entered the room. She had full, long-flowing, dark black hair that hung attractively inches below her strong-looking shoulders, and a feminine figure that her police uniform failed to hide. She gracefully entered the kitchen with a portable video camcorder in her right hand and a pad and pencil held in her exquisite left hand. Her eyes met mine. I saw her look of surprise before she looked away. There was recognition in her surprise. She turned on her camcorder and aimed it at me. I noticed that she wasn't wearing a gun.

Pierre asked her, "Michelle, are you recording?"

"Yes sir," Michelle Orleon answered in a silky voice.

Michelle was gorgeous. Her face was triangular except for her square chin with a slight cleft that matched the cleft on her sexy upper lip under her perfect nose. Her cheekbones were high but not like high-priced models. Her eyes were her best feature. They were not the large almond-shape that attracted immediate attention. They were spread wide toward the side of her face. She didn't have an Egyptian nose, but it was thin, prominent with a sexy slant, and perfectly straight. She didn't have a wide mouth or voluptuous lips. None of her features were exceptional, but all of her features fit together perfectly—exquisitely: the whole better than the individual parts. She was one of the most beautiful women I had ever seen.

Chapter 16
Michelle

Michelle Orleon watched intently as Pierre encouraged the older O'Sheen to lead them through the crime scene. O'Sheen was old enough to be her father. Something exploded in her body when their eyes met. She wondered why he had held her gaze for so long. Most men would have broken eye contact to admire her body.

Michelle graduated at the top of her class in forensic pathology at George Washington University in D.C. She was the president of the photography club, which was still her favorite hobby. She recorded everything as the older man walked Pierre through the mayhem. The description of the events that he described was surreal. No one man could have survived such an onslaught, but his explanations to Pierre somehow made perfect sense, and the timing of each event was logical and believable. The man turned away from the window by the back door and explained his uneasiness with Spellman as he recounted Spellman's guided tour of the house. He explained his logic for leaving the back window up and the protective louvers slightly open. He glanced sideways at Michelle, and she suddenly realized that this dangerous man was a threat to her.

She was relieved when he turned away and started down the hallway. When he suddenly turned back to her, he gave her a look that turned her blood both hot and cold. She had to separate herself from this man so that she could transmit her report. She asked Pierre, "May I use this water closet?" Pierre nodded in the affirmative.

When she entered the bathroom and closed the door, Pierre was shocked when Pat walk up and put his ear to the closed door. Lieutenant Sabadeaux was about to object when Pierre raised his hand.

Michelle punched a speed dial number into her cell phone as she lowered her pants and sat on the cold commode. After encountering O'Sheen and seeing the results of his talents, she was enthralled. She was seriously relieving her bladder when the voice mail tone engaged without instructions. She relayed, "P1 alive and unharmed. A2 and MF not accounted for. No other survivors."

***

I moved away from the door, approached Pierre, and whispered, "We need to talk privately."

Pierre hesitated while he formulated a plan in his mind. He decided on the truth. He told Lieutenant Sabadeaux as Michelle exited the bathroom, "I've known this man for almost twenty years. I need to talk to him privately. Moe, do you have any objections?"

Without objection, we walked down the hallway, and I led him through the door to large bedroom on the right. I noticed Michelle following us.

She tried to enter the room with us when Pierre turned, looked at her, and said, "Did you misunderstand the word 'privately'?"

Pierre was knocked off guard when I reached past him, grabbed Michelle's wrist with my cuffed hands, and pulled her into the room. Pierre turned on me, the sensibilities of his patience having been exceeded. He was not going to let me treat one of his men, well actually this beautiful subordinate in such a manner.

I closed the door and immediately backed away from Pierre and Michelle. I demanded, "Take her cell phone."

Pierre noticed her movement toward the door, slammed his hand against the door, and held it shut while he reached across her body for her phone. The force of her left hook to his right jaw stunned him, bringing stars to his eyes.

I moved in and pinned her against the wall while Pierre took her cell phone and punched a button to view her last call. It was made a minute ago.

I said, "She was reporting my status to the attackers."

Pierre opened the door and yelled, **"Moe."**

Lieutenant Sabadeaux tensed at the unusual force in Pierre's voice and ran down the hallway while drawing his weapon. Entering the door he saw Pierre standing a few feet inside the doorway. O'Sheen held Moe's beloved Michelle in a compromised position. He started to raise his gun toward O'Sheen, but Pierre's hand stopped him.

"Arrest this woman."

Moe wondered if had heard Pierre correctly? He shouldn't refer to her as *this woman*. Moe turned toward Pierre with animosity and noticed a bruise developing on the back of his right jaw. He turned his focus to me with hatred building in his stare, aware that I was still cuffed and apparently unarmed. Confused, he looked at Michelle. Her beautiful eyes looked pleadingly into his. He barely heard Pierre's order to cuff her, but Moe Sabadeaux did what he was ordered to do. He cuffed Michelle and followed Pierre's command to take her to the kitchen for questioning. Moe's heart was squeezed by Michelle's betrayed and angry glare as he cuffed her.

Pierre turned to me with anger, frustration, and confusion all written on his face at the same time. I spoke first, "You need to trace that last call she made. It will prove that she is working with the group behind these attacks against me."

Still frustrated, Pierre challenged, "Pat, this has gone too far. I am not helping you any further without a full explanation. You are the only one we can blame for all these dead bodies. I already told you that I couldn't protect you from my superiors again. You have to give me something . . . something to prevent them from forcing me to put you in jail until a hearing can be arranged."

I understood Pierre's dilemma, and I disarmed him by stating, "So we now have to be more worried about supervisors than terrorists?"

I stung him deeper, "You could have had me followed from the prefecture. You knew they were watching and waiting for me to make my exit. I warned you of the eminent attack against me. Why didn't you have me covered?"

Pierre defended himself, "Where is your beloved CIA that was going to act illegally in my country to capture the terrorists? You would have asked for my backup if you wanted it."

I nodded in understanding, "I was betrayed. Pierre, I have a folder with three pictures in the seat of my pants. I have one of the men in the pictures in custody, and he will die soon if you don't let me get to him."

Pierre recoiled in disbelief. "You have a man in custody? Impossible! Where is he?"

I wagged my backside and turned my head toward it, reminding Pierre of the folder location. I turned as Pierre reached down the back of my pants and said. "Be gentle, Pierre."

Pierre chuckled. How could Pat so easily disarm his anger? Maybe a dozen men were dead by this man's cuffed hands, and he made an extraordinary claim that he had a man in custody, when there was obviously no place to hide a captive in the building. Pat had just uncovered and exposed one of his most treasured new employees. And yet, he was still able to joke about someone reaching down the back of his pants.

The French government always encouraged Pierre to develop a friendly relationship with Pat O'Sheen. They knew he was an incredibly talented covert agent. They even suspected that he might be the legendary covert agent codenamed Coyote. After what he just observed in this safe house, Pierre believed that they might be right. But that was not why he had befriended Pat. On the first night they met, Pat had saved Pierre's life, held his hand as he recovered in the hospital, and over the years became one his most beloved friends.

Pierre extracted the folder and pulled three pictures from it. He spread the pictures out on the double bed in the room as I approached. He recognized the pictures that his superiors had given to Agent Kamper.

I pointed to the center picture with my cuffed hands; "Mohammed Faisad."

Pierre said, "He was one of those watching for you to exit the prefecture."

I was tempted to chastise Pierre again for not covering my departure from his office, "He is the one I have in custody. You need to allow me to interrogate him before his injuries overcome him."

"Where is he, pray tell."

I noticed Pierre's disbelief again. "Hidden."

"I need to interrogate him with you."

I said, "Pierre, I'm sorry, but I can't allow that. The questions I have to ask him are classified 'top-secret' in America, and I refuse to involve you and your family in my current nightmare."

After a stare down with O'Sheen, Pierre said in acquiescence, "After you interrogate him, you must turn him over to me."

"I promise that I will do that."

Pierre pointed to another picture, "This man was watching for you to leave the prefecture too."

I said, "Abdul Faisad, Mohammed's cousin. He got away.

Pierre removed the handcuffs while I presented my plan. After a few modifications and Pierre's cell phone call, we left the room. I noticed curious but non-threatening policemen's eyes following us to the back door.

Pierre and I watched a police car pull up to back gate. I went down the back stairs, through the back yard, and opened the back gate after reaching down and extracting a small metal stake with a three-inch diameter, thin metal flower. I closed the gate and entered the opened back door of the awaiting police cruiser. I told the driver to move forward slowly.

The driver told me, "Sir, your door is not closed."

I commanded the driver to start moving as I slammed the door. The back seat doors locked automatically when the car moved forward. I knew that they could not be opened from inside the back seat.

Chapter 17
Manage the bizarre

Pierre watched Pat enter the police car, satisfied that he would be able to talk some sense into Pat later. He knew that Pat wouldn't leave a dying man alone. He had to get away from scrutinizing ears so that they could interrogate Mohammed together. He hated that he had deceived his friend, but the stakes were getting too high, and Pat hadn't been totally honest with him. Pierre could tell from the crime scene that Pat had help from someone. Pierre assumed that the man or men who helped Pat were holding Mohammed somewhere. Pat had to get the pictures from agent Kamper when he entered the safe house. Kamper would not let Mohammed die.

When Pierre reentered the house from the back deck, he spat out his commands for an immediate meeting. He brought the forensic specialist from the back yard with him.

When they entered the kitchen the team was assembled. He looked at Michelle sitting on a chair handcuffed. She threw her most attractive and sensuous smile at him for all the men in the room to see: which was contrary to what a guilty person would do.

Before Pierre began, Lieutenant Sabadeaux asked angrily, "Where is O'Sheen?" Moe Sabadeaux was pissed. Pierre had been his mentor for ten years. O'Sheen was driving large holes through their peace and harmony . . . well maybe harmony wasn't a proper description of Moe's present life. *But why would Pierre turn against Michelle? What hold did O'Sheen have over him?*

Pierre responded, "I had a police car pick up O'Sheen to put him into protective custody."

Sabadeaux was incredulous and glared at Pierre. He looked at the forensic specialist he had brought in from the back yard. The man nodded in agreement, and to Pierre's relief the specialist added, "O'Sheen left in the back seat of a police cruiser from the back gate."

Pierre still noticed the disapproval in the room. Most of the men were watching Michelle and showing anger in their eyes at her captive state. The sentiment in the room was in her favor.

Pierre had to regain control. "We will interrogate O'Sheen at the station. O'Sheen said Michelle made a call on this cell phone from the bathroom." He held the phone up. "When I tried to get this phone from her, she slugged me right here." He rotated so that everyone could see the swelling. "She did make a call from the bathroom. O'Sheen believes she was making a report to his attackers. Lieutenant Sabadeaux, what do you think? Why would she make a call from the bathroom?"

When too much hesitation ensued, Pierre, in a very calm and soothing voice addressed Sabadeaux less formally, "Moe, give us your insight into this mess?" He noticed that his change of tone effectively reduced the tension in the room. The hateful look in Moe Sabadeaux's eyes seemed to dissipate. Pierre noticed it returning when Moe looked at Michelle, whose eyes radiated her pleading.

Pierre observed the power she possessed over his lieutenant. He queried again softly, "Moe?"

Suddenly, Moe stood up. He tore his eyes away from Michelle, realizing that he had been duped by man's most primal weakness.

He had stood up to defend her, but the bizarre circumstances of this killing field and his experience on the street brought him back to his senses. He looked back at Michelle and realized that he had almost given up his wife, kids, and his career for her. And that he didn't even know who she was. Words suddenly came into his mouth from nowhere. "Inspector Boudreaux, based on the recent events surrounding Pat O'Sheen, he is an obvious target of a large organization with substantial financial backing." He paused as he repelled Michelle's control over him. He recalled many of her questions concerning O'Sheen in the last few days. He reeled at his recollections of the research on O'Sheen he had done to answer her questions. He glared at Michelle and bit his tongue to stop a self-deprecating monologue that was fast-forwarding in his head, and that if put into words could ruin his career. He simply added, "You were right to remove O'Sheen from here into protective custody."

Pierre smiled at Moe's recovery.

Moe pointed at Michelle, "That woman has attempted to manipulate our entire department, and I think she may have assisted in this organized attack on O'Sheen. She has asked me several probing questions about O'Sheen during the last few days."

Pierre said a silent prayer of thanksgiving. He wondered how Pat saw through Michelle's facade so quickly.

Pierre understood how Lieutenant Sabadeaux had been compromised by Michelle's enticements. Her exceptional beauty and her seductive ways had also tempted Pierre. His wonderful wife and family, his strong Catholic upbringing, and the taboo of friendship between management and subordinates had helped him to reign in his passion.

Pierre commanded forcefully, "Moe, you are in charge now. I have to follow up with O'Sheen at the station. Do you have any questions before I leave?"

Pierre saw Moe Sabadeaux react with pride at being put in charge. Pierre realized why his favorite lieutenant was not living up to expectations lately. He watched as Moe picked two female officers to take Michelle to "lock up" at the station, and directed other teams to investigative assignments. Pierre recognized the resolve in Moe that had been missing over the last few weeks: the weeks that followed Michelle's assignment to his department. Pierre thought, *I have to find out who assigned her to my department.*

Chapter 18
Failure

This time Abdul had to make the call. He was wondering how to explain to Sheik Faisad the failed mission and that that his grandson was captured. He punched a three-digit speed-dial number into his cell phone. Even though his mind had rehearsed his report, the cell phone was shaking in his hand as he raised it to his left ear.

The sheik answered, and as expected, Abdul's report was received with vitriol. A familiar commanding voice that Abdul had only heard once before, questioned him in English with an American accent, "Abdul, are you telling us that Pat O'Sheen survived, that he may have possession of the yellow belts, and that Mohammed was captured?"

"Yes. I warned you about O'Sheen's skills. He may be the best warrior on this planet. O'Sheen is too talented for an assault team. Somehow he figured out how to defeat the men wearing the hologram belts, and he killed most of my fourteen well-trained men on the assault team. I explained my concern after our first attack against him. Review my written report on the first attack and my recommendations."

Abdul listened to another American voice, one he had never heard before. "If they have the belts and if Mohammed is still alive the situation is further compromised. If Pat O'Sheen survived, we don't want him dead. We need to interrogate him."

Abdul made the most dangerous decision of his life. He was not going to work for Americans trying to kill O'Sheen. He said, "I will handle this in my own way."

"You will handle it our way or you will not be paid."

Abdul growled, "I don't want your satanic American money."

The smooth American voice warned, "If you don't follow our instructions, you will be eliminated."

Abdul laughed for several seconds. "You better send many of your best against me. Like Pat O'Sheen, I can handle them." He disconnected.

***

As the police officer drove up the alley away from the back gate of the CIA safe house, I ordered, "Stop at the next gate."

Instead of hitting the break, the driver accelerated.

I couldn't believe that Pierre had betrayed me. I rammed my left shoulder against the door hoping that the thin metal flower that I had inserted into the door lock mechanism served its intended purpose. When the door sprang open, I rolled out of the accelerating car and tumbled into the alley.

As I stood up painfully limping on the reinjured ankle that I had hurt scaling down the fire escape, I approached the back gate of the house four doors down from the safe house. The police car screeched to a stop two gates down and the driver's door flew open. I opened the backyard wooden gate toward the driver, shielding me from harm.

I closed the gate behind me and tripped clumsily to the ground. A severe pain in my right rib under my Kevlar vest from the bullet that hit it made its presence known. *I was getting too old for this*!

I heard the policeman say on his radio. "O'Sheen has escaped through a yard toward Roux Deux. I'm driving around the block in pursuit." I heard the car speed away.

I removed my polo shirt as I stood up and hurried up the stairs. I wrapped my right elbow in the shirt and reached for the doorknob. The knob turned, but there was a bolt lock preventing entry as expected. This house didn't have a steel back door, and the door had four small windows.

I considered what I was about to try based only on what Spellman had told me. My gut was not aching which was encouraging. I smashed my right elbow that was covered by the shirt through the bottom left corner window panel next to the doorknob. I sensed a vibration. Maybe an alarm on the broken window would finally bring in the CIA cavalry that Agent Kamper had expected. I reached through the broken window and retracted the middle bolt on the door. Its similarity to the bolt at the safe house was encouraging.

The door would still not open.

I jumped up and crashed my elbow through the upper left glass panel on the door. The pain at impact went down my arm numbing my right hand. I landed with most of my weight on my left foot, but my right ankle still screamed out in pain. Because of the numbness in my right arm, I had to reach through the broken window with my left hand to slide open the top bolt. I did not have a plan to reach a bottom bolt, hoping there wasn't one, or hoping for laziness on the part of the last person that bolted the door. I twisted the knob and sighed in relief when the door opened. *My guardian angel!*

I remembered Spellman's claim of having men in adjoining houses. He would have stationed men in this house too. Otherwise, he would not have told me about the underground escape route. I almost laughed out loud at the realization that I had lost my only weapon: a painted metal garden flower.

I hurried through the door toward the top of the staircase, descended the staircase, jumped to the floor in the living room, and grabbed a decorative poker from a fire-tool stand, and coiled for an assault.

My ankle cried out in agony, but the house was quiet. No assault came. The front door was partially open. The assault team had left in a hurry.

I felt the vibration again when my elbow hit the top pane on the back door and realized that it was my cell phone. I retrieved it from my front pocket. I recognized Jody's number calling from his assignment in Australia and connected, "Jody, is everything alright?"

"Dad, I identified one man shadowing us when we got here. Now there are three. What do you recommend?"

I replied, "Put the family on Code 2 and activate the full Australian backup team." I explained, "Jody, they attacked me again in Paris with a much larger force than the last time. I captured one of my attackers and a strange yellow belt worn by two of the attackers. I am about to interrogate my captive. I'll keep you informed."

I closed and locked the front door while making a call to Cory Webb, an agent friend with MI-6 who lived in Australia, and who had helped me in covert operations in the Far East. I apologized for waking him up, and I updated him on Jody's situation.

Chapter 19
Mohammed Faisad

After I disconnected from Cory Webb, I ran down a familiar looking hallway and reached under the chair-rail wainscot. The panel cooperatively slid open. It had the identical lift as the other safe house. *If Spellman was the enemy, why had he revealed so much?*

I started to enter the lift when my instincts made me recoil and forced me to step back into the hallway. My heart was racing. *If Spellman wasn't the enemy, was Gene Kamper?* I closed my eyes and took three deep breaths. I checked under the wainscot across the hallway to see if it had another weapons room: *no such luck.*

I stood motionless, closed my eyes, and prayed for inspiration. I was drawn back toward the front door. To the left of the front door, in what could be described as a small living room, was a paneled entertainment center eerily similar to the arrangement in my house in Alabama. I pressed the panel that opened the consol. The green LED lights on the electronics were steady, not indicating a security warning. I found a Colt 38 revolver hidden in the right side of the consol.

I hit the release on the revolver and rotated the magazine open to expose the back of the bullet cartridges. I extracted two of the bullets, was satisfied with their weight, re-inserted them, and slammed the revolver into alignment. I searched the surrounding areas for more cartridges to no avail. Six shots would have to do. I found a flashlight in the console that tested positive, and found a large butcher knife in the kitchen. I approached the lift, and then backed off again.

Three questions: First, *what had happened to the CIA sting operation that I helped plan? Second, was the CIA double-cross designed to silence my knowledge of a top-secret hologram security leak?* Third, *was Gene Kamper at the safe house to make sure I would no longer be a threat to expose the top security leak?*

Gene had killed Spellman. *Was Spellman planning to shoot Kamper and not me?* Kamper was obviously not on Brett Spellman's side, or on the side of Mohammed's group who shot him in the chest.

I recalled that Gene had sufficient opportunity to kill me while I dragged Mohammed to the lift. But Gene wasn't present when Spellman showed me the location of the lift-panel's opening button. *Yet Gene had opened the panel before I arrived with Mohammed's body.*

Dear God, I have to trust someone.

I entered the lift. As the slow mechanism lowered me to the sublevel, I replayed Gene's every word through my audio-graphic memory from the first moment we met. I was at full alert when the lift stopped. The lights in the underground hallway were on. There was no immediate threat on the lower level.

I set the flashlight on the floor inside the lift and walked through the narrow passageway under the three intervening dwellings while counting my steps in case I was forced to retreat in darkness. I approached a closed door that looked like a WWII bunker.

I studied the door. Opening that door could be deadly. Gene and Mohammed should be in there, if they hadn't already fled the same way I had just entered. *Are they working together? Not likely. But why did Kamper close the door.* I reached for the door handle.

***

Robby Clark, who had accompanied Jody to Melbourne, listened as Jody relayed what little he knew of the attack on his dad. Jody went silent; his mind was totally absorbed into a reverie. Robby had seen Jody's dad do the same thing many times before.

Recognizing Jody's tension, Robby tried to distract him, "How is Keisha feeling today?"

The ploy didn't work. Jody's mind was totally occupied. Robby released the magazine on his Sig Sauer P-226. When he jammed the magazine noisily back into the handle, the threatening sound brought Jody out of his reverie.

Jody initially responded angrily. "We have 12 hours to prepare for this concert, and we know we have adversaries that have us under surveillance."

Jody recognized that Robby knew the concert wasn't the main issue. Someone had launched another major attack on his dad. Because they failed, his dad had warned him that they might come for the family: that he might be a target again. The sudden increased surveillance against him in Australia supported his dad's concerns.

Jody shared his apprehension, "Robby, I'm not sure how to proceed. Our primary job is to protect Keisha, but I can't ignore the increased surveillance."

Jody decided before Robby could respond, "Robby, I am going out as bait. I want you to arrange the capture of some of the surveillance team following me and find a proper place for an interrogation."

Robby stood up immediately. "Give me an hour to set it up." He smiled at the young O'Sheen before he left the room.

Robby would normally be in Alabama protecting the family. He liked this role better. He liked Jody and noticed that after the Paris encounter, Jody had started acquiring some of his father's aggressive traits.

An hour later, Robby and Jody finished reviewing the plan. It was perilous, and Jody said a small prayer knowing that some future events were out of his control.

***

I turned the handle on the bunker door and considered busting through the door with the Colt 38 blazing. Instead, I slowly opened the door. Gene Kamper was standing inside the door with my silenced Glock aimed toward the opening door. I backed up a step, allowing the door to close under the weight of gravity.

***

Gene noticed the 38 Special in O'Sheen's hands through the slightly opened door. When the door closed, he knew that O'Sheen still didn't trust him. He knew that he would have to open the door and expose himself before O'Sheen would feel comfortable.

He lowered his gun to his side and slowly opened the door. A Colt 38 was aimed between his eyes. Gene smiled, "Come in, Major O'Sheen."

***

I noticed that my captive was lying on a cot still wearing the cuffs. I told Gene, "I need to interrogate Mohammed alone."

Gene objected, "I have to make sure that any interrogation is done according to the Geneva Convention."

I chuckled. "Okay, you covered your politically-correct ass." I pulled back the hammer on the Colt 38 knowing that Kamper would hear the click and understand the warning. "Now get your ass out of here and close the door behind you."

Gene exited and closed the door saying, "I'll be right outside if you should need me." I slid a bolt lock closed on the inside of the door as an answer to Gene's offer.

Mohammed watched me with hatred radiating from his eyes while I placed three pictures face up on the floor in the middle of the room. I approached the foot of his cot with the large butcher knife in my left hand and the pistol in my right. While approaching, I feigned with the knife toward Mohammed, who instinctively curled his knees up toward his stomach and raised his cuffed hands. When I backed off, Mohammed's ankles were no longer cuffed together. I slid the pistol inside the back of my belt as I crossed the room and stood next to the bolted door. I tossed the knife into the far front corner.

I told him in Arabic, "Mohammed, I want you to stand up and slowly approach the pictures on the floor."

Mohammed did as he was told realizing that the approach would put him only five feet from the careless old man. He stooped to look down at the pictures.

I knew that in any interrogation it was important to get a truthful answer to the first question. "Identify the man in the picture on your far left."

Mohammed looked at me and hissed, "You know that is a picture of me."

I demanded, "Identify the man in the middle picture."

Mohammed lowered further into a crouch, feigning an attempt to get a closer look at the picture. He looked at the third picture, paused, and charged, swinging his cuffed hands at my head. He yelled in pain as I ducked and his knuckles hit the solid concrete block wall. When he turned to me, I broke his nose with a left-handed punch and flipped him over my shoulder to the floor. I heard his left humerus bone break when he reached out his cuffed hands and elbows to protect his face from slamming into the concrete floor. He screamed out in pain.

I retrieved the pistol from behind my back and from three feet away aimed it between Mohammed's eyes.

I explained, "It would have been a lot less painful if you had just told me that the man in the middle picture is your cousin, Abdul Hussein Faisad."

I asked threateningly, **"Who are the men in the third picture?"**

Mohammed cleared his throat, glared at me with hatred, and spat a wad of spittle.

I had heard him clear his throat and anticipated the action from previous experience with men from the Middle East and avoided the wad of phlegm by moving to my left as it passed over my right shoulder.

Mohammed was upset that he missed me and hollered in English, **"You killed my father, you rotten motherfucker, asshole, son of a bitch."** He voiced expletives that would be used under the circumstances in the West, but not ones that a zealous Muslim would use.

But the accusation made me back up several steps. The missing link struck me like thunderbolt. My mind finally connected to the name *Faisad.* Before the first Gulf war, after I spent a month undercover in Iraq, I warned our government of Hussein's impending invasion of Kuwait. I led a Special Forces unit into Kuwait to try to stop Saddam Hussein's invasion by thwarting an advanced group of saboteurs who were sent to Kuwait to disrupt their communication system. The lead saboteur was one of Saddam's many nephews. Second in command was Mohammed Kareem Faisad, who I now realized was the father of the man who lay on the floor in front of me. I now understood why the sheik was targeting my family.

I asked in a soft tone, "Who is the man standing with your grandfather?"

Mohammed blinked repeatedly when he realized that I had already identified his grandfather, and that he was not being asked to betray his grandfather's identity. He had already decided to answer when I pressed my foot against his broken arm.

He yelled, "He is the man who supplied the yellow belts."

"Who is he?"

When Mohammed hesitated, I pressed down harder, sending pain through his entire arm. He screamed. "He calls himself Jonathan Booth. I think he works for an American defense contractor."

"What is the name of the contractor?"

When I lowered my foot again, Mohammed screamed, **"I don't know the name of the contractor. I swear to Allah."**

I believed him. I now understood the motives for the attacks against me, and I knew how to proceed with this new knowledge.

I retrieved the knife from the corner, and the picture of the grandfather and Jonathan Booth from the floor and left Mohammed's picture and Abdul's picture in place. I slowly opened the door being careful not to expose my body and glanced out.

Gene had again raised the silenced Glock toward the opening door. Recognizing me, he lowered it immediately. I opened the door and Gene smiled as he looked down the barrel of my revolver again.

I lowered the weapon and asked, "Did you hear any of that conversation?"

"I heard some of it, but I only know a small bit of Arabic."

"Good. Grab the yellow belt and let's get out of here." I closed the door and lowered the three foot steel bar hinged beside the door down into the metal channel by the doorknob, preventing Mohammed's escape. Gene retrieved the yellow belt from near the ceiling between two floor joists on top of a concrete block wall—a good hiding place.

Gene pointed to the room wondering if Mohammed was still alive, and if so, whether he would survive without a means of escape; "What about him?"

I pointed down the hallway toward the lift four buildings down and hurried down the subterranean hallway. I pushed Gene into the lift, reached down and picked up the flashlight off the lift floor, and squeezed in beside him while activating the lift. I realized that I was vulnerable to the younger, stronger agent in the cramped space.

It was totally dark when we reached the main level. I snapped on the flashlight, and we ascertained that the first floor was clear.

I hit a speed dial number on my cell phone. When it was answered I said in English, "Pierre, I am very disappointed in you. You should have trusted me."

"You lied to me, Pat. I could see evidence that someone helped you during the attack."

I sighed loudly, "Touché.

"Mohammed Faisad is in a bunker below you. The lift switch is under the chair rail to the right of the decorative panel in the hallway leading from the bottom of the stairway to the kitchen. Be careful entering the bunker. Mohammed has a broken arm and nose, and he is pissed."

Gene was relieved to know that Mohammed was alive and was not going to die of dehydration locked in the bunker.

He heard Pat say, "No. I won't surrender. I have to leave to protect my family. I'll be in touch." He disconnected.

Gene followed me to the second floor, and we searched it. I grabbed a towel out of the bathroom and told Gene to wrap the yellow belt in it. "Follow me and maintain absolute silence until I speak to you first. If you need to get my attention, tap me on the shoulder. Do you understand?"

Gene nodded. He wanted to get away from the area too. O'Sheen was his best bet at getting away.

We went out the back door and through the alley. Five blocks away, I turned to him knowing that we were not being followed and asked, "What do you want to do now?"

"I'm tempted to activate my panic button again," Gene replied.

I countered, "After today? Are you sure you can trust anyone with the CIA in Paris?"

Gene asked. "Where are **you** going?"

I was surprised, "Do you want to leave here with me?"

Although Gene missed most of the action at the safe house, after seeing the aftermath, he no longer considered the stories of the agent, Coyote, unbelievable.

Gene said, "After today, I'd follow you to hell."

I chuckled and replied, "I would never lead you there."

Chapter 20
Cory Webb—Australia

Jody was following the plan that he and Robby developed. The plan was for Jody to lead the enemy surveillance away from the hotel. Two cars filled with the men from the Australian backup team that his dad told him to activate would follow him at a distance to cover his back and hopefully capture some of the adversaries threatening him.

Jody took a deep breath as he started the car. He knew his backup was in place, but he had second thoughts about exiting the hotel in the rent-a-car as bait. He overcame his fear and rolled down the window, exposing his head in the parking lot.

As he drove alone along the planned route, his cell phone rang. His caller ID didn't identify the caller. Jody pressed the receive call button without speaking. After a short hesitation, a deep voice blurted out, "Jody, there are two vehicles following you. Take a right at the next intersection and head up the mountain."

The man calling had an Australian accent, but Jody was almost sure that he wasn't with the Australian backup team who knew the plan and would not have to tell Jody to turn. Jody and Robby's plan was to turn at the next intersection. The man's recommendation that he take the mountain route raised a red flag. Jody felt the handle of the Sig Sauer pistol on the seat next to him as he turned up the road.

Jody didn't underestimate his adversaries' capabilities of discovering his cell phone number. There were only three ways off the mountain. That was why they chose this route to entrap the men following him.

The two cars following him before he turned right were probably Robby's people. Only one was going to follow him up the hill. Robby's car was going to set up a roadblock on the road where they had agreed that Jody would drive off the hill.

Jody asked as he turned right up the mountain, "Who in the hell are you, and how did you get my cell number?"

"I am a friend of your dad. Jody, they both turned and followed you up the mountain. I'm in the Hummer following them. I plan to ram them off the road. One mile up the road, there is a switchback road on your right. Even if I fail to wreck both sedans, the distraction will allow you to escape." The phone went dead.

Robby Clark saw Jody turn up the mountain road. Two sedans and a Hummer followed Jody up the road. He gave instructions to his other team car to block the east pass. Robby sped forward with his men. He hit a speed dial number and was upset that Jody's phone was busy.

Jody saw two sedans and a Hummer a quarter mile behind him and was considering his options when the right turn switchback road arrived too quickly. There was something in the tone of the unknown man's voice on the phone that convinced him to stop: *a friend of his dad.*

He had to back up to maneuver into the switchback. He positioned his vehicle to allow all three avenues of escape off the mountain. When the two sedans didn't speed past the switchback, he concluded the voice from the Hummer had probably set him up. Jody's trap had failed. *The Hummer was probably planning to ram him.*

Jody rolled down the window and put the car in drive with the intention of speeding to Robby's location at the east pass. Then he heard gunfire below. The gunfire convinced him that the deep voice on the phone was indeed trying to protect him.

Jody sped back down the curvy road. His cell phone started ringing, but he couldn't answer on the curvy road at high speed. After rounding a sharp curve, he saw a sedan facing uphill in the left lane of the road, and saw a large black Hummer further down crashed into another sedan on the left. Two men were shielded next to the car in the middle of the road and were shooting toward the crashed Hummer.

Jody was speeding too fast to stop. He aimed his vehicle toward the two men in the road. The man closest to him rose up and fired at his windshield. Jody ducked toward the center console and lost control of the car. He sat back up in an attempt to take control of the car just as the man that had shot at him was smashed between his car and the sedan's front door. A few milliseconds later, the front of Jody's out-of-control car rammed the second man that was attempting to jump into the air to avoid certain death. In surreal slow motion, Jody saw the hood of his car contact the man's knees, and in even slower-motion watched the man's head hit the bottom of left side support of his windshield, spattering blood across the glass.

Seeing the steep drop-off into the trees on the right side of the road, Jody turned the power steering hard to the right and slammed on the breaks, causing the car to skid toward the ditch on the left past the Hummer. The car did a 90-degree sliding spin, with his driver's door facing downhill—away from the uphill gunfight. Instead of careening into the ditch on the left, the car came to a stop sideways in the middle of the road.

Jody fumbled to pick up the Sig Sauer P-226 that fell off the seat. Hearing more gunfire, he dove out of the driver door with the pistol in his right hand. Lying on the ground, he maneuvered into position to survey the battle. From his view under the front bumper of the car, he saw a sedan screech up the hill away from his position.

Jody jumped to his feet and watched a big man cautiously leave the cover of the Hummer. The man surveyed five unmoving bodies, recovered their pistols as he walked between the bodies and threw the weapons through a broken back window of his Hummer. The big man approached Jody while casually tucking a pistol into his belt next to his left thigh. He yelled, "Jody, your dad, Pat O'Sheen, gave me your cell phone number. I know Dale, your mother."

Jody moved from behind his vehicle with his gun aimed at the man's large head. The man didn't flinch. He walked around the car and stopped five feet from Jody while looking down the barrel of his gun without fear.

He volunteered very formally in an exaggerated Australian accent, "Aye Mate. I'm Cory Webb." He bowed ceremoniously.

Jody didn't lower his weapon and demanded, "Who in the hell is Cory Webb?"

"Wow. You look like your dad when I first met him, and you already have his attitude." Cory explained, "Your dad called me from Paris and asked me to watch your back."

Jody lowered the pistol. The large man approached him and threw big arms around him in a crushing hug. "Why did you come back? I was supposed to be protecting you. You weren't supposed to protect me."

Instead of returning what seemed to be a loving hug, Jody stuck the barrel of his pistol into the large man's ribs to regain control.

The big man wasn't surprised or intimidated. He backed off and looked kindly into Jody's eyes. "I had you covered. The men pursuing you were better trained than I anticipated. I was expecting my demise until you reentered the melee."

He took two steps back and continued, "I had accomplished your escape. That was the mission I owed your father. Your reentry threatened my success. Jody . . . I . . . ah . . ."

Cory had been rattling off so quickly that he had started choking on his own words. He finally spat out, "I fulfilled my obligation to your dad, but now I owe you. You saved my life."

Jody said, "You don't owe me anything."

Jody pulled his cell from his pocket and hit his speed dial. He held up his hand when Cory tried to continue speaking.

Jody spoke into the phone, "Robby, did you see a black Hummer following me up the mountain?"

After the affirmative answer, he said, "The driver of the Hummer rammed the sedans that were following me. There was a gunfight and we have several fatalities. One of the sedans is heading your way. You should easily recognize it by the missing door on the driver's side and its busted windows. I want a man in custody for interrogation. I am about to pursue the sedan from behind. I'm not sure how many are in the vehicle, but . . ."

Cory Webb interrupted, "There is only one."

Jody relayed, "We believe the driver is alone."

Robby promised, "We will intercept him."

Jody said, "Mr. Webb, I hope you can get that Hummer out of here. You interrupted a sting operation. I was hoping to capture one of my pursuers. I have to hurry."

Cory was starting to understand Jody's plan as he watched Pat's son jump behind the wheel. Cory said, "I'll cover your back."

Jody rolled down the driver's side window as he shut the door. "What if I don't want you behind me?"

"Then you won't know I am there."

Jody took the time to smile at Cory through the open window before accelerating away.

Jody cleaned most of the blood off the windshield with the wiper spray as he sped in pursuit. Minutes later he glanced in his rearview mirror and saw the damaged Hummer following at a distance. He pondered Cory's willingness to sacrifice his life to protect him. Jody had met many people that lovingly accepted him because he was Pat O'Sheen's son. *How had Dad earned so much loyalty?*

Robby had the man from the damaged sedan in custody when Jody approached. When he got out of his car, he waved Cory Webb in as he surveyed the young prisoner. He was younger than Jody. No one had ever looked at Jody with so much hatred in his glare.

When Webb walked into the scene, Jody introduced Cory to Robby by first names only.

Robby put out his hand and addressed Cory by his last name, "Mr. Webb, it is a pleasure to meet you. Pat and Dale speak very highly of you."

Jody was shocked. He had never heard the man's name before. But he was pleased that they had a man to interrogate. He hoped the interrogation would help his dad discover the reasons behind the recent attacks in Paris. After he and Robby agreed to proceed to the next phase of the plan, Jody explained that Keisha's manager had paged him: that he needed to get back to the hotel. He trusted Robby to follow the plan. *At least he did until Robby invited Cory Webb to the interrogation facility. Why would Robby do that? Had his dad told Robby about Cory Webb? **Why wasn't he informed?***

Webb seemed like a hard-ass. Jody instructed Robby to detain the prisoner and to wait for him to return before starting the interrogation.

Most of the Australian team followed Jody back to the hotel.

Jody had stopped at a self-spray car wash and washed the blood off of his car. He wanted to calm down before calling his dad and before returning to Keisha and Jonny. He was still unnerved when his dad answered the call. He asked, "Dad, are you safe?"

"Yes, I'm on the charter plane. I am talking to your mother on the other line."

Jody quickly relayed an abbreviated story of the pursuit, about Cory Webb covering his back, and Robby capturing one of the men following him. He didn't tell his dad that he had killed two more men with his car.

Jody finished, "We are in control here. You'd better get back to Mom. I'll keep you updated."

He had hoped to get his dad's input on Cory Webb and how to interrogate the prisoner, but his mother's concerns were more important.

Jody walked into Keisha and Jonny's suite. Jonny asked where Jody had been for the last hour.

Jody said, "There are too many people milling about that were not on the approved list. I checked them out. I didn't find any problems."

Keisha didn't share Jonny's paranoia about her safety. She had no qualms about Jody O'Sheen providing her protection, despite the attack in Paris that Jonny was convinced was caused by Pat. Paris is where Jody won her respect. She marveled that Jody survived an attack by four mercenaries and killed three of them. It was in Paris that Keisha Steele recognized Pat O'Sheen's characteristics in his son, Jody. Something had changed in Jody after the attack in Paris. Jody was much closer than Pat to her age—and he wasn't married.

***

Kathie Boudreaux couldn't help but notice the long face on her husband Pierre when he walked into their house. He hugged her longer than normal, and then he immediately went to the kitchen and made a drink.

She said, "What is wrong?"

"I betrayed Pat O'Sheen today."

She objected, "You would never betray Pat."

Pierre started telling her the story. When he started describing the scene at the CIA safe house when he arrived, Kathie stood up from the dinette table and made herself a drink. Pat was such a nice man. She couldn't fathom that he could kill so many men.

Pierre told her about Pat walking him through the house explaining almost a dozen dead bodies. He said, "Michelle Orleon filmed all of Pat's explanation." He explained how Pat exposed Michelle.

Kathie was incredulous, but she was becoming impatient. "How did you betray Pat?"

"Pat told me that he had a captive that he needed to interrogate before the captive bled out."

"Where was his captive?"

"That's where he lost me, Kathie. When I arrived at the safe house, the smell of gunpowder was still overwhelming. Pat couldn't have hid a captive before we arrived. I called a police cruiser at Pat's suggestion so that he could leave to interrogate his prisoner. He refused to let me go with him under the guise that the interrogation would disclose top-secret American intelligence."

Kathie waited. When Pierre grimaced and his eyes moistened, she asked again, "So how did you betray Pat?"

"I told the driver to take Pat back to the prefecture and hold him until I got there. I knew Pat must have an accomplice controlling the prisoner. Pat realized that I had double-crossed him and somehow opened the locked back door of the cruiser and jumped out, climbed over an eight-foot wooden fence and disappeared."

"So what happened?"

"Pat called me thirty minutes later. He chastised me for betraying him and told me how to find his captive.

"Kathie, I broke twenty years of trust and friendship. I don't think I can ever recover that trust and friendship again."

"Where is Pat now?"

"His private plane left French airspace before we tracked him down."

"Wow! He is really good?"

"Better than I ever imagined."

They talked for another hour. Pierre made a third drink. He never did that. Kathie had never seen her husband so despondent. "Honey, Pat loves you."

"He will never trust me again."

"Yes he will." She stood up. "I'll warm up the supper."

He stood up poured his drink in the sink and left the kitchen. She assumed he was going to the bathroom.

When he didn't return, she went to their bedroom to check on him. He was snoring fitfully on the bed. She closed the door silently, poured a glass of wine, and called Dale: it was the middle of the afternoon in America.

Chapter 21
Bagdad

Gene followed Pat up the stairs of his chartered jet. Pat had offered to drop him and the hologram belt off in D.C.

After they were airborne, Pat called Brendan to see how his wife and unborn child were doing following the car accident. He was happy to hear that she had been released from the hospital that morning. He explained that he was airborne and leaving France.

Brendan sighed with relief that Pat survived without his backup.

When Gene took his cell phone out to report his status to the CIA, I snatched the phone from his hand and said, "I can't let you report to the CIA yet. We were betrayed by your CIA."

Gene wondered how O'Sheen knew that he was going to report in. "Mr. O'Sheen. I'm not sure what happened back at the safe house . . . except that you saved my life. I don't know how to properly thank you."

I wasn't good at accepting compliments. I failed to save my partner, Mike Burkowski, in Nam. I deflected, pointing at the yellow belt lying on the seat across the aisle. "We need to talk about that yellow belt before you report in."

I liked Agent Kamper. I wasn't yet sure that I was ready to trust him, but I no longer considered that he was part of the hologram conspiracy. "Think about that yellow belt while I call my wife." I stood up and retreated to the back of the plane.

I called home. Dale's anguished voice answered the phone with the latest Code 2 protocol, "Two gray mares."

"Pasturing in the field," I answered trying to hide my emotion at the sound of her voice that, during the attack, I thought I might never hear again. I corralled my emotion while she punched the secure code into our home phone. The phone seemed to go dead. That was normal.

She came back on, "Eddie, are you okay?"

"I'm fine." Anticipating her next question I added, "I'm in the chartered jet and just left Paris."

She expounded her relief, **"Thank God!"**

The relief quickly changed to concern, **"Why am I on Code 2?"** The concern turned to fear. "Is our family still in danger?" The fear turned back to love and appreciation. "I am so happy to hear your voice and hear that you have left Paris." The sudden changes in emotion from relief, to concern, fear, and love, turned suddenly to anxiety, "Are you coming home?"

The many emotions expressed in less than twenty seconds brought tears to my eyes. *What an incredible woman.* She wasn't ready for me to answer her questions. I diverted her anxiety, "Can you see all the monitors?"

Dale calmed as I made her report all the visuals and audios involved in the Code 2 procedures. I could tell that she sensed a high level of concern in my voice. My initial calming effect was waning and her emotional level was rising again.

It didn't help when I said; "I'm sorry, Dale, I need to put you on hold." I switched to get Jody's report. I switched the phone back. Dale yelled, **"Damn it. What is happening?"**

I calmly explained that Jody called while we were talking. We talked for another five minutes. I told her about meeting an agent named Gene Kamper at a CIA safe house in Paris—she was familiar with safe houses. I explained that Pierre and the Parisian police force got involved, and that they took charge of one captured leader that tried to attack me. I disclosed that during an interrogation, the leader had exposed a threat against our family, which was why she was on Code 2 security level.

Dale asked, "So who is the leader. Who is threatening our family?"

Silence was her answer—top secret.

I knew she understood. I said, "I really want you to meet Gene Kamper. You will love him."

Dale couldn't believe it. *Eddie was acting like he was just finishing an ordinary business trip where he had met a new business friend that he liked.* She knew that wasn't true, but his calm diversion was comforting. "Are you on the way home? Can I get off Code 2?"

I said, "Move to Code 3, I have one more stop to help clear up this mess before I can get you off of Code 3."

Dale knew by his intonation that he would tell her no more.

When they finished their conversation, and she put the portable phone back on its charger, Dale was calm. Eddie had that effect on her. He acted like it was just another ordinary day at the office.

Well, this was not an ordinary day for a housewife—having to stay in a one-room, lonely bunker. But Eddie said that he would be home in two days. She could handle that on Code 3, which gave her access to the whole house. Eddie was alive and his voice and demeanor had calmed her . . . *again.* She didn't approve of her husband's covert career, but knew that he was very good at it. He had personally known every president since Nixon. Pat and she were close friends with the Secretary of State and his wife. Dale took a call from Paris.

***

Jody entered the warehouse where Robby held the captive. Jody approached the restrained prisoner and demanded, "Why are you after me and my family?"

Jody's answer was a large wad of spittle expertly ejected into his face.

Robby moved forward, placed his pistol on the man's knee, and pulled the trigger. The deafening report from his pistol echoed off the metal walls of the small warehouse. Jody and the captive were both shocked.

Robby very calmly asked the man, "Who is responsible for the attack on this family and why?" When the man hesitated, Robby placed his pistol back on the man's knee and was instantly rewarded. The man explained with an Australian accent that Pat O'Sheen was responsible for the death of a rich oil sheik's son, and that Jody was to die in retribution. He looked up at Jody.

"What is the sheiks name?" Robby demanded.

"I swear to Allah, I don't know." Robby pulled the trigger, but again, deflected his aim, causing only slightly more injury.

Jody hollered, "**Enough**. I believe him."

Jody saw Cory Webb enter the room. *Why was he still here? And why was he hiding?*

Jody saw that Robby wasn't surprised. Jody was pissed that he was always kept in the dark. *Why wasn't he told everything?*

Cory said in support, "I also believe him. Jody, pass the information the captive just disclosed to your dad. I'll clean up the mess here in my country."

Jody did not like the implication. He turned to the captive, "Do you live in Melbourne?"

The man nodded. Jody turned to Cory, "I want this man escorted back near his home and released unharmed."

When he saw the surprise and then the refusal in Webb's eyes, Jody barked at Robby, **"Robby, am I making myself clear?"**

"Perfectly."

The man who had spit on him earlier looked up at Jody with surprise. Jody met his gaze and nodded his assurance.

Jody glared at Webb who glared back. Jody said, "You said that you owe me. I am calling in that marker. I don't want this man hurt." He pointed.

Webb nodded in agreement.

Jody left the warehouse, still pissed that he was not being totally informed. If he found out that they failed to follow his order, Robby would have to find another job.

Jody decided to make it clear that from now on he would be fully informed of all operations, or he would fire anyone who had knowledge of a part of an operation without sharing it with him.

Well, he might give his dad some leeway.

***

I made several more cell calls before I sat back down across from Gene and retreated into a reverie.

The night sky was clear and Gene recognized the pattern of lights on the ground abruptly stop as they crossed a coastline. He noticed Pat relax as the plane flew over what Gene assumed was the Atlantic Ocean, leaving the European Continent behind.

O'Sheen laid his seat back and was asleep in minutes.

Gene was still wound up as tight as a spring in an old grandfather clock.

A little over two hours later, Gene saw that they were paralleling another coastline. That made no sense if they were over the Atlantic Ocean flying toward America. He woke Pat up and pointed out the right side window and asked, "Where are we going?"

I noticed Gene's discomfort and raised my seat. I looked out the window and saw the night lights glowing on a coastline. I hid my smile as I looked back at Gene. I could see that he read the amusement in my eyes. *He was good. Very good!* It was ingrained in my nature to look for exceptional talent that I could trust.

I told him our destination, "We are going to Baghdad, by way of Kuwait. I'll drop you off in D.C. after that."

Gene was unsettled, "Why Baghdad?"

I said, "I need to have a short visit with an oil sheik. I am hoping that you will help me locate him."

Gene's eyebrows raised and concern crossed his face. I was learning to read him. But I wasn't ready to share details of my plan in Iraq with him.

I changed the subject and pointed to the half-melted, yellow belt in the seat across the aisle. "The CIA double-crossed me at the safe house in Paris. I'm not sure who I can trust at Langley. You will have to explain that belt to them."

"Sir," Gene respectfully replied, "I never saw that belt in action. You should go with me." He reached across the aisle and retrieved the yellow belt.

I recalled that Gene was unconscious when the dying bodies wearing the belts appeared from thin air. I ridiculed, "I heard you firing your AK-47. Are you so bad that you missed everyone?"

Gene said. "At first I thought that some of the munitions must have been loaded with blanks. I couldn't have missed the first two men entering through the hole at the front of the house. But they were the only ones visible in the room who could have fired the bullets at my chest?" Gene rubbed his sore chest where the bullets hit his Kevlar vest.

I explained to him what he missed while unconscious at the safe house, "I saw a man approaching you with a SW 1911 aimed at you as you lay unconscious on the floor. I ran down the stairs, firing at the man's hologram projection with no effect. And then I swept the room to the man's right—my left—I could hear the difference in the sound of the bullets that hit the floor in the room versus the bullets that stopped before hitting a wall or floor. I heard him fall to the floor even though I was firing about 10 feet to the left of his hologram image.

"Then my bullet-proof vest was hit on my right side from the position of the man who had approached the kitchen. I dove down the remaining stairs to the floor. When I saw his projection near the kitchen door, I started my bullet spray about twelve feet to his left and he went down in a hurry.

"When I looked back where the first man fell, he was materializing out of thin air while his hologram projection was fading."

I sighed, finding my own story hard to believe.

"His belt, the one in your lap, started smoking. I'd bet that all of the electronics in it are fried. When I went around the couch, the other man was visible, but still alive. He pushed the center button there." I pointed at the middle button on the belt on Gene's lap. "That button set off an explosive in the belt. Did your briefing explain any of that?"

Gene replied, "My briefing described a projected hologram image: a real lifelike projected image of the one wearing the belt. The picture showed a belt with only three buttons. Not five buttons like this one."

"Well . . ." I hesitated, still unsure of my hypothesis, ". . . the belt uses some kind of deflective ray technology, sort of like a cloaking device—a device that renders its wearer invisible."

Gene smiled, "Pat, I'm a 'Star Trek' fan. I know what a cloaking device is supposed to do. Do you honestly believe that we have developed that level of technology?"

I replied, "We have a 'stealth bomber' that is invisible to radar. I don't know how else to explain what I witnessed. The belt must also sense the life of the one wearing it: maybe his heartbeat. The one in your lap quit projecting the hologram after the man died, making him visible to me. Then the belt smoked as it went into meltdown."

Gene argued, "But you said the other man was alive and visible and able to explode the belt by pushing this middle button? He wasn't dead, but he was visible to you. Your analysis is inconsistent."

"Kamper, I wouldn't have been assigned to the field if I had Einstein's brain. If I come up with any more theories, I'll let you know."

I continued, "But now you know as much as I know. I suggest you share what I witnessed with the right people in your CIA. But, if I were you, I wouldn't let them know that you are bringing that belt in until you arrive at the gate at Langley. We were both double-crossed by someone in the CIA."

I changed the subject, "Let's talk about Baghdad." I explained what I needed in Iraq.

I wasn't surprised by Gene's reaction. He said, "I can't operate in Iraq without CIA authorization, and I doubt I'll get approval to help you kill an oil sheik."

I let him off the hook, "I can accomplish the objective without your help. It may take me an extra day or two. You can wait in Kuwait with my plane or find another ride to Washington." I stood and headed for the plane's bathroom to call Jody.

I turned back to Gene, "I have no intention of killing the sheik. I just want to talk to him."

Gene remembered the carnage that Pat inflicted in the safe house. He couldn't imagine that Pat would travel to Iraq without the intent of killing the source behind the attack. Gene would do the same to protect his family.

Gene considered, *O'Sheen just saved my life. I need to help him. I don't want to sit in Kuwait for two or three days wondering what was happening in Iraq.* Gene called a friend who went through CIA basic training with him, and who worked in the "Green Zone" surrounding Iraq's Baghdad Airport.

When I returned from the bathroom, I laid my seat back and fell asleep. When I awoke, I was looking into Gene's deep-blue eyes. If I had

Gene's attractive features, I would never have been able to blend into a crowd; therefore, in undercover operations, my life would have ended many years ago. My survival relied on my average, hard-to-remember, and easily disguisable appearance.

I was always careful to avoid being photographed. But Jody was so enthused when starting the new protection business that he put my name and picture on an Internet ad. I had Jody remove my picture from the advertisement as soon as he showed it to me. Maybe not too many of my enemies saw it or could connect my picture to my alias "Coyote." Sheik Faisad had apparently made the connection.

When Gene saw that I was awake he declared, "I couldn't get clearance for your plane to land in Iraq after leaving Kuwait. You need an alternate plan."

I smiled at Gene. I was happy the he had decided to help me. "I've already worked out that plan. I won't have any problem landing in Bagdad."

I knew that Gene was thinking, *I'll believe you after we land.*

I said, "I am flying into Baghdad on an Army supply flight from Camp Arifjan in Kuwait."

Gene chuckled. He should never have underestimated O'Sheen.

Gene told me about his contact with his CIA friend in Baghdad.

When we landed in Baghdad, a man in an army uniform met us. Gene introduced him as Bill Cameron.

Bill told us that Sheik Faisad was in Al Kut, twenty miles up the Tigris River: about a forty-minute drive south. We all jumped into an armored Hummer. Bill gave Gene and me army uniforms. He explained that we should be able to make it to Al Kut before noon prayers at the mosque.

I was very impressed with Bill Cameron.

Chapter 22
The Sheik

Sheik Faisad had tried for years to identify the man who had taken his only son's life, which made it impossible to live a day of his life without thoughts of revenge. For years, he patiently had his grandson, Mohammed, trained to avenge his father's murderer. He hoped that Allah would eventually expose the murderer's identity.

Recently, Allah answered his prayers. A most trusted source had seen Pat O'Sheen's picture on a website advertising O'Sheen's celebrity protection business. The trusted source was a man who had been with his son in Kuwait on that fateful day. He convinced the sheik that O'Sheen was the leader of the American Special Forces unit that had killed his son.

The opportunity to fulfill his lifelong desire to kill his son's murderer materialized when it was disclosed that the O'Sheens would be in Paris to protect an American singer.

His initial plan was to kill Pat O'Sheen. But he changed his mind and decided to kill O'Sheen's son, so that O'Sheen could experience the same pain that had enraged him over the last twenty years. He thought that O'Sheen's age would give Mohammed the advantage, particularly with his grandson operating under the proven mercenary skills of Mohammed's cousin, Abdul.

He had been wrong. Even though the hologram belts should have given Mohammed a distinct advantage, O'Sheen had somehow survived. Not only did he kill most of the assault team—but to add insult to injury—O'Sheen captured his grandson.

Abdul had advised against an open assault force, but the sheik had brought up his grandson, Mohammed, to kill O'Sheen personally.

Abdul had used such a large force on the second attack that O'Sheen's survival was a hard concept for the sheik's mind to comprehend. Perhaps he should temporarily withdraw his Fatwa against O'Sheen. The Koran taught patience.

The next morning, Sheik Faisad was walking down a side street in Al Kut toward the mosque for noon prayers. Al Kut was a medium sized city in Iraq about twenty miles south of Baghdad on the Tigris River. It was in Al Kut that the sheik got the news of the second failed assault against Jody O'Sheen in Australia. Apparently, all the O'Sheens had the nine lives of a cat. The sheik was perplexed by a call this morning. The only surviving man in Australia sent to kill Jody O'Sheen was captured and released. The released man was singing Allah's praises for Jody O'Sheen who had ordered his release instead of demanding his death. *Maybe Jody wasn't like his dad.*

The sheik's two guards were walking next to him when three American soldiers approached on the same side of the street. He was not yet comfortable with the dreaded sight of armed American invaders in his homeland. As they passed, one of the soldiers grabbed his arm and stopped him while the other two escorted his guards twenty feet away. When he angrily turned to face the man holding his arm, he almost fainted. *Pat O'Sheen! Impossible. Only yesterday, he had killed eleven of his grandson's best men. He couldn't possibly be in Iraq today.*

The sheik considered screaming.

***

Gene was worried when Pat approached the sheik on the street. Should he have put his CIA friend's career at risk to accompany Pat on this mission? He had known Pat for less than two days. What was Pat going to do to this man who had signed a Fatwa for death warrants against his family? Gene was prepared to restrain Pat if things got out of hand—a task that he was not sure that he could accomplish. He listened to the conversation, but he wasn't able to understand the Arabic.

***

I spoke calmly in Arabic, "Good morning, Sheik Faisad. I see that you recognize me. Why do you have a Fatwa against my family?"

The old man stiffened in defiance when my grip on his arm tightened, so I quickly loosened the grip and said, "My reason for being here is to ask you to withdraw the fatwa against my family. This conflict is between you and me, not our families.

The sheik was amazed that his defiance brought a conciliatory reaction from this dangerous man who had traveled over a thousand miles to kill him. O'Sheen had *asked* him to leave his family alone: *not demanded.* O'Sheen's threatening look had changed to an eerie calmness.

The sheik expected that his death was eminent. He barked, "**You killed my son.**" *Defiance had worked once.*

The sheik was shocked when O'Sheen apologized, the sorrow expressed in O'Sheen's eyes seemed sincere. "I am sorry that your son was killed. He was cavorting with very bad company."

The sheik knew that the statement was true. He had warned his son against his affiliations with Saddam Hussein and his Republican Guard.

Sheik Faisad became confused. *What did this man want?*

O'Sheen said to him in very calm voice, "I am truly sorry for causing you so much pain. I wanted to capture your son and his men to interrogate them. I did not want to kill them. They refused to surrender and we got into a firefight."

The sheik was starting to believe that this warrior did not intend to kill him, nor had he intended to kill his son.

The sheik was shocked when O'Sheen said "I will leave you now. I have made my apology. I've said what needed to be said. Please leave my family alone. I don't want to have to come back here. There is no reason to involve my family or yours. If you hurt my family, I will hurt yours. If you kill a member of my family, I will kill every member of your family . . . your two brothers, three sisters, and all of your nephews and nieces," O'Sheen turned and started to walk away.

The sheik had no doubt that O'Sheen could back-up the threat. He proved his capability by confronting him so quickly after the attack in Paris. O'Sheen could have killed him easily in this surprise encounter. The sheik's deep thoughts were interrupted.

O'Sheen had turned back to the sheik and said, "You would have been proud of your son. He stayed behind to slow our progress, sacrificing his life so that his friends could escape. He was a very brave young man."

O'Sheen started to turn away, and then turned back again. "I will try to help get your grandson released from police custody in Paris so he can return to you if I am still alive, and if I learn that my family is no longer in harm's way."

Sheik Faisad took a deep breath as he watched the three soldiers walk away. He exhaled heavily and some of the hatred that consumed him for almost twenty years seemed to exit his body with his exhaled breath. After meeting him in person, O'Sheen was a man that he respected and not a man he could easily hate.

The sheik considered that O'Sheen's son had shown the same mercy in Australia to a man he had captured. Both of the O'Sheens had demonstrated mercy.

At the mosque, when Sheik Faisad bowed toward Mecca during the noon prayers, the heavy weight that he had carried for twenty years lifted from his shoulders. He was able to let loose of the pain of losing his only son. He was exhilarated at hearing that his son had bravely sacrificed his life to save his comrades.

When the sheik left the mosque, he grabbed his cell phone from his pocket and started reversing the wheels of revenge. He withdrew his Fatwa against Pat O'Sheen and called off the attack against Jody O'Sheen in Australia.

***

Gene had tried to listen to Pat's conversation with the sheik and still keep his focus on the sheik's guards while his friend reassured the nervous guards in Arabic that the sheik was in no danger.

Gene was expecting to hear a heated conversation between Pat and the sheik. The Arabic dialect they were speaking was too difficult for him to understand, and O'Sheen was speaking too softly at times for his voice to be overheard. Gene was surprised by Pat's calmness, and he was shocked at how quickly the conversation ended. *Was that a look of admiration on the sheik's face when they parted? That didn't make any sense.*

But it seemed that the confrontation he dreaded was avoided. They had come a very long way for so few words.

On the drive back to Baghdad, Gene was relieved to join a military convoy. This was his first time in Iraq. He was worried about improvised explosive devices (IEDs), or a suicide bomber ramming into them with an old truck loaded with explosives, and he worried about sniper fire. The counterinsurgents were not giving up as easy as the Iraqi Army.

Gene looked across at Pat. For the first time since they had met, Pat seemed totally at peace. He was oblivious to the dangers on this road. He remembered the same look on the sheik's face and wondered, *how could such a short conversation with such an avid adversary result in such personal peace?*

***

When their plane reached cruising altitude, Gene spoke. "Pat?"

"Yes, Gene," I responded. My eyes were barely open. When Gene didn't respond, I opened my eyes and turned to look at him.

Gene asked, "Why did we travel over a thousand miles for a three minute conversation?"

I replied, "The conversation was secondary. My ability to confront Sheik Faisad so quickly after the attack in Paris, and my apology for his son's death twenty years ago, communicated the message I wished to convey." I leaned my seat back.

Gene couldn't let it go, "He hired men to kill you and your son. You had an opportunity to kill him. You talked to him in his native dialect for a few short minutes and now you are both at peace. Give me a break. What I just witnessed was not logical."

I shrugged. "It makes perfect sense to me."

Chapter 23
Success

On the other side of the world, there was no apparent threat against Keisha at the concert in Australia. Jody had to bump up against one man who thought he was a 'hot shot', and who had too much to drink at the party following the concert. The man looked at Jody angrily until he saw the look in Jody's eyes and saw the wire running from his shirt collar into his earpiece. He moved on to mingle with the other celebrities in the crowd.

After the late night party ended, and after Keisha was safely tucked away, Jody's cell phone vibrated. The number was vaguely familiar. He pressed the connect button and listened. Cory's now familiar deep voice bellowed, "Jody, your adversaries have retreated. I'm going home to my family. Please convey my loving sentiments to your parents. And Jody, please call me day or night if I can be of service to you." Cory disconnected before Jody could respond.

Jody was perplexed. He looked up to see Robby smiling. He must have overheard the man's strong bass voice.

Robby offered, "You have made a life-long friend. Don't forget him." Robby's phone vibrated and after listening he said, "Our group confirms Cory's analysis that the adversaries have withdrawn. You can relax now."

Jody queried, "What changed?"

Robby answered, "I don't know. But I would bet that your dad has something to do with it."

There it was again. Could he ever measure up to his dad?

Jody responded defensively, "Maybe my granting mercy to the attacker we captured helped, or that our organized aggressive action against them scared them away." Jody looked at his watch, figured the time difference, and called his dad to give him the good news.

Chapter 24
Homeward bound

The Yellow belts. Gene Kamper was obsessed with the implications of a top-secret leak. When the jet was airborne, Pat immediately pulled out his cell phone. The guy's cell phone was probably more secure than Gene's CIA issue. Gene lost interest in the conversation when Pat again addressed a man named Brendan. He still didn't understand Pat's concern about Brendan's family, but apparently the outcome was satisfactory to Pat. Pat requested Brendan's help about something dealing with Code 3. *Apparently O'Sheen ran his household by CIA type codes.*

Gene wondered if Pat would lean back in his seat and sleep again. The older man knew how to grab his sleep when time permitted. But instead, after reflecting on his phone conversation for a minute, O'Sheen leaned toward him and stabbed a compliment deep into his psyche, "Gene, thanks for your help. I would have died in Paris without your help, and your help in resolving the issue in Iraq has put me forever in your debt."

Gene didn't know how to respond to O'Sheen's absurd proclamation. He had not yet learned of the total body count in Paris, but he knew his effective kills were only one: Spellman. He may have served as an effective decoy, and his contact in Iraq did help Pat confront the sheik. Gene sensed that Pat wasn't the type of man that doled out praise easily. The comment *'forever in your debt'* flabbergasted him.

All Gene could manage to say was a weak, "Thank you, sir."

***

I sensed that Gene hond I would be life-long friends. He accepted my thanks gracefully, although I could read in his face that he wanted to belittle his contribution. He must have been raised by very good parents: being gracious was hard to learn later in life.

Before I could continue my conversation with Gene, my cell phone vibrated with an incoming call from another secure phone. I connected without speaking.

Jody said, "Can you talk?"

I could tell by his relaxed tone that the concert went well. "Yes, Jody. We are in the plane heading back to America. How was the concert?"

"Keisha blew the audience away. They demanded encore after encore. Jonny only let her do three. Dad, she is incredible."

I smiled, "I agree. Tell me about the surveillance threat?"

Jody's elated tone changed, "You should have told me that you asked Cory Webb to cover my back. I was tempted to shoot him."

When I didn't respond, Jody continued. "I don't want to get into that whole story over this insecure phone. The surveillance threat withdrew after the concert. Robby thinks you had something to do with that. Did you?"

"Maybe. We can compare notes when we get home. Love you."

Jody realized that his dad had other ears listening and was cutting the call short. "Love you."

I leaned my seat back and fell asleep.

Gene held the towel containing the yellow belt while I walked him to the top of the stairs on my charter jet in D.C. He tried again to persuade me, "You need to come with me to Langley to help explain this belt."

I shook my head, "Family always comes first, Gene. Langley will try to pull me in soon enough." I grabbed Gene by the shoulders and pulled him into a hug.

Gene had never been hugged by a man, but he left the plane elated. He knew the next few days at Langley were going to be intense . . . *insane might be a better word.* But after spending a couple of days with the legendary Coyote, he knew he could handle it.

Gene knew that CIA covert operatives could disappear for days without arousing too much concern. But approaching a sheik in Iraq without prior approval probably crossed the agency's boundary limits. He would fully disclose the Iraq encounter. He had learned early in life that honesty was the best policy, and Pat had not asked him to alter the true story. But how was he going to present the incredible O'Sheen story. Would anyone at the CIA believe him? The yellow belt wrapped in the towel would help.

Part Two
Investigation

Ed Sheehan

Chapter 25
Michelle–Paris

Michelle Orleon was angry about her arrest, but she knew that they could find nothing to legally hold her past the maximum 72 hours allowed by French law and would have to release her. With the impact that she had made on the rank and file in the Prefecture de Police, most of the police officers would cheer her release. She couldn't legally challenge her dismissal even if she wanted to, because she had struck a superior officer: one that she had failed to control. *I'm sorry, Abdul. We all failed you.*

Was her fascination with O'Sheen the cause of her demise? He had captured her imagination when their eyes first connected. When she followed him through the killing field, she was drawn to him by his amazing charisma.

Amazing wasn't the word that described the gnawing, longing, pent-up feelings that were tattooed inside her; feelings that O'Sheen rekindled, feelings that she hadn't felt for years, feelings that she had tried to forget. For two years after she reached puberty, her stepfather had affected her in a similar way.

Michelle gained her independence shortly after her fifteenth birthday. Michelle's stepfather had again, late at night, come into her bedroom. Michelle came close to doing major damage with her teeth to his manhood that night.

Weeks later, Michelle noticed that her stepfather was devoting his attention to her mother again and treating her mother like a queen. But he still looked at Michelle with passion.

She was able to convince her rich stepfather to send her away to a high-priced prep school in America. When she graduated from the prep school in Washington D.C., she was admitted to George Washington

University where she met Abdul Faisad. She fell in love with Abdul on their first date. Her relationship with Abdul progressed quickly to the bedroom, but she wasn't able to captivate his full attention or much of his time. She sensed that she had bedded the religious, Islamic man too early in their relationship for her to capture his heart. She later learned that he was permitted by his religion to go to bed with her because she was not a Muslim. But her loose morality was not acceptable to be a marriage partner.

When Abdul befriended Professor Steadman, her nights spent with Abdul trickled off to rare nights in bed together. Then Angela from Alabama captured Abdul's heart, and Michelle was cut off completely from sexual pleasures with him.

Patience, her high IQ, and her planning ability were Michelle's best strengths. But it was always her beauty that first got people's attention. She never stopped loving Abdul, and she was pleased to hear of Abdul's startling separation from Angela, hoping that her opportunity had arrived. She didn't believe the rumors on campus that Abdul had beaten and raped Angela. Her investigation found that no assault or rape charges were filed. But Abdul had disappeared.

She had been unable to track Abdul down over the next five, years and became discouraged.

Her American education in forensic pathology landed her a good job in the morgue in her native and beloved City of Light, Paris. She quickly gained respect with her ability to determine the cause of death, which moved her career into the arena of homicides. Her career was doing well and was quite rewarding despite the low pay. Her skills developed rapidly during her sixteen-hour workdays, but her personal life was barely existent despite the many lustful looks that she received from many of her male coworkers.

She didn't discourage the advances from several sexy homicide detectives that were required to monitor her autopsies on their cases. She had even shared her body with a couple of them. But she learned that they would never consider marrying a woman who cut up dead bodies every day in her job.

Her closest girlfriend, who was somewhat comely, disclosed at a bar one night, "You are great trolling bait, but I'll never find a man if you only join me once a month."

Trolling bait. She felt used. A common feeling during the many years since the first time her stepfather came into her bedroom in the middle of the night. *Her friend had only invited her because her beauty attracted men.*

That night when she arrived home, Michelle saw a man lingering near the entrance to her apartment. She was cautious but not scared while exiting her car. She discreetly pulled a can of mace from her purse when she noticed that he was totally focused on her. After walking half of the thirty-feet across the parking lot toward her apartment, his confident stance alarmed her and made her stop in her tracks. She sensed that he was serious trouble and that mace may not be adequate. She started running back to her car when a voice called after her, "Michelle."

The call of her name was beseeching. She might be willing to talk to the man from the safety of her car.

Her panic level reached an apex when she heard the man running after her while she unsuccessfully searched the key ring for her car key and realized that she would not find it in time. As he rounded the front of her car, she gripped the mace canister and aimed.

He abruptly stopped, "Michelle. It's me. Don't you recognize me?"

Her heart was throbbing in her chest so hard that she failed to understand what he was trying to say. She knew that she had the training and skills to incapacitate normal men. She also knew that skilled men had the strength advantage. Instinctively, she knew that this was not an ordinary man. When he slowly started approaching her again, she focused on his vulnerable crotch area for an aimed kick. But damn it, he again stopped too far away.

Instead of approaching further, he said," Michelle. We were lovers years ago in college. I recently heard from a mutual friend that you searched for me after I left GWU. You're not in danger. Look at me."

Although her heart was still racing, the words and the voice from her past started to meld. She looked up and didn't recognize him.

"Michelle, look at my eyes. I am Abdul Faisad."

Without his beard, his appearance had changed, but the eyes were the same, and the realization that her almost-forgotten dream had suddenly materialized out of the blue, coupled with the stress she had just endured made her dizzy and she staggered. He cautiously put out his hand to steady her. She looked back up into his eyes. Then she threw her arms around him, "Abdul?"

Soon after their reunion, Michelle was collaborating with Abdul on mercenary projects. Abdul was right when he said that her personality and assets were ideal for covert operations, and she loved the work: it sure beat cutting up dead bodies in the morgue. She still adored Abdul and their time together was physically and emotionally rewarding. His planning was complex, and her role was always challenging and exciting.

When he had asked her to use her talents to get a job with the Prefecture de Police in Paris, she had at first laughed before realizing that based on her forensic background with the city, and the fact that she knew many of the detectives, the acceptance of her application was very plausible.

Her connections, her education, and her seductive interview skills got her hired as an intern while her application for the police academy was being processed. She enjoyed the new challenge of honing her skills in the law enforcement environment. She was disappointed when Abdul told her that her successful infiltration efforts were aimed at only one man, Pat O'Sheen. But she knew that O'Sheen must be important for Abdul to go to so much trouble.

Weeks later, after she encountered Pat O'Sheen at the safe house and saw all of the mercenaries that the American had killed, she understood Abdul's cautious preparation. O'Sheen was not an ordinary target.

Chapter 26
Prefecture de police

Michelle entered a private interrogation room with Inspector Pierre Boudreaux and his supervisor. She explained that her phone call from the bathroom in the CIA safe house was made to her message machine at her apartment. Pierre handed the phone to her and had her call for her messages with the speaker feature of her cell phone activated. Pierre listened to the phone go dead after the fourth ring. Michelle spoke the word "retrieve" into the mouthpiece. Seconds later the machine responded, "No messages." She handed the cell phone back to Pierre, who looked at the screen, shook his head, and hit the disconnect button. He opened the room's door and handed the cell phone to a subordinate in the hallway.

Pierre said, "Most cell phones keep the last numbers called in memory. Why doesn't yours?"

Her excuse was lame but workable, "I don't know. I've only had the phone for a few weeks. I've intended to call the phone company but haven't taken the time."

Then Pierre asked the indefensible question, "Why did you punch me?"

Pierre's superior leaned forward as Michelle squirmed in her seat before answering.

She responded, "Instinctive reflexes. I followed you and O'Sheen to the bedroom because you had ordered me to film **everything**. When you allowed O'Sheen to pull me into the room, I was confused. When you turned against me and tried to grab my phone, I reacted defensively. I'm sorry."

Pierre didn't believe her concocted story, but he had to admire her. She would be exonerated in a formal inquiry.

Pierre had no real evidence to make her complicit in the attack on O'Sheen. He said, "If you resign now, I won't file assault charges against you." He knew that she wanted out as bad as he wanted her out of his department.

He wasn't surprised when she stood up and said, "I resign. May I go now?"

Pierre's superior interrupted, "After you fill out some paperwork."

Pierre had already arranged for a tail to follow her, and he sensed that she would be expecting it. He also sensed that Michelle had experience that wasn't disclosed in her resume and job application.

Michelle went straight to her apartment and threw a TV dinner in the microwave, packed, ate for the energy she would need later, and went to bed.

She arose before daylight, showered, and dressed for colder weather. She waited until the traffic patterns in Paris would best suit her purpose and carried her bag to the car. She let the government issued sedan follow her long enough for her to be convinced that she only had one tail. Pierre must have suspected that the tailing effort would be fruitless. She quickly lost the tail and drove out of Paris.

The officer assigned to follow Orleon reported back to Pierre that she noticed the tail and aggressively shook him. Pierre thanked the man for his report. He was now fully convinced the O'Sheen was correct when he said that she was working with Faisad.

Michelle carefully drove up the curvy narrow road through the beautiful trees and mountains of Switzerland. The directions she had memorized proved accurate, and she arrived at the small chalet without missing a turn. She didn't take the time to put on her coat even though the mountain air was cold. She ran toward the stairs. Abdul opened the front door before she reached the stairs and walked onto the small front porch. She ran up the stairs and threw herself into his outstretched arms. He easily picked her up and carried her across the threshold like a bride. He kicked the door closed and carried her straight to the bedroom, while their lips kissed hungrily. He gently laid her on the bed, and without releasing her, he laid down beside her. His lips sought hers while his hand went to her breasts. She sat up and removed her sweatshirt exposing her bra-covered breasts. Abdul smiled as she rolled him onto his back and straddled her long legs in a kneeling position over him while reaching behind her back to unfasten the bra. She teasingly held the front of her bra to cover her and smiled. She relaxed her knees to lower herself from the upright kneeling position onto his expanded crotch.

She waited until he started reaching for her bra before she snatched it away, exposing the beauty he was so desirous to behold. She lowered her pelvis onto his thighs so that his expansion was unimpeded. His hands were full of her breasts. He tried to sit up, but knowing his desire, she pushed his hands aside and leaned forward offering her right nipple to his awaiting lips and tongue.

When they finished the ritual that Adam and Eve started to populate the earth, she opened a bottle of wine. They sat naked beside each other on the couch, his manhood reduced to its normal size.

Michelle started to describe in detail the scene she had filmed for Inspector Boudreaux in the safe house in Paris. Abdul asked many questions. He returned to an early part of her story. He asked, "How did he make you?"

He noticed her nipples harden as she described how O'Sheen stared at her when their eyes first made contact. She continued describing the killing scene that seemed incredulous, considering that Pat O'Sheen was the only one alive in the house.

Abdul had to stop her and ask, "O'Sheen was alone?"

Michelle raised her hands toward the ceiling, "I know it seems impossible. But if he had any help, his help somehow vanished into thin air."

She continued the story by describing the carnage on the second floor and repeated O'Sheen's logical description of the carnage down the back stairs to the yard behind the house. She described how his eyes locked with her eyes again.

Abdul noticed her nipples hardening again.

She said, "I was suddenly frightened and excused myself to use the bathroom to make my report, fearing that he would not allow me much more time. The scenes that I had observed made me aware of how dangerous O'Sheen could be, and somehow I suspected that he made my connection with you when I first walked into the kitchen."

Abdul noticed her nipples harden again. This time it started his manhood springing back to life. Michelle noticed.

Though distracted, Michelle continued her story, describing the confrontation with Inspector Boudreaux in the bedroom, O'Sheen's interference, and her arrest. She smiled at his fully-grown interest. She slipped off the couch to her knees on the floor between his feet.

Later, after they were dressed, Abdul asked her to help formulate a plan. The plan's focus again involved Pat O'Sheen, and more specifically, his son, Jody.

Chapter 27
America

Dale had gone to bed after Pat called to tell her that he had just dropped off Agent Kamper in Washington, DC and would be arriving home in the middle of the night. Hours later, she heard Pat enter the darkened bedroom where she had been peacefully sleeping, and watched him walk to the bathroom. His normal routine was completed in half the normal time. He exited the bathroom as he had for the last thirty years—naked except for his tiny briefs. His unusually slumped shoulders concerned her. He attempted to imperceptibly slide under the sheet beside her so as not to awaken her: his considerate custom.

She shuffled in the bed, and following the same routine that had been repeated thousands of times over the years said, "Hey honey. Welcome home."

He squirmed through the sheets in the dark with his left hand seeking her jaw to safely align the good night kiss in the dark. She could tell that he was exhausted and was surprised when he drew his almost naked body tightly to her side and laid his arm across her granny-gown covered abdomen. She reached her left arm around his head and pulled his right cheek against her in a motherly way. While holding him she felt tenseness slowly leave his body. She thought he had dropped off to sleep when he suddenly squeezed her and said, "Thank you for raising such wonderful children." Before she could respond, the first soft snore exited from her loving man.

***

Gene Kamper's report and the yellow belt he brought from Paris put CIA's headquarters in a frenzy. The next day, Gene's security level was raised to "need to know". He was in the most secure room the next day when the call was made to Pat O'Sheen's residence.

Dale saw the caller ID, "Unknown". *Another phone solicitation.* Then she noticed their caller ID also indicated that the call came from a secure line—government business—so she answered, "Hello."

Gene took the lead, "Is Pat O'Sheen available? This is Gene Kamper."

I recognized the voice and moved next to her while shaking my head and hand in a "No" gesture. I punched the speaker function on the phone and nodded for Dale to proceed.

"Mr. Kamper, I'm sorry. He is not available." Dale remembered that Gene was with Pat on the flight from Paris. Pat wanted her to meet him.

Gene noticed that the phone was put on speaker and believed that Pat was listening. Gene didn't want to deceive his new friend and declared, "Pat, I'm with Gene Tanner, Director Collins, and the Deputy Director Bob Hill. Can you secure this call from your end?"

Pat nodded to Dale.

"Hold on." Dale responded, her tone expressing aggravation. Gene punched the voice mute button and explained to the director that he thought Pat was listening. The O'Sheen line seemed to go dead and then came back to life.

"My end is secure," Dale said. She still sounded aggravated.

Director Collins took over the dialogue. "Mrs. O'Sheen, this is CIA Director Collins. This discussion will be classified. Please put your husband on the phone and leave the room."

Dale didn't like her condescending attitude. The female director seemed to believe that southern women were ignorant.

The director was surprised when the lady of the house came back in an exaggerated southern-belle accent, "Madam Director, as I already conveyed with sufficient clarity to Mister Kamper, my beloved husband is not properly situated to converse with y'all." Dale's dander was rising. She might never get an opportunity to talk to a CIA Director again. "My beloved is no longer employed by you, nor does he have reason to trust your organization. Recent events by your organization have put my family in unparalleled jeopardy—the likes of which I have never been so frightened by before. When he becomes available, I may refuse to let him converse with you outside of my presence." Her aristocratic old-southern accent was thick.

The director responded, "Mrs. O'Sheen, I apologize, but I have to put you on hold for a minute." She pressed the mute button and looked at Tanner demanding an answer without asking a question.

Tanner relayed, "Dale is an extremely strong-willed woman and a major contributor to Pat O'Sheen's resolve. She is putting you on with the accent, but I suggest that you don't cross her." He almost criticized her for not starting out more politely, but thought better: *too late now.*

She looked around the room for help. None was forthcoming. "Kamper?"

Gene nodded, "I may have some influence, if she allowed Pat to remain in the room."

"**If she allowed him**?" the DCI declared in frustration "O'Sheen's reputation is iconic around here. He is not the type to let a woman control him. Gene, get her to leave the room so we can conduct our business." She impatiently punched the phone to disengage the mute button and nodded for Gene to proceed.

Gene tried again, "Pat, we need to talk to you."

When he didn't respond, he addressed Dale, "Mrs. O'Sheen, you put us on speaker phone, so I assume that he is listening."

In the exaggerated southern accent Dale said, "I am shelling peas. The speaker phone allows me to continue my household chores without wasting my time while talking to y'all."

I had to walk across the room to conceal my laughter. *Shelling peas!*

Dale offered, "Mr. Kamper, somehow you have captured my man's heart as if you were one of his offspring. But the recent goings-on by your compatriots in the CIA have put my family in unheralded peril. The master of the house is not currently available, but he would want me to greet your unwanted intrusion with utmost kindness. But, I dare say, your present accompaniment disillusions me to the probability of successfully completing his wishes."

Dale was laying it on. I had to retreat farther and cup my mouth in the crook of my arm to conceal my laughter.

Director Collins pushed her chair back from the table and surveyed the listeners in the room. Deputy Director Hill twirled his right index finger around his right ear indicating that Mrs. O'Sheen must be crazy.

The director suggested, "Mrs. O'Sheen, can you recommend a course of action whereby we may discuss this national emergency with your husband. We really need him to come to Washington."

"Madam Director, as long as my family is in jeopardy, my husband's solicitude and presence is required here to assure a resolution to our current precarious predicament. Perhaps you could seek his accompaniment in Alabama."

The director looked at Gene bewildered and noticed a smile on his face. She nodded for him to proceed.

Gene proposed, "Mrs. O'Sheen, please tell your beloved husband that my plane will arrive shortly after sunset to arrange a meeting." He looked at the director for approval. She nodded.

The response came, "Mister Kamper, I am sure my beloved will welcome your arrival with open arms."

I reached over to the phone and broke the connection.

Dale looked at me and saw the tears of restrained laughter streaming down my face. I let the now-uncontrollable belly laugh release. She couldn't help but laugh with me, despite the fact that her nerves were on edge after talking to the Director of the CIA for the first time. Her nervous laughter caused me to laugh so hard that I rolled onto the couch barely able to breathe. She pounced on top of me, her laughter also becoming uncontrollable. It was minutes later before any sense of composure returned to either of us.

I took Dale into my arms and kissed her tenderly on her lips and proclaimed, "My dear Miss Scarlett O'Hara . . ." the effect of which was another minute of uncontrolled laughter.

I finally got up and went to the kitchen and poured us each a glass of wine even though it was just noon. Dale would know that when I returned, a more serious subject would ensue. I handed her a glass of wine before sitting down. I struggled between giggles, "Why did you speak to the director in that old-fashioned, southern style?"

Dale became serious, "She addressed me as if I were an ignorant redneck southern housewife. I decided to meet her expectations. My grandmother spoke in that southern fashion and I hated it . . . until now."

She continued. "But inform me from your superior male intellect, why the director herself is seeking your expertise?"

I laughed again at her return to the southern accent. I retreated into my normal thinking mode, measuring every possible word, deciding what I could say that wasn't classified.

Dale knew how to jump-start me, "Spit it out damn it."

I started slowly, carefully, in recognition of the effects of my somewhat desperate disclosure to her before I left for Paris concerning my inadequacies during the first attack. "The first attack in Paris was aimed at both Jody and me." I hesitated and went close to the truth. "Dale, Pierre helped me thwart the second attack and he arrested their leader, Mohammed. I interrogated Mohammed. He accused me of killing his father in an operation that I was involved with in Special Forces in Kuwait almost twenty years ago: before Operation Desert Storm, the first Gulf War with Iraq."

"My undercover Special Forces unit intercepted an Iraqi Republican Guard unit sent to sabotage Kuwait's communication systems before Saddam Hussein attacked Kuwait. When my unit intercepted them, they refused to surrender and fired on us in an attempt to escape. Some of them did escape because one man set up in a strategic position and pinned us down. He died in his effort. We later identified him as Mohammed Kareem Faisad. It was his son, Mohammed Faisad, who attacked Jody and me."

Dale was bewildered, "What does that have to do with what is happening now?"

I explained. "Mohammed's grandfather is a rich oil sheik who lives in Iraq. He blamed America for his son's death and trained his grandson to exact his revenge if the identities of the men who killed his son were ever discovered. I assume that someone connected to the rich sheik, and who was on the sabotage mission with his son, recognized my picture that Jody put on the internet to advertise our security protection business."

"Did you kill the sheik's son?" She saw in her husband's eyes that he did.

I warned, "The fact that America had forces in Kuwait at that time is still highly classified."

"Eddie, I asked you if Pat killed the sheik's son."

Eddie nodded. "Pat had to protect the men in his Special Forces unit." He often referred to his alter-ego in the third person.

Dale conjectured, "The sheik must be even madder now that his grandson is in custody. I understand the concept of revenge, and I heard Jody's report of the threat withdrawing in Australia. Before you got home, you withdrew all the code warnings. Tell me what you did to suddenly assure our safety?" Her statement wasn't a question: it was an accusation.

I explained, "When I left Paris, I went to Iraq and had a short face-to-face visit with the rich sheik. I convinced him that reconciliation was in our mutual interest. The pullback of his aggression against Jody in Australia was evidence that my conversation with him had the desired effect."

Dale's look at me was incredulous. "You said he planned this for decades. How were you able to get this angry sheik to meet with you so quickly?"

"Gene Kamper arranged the meeting." *That was partially true.* "The sheik didn't agree to meet with me. We intercepted him on his way to the mosque for noon prayers, and I confronted him. Apparently, he expected that I was there to kill him.

"I explained the circumstances around the death of his son, apologized, and I told him that his son died heroically, sacrificing his life so his comrades could escape. He withdrew his fatwa shortly after I left." I expected that the terminology would confuse Dale enough to end her inquisition.

Dale was comforted but still confused, "How was Gene able to find the sheik so soon after his grandson's arrest?"

"You will meet Gene tonight. He is quite an incredible young man."

"I'll be the judge of that," Dale responded. "You too freely drape your admiration upon the undeserving shoulders of acquaintances that you have companioned."

Realizing that her words and accent relapsed into her recent actress roll, I laughed aloud, "Yes, Miss Scarlett. I am in total agreement with your experienced and expert analysis." We laughed heartily into each other's arms, and then embraced more intimately.

What an incredible woman! I breathed easier knowing that she had again allowed me to cover my covert operations. The intimate contact with her was starting to take my breath away.

Chapter 28
Reunions

Jody arrived from Australia the day after Pat arrived home from Paris and Iraq. He still wasn't sure why the threat had retreated in Australia. He knew that Robby's short analysis that his dad was somehow involved in the pullback was probably correct. After getting resettled in his house, he called his dad and then headed through the woods to the back door of his parents' house.

After sharing hugs, both Dale and I could tell that Jody wanted to talk to me in private. He and I retreated to the computer bunker.

I wasn't sure how much to tell Jody: some of my knowledge was classified and could put his life in jeopardy.

When they were alone in the bunker, Jody blurted out, "I read a story from Paris on the Internet describing a gang war that left eleven people dead. **Were you involved**?"

The directness and the emotion in his question went to the heart of the issue and made me realize that Jody was ready to hear the truth. After all, he had survived his first kills as a result of the same threat.

I asked, "Are you sure you want to know?"

Jody cackled without humor, "I guess your question answered mine." Jody looked away aggravated.

Jody was starting to understand who I was. I decided to tell him, "Yes, I was involved."

Jody looked back at me amazed that I actually admitted it.

I started, "I anticipated the second attack and arranged CIA back-up to entrap my adversaries. I was double-crossed, except for a CIA agent named Gene Kamper, who was also betrayed. If Gene hadn't backed me up, I would not have survived."

I considered what I could and could not tell him.

Jody asked, "Dad, can you tell me what started this nightmare? What this is all about?"

I deflected the question and continued sharing the betrayal in Paris, and without going into too much detail about the confrontation, I explained Gene Kamper's role, Brett Spellman's role, and the CIA betrayal. I told of my capture of Mohammed, and that I had interrogated him before Gene and I left the area.

I explained who Mohammed and Abdul were and their relationship with a rich oil sheik in Iraq. I told him about Kuwait, my Special Forces operation before Desert Storm that resulted in the sheik's son being killed, and that vengeance for the sheik's son death sparked the attempt on our lives in Paris and in Australia.

To answer Jody's ultimate question, I added, "Gene Kamper's contacts in Iraq helped me intercept the rich sheik the day after the second attack against me in Paris. The sheik and I talked and apparently he accepted my apology for killing his son twenty years ago."

Jody asked, "And that is why the threat against me in Australia retreated?"

I nodded, "Possibly."

I stood up and told Jody about the expected arrival of Gene Kamper at the Birmingham airport.

When Jody stood, I hugged him like the dear son he was. "I love you, Jody, and I hope the worst of this nightmare is behind us. It may not be for me. But I believe that the family is now safe from the rich sheik who put a fatwa against us."

***

Jody noticed that his dad hadn't mentioned the mercy that he administered to his captive in Australia, and he concluded that his dad didn't know. Jody decided not to tell him. Not yet.

Jody called his fiancé, Lacy, while walking back through the woods to his house.

Lacy answered her cell phone, "Hey Honey, are you back?"

"Yes, and I need your TLC tonight."

She said, "I get off in twenty minutes. I'll be there in forty." Lacy smiled as she change her evening plans.

Chapter 29

It is not over yet.

Dale slowed her pace to allow Pat to advance alone toward the young man in the Birmingham, Alabama airport. Pat was correct in describing him as the young James Bond in the early Bond movies. She watched as Pat extended his hand, and she was surprised to see it slapped to the side as the man embraced her husband in a bear hug that was calmly returned. *They have only known each other for a few days.*

The gorgeous man looked up and smiled at her while releasing from the hug with her husband. She approached slowly as Pat turned toward her, but before he could initiate an introduction, the young man blurted out, "Pat, this must be your Miss Scarlett."

She looked at Pat in realization that this man wasn't fooled by the ruse. Pat broke out into a hearty, contagious laugh that the gorgeous man joined, and from which she could not refrain. Her mind was going into the character.

I took the lead to introduce them. "Gene, this is my wife, Dale. Dale, this is Gene Kamper."

Gene exclaimed, "I'm not surprised by your beauty." He grabbed her extended right hand and twisted it palm down, bowed down, and kissed the back of it.

"Oh my!" escaped involuntarily from Dale's lips.

I gave Gene a friendly shove. "You will not steal her from me without a fight," We all laughed again.

When I drove from the Birmingham airport, Gene broke the silence, "Laughter makes me hungry. The U.S. government will buy you both the best steaks in Birmingham."

From the back seat Dale asked, "Eddie, are you thinking of eating where I am."

I saw Gene's confusion and explained. "I grew up being called 'Eddie', and I am still Eddie to Dale and most of my childhood friends."

"Well Eddie, where are we going to eat?"

I smiled. "You will see soon enough. The place is not far."

In the ensuing silence I mused, *Dale accepted him without question. Her judgment is not tainted by my paranoia. I hope she's right.*

The O'Sheens made Gene miss his parents. He was overdue for a visit to their home.

Gene was surprised when Pat pulled into the parking lot of what once must have been a curb-hop, fast-food, teenager hangout in the 60's. The large neon sign read 'The Original Golden Rule." He looked questioningly at Pat.

I was expecting the unspoken query and said, "I bet you have never had Alabama barbecue. That lack of experience is about to change. Good steaks are available everywhere in the world. You need to taste great Alabama barbecue. This is one of the best."

Gene enjoyed one of the most memorable meals of his life. The food and the company were priceless.

Dale and Gene were laughing again as we left the Golden Rule. I steered Gene to the side and suggested that he spend the night at our house. "I've already cleared it with Dale."

Gene countered, "I'm not sure your delightful wife would be safe from my advances overnight." Pat's warm response sealed the deal.

Gene said, "I will have to call in and report my location. Is that a problem?"

I replied, "We have time to discuss issues tonight before you report in." The three of us climbed into Dale's Rendezvous.

Gene watched as I punched a code into my cell phone. From his shotgun seat, he stared in his side mirror at the Land Rover that pulled up behind.

I informed Gene, "He's friendly."

Dale apparently understood Gene's apprehension. From the back seat she drawled, "Master Gene, my notorious husband would not allow a man of your caliber to have access to his beloved wife without sufficient backup." Her exaggerated southern belle impression broke the tension into another group laughter.

The conversation in the SUV quieted as I drove out of the city.

*****

Gene reflected on the woman seated behind him. The lovely woman had outmaneuvered the director of the CIA; otherwise, he wouldn't be in Alabama. Dale had won him over with her personality faster than Pat had won him over with his special talents. In the silence, he reflected on his first days with Pat O'Sheen. The intimate and kind moments with Pat reflected the personality of his wife in the back seat.

Gene noticed that the Land Rover was no longer in sight after they exited the interstate highway.

Pat's cell phone echoed a strange sound.

"Hold on tight." Pat declared as he went to full acceleration. He yelled at Gene, **"Find out if those are your CIA people following us. If they are, explain that they are in mortal danger."**

Gene anxiously punched a specially encoded three-digit number into his cell phone. He held on as Pat recklessly turned right at the next intersection. He heard Dale scream a warning, **"Eddie, this is a dead end road**."

Gene watched Pat retrieve a pistol from under the driver's seat, and recognized the same fire in his eyes that he had seen in the Paris encounter. Pat popped the center console on the Buick Rendezvous and withdrew another pistol.

Still waiting for a CIA response from his emergency call, the unarmed Gene took the weapon that Pat placed on his lap. He watched the empty, undeveloped cul-de-sac approaching too quickly for this SUV to handle. Still waiting on what was supposed to be a quick response code in his cell phone, he held on to the handle above the door that was designed to assist the elderly to enter the vehicle, and he braced for the inevitable crash into the woods.

The Rendezvous should have flipped-over, but somehow Pat managed to control it through a 180-degree turning skid. The front of the now immobile vehicle was facing the pursuers and opened front doors would provide cover at this angle.

Pat punched one of the several buttons in the front center console that audibly released the lock on the rear hatch door. Pat told Dale to get on the floor as he jumped out, aimed his Glock 22, and shot the left front tire of the pursuing vehicle speeding straight at them, forcing it to stop about sixty feet away. Pat ran to the back of the Rendezvous and opened the hatch.

Gene's patience for CIA response expired as he noticed a Land Rover rushing into the scene and stopping twenty feet behind the pusuing vehicle. Gene jumped out of the SUV, raised his pistol and yelled, **"FBI, freeze."** He pointed the pistol that Pat had set in his lap toward the driver who had exited an old Impala. The black man had a long-barreled Colt 45 in his right hand.

Gene shouted again, **"FBI, drop your weapon,"**

The driver's lack of reaction to Gene's warning ascertained that he was not CIA or FBI. When the man turned the barrel of the 45 in his direction, Gene fired. The report from Gene's pistol was less than a second behind another pistol report. The man's head jerked forward instead of backward, and the driver's body fell limply to the ground.

Another black man exited the passenger seat with a pistol and ran toward the woods. Gene was startled when a blast erupted from behind him. The man running toward the woods left leg caved, and he collapsed awkwardly into the roadside ditch. A large man, one of the two who had exited the Land Rover, ran forward with his gun aimed at the man in the ditch while the other man was running to where the driver had fallen.

I walked quickly past Gene with a high-powered Remington rifle still aimed at the man in the ditch.

Gene followed. The man in the ditch saw us approaching, rolled onto his stomach, and stretched his empty hands out on the edge of the road in front of him. He wanted everyone to know that he was no longer a threat. The large man from the Land Rover reached him first, picked up the dropped pistol by the barrel, and threw it to the side. He reached down and frisked the man's back, roughly turned him over, and completed his weapons search by pulling a switchblade knife from the front pocket of loose fitting, unbelted, cut-off jeans.

I looked over at Robby who shook his head. *The driver was dead.*

We heard Dale running from the Rendezvous yelling in a near panic, "I called 911."

I cursed almost under my breath. I looked at the large man, "Brendan, was he your shot?" tilting my head toward the dead driver. Brendan nodded.

I said, "Robby, I want you to take the Queen home." I turned to embrace my frightened, fast-approaching wife.

Robby moved to her side, stopped and waited until her visible shaking subsided in my embrace. Robby grabbed her upper arm as I started to release her, and he said, "We have to leave, Dale." The words were calm and loving.

"But, but, but . . ." she attempted to protest.

I said, "*Let's* **Go.**" not so calm and not so lovingly, and I regretted my commanding tone before the two words were out of my mouth.

Robby ran as I hurried Dale toward the Land Rover. Robby had climbed behind the wheel and had started the car by the time I opened the back door, helped Dale climb into the back seat, and told her to get on the floor. The vehicle was already backing up before I closed her door. In less than a minute they were off the dead-end road.

I walked back to the black man, who was still lying on his back on the ground with Brendan's pistol aimed at his chest.

"Who hired you?" I demanded.

"Man, I don't know nuttin."

I pointed the rifle at his wounded leg, stepped forward, and inserted the tip of the Remington into the large exit wound on his calf. The man screamed in agony.

The man cried rocking back and forth in agony. "Leroy knows. I jez works for him,"

"What's Leroy's last name?" I asked forcefully.

"Ax Leroy, you som' beach." He replied defiantly.

I informed him, "The next question Leroy answers will be from Saint Peter at heaven's gate."

"Oh sheet, Oh sheet," The man understood my meaning. As I inched the tip of the rifle toward his leg again he said, "Walker. His name is Leroy (he pronounced it Leeee-roy) Walker."

"Where does he live?" I demanded while hearing sirens approaching.

"Ishacooda," he cried as the first of two sheriff's cars rounded the corner at high speed.

***

Gene did not know what to expect when the first sheriff's car pulled up ten feet from the armed group with bright lights from the Sherriff's vehicle shining on them. *Should I drop my weapon? He would if Pat did.*

Surprisingly, the bright headlights dimmed, and a huge sheriff climbed out of the driver's door, while a small deputy jumped out the passenger door with his gun drawn and pointing in their direction.

The sheriff slowly sauntered toward the group with his right hand resting comfortably on the butt of his still-holstered pistol. The black man on the ground cried, "Sheriff, hep me. Please hep me. These guys…"

Shut up, Boy. The sheriff's shout was very politically incorrect.

Gene was reminded of rural southern sheriffs he had seen in old fifty's movies. He saw the sheriff nod at Brendan as he approached.

"Hey, Pat," the sheriff said calmly. Gene relaxed slightly, until two deputies exited the second squad car brandishing weapons. One was running to the dead man on the other side of the street.

***

I said in a calm voice. "Hello, Bo,"

"Who is this gentleman?" Bo looked at Gene and then down at the pistol held by his right thigh.

"A friend," I replied.

"I'll need your weapon, Sir." The sheriff calmly extended his left hand with his right hand still resting on the butt of his holstered pistol. Gene rotated the pistol in his hands with the barrel aiming sideways, and the butt facing up, and he extended it to the sheriff. The sheriff looked in the man's eyes knowing that the man was a professional by the way he handed the gun to him in a way that was non-threatening to either party. The sheriff raised Gene's pistol near his nose and smelled it.

The sheriff looked down the road at the Rendezvous, which was easily visible in the ensuing darkness with both side doors and the back hatch still opened illuminating the inside lights. He called to a deputy, "Cal, what have you got over there?"

"We have a homicide, Sheriff. Black man shot in the back of the head from an area behind your Tahoe."

The sheriff turned toward Brendan and looked at the Sig Sauer pistol still held by Brendan's right thigh, "Is that the homicide weapon?"

Gene was surprised when the response was, "Yes sir."

"Slim," he said to the deputy he had arrived with; "Put some gloves on and retrieve these weapons."

The sheriff said to another deputy, "Bones, call dispatch to get an ambulance and the coroner out here. And get some bandages to wrap this guy's leg before he bleeds to death."

"Thanks Sheriff, sah. These guys tacked us, kilt Leroy, shot me n was tortur'n' me, an vi-latin my civil rights when you pulled up."

"I told you to shut up."

The sheriff pulled a Kleenex from his pocket, grabbed the front wooden grip on the rifle that was cradled in my left arm, and without taking the weapon from me, carefully wiped the blood off the end of the barrel, wadded the Kleenex up, and cleaned the inside of the barrel. He took the rifle from me, sniffed it and handed it to his now gloved deputy.

Gene could not believe what he had just witnessed. The sheriff had just tampered with incriminating evidence.

"Pat, your pistol," the sheriff's request was polite.

I reached behind my back, pulled it from under my belt and handed it to the sheriff with the butt facing forward and down. The sheriff sniffed the gun and handed it to his deputy. "Pat, have you got anything else?"

"Just these," I extracted a pair of night vision goggles from my belt and extracted a large hunting knife from my boot.

"Slim, check Pat's friend here for weapons. And I need to see his identification."

The sheriff addressed me again while inspecting the night vision goggles. "Prepared for a chase in the woods?" The question was rhetorical, not expecting an answer. He took the knife and let me keep the goggles. "Did Dale make the 911 call?"

"Yes, Bo." I anticipating his next question, "I sent her home with Robby for her protection."

"Pat, you know that leaving the scene of a crime is a criminal offence."

Oh no. Gene was suddenly worried, knowing that Robby and Dale leaving the scene of a crime was indeed a violation of the law.

I explained "Bo, Robby and Dale did not participate in the gunfire. I didn't know if other adversaries were in pursuit." The sheriff turned and looked at Brendan who nodded.

The sheriff said, "Pat, I know that you and Brendan are honest men. However, if ballistics and forensics prove that other weapons were involved, the criminal consequences could be severe."

Bo changed subjects, "Where is Jody?"

I replied, "He and Robby just got back from Australia today. Jody is spending the evening with Lacy."

The sheriff nodded and looked back at Gene, but addressed me, "Pat, tell me more about your friend here?"

Gene interrupted this rural southern movie scene for the first time, "Sheriff, I'm Gene Kamper. I'm a federal agent, and I can verify these men's story."

"Son, I don't need a damn Yankee verifying their story. I can see what happened here."

Gene recoiled at the rebuke and was quickly ignored.

"Pat, did the tip of your rifle barrel discover who these guys are, and why they were after you?"

I admitted, "I didn't learn much. It appears that this guy doesn't know why the dead man was hired to attack us." I pointed my thumb at the man in the ditch.

I deflected, "Bo, would you allow me to call home and let Dale know that you have arrived and that we are safe? Then I'll answer all your questions." The sheriff nodded.

I retrieved the cell phone from my pocket and reported in, allowing the sheriff to listen. "Robby, the sheriff is with us, and we are going to be tied up for a while. I need to verify a statement I made to Bo. As you know, things got a little hectic here. Did you discharge your weapon while you were here? . . . Okay, I didn't think so. Dale and you will have to prepare statements. Are you on Code 2? . . . Good."

An ambulance arrived, followed by the coroner in his official vehicle. The deputy nicknamed Bones directed the paramedics to the wounded man, who had apparently passed out. The coroner and a young man whom I didn't know, but who looked like a detective, were directed to the dead body on the ground.

"Pat," Gene addressed. "I need to reverse my emergency call to the agency. My phone is still in your car, and we better shut your car doors before the battery dies."

The sheriff accompanied Gene and me to the SUV. Bo inspected the inside of my vehicle while Gene retrieved the phone. Gene seemed surprised that I did not object to the sheriff's inspection without a warrant.

I asked Gene if he received a response to his emergency call.

Gene looked at his phone, "No, they never responded." Gene and I shared a look: Gene's look of disbelief was accusatory. We both knew that reporting in to the CIA was now out of the question.

We closed up the SUV, and the three of us walked back toward the crime scene. The sheriff stopped us and continued with his last line of questioning, "Pat, I'm sure that you learned something from your rifle barrel probe. Who are these guys?"

"According to the injured man, the deceased's name is Leroy Walker from Ishacooda. The injured man told me that he works for Leroy occasionally, and I believe that he doesn't have a clue who contracted Leroy for this hit job. You showed up before I could get any more background."

The coroner was standing, patiently awaiting the sheriff, while one of the deputies was cordoning off the area with yellow police tape. The coroner addressed me first, "Hey old man. Your life isn't as boring as mine."

Gene let out a small chuckle when he saw the warm friendly smile they shared. *Good-ole-boys.*

The coroner addressed the sheriff, "Bo, the bullet to the back of the head probably killed him, but he was also struck by a bullet in the chest."

Bo spun around toward me not liking this exclusion from our report, remembering the gunpowder smell on Gene and my pistols.

Gene intervened again, "Sheriff, I yelled an FBI warning for him to drop his weapon. I fired at him when he turned his Colt 45 toward me. But I thought I missed based on my distance and the direction that his body fell."

"Where were you standing when you fired?"

"I shot from behind the passenger door of Pat's vehicle," Gene answered honestly.

Everyone looked back at the SUV. Bo did a quick analysis of the distance. An accurate shot with a pistol from sixty feet took exceptional talent.

I anticipated the next question, "Lucky shot. I gave him the gun when the pursuit started. The gun is registered to Stay Safe, LLC."

The sheriff declared, "I'll need to take this Yankee into custody, until this incident is clarified."

Brendan had joined the three of us, standing only inches from the sheriff. "Bo, my bullet killed the man."

Brendan quickly summarized the pursuit, "Agent Kamper's warning to the driver to drop his weapon was ignored, and Kamper's response was to defend the O'Sheens."

The sheriff was huge and probably wasn't used to looking upward into a bigger man's eyes, but he didn't seem intimidated by Brendan's close proximity.

Brendan continued, "We don't know if more hit men are nearby. And perhaps, Agent Kamper was the target, not the O'Sheens. These two need to get to the safety of Pat's house to investigate. I'll ride with you to the station."

I added, "When we get back to the house, all of us will write out our statements on the details of what we witnessed here tonight, sign them, and have them on your desk in the morning."

The sheriff corrected me, "Dale and Robby can do written statements. I'll need you and Agent Kamper to come in and answer some questions in front of a court reporter. I'll return Kamper's ID at the office tomorrow."

I nodded, "We'll be there at eight."

Chapter 30
Trustworthy?

Gene Kamper watched and listened intently as Pat went through all of the security procedures to pass through the gate and enter his homestead. The last words from Pat were "Put the Queen on Code 3 and inform her of our arrival."

Gene wouldn't have been surprised if Pat pulled into an underground bunker with a group of redneck militia soldiers surrounding a compound. Instead, Pat drove up the driveway and stopped out in the open, twenty feet from the front door of a normal looking middle-class home. Pat casually removed his keys from the ignition, punched the hatch release button on the dash panel, and exited his door.

Gene opened his car door as Pat rounded the front of the car approaching him. Pat grabbed his arm and led him to the back of the Rendezvous and lifted the hatch. "Grab your bag. You will spend the night here." It wasn't a command, but it was no longer just the simple invitation that Pat had made earlier when they left the restaurant. Gene didn't argue.

Gene watched as Pat punched another code into his cell phone, waited a full minute, opened the front door of the house, and stiffly entered. Gene noticed that Pat was more nervous entering his own house than he was when they heard the explosion upstairs in the safe house in Paris, and much more nervous than when he approached the sheik in Iraq.

Gene smiled at seeing Dale cross the floor toward them until he saw the look in her eyes. That fire was the same he had witnessed in Pat's eyes after the battle in the safe house. Gene understood the fire in Pat's eyes in Paris, but the fire he saw in Dale's eyes was totally unexpected.

Dale stopped her hurried approach five feet from them. "What in the hell have you two gotten us into?"

Gene was hoping that Pat would have a good answer, but he remained silent. Dale took two aggressive steps toward her husband, "You are not going to shut me out of this one."

Pat remained uncomfortably silent.

Please handle this, Gene silently implored, while watching this woman who intimidated the director of the CIA, intimidate the man who killed at least ten men in Paris just days before.

Instead of answering her, Pat walked around her toward the couch, apparently unaware how that maneuver fanned the flames of Dale's fire. Gene didn't know whether to move or not. Should he close the open front door behind him, or leave and run like the devil was chasing him. Earlier, he was so enamored with this perfect couple. He did not want to witness the impending explosion.

Dale glared at Pat's back as he sat down on the couch. She closed and locked the front door, and she stomped off toward the kitchen. Gene felt like a fly on the wall that was totally ignored. He hoped that Pat would acknowledge his presence and ask him to sit, but Pat was motionless. He considered following Dale in an attempt to calm her, but that would be inappropriate. So he stood uncomfortably by the front door, unable to decide on an intelligent move.

A few minutes later, Dale reentered the room. She set a mixed drink on the side table next to Pat with a napkin under it. She walked around the couch and handed Gene a glass of red wine. She looked into Gene's eyes and slanted her head toward her husband on the couch. She walked around Gene, opened a door on the entertainment center, punched a button, and stomped out of the room without saying a word.

The fragrance of the wine penetrated Gene's numbed consciousness. Unbelievably, it was his favorite wine. Gene didn't believe in coincidences. Pat or Brendan had somehow researched Gene's background. Gene walked around the couch and sat in an armchair across from Pat. Now he understood Pat's nervousness when they entered the house. He also understood how Pat's fiery wife was at the core of his character. He recalled Gene Tanner warning Director Collins not to cross Dale O'Sheen.

Gene didn't know what to say, so he remained quiet and sipped his favorite affordable wine.

***

I finally picked up the drink that Dale had set next to me, took a gulp, and looked accusingly at Gene.

Gene was alarmed by the look, "What are you thinking, Pat?"

When I didn't answer, Gene pressed, "Pat, what are you so mad about? Did I do something wrong? What is going down here?"

I took another tug on my drink and stated, "Dale was upset with me for contacting the CIA after the first attack against me in Paris. Years ago, she encouraged me to retire from Army Special Forces so that I could spend more time with my kids. When I left Special Forces, I went to work for a local company. I explained to the owner of the company that my Special Forces contract with the government stipulates that I can be called back into government service with a seven-day notice. He allows me to do that without it jeopardizing my job with him.

"Dale knew my CIA work endangered my life, and she despises any contact I have with your agency. She knows that you and I met on the second attack against me in Paris and that the CIA betrayed me during that attack."

I summarized, "Your cavalry never answered your emergency call in Paris. They hung you out to die *(die; not dry)*. They sent you down here to try to involve me once more, which resulted in another attack against me with Dale in the car. They didn't respond to your emergency signal again tonight. They hung you out to die with me again. **You** tell *me* what is going down here."

I saw the perplexed and hurt look in Gene's eyes.

I said in a friendlier manner, "Gene, think about it. Sheik Faisad withdrew his threat on Jody in Australia after my short talk with him. This attack wasn't from him. Abdul Faisad would never hire a local black thug to attack me. Where do you think this threat is coming from? And why does the CIA fail to respond to your emergency calls every time that you are with me and we are under attack?"

When Gene didn't respond, I said, "Take your time and consider all the facts."

I stood up, picked up my drink, and walked toward the kitchen.

***

Gene considered the facts; particularly, as Pat pointed out the lack of response for his panic button call for backup in Paris, and the lack of response during the pursuit tonight. *Was his beloved CIA duping him?*

Thinking back, Gene analyzed his arrival at Langley from Iraq with the yellow belt. He was rushed to CIA Supervisor Gene Tanner's office, and then to a security level that he wasn't even aware existed. They sat in silence until the director of the CIA and her entourage entered the room. Tom Kime, his field supervisor, was excluded from all discussion on the strange yellow belt. He conveyed to the group Pat's theories on the belt, the hologram projection, melt down in case of death, the explosive activation button, and the cloaking device that seemed to fail when the vital signs of the wearer indicated inevitable death. He had disclosed all of Pat's theories in the meeting. *Why not? He was doing his job.*

The supervisors at the CIA meeting the next day were visibly upset when Pat sidestepped their demand to talk to him by allowing his wife to control the conversation.

A light bulb started to brighten in Gene's head. Pat was apparently already enlightened. The knowledge that he and Pat had acquired at the safe house in Paris made them a threat and possibly set them up for extermination. He and Pat knew that their government lost control of a top-secret weapon. The government wanted to put a lid on the leak.

A cold sweat broke out on Gene's body. He realized that if Pat had explained this conspiracy theory to him, he would not have bought into such crazy paranoia. *But he could not come up with any other explanation*

Gene stood up and then quickly sat back down. If he followed Pat down this road, his CIA career could be over. If he didn't, he might be exterminated. *Who were his real friends?*

Do the right thing. Do the right thing. His mom's often repeated advice as he grew up echoed in his mind. Gene stood and approached the kitchen. No one was there. He found a bottle of Bud Light in the refrigerator and twisted off the cap. He slammed the refrigerator door loudly to remind Pat of his presence, and he stood in the kitchen waiting. *Pat didn't arrive.*

Maybe they were watching him. He scanned the kitchen for a hidden camera without finding one. He casually walked back to his seat next to the couch searching for hidden cameras on the way, or for some clue to explain his hosts' behavior. He sat down in his previous position and took a long tug off the long-necked bottle. Maybe Pat was attempting to remove the fire from Dale's eyes. That would be a difficult task. He consciously made his blood pressure and pulse rate lower.

He leaned back in his chair in an attempt to be patient.

He finished his beer and must have nodded off because he was startled by Pat's entrance.

***

When I entered the room, Gene asked, "Did you manage to calm Dale?"

All I would admit was, "She is an incredible woman."

I asked, "Who is my enemy this time?" I stared into Gene's eyes and revised the question, "Who is **our** enemy?"

Gene appreciated his inclusion in the revised question. "Pat, I think we have targets on our backs. The first attack in Paris was focused on killing you or Jody by an angry sheik. After that attack, you challenged the CIA with your hologram theory. The lack of support during the second attack in Paris may have been to prevent you from disclosing the fact that the CIA had leaked the hologram technology. The fact that I escaped with you from the safe house has made me a target with you.

"The attack by the two black men tonight was probably a test to learn how good your security was near your home. Now they know that you are not very vulnerable in Alabama."

Gene continued, "I was duped. I volunteered to come here. Think about it, Pat. Who else has seen the yellow belts in the hands of our enemies except you and me?" He answered his own question, "No one."

"We weren't expected to survive the attack in Paris, and now they don't want us to investigate how the belts got into the wrong hands. I have a feeling that the use of the belts against you during the first attack in Paris was a rogue operation: not approved by the conspirators. Sheik Faisad was surprised that you survived the first attack, and he worried that your survival would expose his unauthorized use of the secret weapon against you, so he ordered the second attack. We need to figure out a way to expose the behind the scene conspirators."

I watched Gene closely to judge his sincerity and listened to the words pouring fast and furious from his mouth. I had already considered Gene's theory. My theory was more focused, but now was not the time to share it, so I played along, "Were you able to pick up any clues from your meetings at Langley? What company is contracted to develop the technology and manufacture the belts? Who is Jonathan Booth?"

"I don't know," Gene admitted. "Director Collins said she would initiate an investigation based on the new information that I brought her."

I knew that Gene knew more and was not willing to share top-secret information that I was not cleared for.

I sneered, **"Bullshit Kamper. The CIA knows who was contracted to develop the hologram technology. Who met with you at Langley?"**

Gene was truthful, "I'm sorry Pat. I love my job. I have a loving wife and a beautiful young son. I can't share need-to-know information with you."

Pat admired Gene for admitting the truth. "You are the one who said we have large targets on our back. I agree with your analysis. We need someone in the CIA whom we can trust."

Gene offered, "My field supervisor, Tom Kime, was not included in any of my meetings at Langley involving the Hologram belts. In fact, I never saw him while I was there. Deputy Director Hill instructed me that nothing about the belts discussed at the meetings could leave the room."

Pat thought, *I didn't know Hill.* He wondered if he was the fat guy that was in his meeting with the Director about the ray deflection technology. I knew Gene Tanner and Director Collins. Now, I had one new name.

Gene and I discussed what to share with his field supervisor, Tom Kime.

I stood up and said to Gene, "Follow me."

Gene stood and followed me down a hallway. I opened a hidden panel and walked down a set of stairs to an underground room blocked by a steel door. I looked back at him, moved to block his view of a keyboard, and punched in a code. The steel door rotated open into a large room.

Gene noticed a young man sitting at a computer keyboard. His resemblance to Pat was obvious. Pat's son turned back to the keyboard, made an entry, and stood up with a tense smile.

Pat started the introduction, "Jody, this is Gene Kamper."

Jody stepped forward and shook Gene's hand firmly while he looked somewhat warily into his eyes. Gene smiled and looked into the eyes of a younger Pat O'Sheen. There could be no question who fathered the young man. But Jody didn't smile. *Why?*

When they released the handshake, Gene took a peek at the computer screen for a clue as to what Jody was doing here, but the screen was covered with a fawn suckling from its mother's teat: a screen saver design. Jody had hidden what he was working on. Perhaps he shared his dad's paranoia.

Pat said to Jody, "I thought you were with Lacy?"

"Mom called and told me about the attack tonight."

Pat brought Jody up to date as well as he could without disclosing top-secret information.

Then Pat explained what he wanted Jody to do, and why he wanted the extra phone security for a phone call.

Gene backed away when Pat asked him to surrender his CIA issued phone to Jody.

Jody explained to Kamper, "The CIA will not be able to discover that your phone was tampered with."

Pat encouraged Gene to cooperate.

Gene said, "I can't allow this. The CIA will know what's happening when we complete our connection."

Jody repeated, "I guarantee that no one will be able to trace the source of our call after I configure your phone. I can't control whether or not the conversation will be recorded on the other end."

Gene was skeptical, but he agreed with Pat that contacting his CIA supervisor, Tom Kime, was necessary, and he didn't want his location to be traced to the O'Sheen residence. He was curious to learn Jody's technology.

He handed Jody his CIA cell phone and watched Jody retrieve a tiny star-headed screw driver from a drawer. Jody removed the back panel from the phone. He flipped the phone over and turned it off and removed the battery and the SIM chip. He retrieved a device from another drawer, plugged it into a USB port on his computer and inserted the phone's SIM card into the device. He retrieved a small cable from the drawer and used it to connect the device to the cell phone. He took some earphones from the drawer, plugged it into the device, and handed the earphones to his dad. He reinserted the battery into the cell phone, turned it on, and handed it to Gene. Gene nodded his admiration and approval.

I listened to the short explanation that Jody gave Gene. The CIA would not be able to locate the coordinates of his secure cell phone call, but his ID number would be recognized and go through normally. I asked Jody to leave the room.

When he left, I instructed, "Gene, tell Kime about the attack on our way from the airport, the one death, and that we will be tied up dealing with the sheriff's office. Don't tell him you are calling from my house. Do you know what else to say? It's after eleven in Washington."

Gene nodded and used the speed dial to call the number. I inserted the ear buds to listen.

Kime answered in a groggy voice. "Gene, where are you? I learned that you were in the building earlier today. Why didn't you report to my office?"

Gene asked, "Tom, is your phone secure."

"Yes. Why?"

"Is it secure from the CIA?"

"I am not sure about that."

I motioned for Gene to proceed.

"Tom, I brought a top-secret package back to Langley last night. I was ushered into a secure conference room, interrogated, and then sent out today on a special assignment."

The now wide-awake and angry reply was, "Why wasn't I informed?"

"Tom, you will have to go up the line of command for the answer to that."

Kime complained, "Gene, my security clearance is way above your level. What was in the package?"

"Tom, you will have to go up the line for that answer, too. I was ordered not to share that info with anyone by people above your level."

"Gene, where have you been for the last four days? Were you anywhere near the safe house in Paris where eleven people were killed? Why didn't you report in after your reconnaissance of the safe house?"

Gene was tempted to tell him about his "panic button" attempt, but that could wait.

I couldn't help but smile. I had never met Tom Kime, but he could fire off questions without waiting for answers faster than Dale. The ignorance in his questions testified to his lack of involvement in this conspiracy nightmare—*or he was an excellent actor.* Pat's gut told him that he could be trusted. He nodded for Gene to proceed as planned.

Gene said, "I was with O'Sheen in the safe house during the attack. The CIA sting that O'Sheen arranged against his attackers never materialized. O'Sheen was double-crossed from inside our agency.

"Tom, when I arrived at the safe house before O'Sheen arrived, I sensed the double cross and hit my panic button. I got no response. Whoever is behind the betrayal of O'Sheen double-crossed me too. O'Sheen and I fought off the attack at the safe house. O'Sheen captured one of the attackers and interrogated him. He also retrieved the top-secret weapon that I brought to Langley."

Gene explained that after escaping from the safe house, he left Paris with O'Sheen on his private jet and was airborne before being informed that the plane was headed for Kuwait instead of Washington, DC. He dutifully reported that he helped O'Sheen arrange a meeting with Sheik Mohammed Faisad who was financing the attacks on the O'Sheen family and he reported the friendly outcome of the meeting.

Gene said, "When the plane finally arrived in Washington, Pat O'Sheen handed me the top-secret package to deliver to Langley. I couldn't talk O'Sheen into coming to Langley with me. After dropping me off, O'Sheen flew to his home in Alabama. After the attack on Pat and me, O'Sheen doesn't trust anyone in the CIA.

"Tom, this morning, O'Sheen refused to talk to Director Collins, forcing me to come to Alabama.

I admired the acumen of Gene. He was reporting all of the relevant facts that would eventually surface, but nothing more. And he didn't compromise the hologram information.

"Where are you now?" Tom Kime asked.

"I'm in Alabama. I was ordered to talk O'Sheen into coming back to Langley.

"Tom, I had dinner with Pat O'Sheen and his wife at a BBQ joint near the Birmingham airport. On the way back to the O'Sheen house from the restaurant, we were attacked by two local black men. One of the attackers is dead, and the other is injured. I fired a shot that hit the attacker who died. I don't think my bullet killed him, but the Shelby County Sheriff is involved. I may be tied up in Alabama for a while. I may need some legal help."

Kime said, "Oh shit, Gene. How can I help?" The concern in his voice was evident.

"Tom. I'm not finished. When we were pursued tonight, Pat initially thought it might be the CIA following us. I dialed my emergency response code. If it was a CIA car in pursuit of us, Pat wanted me to warn them that they were in mortal danger. Pat has good backup protection in Alabama.

"Tom, that was two hours ago. I still have not had a response from headquarters to my emergency response request. I don't think O'Sheen is being paranoid. Someone in the CIA wants both of us dead."

Kime spoke with an alarmed tone, "Gene, I'll get to the bottom of this."

Gene warned, "Watch your back, Tom. I think the CIA has lost control of a top-secret weapon. People way above your grade are trying to cover their ass by eliminating witnesses like O'Sheen and me. Don't indicate that you are protecting us." The concern for his boss was evident in Gene's voice. Pat reached over and disconnected Gene's phone.

Gene turned to me, "Why did you do that?"

"You gave Tom all he needed to investigate. I didn't want you to disclose anymore

"We will see what percolates to the top. I still have contacts at many levels in the CIA who I think I can trust."

"Who are they?"

I shook my head. I didn't trust Gene that much.

I started running conversations with the CIA through my head when Gene asked out of the blue, "Will Brendan be able to deal with the sheriff alone?"

I answered him absentmindedly, my mind far away from Gene's question, "Yeah, Brendan will be fine. The sheriff is his father-in-law."

***

Pat's disclosure hit Gene like a brick. *The sheriff was Brendan's father-in-law.* That explains the sheriff's calmness and a lot of his other peculiar trusting actions at the homicide scene. *Good-ole-boys.*

Although he had to admit that the sheriff captured the whole scenario more accurately in less than an hour with his slow calm approach than most highly trained big-city investigators could have accomplished in a week. He now realized that Bo was protecting his family and friends, and that he had a sophisticated—not a redneck—knowledge of the law. He remembered the sheriff cleaning the blood off the tip of Pat's rifle with a Kleenex before turning it over to his deputy.

Gene watched Pat move to the computer and hit the 'Esc' (escape) button on the computer. Was escaping necessary or was he absorbing Pat's paranoia? A few minutes later Dale and Jody entered the room.

Jody took the CIA satellite phone from Gene, moved to the computer, and skillfully disconnected the cables from the device to retract the phone block. He reassembled the phone, stood up, and handed

Gene his CIA satellite phone. When Gene grabbed the phone, Jody smiled for the first time. The smile was genuine and reminded him of one of Pat's approving smiles.

Dale interrupted the silence after the phone exchange. "Gene, it's late. I have prepared your bedroom." Gene turned toward her and saw that a comforting expression had returned to her face.

She added, "Jody will show you to your room. It's been a long stressful day. I hope you sleep well."

Gene was disappointed that he would have no further conversation with Dale, but the directive sounded final.

Gene followed Jody through the security door that Pat had opened earlier. After ascending the stairs to the main floor, Jody approached the door directly across the hallway from the sliding panel. Jody entered a numeric code into the keyboard next to the door, reached down, twisted the doorknob, and entered the room. Gene followed Jody into a small room containing a double bed, an Oriental dresser, and no window.

Gene noticed his overnight bag on the bed, walked past Jody to an open door at the far corner of the small room, and saw a small bathroom with a toilet, a utility sink with a small six-inch square mirror at shaving height, and a small corner shower with a white vinyl curtain hung from a cheap metal rod: *not Dale's style*. The whole area reminded Gene of a somewhat comfortable, long-term prison cell. He knew that the O'Sheens must have much nicer guest accommodations than this.

Gene took a deep and silent breath before he exited the bathroom. Jody was standing in the bedroom doorway to the hallway. Gene could not read Jody's face. He would not want to play poker with him. He decided to take a direct approach and objected, "I feel too vulnerable in this room."

To his dismay, Jody didn't respond, nor did the expression on his face change. He watched Jody calmly pull out a remote control and punch a button. Gene understood his predicament.

Jody wished him a good night's sleep, stepped back, and the door closed automatically. Gene heard a loud click as the lock on the door engaged. There was not another keypad inside the door.

Gene looked around the room for a means of communicating in case of an emergency. The O'Sheens would allow that courtesy. He saw an intercom button between the bed and bathroom. He pushed it.

Pat answered immediately, "Gene, I'm sorry for the restrictive measures. I don't trust any employee of the CIA around my family right now. We can discuss this further in the morning. Good night, my friend."

Gene knew that he had played every card right. He had earned their trust at the attack earlier in the night. He had helped defend them.

He sighed. He undressed, turned back the covers, and lay almost naked on the bed with the intent of formulating a plan. His stressful, exhausting day caused sleep to overtake him.

Gene was awakened by a knock on the door. He sprung from the bed and unsuccessfully searched the room for something that could be used as a weapon. The door opened exposing Pat's smiling face.

Gene watched Pat scan his almost naked body, followed by another warm smile. Gene knew that he had failed to hide his alarm, but Pat's demeanor was comforting.

"Breakfast will be ready in thirty minutes." He watched Pat turn and walk away, leaving the door open.

Gene entered the bathroom and saw his beleaguered reflection in the small mirror. He had never encountered a family like the O'Sheens. He saw the inviting shower. He hadn't had a decent shower in three days, so he pulled back the shower curtain. A small plastic bottle of shampoo and new bar of Irish Spring soap—his favorite —greeted him. *His favorite shampoo and his favorite soap. Coincidence? Not.* He rotated the shower knob to what he expected would be a comfortable temperature and relieved his bladder while the shower warmed up.

Chapter 31
Gene's end of a Seesaw

Gene Kamper enjoyed the breakfast with Dale. She was cordial and managed to drag out of him that he was married and had a three-year-old boy.

Pat was lousy company: pensive and deep in thought.

Robby Clark was never far away: watching protectively.

Pat's attitude concerned Dale. He seemed to have a handle on this crisis when he returned from Paris. After last night's attack he was unsure again. He was ignoring Agent Kamper, a guest in their home. He had never been rude to a guest in their house before. His temperament was starting to frighten her.

Dale baited him and said out of the blue, "Eddie, don't you agree?"

Pat apologized, "My mind drifted away. What did you say that I should agree to?"

Dale laughed, "Nothing. But I proved that you weren't paying attention."

The intruder alarm went off and then was silenced. Robby announced that Brendan was back.

When Pat drove from the house, Gene expected that most of the morning would be spent in the Shelby County Sheriff's office. He was impressed with the buildings as Pat drove Dale's SUV into the complex followed by Robby in the Land Rover. The newly built, modern sheriff's office building was located next to a recently built, modern Shelby County jail, and an attractive federally refurnished, historic courthouse. Even in Alabama, local control was being lost to the lure of the federal dollar. Gene learned later that the jail was built on liberal standards for the comfort of the inmates. Released prisoners who couldn't succeed on the outside knew what petty crimes to commit to regain the three-meal-a-day, comfortable living quarters inside the prison. Lack of a woman's companionship was a difficult adjustment at first, but prisoners learned that sexual gratification was not necessarily gender related.

In the sheriff's office, Gene worried again about the *good-ole-boy* network. Robby was interviewed first. He entered the interrogation room with his written statement in hand. Robby tried to ignore Gene's eyes while leaving after his five-minute interview.

Gene knew there were only four bullets involved: Brendan's, his, one from Pat's rifle, and the inconsequential bullet that Pat fired to flatten the old Impala's right front tire.

Pat was called in next. Minutes later, Gene was escorted to an empty interrogation room by the deputy he recognized as Slim from the homicide scene the night before.

Gene wasn't concerned until he looked at his watch twenty minutes later. He stood up and turned the knob on the door. *He was locked in.*

He sat down. He was familiar with this interrogation technique for uncooperative witnesses—*or suspects*. The technique forced the suspect to devise answers to the questioning that were evasive so as not to be incriminating. If pressed too far, the suspect would demand a lawyer, in essence admitting some involvement. The technique was effective. Ten minutes later, Gene had changed from his willingness to share his honest observations of the homicide last night to answering only "yes or no" as a lawyer would advise him.

A thought hit Gene like an unexpected clap of thunder. He knew that O'Sheen no longer trusted the CIA. Pat used his wife to draw him to Alabama, and then beguiled him into thinking he was accepted into the family as a friend, and then locked him in a bedroom. Pat could use his friend, Sherriff Hannon, to hold him in custody as a bargaining chip against the CIA. Gene involuntarily smiled. The thought of O'Sheen manipulating the most powerful intelligence agency in the world was inconceivable. But O'Sheen was succeeding.

Finally, Sheriff Bo Hannon escorted Gene to a room where he was told to sit down in the chair facing a mirror that Gene assumed concealed a camera and an audio recording system. A court reporter sat at a small desk in the corner of the room with a stenotype machine.

The sheriff nodded his head as a signal; waited twenty seconds to make sure no technical problems were encountered, and started. He read Gene his "Miranda rights" that was required by a Supreme Court ruling for interrogating a crime suspect.

Gene hadn't committed a crime. The big sheriff was attempting to intimidate him.

Bo asked "Do you understand your rights?"

Gene nodded his head knowing that a verbal response was required. He handed a three-page affidavit he had prepared for the sheriff.

Bo explained, "I need a verbal response. Do you understand your rights? Are you willing to make a statement without consulting an attorney?"

"Yes." Gene replied.

"Please state your name, social security number, and your date of birth for the record."

After Gene complied, Bo continued, "You have handed me a three-page document that you are willing to enter into the record. Is that correct?"

"Yes."

Bo scanned the affidavit. "You had dinner with Pat and Dale O'Sheen last night. After dinner, a high-speed chase ensued and Pat O'Sheen, the driver of the vehicle you were riding in, entered a dead end road with the threatening vehicle in pursuit. A third vehicle followed. The driver of the first threatening pursuit vehicle exited his door and brandished a handgun in a threatening manner. You exited the O'Sheen vehicle with a weapon given to you by Pat O'Sheen during the pursuit. Your intent was to protect the O'Sheen family. You yelled a warning to the driver of an old Impala that you were FBI and to drop his weapon and shot at him when he turned his weapon toward you. You thought your shot missed the assailant. Later, you learned that your shot hit the assailant in the chest."

Bo asked, "Is my synopsis of your report accurate?"

"Yes. But it was incomplete. You left out the fact that the driver of the pursuing vehicle was shot from behind in the head by your son-in-law—and that I am a government employee on assignment to communicate with Pat O'Sheen." Gene didn't want to reveal too much in this recorded meeting, but he was not going to be railroaded.

Sheriff Hannon dropped his bombshell, "According to this fax . . ." he handed it to Kamper, ". . . you don't work for the federal government." A touch of controlled anger entered the sheriff's voice. He had not yet shared this knowledge with Pat O'Sheen.

Gene looked at the fax. Gene raised his two hands to form a 'T', which in a sports game is the 'time out' signal. "I have nothing more to say without a lawyer."

Bo glared at Kamper with contempt, nodded, stood up, and instructed all recordings to stop. He asked the court reporter to finish her transcript, gather her equipment, and leave the room. Bo whispered something into her ear at the door as she left.

Gene stood up to leave. Bo said, "Where do you think you're going? I haven't released you yet." His tone was threatening. "We have more questions off the record."

Gene considered the "we". In deference to the 'good-ole-boy' network Gene sat back down. Instead of asking another question, Bo sat down across from him and remained silent for an uncomfortable three to four minutes. Pat entered the room and closed the door behind him. He didn't make eye contact with Gene.

Gene thought, *Oh shit. Pat heard that last exchange. I hope he knows the CIA protocol for dealing with questions concerning the employment of covert operatives. The CIA always disavows employment when queried electronically.*

Without looking at Gene, Pat put his hands on Bo's shoulders from behind and said, "Bo, the CIA will not acknowledge that an agent works for them until they investigate the reason for the inquiry. Did Agent Kamper's bullet cause Leroy Walker's death?" Gene could tell that Pat already knew the answer to the question.

Bo shook his head. "Brendan's shot to the back of his head killed him."

Bo declared, "But I do have many more questions for Kamper."

Gene said, "In that case you can contact my agency's lawyer."

Bo nodded, stood up, and left the room without looking back at him or Pat.

Gene looked at Pat who was still uncharacteristically avoiding eye contact.

Gene remembered leaving Pat alone with Mohammed Faisad in the bunker below the safe-house in Paris and hearing the agonizing cries from the room. He remembered how relieved he was when he learned that Pat hadn't killed Mohammed. Could O'Sheen torture him to answer questions in a sheriff's office in America? *Maybe in good-ole-boy Alabama.*

Pat raised his eyes for the first time since entering the room and locked eyes with Gene. Gene remained silent, wondering what was coming.

There was no malice in Pat's eyes. But Gene believed that O'Sheen could deceive the devil. A man like Pat never trusted strangers. Obviously, Gene hadn't jumped the final hurdle necessary to be trusted, despite his support in the surreal events that intertwined their lives in the last few days.

Pat shocked him, "Gene, let's get out of here."

Gene followed Pat out of the interrogation room. The female police officer at the desk smiled at Pat admiringly as she pressed a button. The door buzzed and unlocked. She waved at Pat as Gene followed him into the lobby. Gene was relieved to walk out the front door into the fresh spring air.

Pat was silent as he drove away from Sheriff Hannon's office.

Gene's pent up anxiety released in hostility; **"I hope you don't plan to lock me in that small bedroom again."**

"We'll see," was the disrespectful response.

Pat swerved the Buick Rendezvous into a Seven-Eleven gas station that had a convenience mart, and he parked near the roadside curb in the front. "You can get out here if you want."

Gene was shocked. He considered getting out to escape from this bizarre scenario that started a few days ago with this deadly, paranoid man who had the ability to run everyone's emotions up and down like a yo-yo: a man who challenged him deep into the core of his soul.

Gene hesitated. *Do I go with my training and get out, or do I go with my instincts.* He said, "I probably should get as far away from you as I can. But I'm not leaving you. Not yet. I want some answers."

Pat advised, "If you get out now and report back to the CIA, the target may be removed from your back. There is no reason for you to expose yourself and your family by entering into my nightmare. Walk back to Sherriff Hannon's office and make arrangements to get back to Langley. If you turn against me to protect your family, I will understand. It is not uncommon for covert agents after surviving multiple attacks to freak out—and not think rationally. Explain to your superiors that is what happened to us."

Gene glared at Pat, "I can't do that, Pat. I was raised to be honest."

Gene began talking very slowly, "When your jet dropped me off in Washington, and you gave me the half-melted yellow belt to take to CIA headquarters in Langley, I was duped by you. You knew not to expose yourself to the CIA, and you used the excuse of protecting your family to avoid accompanying me. You avoided talking to the director by keeping silent while your "southern" wife manipulated the CIA director on the phone. You wanted the CIA to send me here. Why?"

Gene noticed for the first time since the attack on the back road the night before a look of admiration in Pat's eyes. *Up-down, up-down, like a seesaw.*

Chapter 32
In the radar

Without offering Gene an answer to his question, I pulled the SUV back onto the road and drove toward my house in silence. Gene was starting to gravitate toward my point of view, but I knew he hadn't decided to fully cooperate with me yet.

Gene said, "Why have you turned against me?"

"Because you are standing with the CIA and not sharing information that I need to solve this problem. If you stand with my enemy, that makes you my enemy. You should have left my car at the convenience store."

We reentered my property. I stopped twenty feet from the house in the same spot I had parked in the night before and shut off the engine. I looked at Gene expectantly but said nothing.

When he didn't respond, I jumped out of the vehicle and walked toward the house. Gene had no choice but to follow.

Dale met us at the front door. Gene envied the hug we shared.

Gene followed us into the kitchen. Dale pulled two Bloody Mary drinks in plastic glasses from the refrigerator that had salt around the rims. She handed one to Gene and said with a smile, "I know y'all need to talk alone." Dale gracefully exited the room.

I pulled out two cigars from a drawer and offered Gene one. He declined. I walked onto the back deck, lit my cigar, and sipped on my bloody Mary in silence. Gene followed me as I walked down the steps into the back yard.

Gene finally stated, contradicting his statement from the night before, "I'm ready to violate CIA top-secret protocol with you. Someone in the CIA is setting us up. I don't know who it is, but I have some thoughts that I was not willing to share with you last night."

I sighed audibly and was ready to proceed. "I think we can share public information and what personnel are involved. You said earlier that they took the belt from you when you first arrived at Langley. Did you call ahead and tell someone what you were bringing?"

"No. You had advised against that."

"Did the guard at the gate see the belt?"

"No. One of Agent Tanner's assistants met me at the gate, slightly exposed the belt that was still wrapped in the towel, and told the guard it was for top-secret eyes only."

"What was Tanner assistant's name?"

"Gordon Neil."

Gene added, "Gordon is not the type to get involved in any conspiracy."

I looked sternly into Gene's eyes, "We need to identify all the players before we make any judgments. Who did you meet with next?"

"Quid Pro Quo," Gene exclaimed with a smile on his face. When I looked at him questioningly, he said, "Don't you remember Hannibal Lector's famous line in *Silence of the Lambs*?"

I was still puzzled.

He said, "Apparently, You're not a movie fan?"

I shrugged.

Gene decided not to press his rare advantage, "Who was in your first meeting at Langley after the *first* attack against you in Paris?"

Gene's strange use of the words "Quid Pro Quo" came to me (Latin, the dead language of the Roman Empire, but the root of most European languages. In America, one would say 'tit for tat' or "give and take"". I understood the words when Gene first spoke them, but I failed to catch Gene's meaning: not having seen the movie.)

I complied with the quid pro quo, "Brendan and I met with Gene Tanner. I related the story of the attack on me in Paris. When I asked if the Hologram Project was operational, Tanner got quiet. I knew he was listening to a voice in his nearly invisible earpiece. He stood up and left the room without a word.

"I knew that all meetings held in the less secure rooms at CIA headquarters were monitored, so I used the key word "Hologram" to get in deeper. But we never know who is watching and listening behind the scene in the less secure rooms.

"Quid Pro Quo," I echoed with a smile. I liked the use of the term for bantering. I made a mental note to watch *Silence of the Lambs* with Dale.

Gene replied, "No. Not yet. Give me the lead up to your next meeting."

I nodded. "Thirty minutes later, Tanner returned with two security guards. He explained that Brendan, due to his lack of high security clearance, would be ushered to the lobby by one of the security guards. The other security guard accompanied Gene and me deeper through two security check points to meet with Director Collins."

I nodded my head and rotated my right hand palm up toward Gene indicating that it was his turn.

Gene accepted, "Gordon Neil took me directly to Tanner. Then Tanner and I were accompanied by security through two security checkpoints and the . . ."

I interrupted, "What about Gordon Neil?"

"I guess the next meeting was above his clearance level—like Brendan."

"Describe Neil."

"Six-two, 200 pounds, bald on top, short graying hair on the sides."

Gene continued, "Anyway, I was escorted to a meeting with Gene Tanner, Deputy Director Bob Hill, and Director Collins in a secure room that I had never seen before."

I interrupted again. "Where was the yellow belt at that time?"

"Gene Tanner and I showed it to Director Collins and Bob Hill. They studied it, and Hill handed it through the door to someone who I couldn't see from my viewpoint."

Gene waited for a response, but I remained silent, the gears in my brain were turning too fast for me to respond. I was considering the common players in both meetings, and I couldn't believe that Gene Tanner could be complicit in this. He was one of the few people that I completely trusted during my assignments with the CIA. I ran through the names: Gordon Neil—unknown, Bob Hill—unknown, and the unknown names and faces that saw the belt after it was removed from the secure meeting room. Gene Tanner was a very capable field agent before being severely injured on assignment and moved into his supervisory role. As bad as I hated the thought, I couldn't rule out Gene Tanner's involvement in the hologram conspiracy.

I said, "I don't trust anyone in the CIA right now."

Gene glared at me.

I offered a carrot. "Present company excluded." I watched Gene. He didn't try to hide his satisfaction: like a runner safely clearing the last high hurdle with a sufficient lead to win.

I went back into one of my reveries, replaying every word and inflection in my conversations with the CIA players.

Gene interrupted my private analysis, "An attractive woman delivered coffee to the room during the meeting."

Gene's words pulled me out of my audio recall to rejoin the present, "Describe her."

"She was about fifty, dark hair, nice figure, light skin, and an attractive face. Her name was Carol Motter."

"Why do you remember her name?"

"Her security badge was on her left breast."

I chuckled, "You noticed her breasts and then her name tag?"

Gene chuckled, "She was old enough to be my mother."

Gene explained, "I have . . . well I sort of have . . ." He was apparently afraid to disclose one of his unusual talents. He spat it out. "Pat. I have a photographic memory." His eyes revealed expectation of a skeptical response.

I smiled at Gene's disclosure and decided to share one of my talents with him. I was starting to trust Gene and needed his help to negate the high-level threat from the CIA against me and my family, "Does Gordon Neil have a deep voice?"

Gene seemed confused at my change of subject, but he acknowledged, "Very deep: like a TV anchorman."

I nodded, "I passed Gordon Neil in transit from my first meeting with Tanner to the second meeting. I didn't know that he was one of Gene Tanner's assistants. Based on where we passed in the hallway, he was probably in the film and audio room next to our first meeting. I remember his deep voice when he said 'hello' to me."

I explained, "Gene, I have what you might call an audio-graphic memory. I have always aggravated people when I replay past audio recall in my mind. Replaying the audio helps me recall the video. Given enough time to rerun my encounters with you, I can recall every conversation you and I have had since our first meeting in Paris. The talent has caused me problems since my childhood, because I tend to go off into my own world as I do fast replays of previous conversations while searching for connections and inconsistencies."

Gene marveled at the revelation. Now he understood Pat's long reveries. "That explains your incredible language skills? Your audio recall transcends language."

I nodded. "I trust that you won't share that with anyone." I continued, "What do you know about Bob Hill?"

"He's smart, He has a law degree, and he has aggressively climbed the ranks in the CIA. He is a bit scary."

"Scary in what way?"

"In the 'you better watch your back' way."

I surmised, "Well, if he is a lawyer, he fits that stereotype."

I pointed out the obvious, "Director Collins seems too involved in every meeting on the hologram belts. Have you met her before?"

"Not before I brought in the yellow belt."

I agreed, "Since I mentioned the deflective ray project on my first meeting with Director Collins, she has been personally involved in every meeting or correspondence on the hologram weapons. And when you called my house, she personally got on the phone to confront my wife in an attempt to get me on the phone. She is in a serious damage-control mode. Exposure of the hologram technology leak is the damage that she is trying to control, and our knowledge of the security leak makes us the most serious threats of exposing the leak. We are dead center in the government's radar on this leak. We may need to find two of those yellow belts and start wearing them ourselves."

I leaned back in my chair and started replaying all of Director Collin's words. When I finished, I was pretty sure that she wasn't involved in this conspiracy. She was a new presidential appointee with no covert experience.

Gene formulated a plan during my reverie and presented his plan to me. I liked the psychology of his plan, but it had too many weak links. We discussed it for an hour and arrived at a workable plan.

I made Delta Airline reservations for Gene to return to Washington. I alerted my charter jet pilot to be available on short notice. I had to pay for stand by time. This crisis and the cost of the charter jet was digging into my money stash that I had accumulated in a private bank account in Geneva, Switzerland during my covert career. I never used the money for personal use. I was using it now because my covert government career was at the root of this crisis.

Part Three

Resolution

Ed Sheehan

Chapter 33
Michelle's job interview

After clearing customs in Atlanta following her flight from Germany, Michelle Orleon grabbed her suitcase when it approached her on the circular conveyor belt in the baggage claim area, and then grabbed her garment bag. An amusing thought entered her mind. *Why is the suitcase used to carry garments, and the garment bag designed to hold suits?* She was feeling good—happy to be back in America. She wheeled her luggage through the Atlanta Hartsfield-Jackson Airport to her rent-a-car and drove toward Birmingham. She had a job interview with an electronic home-security company that Abdul had selected as the best local company he could find on the internet. It was unlikely that they were the ones that installed the security systems at the O'Sheen residences, but she looked forward to learning about security systems. Her revised resume had already been reviewed by the security company and her interview confirmed.

She arrived at the late Friday afternoon appointment modestly dressed. She had applied for the job under the pseudo name, Michelle Musso. A matronly-looking woman from the personnel department greeted her in the lobby. *Not good. Her charms worked better on men.*

She was aware that she had caught the eye of an older man that was carrying a cup of coffee to a corner office. A minute later, a man who appeared to be in his forties entered the lobby, and exclaimed, "Mrs. Dees, I'll handle this interview."

Mrs. Dees looked at Michelle apologetically and said, "Yes sir." She huffed out of the lobby.

"Miss Musso, I'm Bill Sharp, head of Employee Relations," He extended his hand. Michelle thought as she shook his hand, *he didn't handle employee relations very well with Mrs. Dees*. Her initial judgment was that the man was obnoxious because of an insecure ego.

Sharp said, "Please follow me to my office."

Bill Sharp pretended to review her resume and asked a few meaningless questions to judge her response. She asked a few appropriate questions about company goals and benefits.

Mr. Sharp answered his phone. "Yes."

He offered, "Yes sir. She is qualified." He looked at her and smiled, "Well, I haven't finished the interview yet. . . . Yes sir."

Michelle noticed the disappointment in his face.

Sharp explained to her, "The owner, Mr. Monroe, has to leave shortly. He wants to interview you personally." He escorted her to the corner office that she had noticed the older man enter earlier and wasn't surprised to recognize the older, coffee-carrying man.

After formal introductions, Monroe said, "Thank you, Bill, I'll take it from here." Apparently, Bill knew to close the door on the way out.

Walter Monroe studied her resume. Twice he looked up without speaking and stared at her without reservation, and then his eyes returned to her resume. He pushed his chair back from the desk with a professional air and said. "Miss Musso, you have an impressive international resume. Why would you want to move to Birmingham, Alabama?" He said it with a clear knowledge of the negative international perceptions of his city and state.

Michelle realized that despite his southern accent, she was dealing with a very intelligent, analytical man. His first question went to the heart of the interview and was the hardest to answer, but one that she had anticipated.

"Mr. Monroe, I'm going to be honest with you." She batted her eyelids at him and enabled moisture to enter her eyes. "I am just getting out of a very abusive relationship in Paris. This simpler, more obscure environment is very attractive to me. I doubt if he'll ever find me here."

"But why Birmingham?"

He wasn't going to make this easy. "I became very close friends with one of my roommate's friends at George Washington University. She lives near here."

"Why didn't you apply for a job with the city or the county? Your credentials would have assured your employment."

Damn. Southerners were obviously not as dumb as she was led to believe by the beltway crowd in D.C. or as easily manipulated by her beauty.

She answered, "My financial situation is in poor condition. I hoped that your financial package would be better than the government's . . . and I've always wanted to get into sales."

Walter Monroe said, "We are all in sales, young lady. We have to sell ourselves in some ways every day. You will first have to sell yourself to the customer before they will listen to your presentation of our product. I don't think you will have any problems selling yourself."

"Thank you, Mister Monroe."

"Please call me Walter."

The man went into a pensive mood. He raised his eyes to lock with hers. Despite the temptation to take advantage, she looked down at her lap modestly, recalling her encounter with Pat O'Sheen. She had a lot to learn about southern American men. When she averted her eyes, Mr. Monroe grabbed his pen, wrote on the top sheet of a sticky note pad, removed the top sheet, and handed it to her. Written on the sheet was "$50,000 per year". He would never know that the amount wasn't important to her, even though it was more generous than she had anticipated. For the first time since she sat down, she looked directly into his eyes for more than five seconds. She didn't smile as she abruptly stood up. The shock on his face assured her that the maneuver accomplished the desired effect. She stood still as he awkwardly stood up bewildered.

She decided not to wait for him to embellish his offer of employment. She reached across the desk seeking his handshake and enacted her most beautiful smile; "Walter, I accept your offer. When can my employment begin?" She expected him to fall back into his chair, but he regained his composure. She was impressed.

He smiled, "At your earliest convenience." He accepted her extended hand. "I'm sure your move from a foreign country will involve many complications. When would you like to start?"

"Would Monday be acceptable?" She knew by the surprise on his face that she had him. He was tougher to crack than European men, but her feminine charms were universal.

Michelle left the interview with a big smile enriching her beautiful face. She had to find a place to stay, so she stopped at a convenience store for a coke and bought a local newspaper.

She found the classified section in the Friday paper and focused on one ad among several promising ads:

> *Elderly*
> *Homewood woman*
> *seeks healthy female*
> *to rent in-house*
> *room. Chores*
> *involved. 987-5014*

Michelle called the number and connected on the first try. She told the pleasant lady where she was and was pleased when the directions indicated that the house wasn't far away. She arrived at the house fifteen minutes later and rang the doorbell.

She heard a faint voice reply and movement inside. It was almost a minute later before the door opened exposing the smiling face of an elderly woman. The woman had beauty-parlor, blue-gray hair, and was hunched over at the shoulders, leaning heavily on her four-legged, front-wheeled walker.

Michelle introduced herself, "Hello, I'm Michelle Musso." She noticed the old lady look for a wedding ring on her finger.

"And what a beauty you are, Miss Musso. I'm Frances Shilling." She extended her wrinkled-skinned right hand, which Michelle cradled in her two soft hands.

Frances said, "Please come in."

Michelle waited while Mrs. Shilling maneuvered away from the door. She asked Mrs. Shilling in a scolding tone, "Why did you not ask me to identify myself before you opened the door? I could have been trouble."

"Like the boogie man?" The old lady chuckled, "I watched you drive up and exit your car." Her captivating smile showed a hint of gold on a front tooth.

"You are not an American, are you?" Frances continued before Michelle could answer, "Your accent sounds French: very lovely sounding."

For the first time the smile left her face, "Why would a beauty like you want to move in with an old biddy like me?"

Michelle was impressed. She had already learned that Southerners were able to approach key issues quickly. She hoped her fabricated story would be accepted. If not, she could find another place to stay.

She began, "I just got out of a bad relationship in Paris. A relationship that turned violent. A friend of mine where I went college near D.C. arranged a job interview for me here. I was hired today, and I start work on Monday."

"Why don't you rent an apartment?" *A logical question.*

"Mrs. Shilling, I don't have the money for a deposit and a month's rent in advance. I spent most of my money traveling here from Paris for the job interview."

The old lady's inquisitive eyes softened. She said, "Call me Frances. Look around the house, Miss Musso. Your room would be down the hallway past the bathroom on the left. Mine is in the corner. I'll go to the kitchen and make us some tea. Take as much time as you need." The pleasant smile and soft tone of voice had returned. She added an afterthought, "I cannot allow you to bring men into the house."

Michelle smiled as she walked down the hallway. She had noticed the statue of the Virgin Mary in the living room. There was a crucifix over the bedroom doorway in the corner. The bathroom was small but adequate. Her bedroom had a beautiful, but scarred antique four-poster bed. She raised the bottom pane of the double-hung window to ascertain that emergency egress was possible.

Frances's bedroom door was opened so she entered. It was tastefully decorated and had a large, beautifully hand-painted portrait of a young Frances on the wall. She approached it, looked at the painter's signature, and saw that it was a self-portrait. She backed away from the portrait and studied it. Frances was a very accomplished artist.

The bathroom off the master bedroom had been reworked for the handicapped. Michelle headed toward the kitchen looking forward to a cup of tea.

Frances was sitting at the end of an antique dinette table decorated with chili peppers hand-painted on an antiqued white background. She was sipping from a glass. Michelle looked around the kitchen for the teapot and teacups.

Frances said, "Please sit down."

Michelle sat in the chair on the side of the table that had a napkin and a glass of brown liquid filled with ice. When she sat down, her nose detected the aroma of tea. She noticed a gallon jug on the table with the big letters "Milo's" printed on the label.

Frances understood the confusion in the lovely face. "I'm sorry, you were expecting a cup of hot tea. The heat in Alabama has accustomed us to drinking iced tea. Try it. I didn't make it, but it is very popular in Alabama."

Michelle warmed to Mrs. Shilling's perceptive and articulate dialogue. The old woman's body had aged, but intelligence shone from her eyes as brightly as her smile.

Michelle sipped from the glass. The sugar puckered her mouth, but she tried to hide her reaction and looked up at Mrs. Shilling to conduct business. "I can pay one-half month rent if the rent is reasonable. But like I said earlier, I can't afford a deposit. I don't intend to have any men in my life who I would want to bring here. And one more thing, Mrs. Shilling . . ."

"Frances," was the interruption.

"I'm not sure how long I will stay. The new job may not work out, and the man from my last relationship may somehow find me." Michelle watched moisture gather in the old woman's right eye. Frances' empathy melted Michelle's heart.

"Miss Musso, you are welcome in my house for a day, a week, a month, or for years. Although I'm sure a better man will grab you up before a year."

They talked for another ten minutes. Then the old women struggled to her feet. "Did you bring your luggage?"

This old woman was filling a vacant hole in Michelle's heart. Her mother was never protective. She didn't remember her grandmother. The operation Abdul had planned should not endanger Frances. But if their relationship continued to develop at this pace, and the project went badly, she may be subjected to a stressful inquiry: one that may end her life with a question mark. Michelle answered the question, "Yes. My bags are in my rent-a-car."

"Well, bring them in, dear, and give this old woman at least one night of your pleasurable company."

Michelle returned the warm smile, stood up, and walked out to her car. She slid into the driver's seat and pulled her cell phone from her purse. It was getting very late in Switzerland, but Abdul answered on the second ring. She updated him on her successful day, gave him the address where she was staying, Frances Shilling's name, and to Abdul's surprise added, "If our mission causes Frances Shilling harm, I may kill you in the middle of the night while you are sleeping in my arms."

Abdul knew how rare it was for someone in their profession to meet someone that touched their soul. "Tell me about her. How old is she?"

"I didn't ask, but I would guess about eighty. Most of her friends and family have passed on. Her only child, a daughter, lives in Indiana. Her three granddaughters are scattered—none close to here. She is an easy mark after the operation, but I won't allow it. If that's a problem, I'll find another place to stay."

Abdul was moved by the gentle and caring emotions expressed for the old lady by his impetuous lover. He warned, "Don't share anything with her that will compromise our objective."

"I won't."

Michelle recoded the security on her cell phone following Abdul's instructions, grabbed her overnight bag, and entered the small house in this Homewood suburb of Birmingham, Alabama.

Frances smiled when she came through the door with her small bag. "I hope you were able to leave Paris with more than that small bag."

"I have a larger bag in my car. This will suffice for tonight." Michelle's comment was intended to portray to this perceptive old woman that she was exhausted.

Mrs. Shilling allowed Michelle the privacy to rearrange her bedroom in her own style. Michelle realized that it was almost midnight in Germany where she left this morning and that she was indeed exhausted. But she knew she had to make an effort to comfort her hostess. When she entered the kitchen, Frances pulled a small pizza from the microwave oven.

Frances declared, "I heard your stomach rumbling."

Michelle appreciated France's effort. She was hungry.

Michelle chastised her new friend in an attempt to enlighten her to the evil that lurks in today's world. "The small bag I brought in has many implements to quickly end your life."

Michelle's threat drew an unexpected reaction. Frances chuckled. "You underestimate my ability to judge character. Sweetheart, you can't scare me. I've lived eighty-seven years on this earth, and . . ."

Michelle interrupted her dialogue, "There is no way you can convince me that you are eighty-seven years old." When she saw the appreciative smile, confirming the women's truthfulness about her age, Michelle leaned back in her chair even more endeared to Frances. The two of them shared the pizza, drank iced tea that was too sweet, and talked late into the evening.

Michelle spent Saturday canvassing the area around Jody O'Sheen's house and neighborhood. She timed the trip from Jody's house to each type of store he may visit.

That evening, Michelle moved the rest of her meager possessions into Frances Shilling's house, and they talked for hours again.

The arrangement was perfect. Michelle knew that if she had tried to rent an apartment, or an extended-stay hotel room, her every move could be easily traced later if something went wrong. Unless Mrs. Shilling suspected foul play and called the police, this arrangement was untraceable. The added bonus was that Mrs. Shilling was the loving mother and grandmother who had never played a role in Michelle's youth. She would remind Abdul that Frances Shilling was untouchable.

During their long talk on Saturday night, Frances answered her phone. She ended the call saying, "Thank you, Mary."

Frances explained, "That is a younger friend who takes me to ten-thirty Mass at Our Lady of Sorrows Catholic Church on Sundays. You are welcome to join us."

"Frances, I am not religious."

"Okay. But I better warn you that if you stay here, I will try to move you in that direction."

Chapter 34
Men

Michelle arrived at work thirty minutes early on Monday morning. She wore a conservative, long-sleeve, light blue blouse, a navy blue skirt that touched the top of her knees, and short high heels. The blouse was tight enough to accentuate her figure without being too bold. She decided to fasten one more button on the top of her blouse before exiting her rent-a-car.

The owner, Walter Monroe, was already drinking coffee at his desk while sifting through paperwork. She voiced a firm hello from his open doorway.

He looked up slightly startled, broke out in an enthusiastic smile as he stood to greet her, "Miss Musso, please come in and sit down." He pointed to a chair across from his desk.

She said, "Please call me Michelle."

"Very well, Michelle." He looked at his watch, a little embarrassed by his unintended rhyme. "Bill, from personnel isn't in yet, but I'm sure he will have a lot of paperwork for you to fill out. Were you able to find living quarters over the weekend?"

Without waiting for an answer, he repeated, "Please sit." He sat down in a chair on her side of his desk instead of the commanding position from behind his big desk and turned the revolving chair to face her.

She lied, "I have a few good leads for a place to live temporarily, that I'm working on", answering the question he had abandoned. "I hope to be settled by the end of the week."

"Excellent. I have arranged for Tom Fleming to be here at ten. He is the technical representative for our security system manufacturer. He can help you start learning the systems so that you can talk with some expertise to potential customers."

Michelle complemented. "You don't waste time, do you?"

"Young lady, I hired you to improve our profits, not for your good looks. If your resume is accurate, you are educated and should easily grasp the basic concepts of our security systems."

Michelle noticed his eyes wander quickly over her body. It was the first visible chink in his armor. She took advantage, "I would like to review several levels of your customers' security systems. And I would like to help install one, if possible, before meeting with potential customers."

Walter looked at his watch again, stood up, and walked around behind his desk. He knew he had been caught gawking at her, but she didn't seem surprised or offended. He assumed that such a striking beauty was used to men's gawking stares. He picked up his phone receiver and bent over to punch an extension number into the keypad.

"Don?" Walter went off focus, "How was Monica's recital?" He listened and then smiled. "Wonderful, I can hear your pride through the phone line.

"Do you have any appointments this morning?"

Apparently not. "Our new employee, Michelle Musso, is meeting with Tom Fleming this morning at ten o'clock. Can you pull several different levels of our customers' schematics and meet with them?"

The answer must have been in the affirmative. "Good. And plan to take her on your next installation." Walter hung up.

Michelle was impressed. Walter didn't delay taking action to achieve his objectives. She also saw a sincere interest in his employees and their families by asking about Monica's recital.

Walter informed her, "Don Waters is our technical expert. He will join you and Tom Fleming this morning—and I must say . . ." Walter echoed her earlier complement, ". . . you don't waste much time, Miss Musso. You plunge to the meat of the business, and I am very impressed."

The personnel manager, Bill Sharp, stuck his head in the door and said with too much enthusiasm. "Walter, I'm ready to possess her." *Oops,* his face turned crimson at the Freudian slip. His eyes were not on

Walter, who he was addressing, but were lustfully gathering in the Madonna.

"I meant process." Processing her paperwork was obviously not the thought foremost in his mind.

Some men were so transparent. Walter grimaced, walked to the door, and ushered Bill into the hallway. Less than a minute later they entered the room together.

Walter addressed, "Michelle, do you remember Bill Sharp, head of our personnel department?"

Michelle nodded.

Bill averted his eyes away from her until she stood up to greet him. When she uncrossed her legs and stood up gracefully, exposing a bit of muscular thigh. Bill's eyes couldn't resist, nor could Walter's.

Bill acted professionally during the new employee processing: only stealing glimpses at her. She didn't know what Walter had said to him in the hallway, but it had been effective. Something inside her was warmly attracted to Walter. Her mind flashed back to her encounter with Pat O'Sheen, and then, somewhat regrettably to her stepfather. Impressive older men like Walter and Pat O'Sheen had a peculiar effect on her.

Bill Sharp escorted Michelle to a conference room and introduced her to Don Waters. Don was shocked by her beauty, but he recovered more quickly than most men.

Michelle first noticed his green eyes when she entered the room and then his friendly smile. He shook her hand and started preparations for the meeting. She also noticed that he wore a wedding band. He had already spread four blueprints on the large conference table. He invited her to sit in front of the least detailed print. She declined. He was more comfortable in her presence than most men were on first encounters.

Don volunteered, "Tom Fleming called to say he will be a little late. Tom realized that Dad wanted him to do more than the normal first introduction to the security systems."

Don noticed the confusion in her beautiful eyes. He realized that he needed to explain his use of the term 'Dad'. "Walter is my father-in-law. I married his daughter, Billie Sue, after her divorce. My wife died three years ago. My kids are in college. Billie Sue and I are raising her two kids from her first marriage. Billie Sue calls Walter 'Dad' and he never objected when I started calling him Dad. You probably noticed that he is an exceptional man."

Michelle was shocked at such a complete disclosure on an initial contact. Alabamians seemed unusually open, apparently not concerned that their openness could be ridiculed.

She didn't plan to say what spilled threw her lips involuntarily, "I sense that Walter has an exceptional son-in-law."

She saw Don blush. She wouldn't bat her eyes and use her charms to disrupt this functional family. Her life experiences dealt mostly with dysfunctional families. Her new landlady, Frances Shilling, was already affecting her perspective on life.

Don said. "Dad said you would like to watch a security system installation." The word Dad came out of him so comfortably that it was warming to her heart. "We don't have a new installation this week, but I will be installing an upgrade on one of our most sophisticated systems tomorrow. That is the new schematic for the system," he pointed to the blueprint across the table.

Michelle walked around the table and looked at the perimeter of the blueprint to find the owner's name. The name sprung out at her so unexpectedly that it almost knocked her off her feet: the name was *O'Sheen, Joseph.*

The shock sent her into a coughing fit and she managed to choke out the words, "Please excuse me."

She ran to the bathroom. When she looked in the mirror her face was beet red. She was smart to leave the room in a hurry. Abdul had emphasized that there may not be much time for her to accomplish the goal of being able to penetrate Jody O'Sheen's security system. What could have taken weeks materialized before lunch on her first day of work. She shook her head in disbelief. It took her five minutes to calm down.

When she returned to the conference room, she apologized and blamed it on a girl thing. Men never push for a more detailed explanation.

Michelle returned to the drawing and started running her index finger over the blueprint, "This is going to be more complicated than I expected."

Don smiled, "You just need to learn the concept not the technology. I'll handle that with the customers."

He hesitated and then added, "You are obviously very intelligent. Dad's genius in selecting his personnel always impresses me. You are exactly what our company needs right now." The compliment was heartfelt.

Michelle smiled her appreciation as she heard some commotion and a loud voice in the hallway.

Don advised, "Tom has arrived." Don's disappointment was apparent, "I should warn you that he is not married. You may have a time trying to control his advances." Don looked concerned. "I'll stay with y'all for a while."

What a nice gesture.

Chapter 35
Tom

Don left the conference room and met Tom in the hallway out of her sight and hearing range. She couldn't decipher Don's mumbled monologue, but she suspected that his dialogue was attempting to prepare Tom to meet a beautiful lady. When Tom saw her he quickly averted his eyes enough so as not to stare. She knew by his reaction that he was not gay and remembered that Don said that he was not married. *Fair game*! She had found her mark.

Tom looked Irish, except for his large, square, Norwegian chin. He stood erect at about six-foot two, with broad shoulders. She could easily envision the bright red hair and freckled whiter-skin that adorned his youth. She knew that redheaded boys toughened at an early age, and many had redheaded tempers. She could also see that he was not an exercise freak. His jowls were a bit fleshy and his midriff carried extra pounds. His blue eyes were enticing. After Don's semi-formal introduction, she crossed the room and shook his hand firmly. Tom's hand was slightly shaking in hers. *How cute. Her beauty intimidated him.*

Tom turned toward the blueprints on the table in an attempt to recover from his embarrassing reaction to their first encounter. She was the most enticing woman that he had ever met in his life. And she seemed interested in him. *No! Don't make a fool of yourself.*

Tom lost his wife to cervical cancer two years ago and he had not been sexually active since her death. He toyed with women he met in his job, but none of them could raise his libido like his wife, Mary, had done for many years. Just seeing Michelle reinvigorated his inactive libido. How embarrassing. *How exciting.*

Michelle relieved Tom's tension by addressing Walter's son-in-law. "Don, please continue to tell me about these drawings you have spread out on the table."

Don walked to the first drawing that he had arranged on the table so that more complicated systems progressed in a counter-clockwise direction.

He traced his index finger over lines on the first blueprint. "This is the basic security unit: our bread and butter. Eighty-percent of our customers buy this basic system."

Tom rediscovered the brain in his upper head when the discussion turned to his expertise. "Our basic unit is better than some of the highest grade units that our competitors offer." He went into his sales pitch.

Michelle noticed that Don was backing out of the room. She interrupted Tom's pitch to stop Don, "Don, please don't leave." When he hesitated, she pointed to the perimeter blocks on the second blueprint with a questioningly look.

Don walked up to see what she was questioning. Her manicured fingernail pointed to the initials "D.W." signed in the block in the bottom right corner. He answered her unasked question, "Yeah, D.W. is me. I redesign all our security installations for those that order more than just the basic unit." He backed off from her enticing fragrance and overwhelming presence.

Michelle asked him, "What is the significance of this large number." She pointed to the most significant block on the bottom of the page.

He answered, "The first four digits identify Tom's unit number, and the next three digits following the dash is my design modification number. The last six numbers identifies the customer."

She seemed satisfied, so he backed up again. She turned him on. But he would be no match for Tom's charm even if he were not happily married.

Michelle looked inquisitively at Don again, and her look stopped him. She slowly walked around the table with a quick study of the blueprints. The men's eyes followed her. When she reached the last blueprint, Jody O'Sheen's, she looked up. "Don, as I walked around the table, each print is more complicated. This last one has twice the lines of the others and has a lot of red markings on it?"

Don walked around the table toward her and the blueprint. "As I said earlier, this is one of our most sophisticated systems. The red lines are an upgrade that I am adding to the system tomorrow."

Michelle looked up into Tom's eyes, "Can you come with Don and me to this job tomorrow if Walter approves of my going with him?" She assumed that Don would check with Walter before agreeing to let her accompany him.

Don didn't mind that she was drawing Tom into tomorrow's plan.

Tom responded, "I'll need to call my office and determine if I can postpone a couple appointments." He didn't want to blurt out that the answer was a very enthusiastic *Yes*.

Don saw the connection developing between Michelle and Tom, and this time he successfully left the room.

Tom was more than willing to show her the security secrets of the more intricate systems. When he hesitated before answering one of her more probing questions, she worried that she may have been too probing until he said, "Follow me." He grabbed the simplest blueprint from the table and exited the room.

She noticed that he had a nice derriere as she followed him out the door, down a hallway, and through a wooden door into a concrete floored warehouse. He led her to an eight-foot wide by four-foot tall pegboard with security components and connecting wires neatly arranged across it. He looked at her, smiled, and unfolded the blueprint. He held it underneath the display and explained each item on the blueprint and pointed to each real-life component on the display. He answered Michelle's questions which mostly involved activating and deactivating the system, and dealing with false alarms activated by pets, carelessness on the part of the owner, and power interruptions. He recognized that she had already put herself into the customer's shoes and was asking questions that an intelligent customer should ask. Tom was very impressed. Beauty and a heavenly body were not her only assets.

When they returned to the conference room, she asked about the upgrades to the system they were visiting tomorrow. He proudly put his expertise on display.

He explained the redundant systems to be installed on Jody O'Sheen schematic and how they would tie into the basic unit on the panel next to the front door. The lesson continued for another hour until Tom became alarmed at her more probing questions.

Michelle noticed his concern and asked if they could take a break for lunch.

Tom looked at his watch. It was already noon. Time flies when you're having fun. His heart quickened every time she touched his arm or his hand or softly rubbed up against him. He asked, "Can I buy your lunch? There is a great place not too far from here."

Michelle's response was timid, "Okay. But this is my first day at work here. I don't want to be absent for too long."

She expected Tom to take her to a glamorous, knock your panties off restaurant. Instead, he had trouble finding a parking place next to a busy railroad track. When he escorted her across the street, Michelle didn't notice any American neon sign attracting customers to a nice restaurant. She did see a long line of people on the sidewalk across the street. Most of the people in line were businessmen, but many others appeared to be older retired couples. The buzz of conversation stopped as they approached and all eyes turned to her. She was used to that reaction, but Tom wasn't. He straightened his posture, wrapped her hand through the crook of his elbow, and proudly strutted up to the back of the line.

After lowering his peacock feathers, Tom explained, "This is the Whistle Stop Café that was in the movie *Fried Green Tomatoes*." When he looked down at Michelle, he realized that she didn't have a clue.

"They have all kinds of food served cafeteria style. If you are on a vegetarian or on some special diet, you will love this place."

Michelle replied, "I am not on any special diet."

Michelle enjoyed listening to the many conversations she overheard from the people on the street in the fast-moving line. The southern drawl was evident everywhere. She could learn it easily if she spent time here. When they approached the food counter, Tom suggested that he order for her, and she agreed. The whole setting was busy, but comforting. All of the customers seemed happy and unpretentious.

Tom studied food bins behind the counter-glass partitions and ordered them fried pond-raised catfish filets, black-eyed peas, and of course, fried green tomatoes. At the end of the counter, he selected corn bread for both of them.

A pleasant looking, older lady sitting behind a register punched in the food selections on both plates and handed a rollout paper bill to Tom. The lady stood up and hugged Tom. When Tom returned the hug, she whispered something in his ear that reddened his face. He picked up the trays and walked out to find a table. All of the tables in the adjoining room were occupied.

Michelle followed Tom through a doorway that opened to a larger seating area. All of those tables were occupied, too. She was starting to feel embarrassed for Tom, but he sauntered through another doorway to another large room and set the trays down on an empty table for two. He pulled a kitchenette-type chair out from a cheap table, and in a grandiose gesture, waved his arm inviting her to sit.

She thanked him, and after they both sat, she asked, "Who's your sweetheart at the counter."

Tom chuckled. "She is my mother's best friend. She has always been like an aunt to me since I was a kid."

"What did she whisper in your ear?"

Tom's freckled face blushed again. "She said, 'It appears your love life has become much more interesting'."

She was amazed at his honesty and the refreshing openness of Alabamians with their unguarded vulnerabilities.

When they finished eating, she vowed that she would never forget the food or the companionship that were both so delicious. Unfortunately, Tom had another appointment, so when they got back to the office, he just dropped her at the front door.

When she entered the lobby, Michelle was approached by a man with a captivating smile and movie-style dark brown hair that was combed straight back. His hair stood up high and was dry, not slick.

"Hi. I'm Jim Cooper, head of sales." He did a kind of exaggerated bob and weave with his head as he accepted her firm handshake. He appeared to be in his mid-forties. His eyes shone even brighter than his smile in a delightfully teasing way.

"Hello, Mr. Cooper. I'm glad I'm finally getting to meet my new boss." It was easy to return his contagious smile. In fact, it would have been difficult to do otherwise.

"Mr. Cooper is my dad. Call me J.R., Miss Musso."

He knew how to get past formalities. "Okay, if you will call me Michelle." She noticed the wedding ring on his finger.

"Well, Michelle is a gorgeous name: very appropriate in your case."

Without stuttering after the aggressive compliment, he continued, "I'm sure Walter told you that I have been traveling. I'm sorry I couldn't be here for your interview. Walter is better at interviews anyway: I'm a pushover. I would have agreed to hire you when you walked through the front door."

He actually blushed a little, but disguised it with a "you know why" knowing smile and the cute repeat of the bob and weave of his head. "And so will our customers," He added.

Michelle noticed that he was very comfortable around her: not at all intimidated like most men. She guessed that his wife was beautiful.

"Please follow me to my office." J.R. opened the glass door that entered a hallway and held the door open for her to enter first. When he watched her from behind while following her through the door, it became clear to him why gentlemen had developed this custom. As usual, J.R.'s private thoughts escaped from his lips, "Opening doors for women is magnificent gentlemanly custom, don't you think?" He admired her voluptuous rear end. The question was rhetorical.

She understood his meaning and was becoming more enamored with his honesty and lack of intimidation. She stopped to allow him to pass her in the hall since she did not know where his office was located. She noticed that he had a nice derriere too. She returned his barb, "In many societies, the women are required by law to walk behind their man. In this case, it is not an unpleasant experience."

J.R. burst out laughing. The boisterous laughter was so contagious that she had to join in.

He stepped aside with a slight bow and a sweeping-hand motion inviting her into his office. The humorous smile on his face said more about his joy-filled outlook on life than words could convey.

Michelle walked into a small corner office with windows on two sides that looked out at the front grills of cars in the parking lot. The windows gave a lively brightness to the neatly kept room. On the wall behind the desk were family photos. On his desk was a large photo of a woman which was signed, "Jimmy Ray, I love you, Paula." She had guessed right: his wife was beautiful. *Jimmy Ray explained why he asked to be called J.R.*

J.R. noticed her attention focused on the picture. "I call her 'Love'." He bobbed and weaved his head again. "She doesn't like me to call her 'Love' around strangers, but she is the love of my life." He said it with heartfelt sincerity and perhaps as a strong hint that he was not available.

Michelle was starting to love Alabama. The men didn't seem to play games like Parisians or the men around Washington, D.C. She switched the conversation to business. "Can you give me a demographic of our existing and potential customers?"

J.R. looked amused that she was the one to turn the conversation to business. He started to say something, but instead he leaned over and typed on the laptop computer on his desk without sitting down. He spun it around facing her. He gestured to the upholstered chair by the window and sat down next to her in the matching chair. He pulled the laptop screen closer.

Michelle leaned forward to better see the screen, giving J.R. a better view of her. The screen had a page of names with all the last names starting with the letter A. She reached her right hand toward the mouse, stopped, and looked at J.R. for approval.

He nodded and still donned his amused smile.

The man probably always smiled. She put the mouse arrow on the scrolling bar and slowly panned through the names. The list was extensive, so she moved the curser over to the scroll bar and moved it down to the end of the data base and clicked on the last name, Ziggarelli. At the bottom of the screen was the line number on the spread sheet.

"Wow!' she exclaimed, "You have over thirty thousand customers?"

J.R. clarified, "Not all of them are active, and only twenty percent of them pay the monthly fee for a telephone response when security is breeched."

Michelle tapped the scroll bar up a couple of times until she got to the 'O's'. She highlighted the name O'Sheen, Joseph (Jody).

She explained, "This is the system I am going to visit tomorrow with Don and Tom if Walter approves."

J.R. nodded and appreciated how quickly she understood how to manipulate the database.

Michelle went to the next name higher on the list "This O'Sheen, Edward Patrick, is that Jody's brother? Did we install his system?"

"No, Pat is Jody's dad. He was a Special Forces major and a CIA agent. He buys a lot of high-tech equipment from us, but he installs it himself." J.R. reached up to the computer and changed programs. "This spreadsheet breaks the customer list out by security level and yearly sales. And now we begin your training."

Over three hours later, at 4:30 p.m., J.R. looked at his watch, "I'm sorry, Michelle. We will have to continue this later. I have to meet Paula." He added, "My love", emphasizing again that he was not available.

She smiled. Not one time during the long uninterrupted session had he rubbed up against her or looked at her lustfully.

"Will I see you tomorrow?" She asked hopefully. J.R. was very entertaining.

"I have appointments tomorrow, but we can make some calls together on Thursday. I'm anxious to see what you learn from Tom and Don." He stood up and walked his fine derriere out the door, leaving her alone with the computer still connected to the database. *Very trusting.*

She sorted the list by Jody's area code and opened Google Earth. She located Jody and Pat O'Sheen's houses. Three other security systems were close to the O'Sheens' homes: Clary, Clark, and Jacoby. She found five more close to the others. She sensed that Pat and Jody O'Sheen knew all of them personally. She realized that an assault on Jody's house would have to be completed quickly and covertly with so many friends close by.

An hour later, she saw Walter walking to one of the few cars left on the parking lot. He noticed the light in the corner office and probably saw her through the large window, and he walked back toward the front door. She clicked off the company database, opened a guest internet site, and was composing an e-mail message when Walter entered the room with a large black man in a security guard uniform. *Oh no!*

Chapter 36
CIA

Agent Gene Kamper was nervous when he got to CIA headquarters at Langley. He had called his boss, Tom Kime, on his cell phone informing him of his ETA, and answered his unasked question, "Pat O'Sheen isn't with me", knowing that his boss would be disappointed.

Gene had planned his arrival after most of the staff had gone home. The guards at the gate informed him that he was expected in conference room C. After being escorted through the checkpoints, he entered a room in which Director Mary Collins, Gene Tanner, and Bob Hill already occupied seats. His boss, Tom Kime, was absent.

Hill started the accusations. "O'Sheen refused to come back with you? I think we need to classify O'Sheen as a rogue agent."

Kamper countered strongly, "**That's bullshit, Deputy Director Hill. O'Sheen is an American hero**, although the American public will never know how much of a hero he is." He forced calmness in his voice, "Only a few of us in this organization and high-level Army officers know of his many accomplishments."

Mary Collins looked at Gene with concern for his outburst. She could tell that O'Sheen had won him over—like O'Sheen had won her trust during their first encounter a week ago.

Kamper began a review, "I was ordered to verify that O'Sheen had CIA backup at our safe-house in Paris to help him capture his attempted assassins. We hoped to trace the hologram technology trail back from the assassins to the source of the leak and to the rogue manufacturer.

"When I inspected the safe-house, the precautions didn't make sense. When the man in charge, a Sergeant Spellman, attempted to delay my departure, I hit my panic button on my CIA alarm."

Bob Hill rudely interrupted, "I've heard all of this before. Why didn't O'Sheen return here with you?"

Agent Kamper addressed the director and continued as if Hill hadn't interrupted, "After I activated my panic button, the CIA cavalry never arrived."

Hill interrupted again, "We have discussed that before. The assassins were using a communication jamming device."

Kamper ignored Hill again. "I was with O'Sheen and his wife when we were attacked two nights ago in their car. I activated the emergency code when the pursuit started. Again, I got no response from the CIA. I've still had no response two days later." Gene looked into Hill's eyes, "Did the Arabs electronically jam me on a back street in nowhere, Alabama?"

Gene further explained, "O'Sheen is being extremely cautious. After our agency's failure to back him up in Paris, and the lack of response to my emergency response signal in Alabama, I don't blame him."

Bob Hill complained, "O'Sheen has gone rogue. We need to pick him up or neutralize him.

Tanner interrupted, "Bob, you are underestimating Pat O'Sheen. We can't just pick him up without his approval. And neutralizing him is out of the question."

Hill got more animated, **"Damn it, Tanner, we are the CIA.** He is just one man. Figure it out."

The director finally spoke, "Bob, Pat O'Sheen is not the enemy. Let Gene continue his report without any more of your interruptions.

She said, "Agent Kamper, I assume that you and Pat have a plan?"

Gene explained Pat's plan for their return to Paris.

When he finished, the Director slowly scanned the powerful men around the table. Hill didn't look at her. No one in the room offered an opinion. She rested her calm eyes on one man, "Agent Kamper, proceed according to O'Sheen's plan."

She commanded, **"Hill,** give Kamper any support he requests and upgrade Tom Kime to Gene's elevated clearance status on this project. I want a comprehensive report on my desk before noon tomorrow explaining how we failed O'Sheen at our safe-house in Paris, and how we will ascertain that we won't fail to support him again." She stood up and stomped out of the room.

Hill looked at Kamper with smoldering eyes. He was not used to subordinates getting their way.

Tanner watched Gene Kamper glare into Hill's eyes. Satisfied that Kamper could hold his own, he stood up and left the two of them alone. As soon as he was out of sight, he stopped outside the door to listen.

Bob Hill glared at Gene, his smoldering eyes betraying his calm voice. "Young man, you are putting your trust in a very dangerous man. Your association with O'Sheen will ruin your career and might get you incarcerated. I can help you. Meet me later tonight and I'll put you on the right path."

Gene said, "I'm Sorry, Mister Hill. I can't. I have another matter that needs my immediate attention."

"You're making a huge mistake by aligning yourself with O'Sheen."

Gene smiled, stood up, and left the room. He saw Tanner hurrying away from the door and around a corner in the corridor.

***

Walter Monroe entered the corner office with a huge security guard.

Michelle rolled her chair back from the computer, "Mister Monroe, is there a problem with me staying after hours? Have I violated a company rule?"

"No. But you are the last one here, and George doesn't know you." Walter handled the introduction.

Michelle offered her hand. When it was accepted, the big black fingers reached almost halfway to her elbow, but he didn't apply any pressure.

While Michelle shook the huge intimidating hand, Walter walked around Michelle to see the screen on the computer and saw a Gmail page.

Michele apologized, "Walter, I wasn't able to bring my personal computer from Paris. I was retrieving my personal emails. I hope that you won't fire me on my first day here."

Walter smiled at the beautiful lady. "Do whatever you need to do. When you are ready to leave you need to find George to let you out without setting off the alarms."

It was almost eight o'clock when Michelle returned to her rented room. Frances Shilling was waiting for her. Frances opened the door as she approached, and when Michelle entered the house, Frances announced, "I made a cake."

Michelle smiled. She was looking forward to another evening of conversation. She took her normal seat at the kitchen table that contained a large piece of chocolate cake.

After a few delicious bites, Michelle explained her successful day without disclosing her motivation.

After they finished their cake, Frances said, "I'll leave you in peace. I'm sure you don't want to spend another night talking to an old biddy like me."

"I enjoy talking to you, Frances. You have the most interesting stories about how America used to be. You should record your stories."

Frances smiled, "My niece, Dale O'Sheen, gave me a hand-held recorder to do that. But I can't comfortably tell stories to a non-responsive recorder."

Michelle almost panicked at the name O'Sheen. She recovered, "I thought your husband was named Dale?"

"Yes. You have a very good memory. My niece was given his name. It didn't seem that God was going to bless me with any children. My sister was pregnant with her third child at the time, and she agreed to name the baby after my husband."

Michelle said, "And your niece, Dale, married a man named O'Sheen?"

"Yes. Eddie O'Sheen, her high school sweetheart, is an exceptional man. He knows the President and the Secretary of State."

Frances got worried when Musso paled, "Michelle, are you alright?"

Michelle recovered. "Frances, I had a stressful day on my first day of work. As much as I enjoy your company, I need a good night's sleep to function properly tomorrow."

Frances said, "You do look stressed out. Go to bed."

Michelle couldn't believe that on her first day of work that she saw the schematic of Jody O'Sheen's security system, and that tomorrow she was going to see the installation upgrade on that security system. And now she learned that she has rented a room in answer to an ad in the newspaper from Pat O'Sheen's wife's aunt. *This was all too unbelievable.*

Michelle forced herself to recover. "I'm alright Frances. I'm just tired. I didn't sleep well last night because I was worried about my first day of work."

Frances said. "Of course you were worried. Maybe we should both turn in early tonight?"

Michelle loved this woman and stood up and retrieved a beer from the refrigerator while saying "What is your sister's name?"

"Mary Banker. Our maiden names are Mahon. Mary actively encouraged her daughter, Dale, to court Eddie O'Sheen."

Michelle managed to keep her shock under control.

Michelle learned all about Frances' daughter and her grandchildren in the very pleasant evening spent with Frances Shilling, and she was rewarded with a good night's sleep.

Michelle got up early the next morning and put her suitcases in the trunk of the rental car. In the conversation with Frances the night before, she learned that Pat O'Sheen was her favorite friend, and that he often came by to check on her on his way home from work, and often spent hours keeping her company. Michelle would have to come up with an excuse for why she had to move."

Michelle arrived for work early. To her surprise, Tom was already there. He looked like he had not slept well. His blue eyes were slightly puffy, and his red hair wasn't combed quite right, but he greeted her warmly.

She gave him a warm, sexy smile that changed his whole demeanor. His face brightened, and his posture improved. She asked, "Can you finish explaining the installation we are doing this morning?"

The blueprints were no longer on the table, so Tom excused himself to retrieve the blueprints of the upgrades of Jody O'Sheen's security system. He spread the sheet on the conference table. He didn't attempt to rub up against her while reviewing the redlined alterations to the design. To his surprise she rubbed against him ever so slightly and looked up into his deep blue eyes on more than one occasion. Don Waters entered the area interrupting her advances. Don pointed, "I have to leave now. I'll need that blueprint. Does anyone want to ride with me?" He looked at Michelle protectively—or perhaps hopefully.

Tom spoke first, "I have to take my vehicle. I am not sure how long I can stay. I have other appointments."

He looked at Michelle and offered, "Would you like to ride with me?"

Michelle handled the quagmire diplomatically, "I'm still trying to acquire adequate living arrangements. I need to take my car in case I get a call to view an apartment."

She followed Tom's car closely, pretending that she needed his lead to find Jody O'Sheen's house, even though by now she could drive there blindfolded. She had spent the whole weekend traveling back and forth to Jody O'Sheen's neighborhood in an attempt to answer all of Abdul's questions of what was nearby.

When they entered the house without Jody meeting them at the door, she asked with concern, "Shouldn't we wait for the homeowner before we enter?"

Don explained, "Jody cleared me with his cell phone when I entered my security code."

Michelle wondered if she could get that code.

Michelle and Tom watched Don make a splice into the main panel and two slave panels, and Tom helped Don add wires for the upgrade.

Later, Tom went and picked up some BBQ sandwiches for lunch. After they ate lunch on the back deck, Tom got a call on his cell phone and had to leave.

After another hour of watching Don's installation, Michelle knew how to override the security system. But she stayed to make sure she understood the function of the rest of the system.

She reached into her purse and covertly activated her cell phone, pulled a tube of lip-gloss from her purse, and applied it to her lips. She noticed in her make-up mirror that Don watched as she applied it.

As expected, her cell phone rang. She walked off to answer it, faked a conversation, and returned to where Don was working. He often admired her now that Tom was gone.

Michelle was explaining to Don that she had to meet a potential landlord when a handsome young hunk walked through the front door.

Michelle recoiled as she recognized the young man's resemblance to his dad. She chose an aggressive approach. "You must be Joseph O'Sheen." She extended her hand.

Jody's eyes panned the room nervously and saw Don. He took her hand delicately as his eyes panned the beautiful face and magnificent body. "Yeah, I'm Jody. This is my house. What are you doing here?" His voice and demeanor were threatening.

Without waiting for an answer, he left her and ushered Don into an adjoining room and closed the door. She approached the door to listen.

Jody said loudly, "**Don, who is that woman**? **Only you and Tom are allowed near my security system.**"

Don whimpered, "She's a new employee. Tom brought her here. I thought Tom cleared it with you. She is definitely not at fault . . . nor any kind of threat."

Michelle was tempted to run out the front door. What would she do if Jody pegged her affiliation with the enemy like his dad had done on their first exchange of glances in the Paris safe house?

She tried to remain calm when Jody stormed back into the hallway. She took the lead to disarm him, "Mr. O'Sheen, I'm sorry if I have invaded your privacy. I was just about to leave when you entered." She gave him her most pathetic look.

He stammered at her beauty, "Don explained that this wasn't your fault. I'm sorry that I overreacted. Please stay." Jody wasn't just being polite: he wanted time to judge her.

Michelle was insistent, "No, seriously. I just arrived in Birmingham on Friday and accepted this job. I have to meet a potential landlord, but thank you for your courtesy." She smiled.

Don backed her up, "Michelle was just telling me about that when you arrived."

She saw doubt in Jody's eyes, but he allowed her to leave the house.

Whew! That was intense. Michelle had to assume that Jody would be on a higher alert level after that encounter. She discarded the cell phone into the trashcan at her first stop, retrieved another from the glove compartment, and called Abdul.

After listening to her analysis, Abdul responded, "Are you sure you can handle the security system?"

"Yes, if I have access to the house for at least twenty minutes."

Abdul considered, "Jody will eventually share his concern with his father. We can't wait. We need to move today."

Abdul reiterated his main concern, "Michelle, you haven't had much time to learn security systems. Now is not the time to falsely brag about your intellectual talents. Convince me that you can handle the security system."

She explained the components of the system and the upgrade, the triggers, the activation sequences, and her plan to enter the house to deactivate the system. She knew Abdul couldn't totally understand the explanation, but she successfully assured him that she was capable.

Abdul said, "I have the house under surveillance. Drive to a store nearby and linger. I'll let you know when it is safe to approach."

Michelle stated, "I need to go to a nearby Lowes to purchase what I need to break into the house." She heard Abdul typing on his keyboard.

She interrupted, "Abdul, I know where the nearby Lowes store is located."

Chapter 37
Seizure

An hour later, Jody and Don had tested the upgrade to the security system, and then tested the whole system many times in a variety of ways. Lacy was coming over tonight, so Jody left the house to pick up some steaks and baking potatoes at the supermarket. Life seemed to be calming back to normal. He was finally able to spend some time with the love of his life.

After being notified by Abdul that Jody had left the house, Michelle saw Jody's pickup pass by her strategic viewpoint. Following Abdul's instructions, she drove directly up into the driveway of Jody's house, walked onto the front porch, and rang the doorbell. There were only two neighboring houses within sight. Both had the same company's security system and might be connected to Jody O'Sheen. If they were nosy, they might have seen her car there earlier. She rang the bell again and waited another half-minute, exited the porch, and walked to the back of the house. She removed the glasscutter that she had just purchased from Lowes from a large handbag and walked up onto the back deck. She cut a hole in the master bedroom window large enough for her to crawl through. She knew that there were no motion detectors in the master bedroom (too inconvenient for middle-of-the-night bathroom visits or romantic rendezvous). The magnetic strips on the windows were only activated if the windows were opened.

There was a small keyboard on the bedroom wall next to the hallway door. The homeowner set the numeric code, a code unknown to the security company. Entering the hallway would trip the motion alarm timing mechanism. Once she entered the hallway, she would have only forty-five seconds to disarm the main security panel. She felt up to the challenge.

***

Jody saw a car following him when he left his driveway. Out of habit, he slowed as he passed the side road to his dad's house and checked for anything unusual in the cul-de-sac. The car behind him didn't slow down—a good sign—and narrowed the gap to 40 feet: still too far away to see the occupants.

Jody turned right toward the market at the stop sign and watched in his mirror as the other car turned left. *Good.*

It took him ten minutes to get to the grocery store. Since he knew exactly what he wanted, he was at the checkout counters quickly, but even the express lane had a long line. He finally got checked out and headed back home.

***

Michelle had retrieved her tools before entering the hallway where a motion detector would trigger the 45 second alarm delay that gave someone entering the door time to enter the deactivation code. She set her personal timer to 40 seconds. She ran toward the security panel next to the front door. She dropped her bag on the floor below the panel and used a small star-studded tipped screwdriver that was already in her hand to remove the four screws on the main panel. She removed the panel cover, grabbed a wire that she had draped over her shoulder, and attached an alligator clip to the input power terminal. She counted each terminal and attached the other alligator clip to the third terminal from the right. The red light on the panel turned green.

She looked at her timer and smiled: eight seconds to spare. She took a few seconds to congratulate herself, ran onto the back deck, and did two full-pirouette turns. Three men exited the woods and ran across the backyard. Once they were in the house, she closed the back door. She positioned one man in the master bedroom, one in the coat closet near the front door, and one crouched behind an entryway heirloom: a Grandfather clock that would hide him from the motion detectors and from Jody when he entered the front door. She spoke to the man behind the clock while pointing to the motion detector and told him to stay out of its line of sight. They all understood her instructions not to move until Jody punched in the code to deactivate the security alarm.

Now she was confronted with her most difficult challenge. Once she removed the alligator clips from the alarm, she had forty-five seconds to reinstall the panel cover, exit and close the front door signaling the alarm to rearm without causing a warning. Installing four screws was much more difficult than removing them. She picked up the panel and the four screws, slightly opened the front door, and twisted the door knob lock mechanism so that when she exited, the door would lock behind her. She took a deep breath.

She set the timer on her waist and removed the bypass wire alligator clips from the panel starting the countdown. She positioned the cover and threaded the first and most difficult screw into place. She succeeded until the fourth screw cross-threaded on entry. She had to back it out to try again. She almost had it in when her seven-second warning beep sounded from her belt. *Damn! Not enough time to tighten the screw all of the way.*

***

Jody slowed at his mom and dad's street again, looked left to survey the cul-de-sac, which was clear, and turned right instead of going straight to his house. He was following his normal precautionary habit. The road circled back to Robby Clark's house across the street from his own. He normally stopped for a minute to observe. This time, however, there was a car in his driveway. He momentarily thought about calling for backup, but then he recognized the car. He couldn't see his front door from his angle, so he drove down the street and into his driveway. The beautiful woman, Michelle, was standing on the front porch punching his doorbell.

***

Michelle had grabbed her bag, which looked like a large purse and rushed through the front door slamming it behind her. Two seconds later her timer beeped the signal ending the time limit. She knew the blinking red light on the panel had already turned green. She took a slow, deep, relieving breath.

Her relief didn't last long. She heard a car entering the driveway. *Oh shit, Jody can't be back already. What should I do?*

216

Instinctively, she reached up with her right hand and pretended to press the doorbell, and then turned toward Jody's approaching pick-up truck.

She started walking down the front porch steps as Jody exited the vehicle. He noticed her approach and leaned back into the car to retrieve something: *probably a gun.*

***

Jody saw the concerned look on Michelle's face as she approached. He reached into the pick-up truck and retrieved the grocery bag from the seat and closed the car door.

The gorgeous lady looked surprised when she saw the grocery sack in his arms, relaxed suddenly, and then a smile crossed her beautiful face. Before he could ask a question, she explained, "Mr. O'Sheen, I am so sorry for intruding on your privacy for the second time today. I hope I left a small makeup purse in your house. It contains my license and Visa card."

She feigned distress. "I can't find my little bag anywhere else."

"I didn't see it anywhere in the house," Jody advised kindly.

Michelle said, "It would probably be in the half-bathroom off the den."

"Okay, I had no reason to go in there. Guests would be upset if I had security cameras in the bathrooms."

Security cameras: a separate system. In the rush to set this up, she hadn't considered all options. She followed Jody to the front door. He handed her the grocery bag and inserted his key in the bolt lock. She had not needed to retract it, so Jody must have forgotten to engage it when he left the house. She tensed, *please remember.*

He shook his head slowly. He tried the knob, and finding it locked he inserted his key.

She preceded him through the front door at his beckoning. She was still tense when his two hands rested on her shoulders from behind guiding her to one side. He punched in the numeric security code while blocking her view of the panel. She coughed twice and he turned toward her.

***

Jody was still regretful that he had reacted so angrily when seeing this innocent and very beautiful new security employee. He turned off the security system, heard her cough, and saw a touch of fear in her beautiful, brown eyes as he turned toward her. He was about to console her when he felt the sharp pain on his head accompanied by a flash of light. He fell to the floor unconscious.

***

Michelle wanted to search the house for the security camera tapes after giving Jody an injection before he was carried out the back door. She set the grocery sack on a kitchen counter. On a whim, she looked inside the sack: *steaks.* She looked at her watch: 5:10. Lacy got off work at five. If she came straight from work there would not be enough time for her to search for the security tapes. She knew she had to leave . . . or kill Lacy. She decided to leave. If Pat O'Sheen recognized her on the videotapes, Abdul would know how to use that to his advantage. She went to Jody's computer, typed in a code that would give Abdul access to Jody's computer, and left Jody O'Sheen's house.

Chapter 38
Panic

Lacy saw Jody's pickup when she pulled in the driveway and smiled in anticipation of joining her lover. She searched for the front door key on her key chain while walking up the sidewalk. When she reached the top step, she saw the front door ajar, a carelessness that Jody would never allow. He must have seen her arrive. She laughed and said playfully, "Jody?"

She became slightly alarmed. *What kind of game was he playing?* "Jody, you're scaring me."

Lacy sensed that something was wrong. Jody didn't kid around with security. She suddenly became frightened. If this was a joke, she was going to be very angry.

"**Jody**," she screamed forcefully. *No answer.*

Her fear almost made her run from the porch to drive to Jody's parent's house. Her love made her burst through the front door. She stopped in her tracks as the door fully opened and she saw the blood on the foyer floor. She ran through the house abandoning all caution while calling for her beloved.

She ran to his computer room. He spent more time there than anywhere else in the house, but he wasn't there. She started to leave the room when she noticed a big message flashing on the computer screen. The message took her legs out from under her, and she collapsed to the floor.

***

I didn't normally answer the house phone, but Dale was in the shower. I was glad that I did.

Lacy barely made sense through her panicked sobs. "*Jody* and *kidnapped*" were the only understandable key words that she managed to convey. Pat said, "I will be there in two minutes." I opened the cabinet under the sink and punched the orange button signaling Code 3, *Sorry Dale. I can't take the time to explain.*

Shadow looked at me curiously, tilting his head to one side. I commanded, "Shadow, Code 3." Shadow ran frantically to look for Dale, barking loudly all the way.

I ran to my arms room, outfitted myself in ten seconds, ran out the back door, and through the woods towards Jody's back yard. I saw a cigarette butt on the path ahead and came to an abrupt stop. The butt had no filter. I saw several more on the path ahead. I moved sideways, melded into the forest, and pulled my M-16 from my shoulder. I suspected a trap—a trap set for me.

The wooded area wasn't that expansive, and I quickly determined that it was clear. I punched Brendan's speed dial number (Number 3) on my phone for the second time.

Brendan answered before the end of the first ring and said. "I'm in Jody's front yard."

"I need **you** at Jody's front door. Signal me when you are ready to come through his front door."

I checked out the perimeter of Jody's house before I ran to the back corner of the house. I slammed my back against the rear wall in a defensive position. Brendan's signal came across my phone seconds later.

I ran up the steps to the back deck, saw the hole cut in Jody's bedroom window, and tried the door. I was surprised that it was unlocked: *not Jody's style.* I punched the "Go" code on my sat phone, waited for confirmation from Brendan, and ran into the house.

Brendan and I converged on the middle of the house where we heard Lacy crying from Jody's computer room. We both stopped at the open door, one of us on each side. I pointed my left thumb at my chest and rushed into the room. The room was empty except for a shocked and very frightened Lacy sitting awkwardly on the floor. She had not heard us enter the house. I handed Brendan my M-16, knelt down beside her, and put my arm around her shoulders to calm her. She made several efforts to say something through her sobs without success. She finally pointed up toward the computer screen. I looked up and saw the full screen message flashing on and off on the computer monitor. We have your son and the screen flashed an overseas phone number.

I understood the message and without getting off the floor said, "Brendan, take Lacy to Dale and then have her go to Code 1. Call Bo, explain that Jody has been kidnapped, and have his deputies canvas the area for clues. Send Robby here immediately, and once you are convinced that my house is totally secure under Code 1, return here."

I helped Lacy up to the standing position, embraced her, and said calmly. "Jody will be alright. I will get him back safely"

Lacy was comforted. She had never heard so many commands to take control strung together by anyone so quickly.

I reiterated, "I promise you that Jody will be fine. You need to go with Brendan to my house." She grabbed me in a tight hug, released me, and walked toward Brendan while only staggering slightly.

Brendan threw my M-16 to me with the barrel aimed toward the ceiling.

She turned and looked directly into my eyes; the tears had stopped. There was a slight bit of venom in her tone, "Dad, I'm holding you to your promise that Jody will be safe." She turned and gracefully left the room with Brendan.

Lacy had just reminded me of Dale during her feistiest moments. But what really touched me was that she had called me "Dad" for the first time.

Robby entered the room with Sheriff Bo Hannon on his heels. Robby saw the message flashing on the screen and started to approach the computer. I was on my cell phone and stopped him. "Robby, I want to see if I can get Cusimano in on this first, no offense intended." Robby was the best technical man I had, Jody and Brendan were next. I wasn't even a close fourth.

The phone on the other end rang, and I was relieved to hear, "This is Joe."

Joe Cusimano was a computer genius who worked at the government's NSA (National Security Agency) office at Fort Meade, Maryland. Before NSA recruited him, he had helped develop many software packages for Microsoft in Seattle. He was also married to the daughter of one of my long-term friends.

"Joe, this is Pat O'Sheen."

Before Joe could slip into friendly amenities, I pressed forward, "I am at my son Jody's house. He has been kidnapped, and the kidnappers left a message on his computer screen with a telephone number for me to call." I gave him the phone number. "I would like to put you on speaker. Robby, my best computer expert is here with me. Instruct him on what he needs to do to help you trace the source of the message on Jody's computer."

Pat could hear Joe's fingers hammering his computer keyboard.

Joe answered, "I already have the location of the phone number you were instructed to call. It's a pay phone in a rural area of Switzerland, near the French border."

Joe queried, "Robby, are you at the computer?"

Sheriff Hannon reached into his uniform pocket and handed Robby a pair of latex gloves. Someone had to consider preserving evidence left by the perpetrators. Bo knew that in a missing person or a kidnapping case, time was the primary enemy. Bo recognized that Pat, with the help of the NSA, could accomplish more in ten minutes than he could accomplish in a full day.

Robby warned, "Joe, I need to hit as few keys as possible to preserve fingerprints."

"Robby, I am going to guide you through the steps to turn control of the computer over to me. You will have to use the Control and Alternate keys, and the Function keys at the top of the keyboard. The average user rarely uses those keys. Then I need you to punch in an alpha-numeric code to give me access."

Two minutes later Joe was in control of Jody's computer. The mouse arrow darted to the file menu, and then the arrow darted from menu to menu so quickly that eyes couldn't follow—much less the untrained computer mind like mine comprehend. Robby rolled his chair back from the screen in awe.

After five minutes, Joe finally spoke, "Pat?"

"I'm here."

"The message on the computer came from a rerouted secure source that will take time for a trace: more time than you probably want to wait before making the call to the number on the screen."

Joe hesitated, the machine-gun speed of his fingers on his keyboard was still audible. "When do you plan to make the call?"

"Soon, but I'm open for suggestions." I trusted Joe and respected his acumen.

"Make the call from Jody's house phone on an unsecured line. Give me the number you will be calling from before you place the call."

Joe hesitated and reminded, "Pat, you **do** know that the NSA records all of our calls?"

"Yes. But I don't need any interference for at least eight hours. Joe, will that cause you problems?" I continued without waiting for an answer, "It will take Robby a minute to remove the secure status from Jody's house phone." I gave Joe my son's home phone number.

I watched Robby do his magic while listening to Joe still rat-a-tat-tatting on his keyboard.

Robby raised his right thumb.

I proclaimed, "We're ready on this end."

Thirty seconds later, Joe responded, "I've got your phone. Pat, the ball is in your court."

Robby interrupted the big breath that I was exhaling. "Joe?"

"Yes, Robby?"

Robby offered, "No one is going to be waiting for this call at a pay phone in the middle of nowhere. What is your take?"

The men in Jody's computer room waited in silence, except for the sound from Joe's clicking on his keyboard. "Good call, Robby. The pay phone is forwarding calls." Joe was still hammering his keyboard. He finally said, "It is forwarding the call from phone to phone. It may take a long time to break through. It's your call, Pat."

Sheriff Bo Hannon was enthralled. This was way above his training level. He just learned more about how to handle a kidnapping crisis in five minutes than he had learned in twenty years in law enforcement: i.e., stay close to those who have the technology to help. He also realized that he was just a fly on the wall. He walked out of the room and took a call on his cell phone. A minute later, he cleared his throat loudly to get Pat's attention. "Pat, we didn't find any clues in the neighborhood except that it seems that they took Jody through the woods behind here to a back street."

I nodded and turned to Robby for his input. When Robby nodded, I announced, "Joe, I am making the call."

"Give me ten seconds . . . okay, dial the number."

***

Lacy and Brendan entered Pat's house. Based on the code entries, Dale knew that it was Brendan entering. When she saw Lacy, she screeched, **"What is going on? No one tells me anything. Where is Jody?"** Although not articulately expressed, her intuition on seeing Lacy was accurate.

Lacy cried, **"He has been kidnapped."**

Seeing Dale, Lacy's resolve evaporated. Dale grabbed Lacy before she collapsed to the floor, and she sank to the floor with her.

Dale looked up, "Brendan, we will be okay. Help Eddie find Jody." In a motherly fashion she hugged Lacy to her bosom.

Brendan said, "Pat wants you to go to Code 1. Give me a minute to get out of the house before you hit the Code button."

Brendan waited outside until metal shutters folded over all the windows as he ran around the house. Brendan couldn't see them, but he knew four steel bars lowered from the top of each of the two outside doors sealing them off. The O'Sheen house was almost impenetrable under Code 1 without someone using serious weaponry, like rocket propelled grenades.

***

I dialed the number and heard a half of a ring at the first connection before it clicked forward. I tried to count the transfers to successive forwarding numbers before I lost count. I knew I was contacting a professional. Even Joe wouldn't be able to help. Finally, a voice answered the line and said, "O'Sheen, hold for a minute."

The line went quiet. I was so used to music or recorded advertisements in the background while I was on hold and wondered if I had been disconnected. Finally, a singsong voice came on the line, "Hello, Pat O'Sheen." The female voice was drawn out in a seductive manner.

I knew that voice actuators were used on some 900 area code calls used by phone sex marketers. The caller can spend twenty dollars punching through the menu options before reaching the sexy voice that would entertain his perversion. What the caller didn't realize was that he was actually talking to a 6'4" junkie, with a long gray beard, who spent the best years of life on his motorcycle and on drugs. The voice actuators could make the man sound like a young, sexy female in a negligee if the junkie could learn the cadence and the rhythm properly. When used correctly, the voice synthesizer was hard to detect by an amateur.

I was not an amateur. I said, "I was instructed to call this number. You can turn off the voice synthesizer. I have followed your instructions."

The voice actuator was turned off and the voice changed to a male voice. "O'Sheen, I assume that you have properly assessed the situation. Am I correct?"

The speech was too slow and too calm. I didn't respond. Twenty seconds passed, making everyone in the room with me very uncomfortable. I waited. I wasn't going to let this man control me.

Finally, the silence was broken from the other end, "O'Sheen, I know your friends are using every electronic means to locate me. Your friends have less than a one in thirteen thousand chance of tracing this call. Even if they get lucky, no one from your side is near me, so I will no longer be here if someone is successful at a trace. Therefore, we have plenty of time to make sure that we understand each other. Comprende?"

Although the accent was northeastern American, I thought I recognized the well-hidden tone of a foreign accent. After a few seconds I got it. I had heard the man's voice speaking Farsi over a two-way radio in the safe house in Paris.

I said, "Abdul, explain your demands." I asked the question in Farsi.

The silence of surprise confirmed my insight.

Abdul said, "We were never formally introduced in Paris. Despite your age, your skills were most impressive." The response was in Farsi and said with respect. "You do understand the peril that your son is in. You caused my uncle many painful years."

I answered in Russian, "Your uncle and I came to an understanding. You are not acting under his authority."

There was a long silence. Perhaps Abdul didn't understand Russian. I had a suspicion that Russia might be behind the hologram conspiracy—Abdul's response would give me a clue.

Abdul asked me to repeat my last statement in Farsi. If he was dealing with Russia, he was not going to admit it.

When I repeated my Russian statement in Farsi, Abdul replied, "Your ability to confront my uncle the day after the attack in Paris was very impressive. Somehow you convinced him to forgive you, which was even more impressive.

"O'Sheen, you have convinced me that you have the right skills to help me stop a world-wide blood-fest. I have your son. I have your attention. You must follow my directions if you want to see your son alive again."

I answered calmly in English, "Abdul, you are responsible for my son's well-being. Don't neglect that responsibility. I can tract you down and kill you. If you kill my son, I will kill your parents and the rest of your relatives, and then I will kill you." My tone of voice reinforced my threat.

While Abdul and I were bantering, Robby loaded the tapes from Jody's security cameras and put them on Jody's computer screen cued to when the strangers entered Jody's house. I recognized Michelle on the screen immediately. I knew that I had to calculate every word of my dialogue very carefully.

I continued in *French*, "Abdul, I see that you are still working with Michelle."

Another silence of surprise and reflection followed.

Abdul assumed that their conversation was being recorded by the American government at O'Sheen's end, and that O'Sheen was changing languages to delay his government's interpretation of their conversation. He answered in French. "Oui, Monsieur. You noticed that she is very beautiful. She is more beautiful than Angela, the daughter of your friend from Alabama. Angela is still on this earth due to a timely intervention by Allah."

I made the connection. Faisad was the middle-eastern GWU student who fled the country after raping and beating Abdul's college girlfriend, Angela. I had met Angela and her family several years later, after I connected to the FBI in Alabama. Her father had a good friend in the local FBI. The FBI wanted to help in the case, but their hands were tied when Angela refused to press charges.

Abdul's reference was unmistakable: killing Jody would not bother his conscience.

Abdul said in Arabic, "But that was a long time ago, wasn't it?

I replied angrily in Arabic, **"Abdul, you better make sure that I am dead before you hurt Jody."**

Abdul declared, "O'Sheen, I hear hatred in your voice. There are not many people in the world who share our talents. You kill. I kill. In many ways we are the same."

My anger increased. I said, **"I don't kill innocent women and children.**

Abdul said, "You kill for your government."

I hissed in German, **"I kill to prevent you crazy mother-fuckers from blowing up innocent children, crashing airplanes with innocent people aboard into buildings full of more innocent people, and all of your other disgraceful damned religious zealot acts . . . like abusing women by placing them under Sharia law because of your inability to control your male urges. You stone women to death for adultery, but never punish their male participants in the adultery."**

I rarely cursed and realized that I had lost my cool, giving this talented adversary the upper hand. I became silent.

Abdul remained silent, realizing his advantage, hoping to hear more venom from Jody's angry father: a man who obviously loved his son. After a minute, he realized that O'Sheen was using the prolonged silence to rein in his anger.

Abdul finally answered in a Swiss German accent, "O'Sheen, I emphasize that you and I are unique to this world. I also abhor the killing of innocents. But the Jews that returned to Palestine after the Holocaust of WWII defeated the British Empire by terrorizing their troops and their political governors in Palestine. The British would not allow the Jews who returned to Palestine form an army. But the Jews succeeded in recreating an ancient nation that they had been exiled from by the Roman Empire two-thousand years before. They ran the British out by their acts of terrorism. The Palestinians who were driven from the newly created nation of Israel will never forget the effectiveness of the Jews' terrorism."

I replied in the French that he seemed more comfortable with. "The Jews never recruited desperate men, incapable of supporting their families, to blow themselves up in a public area, the success of their effort judged by how many innocent people were killed by their supposed martyrdom, enticing them with a promise of seventy-two vestal virgins in Paradise. How sick is that concept. How can your culture show such disrespect for women?"

Abdul responded in Farsi as if he had not heard my argument, "O'Sheen, I repeat, the nation Israel was recreated against all odds by terrorist tactics. The Islamist will never forget that. The Palestinians lost the homeland that their ancestors had lived in for two thousand years. Was that fair? The Palestinians didn't participate in the holocaust against the Jews.

"The Jews had lost their claim to the land when they rebelled against Rome. Tiberius put down their rebellion and destroyed their sacred temple in 70 AD. The Jews from Palestine were sold into slavery throughout Europe, the mid-East, and North Africa. Why should they be allowed to reclaim the land when the Palestinians have lived there for the last two thousand years? Shouldn't you Americans give a large part of the country back to the American Indians who you stole it from over the last two centuries?"

Abdul didn't want an answer, he continued, "Adolph Hitler's attempt to annihilate the Jews in Europe created an historic quagmire that spanned three millennium of history and inadvertently created the new nation of Israel in 1948. His attempt to annihilate the Jews backfired: sending Jews from around the world back to Palestine with a fire in their hearts to create a nation where they could live isolated from the world's hatred of them."

I went further back in history, "The Jews lived in that land that God gave to Abraham more than a thousand years before the Romans dispersed them from their land, which, not coincidently, was less than a generation after the Jews crucified Jesus Christ. The Prophet Mohammed never doubted the historical accuracy of the Jewish biblical testament. In fact, Mohammed claimed to be a descendent of Ishmael, the first-born son of Abraham by his concubine, before his wife, Sarah, in her old age, was granted the ability to give Abraham a son, Isaac—the son who created the first Jewish Nation." I hoped that Joe Cusimano was getting a fix on Abdul's location.

"Pat," Abdul interjected, cleverly using the familiar address, "The Nation of Islam has made over 500 million converts in the two centuries since your country adopted their ill-conceived notion of individual freedom and liberty, which resulted in uncontrolled capitalism and greed. Islam has converted more followers in the last century than any religion in history. And more recently, America's imperialistic military response to terrorism has become the Jihadists best recruiting tool."

Again, he didn't wait for a response. "Your son is safe for now. If you agree to help me, he will be forever safe from me."

The last words were spoken in Arabic. The language bantering would be confusing to all but Pat: effective against any government agency listening—like Cusimano at the NSA. Abdul sensed that my stalling might be putting his secure connection in jeopardy.

I sensed that Abdul was about to disconnect. I also believed that he was truly seeking my help.

I asked in English, "What are you proposing?"

Abdul avoided my question. "You cleverly arranged a meeting with my uncle the day after our attack against you in Paris. Somehow you gave peace to his troubled heart. You offered to help his grandson Mohammed get released from the Parisian authorities. You must expedite that release for our mission."

I reverted back to French. "What mission?"

"I will contact you with instructions for a meeting place in Europe. You can bring that big man you. The one you had with you the first time in Paris. You will learn more after Mohammed is free. Time is short."

I warned in English, "Abdul, if you hurt Jody, would you prefer that I cut your head off, shoot you between your eyes, or both.

Abdul disconnected.

I closed my eyes in contemplation, ignoring the questioning eyes that were focused on me. Aside from the photographs that Gene Kamper laid on the kitchen table in the Paris safe-house, I had only seen Abdul three times: once in the De Gaulle Airport in Paris, once from a distance across the park from the hotel in Paris, and just for a split second when he rounded the back of the building while I was being shot on top of my head. The man was an intriguing and an extremely intelligent adversary.

I instructed Robby to make copies of the phone call recording so that we could replay it for Dale and Lacy. I couldn't keep Dale in the dark on this international crisis.

Chapter 39
Wheels in motion

Gene Kamper was in his Maryland apartment with his wife and son when his satellite phone rang. He recognized the number on his secure line and answered, "Hello, Pat."

I explained the situation of my son's kidnapping.

An alarmed Gene asked, "What do you need me to do?"

"Gene, I believe this is still related to the hologram belts. Can we trust Tom Kime at Langley?"

"Yes . . . and you can trust Director Collins. She approved our planned rendezvous in Paris. She also raised Tom Kime to a 'need-to-know' security status. Bob Hill threatened me trying to force me withdrawal my support from you. His behavior has made him my number one suspect."

"What about Tanner."

"He met with us, but I couldn't read him."

"That's not surprising." I knew that Tanner was a talented agent.

"Gene, let me call you back in one hour. You call Kime—for his ears only—and explain the kidnapping situation. Do not involve the FBI. If my analysis is correct, Abdul is concerned about the hologram belt technology that they used against me. He may be a very valuable asset in turning this situation to our advantage." I disconnected.

I called Inspector Pierre Boudreaux at the Prefecture de Police in Paris. Meanwhile, Sheriff Bo Hannon's forensic team was collecting fingerprints in Jody's computer room while I waited for the call to go through. Pierre didn't answer. I looked at my watch realizing that I was not thinking logically. It was past midnight in Paris. I called Pierre's home.

"Bonjour?" Pierre answered groggily from a deep sleep.

"Hello Pierre, this is Pat O'Sheen." I was not originally planning to tell my friend about the kidnapping, in the hope of extracting any information that Pierre had gathered about Mohammed Faisad, but I needed to explain the urgency to justify my late-night intrusion. I related the kidnapping story, the flashing computer message, and some of my conversation with Abdul. I concluded with, "What is the status of Mohammed Faisad?"

"We have charged him with attempted burglary based on the affidavits that you and Kamper submitted."

I was surprised, "That is all?"

"We had to charge him with something to hold him past 72 hours. Your affidavits didn't mention enough about his involvement in the attack to invoke other charges. Also, you should know that my superiors still want to talk to you about the massacre. If you return to France, you risk incarceration."

I ignored the last comment, "Can you release Mohammed if proper bail is posted?"

"Actually, I was going to notify you that the bail hearing is set for Thursday morning: two days from now." He looked at the alarm clock by his bed. "Actually that will be tomorrow here in Paris."

"Pierre, I will not be pressing further charges. I need him released as soon as possible after the bail hearing."

"Why?"

"It involves Jody's release from captivity. I'll pay the bail if I need to."

"I'll take care of it, Pat. What else can I do?"

"You and Kathie can pray for Jody."

"You know we will. Pat, be careful, I don't have to tell you that Abdul is not someone to toy with."

"Thank you, Pierre." I hung up.

When I looked up, Sheriff Bo was shaking his head.

"What?" I asked.

"You amaze me." Bo replied. "You are already starting a movement toward another international incident."

"This is already an international incident, Bo."

When I returned to my house with Robby, Brendan was pacing in the yard. I knew that there were other men out of sight during a Code 1. The worried look on Brendan's face spoke volumes of his love for Jody. Robby and Brendan had a short conversation before Robby took over the Code duties outside.

I called Dale, told her I was coming in, and told her to remove the Code 1. When the shutters retracted, Brendan and I entered the house. I reset the security level to Code 3. When I turned around, Brendan stood towering over me. I grabbed my best friend in an embrace.

***

Brendan felt Pat's body shaking and held him gently. Pat was the most courageous man he had ever met. He admired how Pat had taken charge of this unexpected crises by restraining most of his normal parental emotions. He knew that Pat wanted to appear confident and in control when he came face-to-face with Dale and Lacy. If they saw him shaking like this, they would panic.

***

I calmed in my friend's loving embrace. I released Brendan and asked him to have Robby bring in the audiotape of my conversation with Abdul. I turned and walked toward entrance to the bunker.

Dale was already entering the hallway. Fear and tears filled her eyes. She threw herself into my embrace while crying uncontrollably and was uncharacteristically incapable of voicing her concern. I saw Lacy exiting the bunker door behind her with the same fear and tears. I reached out an arm to Lacy, and the three of us embraced. When Robby entered the house, he inserted the audiotape into my entertainment system.

I entered the room with Dale and Lacy under each arm. I was trying to explain that the kidnapping was intended to get our country's attention, and that I might be able to turn the kidnapper into an ally.

I encouraged Dale and Lacy to sit down and listen to the phone conversation. I picked up the remote, knowing that I would have to interpret the many different language exchanges. I located the pause and rewind buttons.

Forty minutes later, the seven-minute taped conversation concluded. Dale stood up and paced the room like a caged panther.

Lacy sat still: more bewildered than ever. *Who was Jody's dad?* She lost count on how many different languages were spoken. She felt better . . . not good, but better. Jody's dad was talented and very confident that he could get Jody back home safely.

Brendan broke the tense silence by saying. "It was a sign of good faith that Abdul invited me to accompany you to the meeting place. He is confident that he can recognize me from the airport in Paris."

Brendan's words seemed to have a calming effect on Dale. She noticed the bewilderment in Lacy's eyes and sat down next to her as Lacy exhaled a big sigh. She calmed Lacy by saying, "Pat will make sure Jody returns safely. Jody's future couldn't be in better hands."

I said a short prayer that Dale's prophecy would come true.

Chapter 40
Reunited

Brendan and I left Birmingham early on Thursday morning in the chartered jet. While refueling in Madrid, Spain, I called Pierre and he confirmed that Mohammed had been released that morning. When we landed in Zurich, Switzerland, I called Abdul to receive final instructions. Brendan drove us in the rental car into the Swiss Alps.

It was almost dark by the time we left the rental car at the designated location. We locked our weapons in the trunk of the car, put the keys on the driver's seat as instructed, grabbed two flashlights, and started the last mile walk to the chalet in the cool mountain air. No vehicles interrupted our walk up the gravel road. I heard people following us. Halfway up the steep road, I spotted a small force of men even though they were well hidden in a wooded alcove in a relatively flat area off to our right. Abdul was definitely in control.

Two men carrying sub-machine guns were visible as we approached the chalet. The door of the chalet opened, and two large men exited and did thorough body searches of Brendan and me.

***

Abdul appeared from the shadows at the corner of the chalet while lowering his weapon. He locked eyes with Brendan and saw intrepidness but no fear in his eyes. He then locked eyes with Pat O'Sheen and studied him in wonder that the average looking man could survive the two attacks in Paris. He had never been this close to him before. O'Sheen's eyes showed no emotion. *Zero. Nada.* He said, "O'Sheen, you're good at following instructions. Join me inside."

***

Abdul turned his back to us, and we followed him into the chalet and entered a dining room. In the middle of the room was a 3' by 6' table surrounded by six chairs. Mohammed Faisad was sitting in one of the end chairs with a cast on his left arm that was resting on a stool. He raised a pistol and aimed it at my chest with anger spewing from his dark eyes.

When Brendan recoiled at the affront, I said to Brendan in Farsi, "Relax." I continued walking calmly into the room toward Mohammed.

Abdul was amused until Mohammed tensed. He warned Mohammed in Arabic to keep his cool.

I pulled a chair from the side of the table and sat down next to Mohammed's end of the table, who then raised the gun barrel less than two feet from my nose. I leaned forward so it was only a foot from my nose and rested my elbows on the table. My eyes never left Mohammed's eyes. I could see the fury building and saw his finger tighten on the trigger.

Abdul yelled "Mohammed. **No.**"

I swept my right hand across the gun barrel deflecting Mohammed's shot toward the kitchen door and snatched the gun from his hand. Mohammed started to stand, but Abdul had already moved behind him and with hands on his shoulders held him in his chair. Three men entered room and aimed guns at me. I pointed the pistol barrel at the ceiling, forced the revolver cartridge open with my thumb and let the bullets fall on the table. The three armed men relaxed.

***

After witnessing the scene, Abdul had little doubt that the man who sat down at the table so calmly under life threatening duress was the best partner he could find to avert a major worldwide catastrophe. This was the first time that he had an opportunity to observe O'Sheen close-up and witness his absolute fearlessness.

Abdul walked around the table and sat down across from Pat. He glared at Mohammed who succumbed to his glare. Abdul motioned for a very tense Brendan to sit.

Pat nodded for Brendan to comply.

Brendan slowly approached the table and sat down next to me. Abdul smiled and looked again into O'Sheen's unblinking eyes. Abdul was beginning to understand how he had underestimated this older man. From a distance, he seemed ordinary. Up close, his eyes were fearless, unshakable, and his hands could move faster than any he had ever witnessed. Mohammed had no clue that O'Sheen was about to snatch the gun from his hand. O' Sheen's eyes betrayed nothing.

Abdul smiled at O'Sheen. Pat's eyes were still void of any emotion.

Abdul gave a long verbal overview of his analysis of the hologram crises.

***

I was alarmed by Abdul's scenario.

An Arab approached Abdul. He was carrying my satellite (sat) phone that I had left on the front seat of the rent-a-car according to instruction. He handed it to Abdul and left the room.

Abdul quietly presented us with a more detailed analysis of his theory. He was direct, and more importantly, was sincere in answering my many questions.

Abdul's scenario had dire international ramifications, and recent events, supported Abdul's theory. Abdul was still in total control of my son's survival. I would probably never trust this man, but if his theory was right, I would have volunteered my support without the kidnapping of my son. I leaned back in my chair and started considering my options.

***

Abdul saw that Pat was buying his scenario. When Abdul raised his right hand, an Arab brought Jody through the kitchen doorway. Jody was shackled in leg irons around his ankles, and his hands were cuffed in front of him.

Abdul watched Pat's reaction. A look of joy crossed Pat's face, but only fleetingly. Brendan smiled and started to stand. Pat told the large man to remain seated, and Abdul noticed that his instruction was obeyed immediately. A chair was brought into the room and Jody was comfortably lowered into it, behind his father, so that Pat could not see his son.

***

Abdul asked me, "Did you arrange for your government to be on standby to accept your call?"

When I nodded, he handed me my sat phone and warned, "Don't deviate from my earlier instructions." He looked past me at Jody conveying an unstated warning.

I dialed a prearranged number. Ten seconds later, Gene Kamper answered the international call on a speakerphone. I relayed the instructions. Gene said he would need fifteen minutes to assemble the group and terminated the call. Abdul didn't trust that my phone would not be triangulated to give away our position. So, he turned off my phone and removed the battery and sim card.

Pat smiled at his very savvy adversary. Fifteen minutes later, Pat was handed Abdul's secure cell phone.

Abdul said, "We have reached a critical moment, O'Sheen. Don't cross me." He put his phone on speaker.

After several rings, Gene Kamper said, "Pat?"

I released a deep audible sigh and asked as Abdul instructed, "What can you tell us about the manufacturer of the hologram belts?"

Abdul wondered if that deep sigh was a signal.

A booming voice came across the speaker. The voice could be in talk radio or in the anchor position for CBS news. The deep voice asked, "Mr. O'Sheen, I have been instructed to ask this before I can proceed, can we assume that everyone in the room with you is aware of the project in question as you indicated?"

Abdul realized he was referring to the deep sigh I had released. I looked at Abdul and recognized that he understood my signal. I returned Abdul's grin.

I responded, "Your assumption is correct."

The booming voice hesitated, probably looking for approval before proceeding. "There is only one contractor for the hologram belts, and I can't disclose the name." He continued, "The belt you returned from Paris has five buttons. The latest prototype we tested only has three, and the contractor is developing a fourth button to manually melt down the electronics. The CEO of the contractor lost a nephew in Afghanistan. He is still livid that President Bush committed most of the troops to attack Saddam Hussein in Iraq rather than concentrating on Afghanistan. He . . ." Pat assumed that a hand signal must have stopped him.

A commanding female voice came through the speaker. "Enough. We have cooperated so far. We cannot proceed until all parties listening are identified."

Abdul recognized the Director of the CIA's voice from CNN broadcasts. He raised his hand to stop me from responding. He leaned back in his small, kitchenette-type chair and steeped his fingers, each fingertip and thumb tips pressed together in a choirboy fashion, but with palms held away from each other. *He hadn't expected that O'Sheen was this well connected. Another underestimation. Abdul considered that his own forces might be surrounded by now.*

When Jody saw Abdul working his palms back and forth like a blacksmith would work a bellows to heat coals, he involuntarily glanced at the back of his dad's head. This man went into a contemplative mode using one of his dad's most aggravating habits.

Finally, Abdul leaned forward. "Madame Director, my name is not important." He paused for emphasis. "A cargo of two-thousand hologram belts has entered an Iranian harbor. They will be in the hands of the Taliban near the Pakistan/Afghanistan border in three days. Thousands of American servicemen will be killed if the shipment is not stopped."

The director's response went straight to the point, "Mohammed, why would you want to help save the lives of American soldiers?"

I looked at Mohammed and then at Abdul, realizing that the CIA had heard of Mohammed's release from the Parisian jail and had incorrectly assumed that Mohammed was behind the attacks on me in Paris and was behind Jody's kidnapping.

Abdul sat back in that same contemplative posture. I could imagine Director Collins doing the same.

The silence lasted for too long, so I said. "Mary, Mohammed (using the name she had incorrectly assigned to Abdul) believes that the belts are rigged to kill its wearers if triggered via satellite from a remote location. His motivation is that the double-cross of the Taliban could result in a violent Muslim uprising around the world, which would cause a worldwide backlash against Muslims."

The people in the room with the director were shocked by Pat's inexcusable familiar address "Mary" to the Director of the CIA. But Mary realized Pat's intent: he was playing the kidnappers. *Smart.*

Mary followed Pat's lead and addressed him by his first name, "Pat, what do you suggest?"

My familiarity ploy worked. I was surprised by the Director's familiar response. She had no covert experience, but she understood my ploy, which raised my respect for her. I read the amazement in Abdul's face. He had no idea that I was so well connected.

I said, "Mary, I would like to know if Mohammed's scenario is plausible."

The bodacious voice responded, "The belt that was brought here from Paris had enough explosives in it to kill the wearer and anyone close to him. Most of the circuitry in the one you sent back here was destroyed, but your *captor's* conjecture is plausible."

I asked for clarification, "So, Gordon, you're saying that technology exists to activate circuits from a great distance that could detonate of the explosives in the belts?"

Gordon recoiled: his name had not been disclosed. O'Sheen was amazing.

After recovering, he answered, "Yes, if configured properly, the circuitry could be activated from anywhere in the world via satellite."

Deputy Director Bob Hill signaled the Director to put the call on hold.

She advised that she going to mute her phone. Hill proposed, "O'Sheen has been involved with this breach of security from the beginning. We would be making a big mistake by trusting him and his terrorist co-conspirator."

To Bob Hill's surprise, Gordon Neil voiced his disagreement, "The belt that Gene Kamper brought here was further advanced than any prototype we've seen. Our technology has been compromised and improved by a very competent, technical adversary."

Gordon paused, allowing the significance of his declaration to register before saying. "I've been technically involved in the Hologram Project from the beginning." Looking at Hill. he said, "But since you changed my oversight duties, we have failed to monitor the company we have contracted to make the belts. I have expressed my concern of the lack of oversight in several emails. I believe that the scenario presented by Mohammed is a logical follow-up to the bizarre use of the belts against O'Sheen in the attacks in Paris. It appears that Mohammed kidnapped O'Sheen's son to get American assistance in stopping the shipment of the belts to the Taliban."

Gordon added emphatically, "And from what I know of Pat O'Sheen, he would never mislead our country or put America in an embarrassing . . ."

Bob Hill barked out, **"You don't know what he might do when his son is in jeopardy."** He looked at Gordon Neil with daggers in his eyes.

Gordon didn't care. He didn't work directly for Hill anymore. At his own request he had been moved to the department under Gene Tanner.

Director Collins had heard enough. She silently agreed with Gordon's analysis. She sensed that Mohammed was becoming impatient at the delay. She punched the mute button, putting them live. "Pat, what help do you need from us?"

Abdul interrupted again, "Incarcerate the CEO, extract the trigger code from him, and blow up the belts."

"What if a lot of innocent people are nearby?" the director asked.

Abdul wasn't impressed by her apparent concern for civilians, but he recognized that the CIA was becoming as politically controlled as the MI6 in Britain. Abdul explained, "Muslims understand that death is the ultimate proof of Allah's acceptance, whether death is voluntarily or by fate."

But Abdul spent enough time in college in America to understand the Director's political constraints, "Madam Director, I have enough contacts to follow the shipment. But I need American support to stop the shipment before it reaches its destination. If you cannot obtain the authority to handle this crisis expeditiously, the blood of thousands of American soldiers and millions of people across the world will be on your hands."

Gene Kamper was afraid that the man who abducted Jody was going to disconnect and spoke up, "Mohammed, I would like assurance that Pat O'Sheen is not being coerced."

The director smiled at Gene. He had asked the question that concerned everyone at the CIA table.

After another interminable silence, a new voice joined the fray, "Gene, Mohammed's analysis is sound." Jody followed the lead in calling Abdul "Mohammed".

I realized that Abdul must have signaled for Jody to be unshackled, knowing that his previous employment with the CIA might add the needed influence to ensure their support.

Abdul smiled. The son understood the purpose of his unshackling, and he had followed the concealment of his identity by calling him Mohammed. *Smart young man.*

Gene Kamper knew Jody's voice, but the others in the room didn't, so he asked, "Is that you, Jody?"

Despite the critical apex that the conversation had reached, the director allowed a short exchange between Jody and Gene, while she considered the meaning of Jody's freedom. *Conspiracy? Was this all being manipulated by Pat O'Sheen? He was capable, and he had purposely avoided meeting with her at CIA headquarters.*

Jody readdressed the group on the conference call, "Yes, Gene. I've been released. My dad is not being coerced."

Jody continued. "Now, consider that this unnamed CEO, who lost a beloved nephew in Afghanistan as Gordon mentioned, can arm the Taliban with two thousand hologram belts. This disillusioned CEO would watch the American soldiers' casualty count increase daily CNN reports it, punishing America for sending the troops to Iraq instead of avenging his nephew's death in Afghanistan. As the death count mounted, the average American citizen's concerns would turn to outrage. The CEO could activate the explosives on the belts saving the day and become a national hero. But knowing that his actions would put him under suspicion, he could provide documents proving that his scientists discovered the solution to the crisis."

Jody continued, "What Mohammed only hinted at in his analysis needs to be included in this equation. There are over one billion Muslims in the world. The Shiite Muslims that control Iran relish the idea of enraging the Muslims of the world against America, Israel, and the rest of the infidels. If the technology to enact Mohammed's scenario exists, the future could be very bleak."

I looked up at Jody with surprise and pride. We had never worked together under this high level of duress.

The director's voice came back on the line, "Stand by while we confer." The connection silenced again.

Abdul addressed Jody with an admiring smile, "Well said, young man. You encapsulated this crisis articulately and convincingly."

I noticed that Jody's look back into Abdul's eyes was not with the anger that should be expected after his kidnapping, but with admiration. Abdul must have explained early on in Jody's ordeal the reason why he was kidnapped. Jody was showing respect for Abdul. I would bet my government retirement pay that Michelle was somewhere in this Swiss chalet with us. Her beauty could make a death row inmate smile while he was being injected with a lethal drug.

The director asked the team at CIA headquarters for an update on the attempt to trace the call. When she received a negative response, she came back on the line, "Pat, what help do you need to intercept the cargo?"

I answered, "I'm not sure yet. But I would like cruise missile capability near the Khyber Pass, drones to protect and guide our movements, and a laser targeting device to direct cruise missiles and smart bombs from a cruising B-52."

I heard a voice laugh sarcastically in the background and assumed it was Hill.

I warned, "Director Collins?"

"Yes, Mr. O'Sheen?" She was answering me by my manner of address.

I was becoming more impressed with her. "Minimal inclusion at your end is a must. You have a mole at a very high level."

Abdul severed the connection.

I immediately stood up, turned, and hugged my son.

***

Mohammed jealously watched Jody's loving reaction to his father's embrace; the reaction that he never was afforded the opportunity to present to his father, because Pat O'Sheen had killed his father. And now, Abdul suddenly trusted the man who Mohammed's grandfather trained him to hate his whole life. Despite his grandfather's retraction of the fatwa, Mohammed's reputation had been damaged at the two failed attempts against the O'Sheens.

Mohammed was glad that he has never been asked to share his opinion on destroying the hologram shipment. *He never had to lie.*

***

I watched and listened while Abdul made his contacts. I was impressed even though Abdul only allowed me to listen to one side of the conversations.

Abdul had to suspect that I could interpret all the different dialects that he used as he contacted one individual after another in quick succession.

When Abdul finished, the five of us sat down to formulate a plan. A sixth man stood watch over us with the Uzi aimed in my general direction.

I asked Abdul where the bathroom was located. I looked at Abdul in a way that caused Abdul to concede that he needed to relieve his bladder, too. In a short minute while peeing together into a toilet, I relayed my concern to Abdul, and a plan to test Mohammed's loyalty was quickly formulated before we left the bathroom.

When I walked back into the room, Michelle was talking with Jody—they were laughing. She looked over and smiled at me. *She looked as gorgeous as ever.*

The next morning, everyone left the chalet. Abdul and his bodyguard went with Jody, Brendan, and me.

I called Robby Clark who was guarding the family and updated him on the situation, and I told him to remove the restrictive codes from the family.

I told Robby, "Tell Dale and Lacy that Brendan and I are with Jody. Tell her we have to help Jody's abductors with a project before we are all free and clear, and that the project shouldn't take more than a week."

Chapter 41
Do or Die

Three four-wheel, all-terrain vehicles (ATVs) crested the top of the hill overlooking Khyber Pass, the mountain pass utilized by most of the traffic that traveled over the mountains between Pakistan and Afghanistan. Jody and Brendan rode together. I was in the second four-wheeler, with an Uzi aimed slightly toward me by Abdul's henchman. Abdul followed in the third four-wheeler accompanied by a small, strange, elderly man. We stopped near the edge of a cliff that overlooked the road through the Khyber Pass. We were about 600 feet away and 300 feet above the pass: Close enough for the hand-held laser targeting devise that we had acquired from the U.S. Army in Kabul, Afghanistan to guide a cruise missile or a smart bomb. Abdul had found a good spot to carry out our plan. The mountain air was cold despite the fact that summer was approaching.

Abdul and I made separate phone calls simultaneously.

I finished my call first and turned to Brendan and Jody, "No B-52 air support backup with smart bombs is available in our time-frame. They will commit to only one cruise missile, and they need a ten-minute launch notice. The cruise missile's arrival to our location will take four minutes and twenty-seven seconds after its launch."

Brendan said, "The military is not taking this threat seriously."

Jody understood the situation, grabbed a set of binoculars, and ran to the edge of the steep slope overlooking the pass. He prostrated his body on the ground with his stomach planted on the perch as he starting scanning the road below. He panned the binoculars to the right, scanning down the curvy road where he knew their target had to make its final approach up the steep climb on the road to the mountain pass. From his vantage point he could identify three exposed areas on the Pakistan side of the border, and he saw an easily identifiable large truck at the furthest bend of the steeply ascending two-lane highway. He clicked the timer on his wristwatch.

Abdul finally got off of his sat phone. He looked at me questioningly while gesturing with his right thumb toward Jody.

I explained the limited resources available and the seemingly impossible timing of hitting the ascending vehicle with a cruise missile that can't arrive until fourteen minutes after we spot the vehicles. When Abdul turned to approach Jody, I restrained him with a firm grip on his upper left arm. Abdul turned abruptly toward me, and the ever alert Arab guard raised his Uzi toward me. Abdul took quick look into my eyes and raised his hand toward his guard in a demand for restraint.

I explained, "Jody is trying to work out the timing for the American cruise missile launch. Don't interrupt him. We need to sit down and discuss our next moves if the missile doesn't destroy the target."

Abdul disengaged from Pat's grip, looked at his little man still sitting in the ATV, and motioned for him to pull his ATV into position for a meeting. The old Arab did as directed. I realized that I had never heard the little man speak. I had seen Abdul speak to him, but I never saw the man respond verbally.

Abdul spoke to the man in Arabic and related the situation that I had just disclosed. The man nodded without speaking.

I considered that the man's tongue might have been cut out. That wasn't an unusual punishment under Muslim Sharia Law. *But who was he? Why had Abdul brought him on this critical mission?*

Abdul switched to the seventh century Arabic of the Koran; the one still used by some Sunni Moslems in Saudi Arabia, the dialect that all Muslims practice before their pilgrimage to Mecca, and the dialect used during their five daily prayers that I had prayed many times in mosques while working in Muslim countries.

The small man suddenly went into a fast diatribe in the old Arabic. I was only able to get the gist of the conversation. When I learned Spanish in Spain, I experienced the same difficulties in interpreting the fast paced, colloquial Spanish dialect in Mexico City. But I interpreted enough to understand why Abdul had brought this quiet old man on this mission. Abdul was still a very religious man. I understood Abdul's ultimate question to his Imam, *Was he interfering with Allah's will on this mission?*

The old man looked into my eyes for over ten seconds before starting to respond to Abdul's question. But Jody ran up to our little group and interrupted. "Dad, we have a two minute impact window based on the ten minute warning time required for the cruise missile launch and the missiles four minute travel time. The target vehicles will be vulnerable about 14 to 16 minutes after the vehicle comes into sight on the furthest curve, depending on the speed of the vehicle. Your laser guiding devise can cover about 1200 feet of the highway. Any interruption in traffic flow during the four minutes after the missile launch would force us to have to choose an alternate target."

I watched Abdul's old friend's reaction. Surprisingly, in broken English, he asked Jody, "Would the alternate target injure innocent civilians?"

Jody looked at me rather than the small Arab, "Only if they are in the remote place where falling debris from the mountain across the pass would hit them. They would have to be on foot in a very unlikely place."

Abdul smiled and turn toward his most trusted Imam and waited for his instruction.

The Imam looked intensely into my eyes again and I understood. Abdul was working with American Christians to stop a shipment of weapons to Muslims who would use them to kill infidel American soldiers—soldiers who had invaded Muslim territory: *a hard sell to an Imam.*

The Imam stated in a slow, clear, modern Arabic dialect, "The father and son have Allah's acceptance in their eyes. The son has Allah in his heart. Abdul, your mission has Allah's support."

Abdul didn't pump his fist in the air physically in triumph, but I sensed him doing it emotionally.

Two hours later, Abdul took a call and informed us the two trucks hauling the shipment were passing through Peshawar, the town on the highway at the base of the Khyber mountains.

It wouldn't be long now. Pat's heartbeat increased. He silently said a short prayer asking God to take care of Dale and his kids if he didn't survive. If the cruise missile wasn't effective, he was prepared to drive an ATV off the hill and attack the trucks alone.

When the shipment appeared on the farthest curve, Abdul pointed out the target vehicle. It was a typical USA-styled Army personnel carrier: a large cab with a flatbed truck covered with canvas tightly pulled over arching metal rails. It could have been mistaken as American military except for the color of the large cab: bright yellow—the same color as the hologram belts. A second identical vehicle followed with four other vehicles separating it from the first yellow truck. The first truck was slowing the traffic behind it, indicating that it was carrying the heavy load of the hologram belts.

Abdul looked through his binoculars and announced, "Mohammed gave me the number of the vehicle. The second truck is carrying the belts."

Jody started the timer on his wristwatch, and started the countdown. The silence on the hill overlooking the pass was deafening.

Jody announced. "Target arrival in about fifteen minutes,"

I hit redial on my sat phone and informed the army captain to prepare to launch the cruise missile in about eleven minutes.

Nine minutes later, Jody had calculated the accent rate, "Two minutes to launch,"

I informed my military contact of the status.

Jody announced, "Thirty seconds."

I relayed the timing.

Jody: "Ten, nine, eight . . . three, two, one, launch."

After I gave the launch command, I approached the hillside with the laser. Abdul was watching intently. This technology was above his experience level. Brendan approached me, reached out his hand for the laser rifle, and I handed it to him without hesitation. I whispered to him to target the front truck, not the second that Abdul identified.

Abdul objected when I handed the laser rifle to Brendan, but I assured him of Brendan's skills. I sat down in one of the ATV's and drove it closer to the crest of the hill giving me a view of the road below. Abdul walked up and sat down next to me in the ATV.

Brendan kept the laser targeted on the back canvas of the front vehicle. A minute later we heard the cruise missile fly very low over our heads, and a second later it exploded into the front truck. Abdul turned to me, "That was the wrong truck."

I aggressively pulled the Sig-Sauer pistol from Abdul's belt, knocked him off the ATV with my shoulder and hip, and sped off the mountain.

Brendan anticipated my move, and he slammed into the guard and ripped the Uzi from him. He aimed it at Abdul. Everyone froze. Jody grabbed a grenade from the guard's belt and held it aloft while jumping into the driver's seat of the closest ATV. Jody accelerated off the mountain after Brendan jumped into the ATV next to him.

***

Abdul wasn't surprised by Pat's move. He suspected that Pat didn't trust him, and he knew for sure that Pat didn't trust Mohammed. He looked down at the road and understood why Pat targeted the first truck instead of the second: the road was blocked and Pat was going to attack the second truck by himself.

When his guard pulled out a pistol, Abdul raised his hand to prevent retaliation against Jody and Brendan as they sped over the crest of the mountain following Pat. Abdul knew that he had chosen his accomplices well—even though they had started out as unwilling accomplices.

***

Brendan held on tightly as Jody sped down the mountain trail in pursuit of his dad. He warned, "You will never catch him."

"Ha! Hold on." Jody turned hard left, leaving the trail and headed in a suicidal path straight down the steep mountainside.

Brendan's head hit the roof twice before Jody rejoined the trail. He was about to chastise Jody, but when he looked over at him, he saw that winner's concentration in his eyes. His eyes had the fire that he had seen so many times in Jody's father. It was the look of concentration of exceptional winners able to sink the winning twelve-foot putt on the 18th hole to win a major PGA event, or the look in the eyes of a college guard shooting two free throws to win the NCAA championship: no hint of fear, no thought of failure; just total concentration. Holding on tightly, Brendan's fear of a fatal crash retreated.

They had narrowed Pat's lead to one hundred yards when Pat slid his 4-wheeler to a stop sixty feet from the solid row of traffic that was blocked behind the truck destroyed by the cruise missile. Before they caught up with Pat, he sped forward without hearing Jody's ATV above the roar of his own four-wheeler engine. Jody didn't follow his dad. Instead, he swerved to the right and approached the swale behind the second truck, expertly drove to the bottom of the deep swale by the road, and slowed the ATV twenty feet behind the undamaged truck. He jumped out while the ATV was it was still moving.

***

The two men in the yellow cab of the second truck saw me coming, grabbed their weapons, and exited the cab. I accelerated to full speed into the roadside swale. Knowing that the ATV would go airborne when it rose up the other side to the edge of the road, I slid off the back just before it crested the top of the slope. The driver of the truck instinctively fired his Uzi at the unoccupied ATV before it slammed into him, fatally smashing him against the metal frame of the cab.

Somewhat skinned-up, I glanced to my right and saw Jody expertly maneuver his four-wheeler into the swale and heard a barrage from Brendan's automatic weapon. I rotated and shot the man from the passenger seat on the bridge of his nose with Abdul's Sig Sauer as he rounded the front hood of the truck firing his Uzi wildly. I turned back in time to see Jody throw something into the cargo hold of the truck and heard him yell, **"Fire in the hole."** I somersaulted down the embankment, proud of my son in what may be the last few seconds of our lives. I hit my head on something hard and apparently lost consciousness. *I had a vision of Saint Peter meeting Jody and me at the pearly gates. Jody was welcomed into heaven. I was being sent straight to hell. Jody grabbed me before I fell into the abyss. Saint Peter advised Jody to let me go, but he refused, telling Saint Peter, "I'll go to hell with him." When Jody started sliding with me into the abyss, Saint Peter* *wasn't sure what he should do. He knew he couldn't let Jody go to hell. So he grabbed us and let both of us enter into heaven.*

***

Brendan saw a man stick a gun barrel through the slit in the canvas at the back of the truck and he fired the stolen Uzi at the back of the canvassed-covered bed. Jody had left the ATV so quickly that he was almost to the back of the truck. Brendan had to stop firing, even though he wasn't sure that more men weren't stationed as guards in the truck bed. He watched Jody pull back the slit in the canvas and toss the grenade inside and heard him shout, **"Fire in the hole."**

Brendan dove to ground, using the four-wheeler for meager cover and cupped the palm of his hands over his ears, not for fear of the percussion from the grenade, but for the massive explosion that would ensue if the two-thousand hologram belts filled with explosives were inside.

***

From Abdul's viewpoint on the crest of the mountain, he watched the whole scene as Jody pursued his dad down the mountain. At least two times he thought that Jody had lost control of his ATV, which would probably have killed him and Brendan if they tumbled in the four-wheeler down the steep mountainside. Pat was almost to the bottom and would confirm whether the missile had hit the right target. Abdul did not have to encourage Pat to risk his life. If the cruise missile had hit the wrong truck, Pat would probably die on the road below, but Abdul would have the needed knowledge and would follow Pat's instructions to make another attempt to stop the shipment. Hopefully, the desired target had been destroyed. Losing Jody and Brendan was not important: collateral damage.

Abdul took a deep breath realizing that he had become attached to Jody. He was a lot more than just collateral damage.

Abdul was handed a camera with a zoom lens as he saw Jody catching up to Pat at the bottom of the mountain. When Pat stopped and then drove forward again, Jody drove his ATV to the right instead of following Pat. He watched Pat make a suicidal run toward the second truck. He was distracted, while putting the camera to his eyes and zooming in. Pat was sprawled on the ground, as his ATV crashed into the driver of the truck smashing the driver into the cab of the truck. Pat shot the other man who exited the cab of the truck on the passenger side. He panned the camera to the right and saw Jody toss the grenade he had stolen from his guard into the back of the second truck. The initial explosion and the many subsequent explosions confirmed that Mohammed had given them the right truck, unless the load had been split between the two vehicles, which made perfect sense. Pat and Jody had accomplished the major objective. The belt shipment was destroyed. But the O'Sheens could not have survived their heroic accomplishment. The older O'Sheen was fearless. Jody just proved that he had his dad's courage.

Abdul watched the scene for another few minutes and was able to hear explosion after explosion. Smoke obliterated the whole scene. He turned away dismayed. Pat and Jody O'Sheen had proven to be great allies. Abdul and his two friends, the old Imam and his most trusted guard rode the only remaining ATV away from the scene.

Abdul marveled at Pat O'Sheen's commitment to Christianity and how easily he made the decision to sacrifice his life for American soldiers. He asked his Imam for an explanation.

The Imam gave him a shocking answer. "Allah knows those who have not been trained in the teaching of the Koran but still have the love of Allah in their hearts. O'Sheen and his son's hearts were forged by God Almighty (the Christian style of referring to Allah). The O'Sheens' work for Allah has not yet been completed."

The last statement by his imam perplexed Abdul. "The O'Sheens died today. In what way can they serve Allah now?"

"Your analysis is premature. Allah will be well served by the O'Sheens in the future. He didn't allow them to acquire their special skills for this mission alone. What you and the O'Sheens have accomplished this day will be recorded in the 'Book of Life' (another Christian term). I thank you for allowing me to witness their incredible accomplishment."

Chapter 42
Survival?

The initial explosion was deafening, but not devastating, and was followed by sequential smaller blasts that lasted for more than three minutes. A West Virginia coal-mine blaster could not have timed the explosive charges to detonate in a more controlled sequence. The belts must have been packaged like detonators in boxes classified "Explosives 1.4" in America, the packaging designed to prevent a mass detonation. Unfortunately, unlike a certified blaster in West Virginia, staying around to ascertain that all charges had detonated was not an option.

Brendan was half-deaf following the blast. His attempt to cover his ears fell short and only accentuated the blast into his hand-cupped ears. He retrieved the Uzi and ran to where he thought Jody might be, and was not expecting a pleasant result. The smoke was so thick that he could only see a few feet in front of him. He gasped gratefully when he found Jody alive and struggling up to his feet. He helped him back to the ATV. Brendan drove the ATV down the swale next to the road towards Pat's last visible location, bouncing almost uncontrollably through the still blinding smoke.

***

I regained consciousness, struggled to my feet, heard the ATV approaching, and made my way toward the noise. Before Brendan and Jody saw me, I jumped on the back of the four-wheeler and shouted, **"Let's get out of here."**

Jody and Brendan simultaneously cheered loudly.

Brendan took a hard left up the slope of the swale away from the road. He proceeded at a very slow pace through the thick smoke, because he remembered the roughness of the terrain and did not want to drive into a ravine and kill them all: particularly after all of them amazing survived the explosions. The fact they were all alive was unbelievable. The visibility improved the further he got away from the road. Brendan found the trail and started up the mountain.

I had him stop near the crest of the high slope, jumped off the back of the four-wheeler, and ran toward the crest with Abdul's pistol in my hand.

Brendan engaged the safety brake, grabbed the Uzi, and followed. He lay down next to me near the crest of the hill.

It was apparent that Abdul had abandoned the position. We stood up together and slowly walked over the crest.

Jody slid over to the driver's seat of the ATV, released the brake, and drove to the top of the mountain.

Once I was comfortable with the situation, I approached Jody in the four-wheeler smiling. My smile didn't last long.

Jody looked down following my stare and realized that the pants leg on his left thigh was covered with blood. He turned his left forearm up and for the first time noticed a four-inch long bleeding gash. He must have hit a sharp rock on the ground when he dove down the embankment after he yelled "Fire in the hole."

I saw more blood on the back collar of Jody's shirt and ran behind him. The back of Jody's head was splintered with debris that caused dozens of small puncture wounds. The back of his shirt was shredded, exposing small blood spots similar to someone who had been flogged with his shirt on.

I returned to the side of the vehicle, grabbed Jody's hand and examined the wound on his left forearm again and exclaimed, "None of your wounds are life threatening."

Brendan retrieved a first aid kit from the ATV.

I looked into Jody's intense eyes and admired his courage to follow me off the hill. I understood how Jody's adrenaline was blocking out the pain. I had been there many times before.

After bandaging Jody's more serious wounds, Brendan bandaged the back of my head. We retraced our inward journey on the ATV back to the road. We were not expecting any form of transportation to be waiting. As expected, the truck and trailer that we used to haul the ATV's to the site were gone.

An old, ragtop jeep with the top down sat next to the road. Brendan examined it to make sure it wasn't rigged with explosives, while I jumped into the driver's seat to look under the dash to see how to hot-wire the ignition. Jody jumped in the passenger door, reached up and lowered the driver's sun-visor. An ignition key fell in my lap. I looked over at Jody and saw a smile beaming on his face.

Apparently, Abdul had left the vehicle in hopes that one or more of our group had survived the truck explosion.

Brendan finished inspecting the jeep, nodded to me, and jumped over the side and into the back seat as I turned the key in the ignition. To all our surprise, the jeep started. I pulled out onto the narrow road.

Jody declared, "Dad, Abdul was never a threat. Why did you knock him off the ATV and go flying off the mountain like that?"

I attempted to respond calmly, "There were hologram belts in the second truck. If I hadn't gone off the hill, American service men would start dying in Afghanistan within a week."

Jody said a bit too challengingly, "**Are you sure? We had a backup plan.**"

I barked back, "**I was not going to take that chance. My life is not worth the life of one volunteer American soldier in Afghanistan.**

***

The forcefulness of his dad's response made Jody recoil . . . and suddenly he understood. His dad had been risking his life for men in uniform for all of his adult life. His dad hadn't considered that he and Brendan might follow him off the hill.

Jody had learned over the past few weeks that his dad didn't worry about his own safety. He was going to do the right thing: *damn the personal consequences.* When Jody saw his dad riding the ATV off the mountain, he saw how unselfishly he made decisions to risk his life for American troops. Jody had reacted with courage to protect his dad, not American soldiers that he didn't know. As his dad drove toward Kabul, Afghanistan, Jody wondered if his dad would have succeeded without his and Bredan's help: *Maybe*! *He had no doubt that his dad wasn't afraid to die trying.*

He had never personally witnessed his dad react in a life-threatening situation before. He had heard tales during his years in the CIA—incredible tales about an agent code-named "Coyote" that now took on believable reality. He recalled Brendan's narration of his first encounter with his dad, and his dad's self-sacrificing action against the overwhelming enemy force to save Brendan's platoon against the FARC rebel forces in Columbia. His dad had volunteered to rescue two Exxon employees held hostage for ransom by the rebel army. One of the hostages was his dad's commanding officer in Vietnam. For the first time, Jody saw in-person how his dad reacted in a "must do" crisis by zoning into another mental state to accomplish a seemingly impossible mission. When Jody looked into the back seat after his reverie, he saw Brendan looking at him with a knowing look in his eyes: as if Brendan had read his mind. Brendan didn't smile: he just gave Jody a slight nod.

Jody would never forget his dad's boisterous rebuke: ***I wasn't going to take that chance,*** or the self-sacrificing courage and determination he had witnessed in his dad that day.

Chapter 43
Traitorous

Three hours later, we boarded our chartered plane in Kabul, Afghanistan. The chief pilot scanned his three passengers. "Are you all alright?" The three were covered in soot and blood. Should I call paramedics?

Pat said, "No Cliff. We survived. Fly us to Tel Aviv, Israel."

After thirty minutes of preparation and the filing of flight plans, the plane was airborne. I noticed Jody's sigh of relief.

I called Robby and told him to put Dale back onto Code 3. I wasn't worried about Abdul. I was worried about the people behind the conspiracy when they learned that we destroyed the hologram shipment.

I pretended to sleep, and as soon the exhausted Jody and Brendan were in a deep sleep. I retreated to the back of the cabin and made three short calls on my satellite phone.

When we landed in Tel Aviv, I ordered everyone to stay in the plane. I instructed the pilots to register a flight plan for home n Birmingham. I lowered the stairs and approached the small private plane terminal. Instead of going to the terminal door, I approached an "Employees Only" door and knocked in an unusual sequence. The door opened and I entered. Twenty minutes later, I reentered the plane and instructed the pilots to get us to Birmingham.

Jody wondered who his dad had met with, "You didn't give away any government secrets did you?"

I feigned astonishment, "We're civilians. Do we know any government secrets?"

We both laughed nervously.

Brendan joined the nervous laughter, but he understood that if the Muslims had more access to hologram belts, the belts would soon be turned against Israel. He knew that Pat had risked a life sentence in prison by his top-secret disclosure to the Israelis. He prayed that Pat's trust in his Israeli Mossad contact would never be betrayed.

Jody understood why his dad was warning the Israelis. Based on recent events, his dad's mistrust of the CIA and the American government was understandable. Many Americans mistrusted the placating Washington politicians who controlled and thwarted the CIA's effectiveness. The small country of Israel had overcome many military campaigns attempting to "drive them into the sea". Their survival was accomplished with the help of American warfare technology and with the information provided by perhaps the most effective intelligence organization in the world, the Israeli Mossad. The present American government would never admit the security leak of the hologram belt technology, and therefore would not warn Israel of the danger. He assumed his dad had just corrected that political error. He knew that his dad would never admit that to anyone.

When Jody fell asleep again, I asked Brendan, "Why did you bring Jody off the mountain with you."

Brendan snorted a laugh. "I had a hard time jumping on the ATV as he followed you off the mountain. At least twice I thought he was going to kill us driving down the mountain in pursuit of you." Brendan took a deep breath and exhaled to emphasize his point. "Pat, he operates with abandon just like you. Your talents are different, but he has your courage."

I smiled and my eyes moistened as pride in my youngest son welled up.

Chapter 44
Bonding

Dale listened on the secure phone and looked at Lacy while Pat relayed the only message that would relieve them. She blurted out to Lacy, "Jody, Pat, and Brendan are in a jet on their way home."

Dale listened to Pat's hurried instructions and stopped him, knowing that he was about to cut the connection. "Lacy needs to hear Jody's voice."

I said, "Dale, he is exhausted and asleep." But then I remembered Lacy's agony on the floor in Jody's computer room. "Hold on."

Dale explained Jody's exhaustion to Lacy. A minute later, I told Dale to put Lacy on the phone.

Lacy queried, "Jody?" She listened patiently for a response.

She heard Jody's groggy voice, "Heloooo!"

Dale saw the tears stream down both of Lacy's cheeks, but her voice was steady.

"Jody, are you all right?" They talked for less than a minute before Lacy handed the receiver back to Dale. Dale put her ear to the phone and realized that the phone connection had been cut, which meant that Pat was still seriously worried about security.

Lacy, recovering from her zombie mental state, walked back to the couch and flopped down. Dale sat down next to her and took one of Lacy's half-lifeless hands between her two palms. She rubbed the back of Lacy's cold hand, and Lacy's quiet tears turned into relieved sobs. Dale reached for her at the same time that Lacy turned to tuck her forehead into the crook of Dale's neck. When she brought herself under control in Dale's loving arms, Lacy felt a big teardrop land heavily on her bare arm. She pulled back and looked at Dale's face. The Queen had her eyes closed and tears streamed down her face as she uncharacteristically let down her strong-willed guard. Lacy laid her cheek on Dale's shoulder again and squeezed her arms around Dale. She heard Dale say "Thank you, Lord" and felt wrenching sobs emanating from the invincible Queen. Lacy hugged her more tightly; realizing that although she had almost lost a fiancé, Dale had almost lost a man that she had adored for over thirty years, and her baby: her youngest child. Lacy sensed the stress draining from Dale in their embrace.

***

Lacy had always been intimidated by Jody's parents and was warned by her parents of their concerns about Pat O'Sheen's secret government background. She was concerned about his background too, and when the CIA hired Jody, she left Birmingham for Oklahoma to wash Jody from her mind with hope to start a new life. She was visiting her parents in Alabama a few years later and ran into Jody, who had traveled from Virginia to visit his parents. The fire in her for Jody erupted, and she moved back to Alabama.

When Jody resigned from the CIA and joined his dad in the new business to protect high profile clients—clients who could not avoid the public without ruining their careers, she still foresaw perils in her future life with Jody. Her divorced parents agreed with her concerns.

Jody presented her with an engagement ring one evening and asked her to marry him. She hated to hurt him, but she just wasn't ready.

After Jody had a very calm year in his new celebrity protection business, Lacy, during a romantic night together at his house, asked him if he still had the engagement ring.

She watched Jody's sleepy eyes widen and brighten up the dim room, and she watched his naked body jump athletically from the bed, turned on the lamp on the night stand, and yank open the top drawer. He retrieved a small box, knelt down beside the bed as he opened the velvet-covered box exposing the ring, and again asked, "Lacy, will you marry me?"

She giggled and said, "Yes."

But month's later, Jody went to Paris with his dad to protect the young singer, Keisha Steele, and almost lost his life. All of the previous warnings from her parents were inflamed and her past fears crystallized again. Jody was like his dad, whom she knew Jody idolized.

Jody's dad, Pat, was likable, but it was difficult to have a meaningful conversation with him. He never shared any personal information. His mom was even more intimidating. *Dale thought that no woman would ever be good enough for her youngest son.*

Before the kidnapping, Lacy had only been in the O'Sheen house once when the "Codes" were called. She recoiled at the names, "Queen and King". The reaction by everyone was surreal . . . movie style. The paranoia caused her to withdraw from Jody again. But her love and passion always brought her back to Jody. She knew that there were very few men like Jody in the world. But her parents were right: his uniqueness was a warning sign. They warned that he was too much like his dad, and that Jody would expect her to be like his mother.

She remembered the comfort that Jody's dad gave her while picking her up off the floor in Jody's house while the computer screen flashed the kidnapper's telephone number. And she remembered his promise that Jody would be alright.

That statement was said with such confidence that her tears had stopped. She remembered challenging Jody's dad to fulfill his promise.

Now her man was coming home. Jody's incredible dad had fulfilled his promise. And the "Queen" was no longer intimidating. Instead, she had shared her vulnerability. Lacy didn't know the whole background, but the "King and Queen" were still together after being married for over thirty years, and they had raised three great kids—and she no longer doubted that Jody's dad knew how to protect the family.

She made a decision: *I am going to marry their baby boy and join the family: marry* **my Jody,** *and give Dale grandchildren for her to dote over.*

Chapter 45
Boom

I was pleased that Jody slept most of the way home from Israel. The drone of the jet engines that would normally allow me to catch up on lost sleep drove me into deep analytical thought; the type of thought that grabs the mind, envelops it, and refuses to let go. My past had caught up with me and was endangering my family. I could have succeeded as a used car salesman and no one would have noticed my "special" talents. Instead, I had honed my unique talents to feed my ego, and I rationalized my absence from important family events to help my government. Dale had raised three great kids.

I almost lost Jody three times in the last few weeks: all because of my past. I also knew that the success in stopping the hologram plot made me a bigger, more threatening target to the manipulating, high-level controllers behind the hologram conspiracy.

When we stopped in Lisbon, Portugal to refuel, I left the plane and walked around the tarmac deep in thought. During my second trip around the plane, I noticed Brendan sitting on the top step of the plane's stairs descending down to the concrete tarmac. I noticed him, because he was looking through the powerful scope of his sniper rifle, panning the surrounding area—always watching my back. *What a great friend.*

I climbed the stairs, smiled my appreciation, and reentered the plane.

As the plane took off, I continued my analysis, replaying every conversation in my head. The first attack in Paris, the meeting at CIA headquarters in Langley, the double-cross at CIA's Paris safe house, the attack on the way home from the restaurant in Birmingham, Jody's kidnapping, the meeting with Abdul, Jody's release, the subsequent maneuvers at the Pakistan border, and the jeep awaiting them during their retreat. I knew that I was the cause of it all. But how could I get out from under my past?

Brendan cleared his throat and got my attention, "Pat, do you recall why I was not able to be with you in Paris during the second attack against you?"

I recognized Brendan's anxiety, "Your wife was in a car accident, and she was pregnant. Afterward, you told me there were no complications. Has something changed?"

"No." Brendan declared, "But who are these people that would hurt my family to keep me from coming to Paris to help protect you."

Brendan was telling me that he no longer believed that his families automobile crash was an accident. I had not previously considered that possibility.

After our plane landed in Birmingham, I walked through the front door of my house that was lowered to Code 3. Dale and Lacy were waiting in the hallway when Brendan and I entered the house.

Lacy lunged into my filthy arms first and said, "I had to stay here to thank you for honoring your promise to return Jody to me. Where is he?"

I hugged Lacy a little more than I normally would, grabbed her shoulders, and held her at arm's length. "He is a lot grubbier than I am, and has more, smaller non-threatening injuries than I do. He wanted to clean up before seeing you and his mother."

Lacy was returning my eye piercing stare as I warned, "Lacy, you must keep your knowledge of this incident inside my family. Share it with no one—not even your family. Do you understand?"

Lacy nodded, hugged me again, hugged Dale, and ran out the back door giddy.

When she left, Dale approached me. We held each other for a long time. I knew she was elated at Jody's safe return. She was used to my safe return.

I asked her, "Is it five o'clock yet?"

She smiled and replied, "Its five o'clock somewhere."

We moved to the kitchen where she made us each a Bloody Mary. She handed me my drink, a cigar, and told me to go sit on the back porch and said that she would join me in a minute.

I exited the back door and stood at the top of the stairs. I contently smiled at the familiar surroundings of my back yard that I wasn't sure that I would ever see again when I drove off the hill at the Khyber Pass, and was taking a sip of my drink when an explosion blew me off the back deck catapulting me onto the manicured grass in the back yard. I used the strength of my arms to roll across the yard to prevent a debilitating injury.

Chapter 46
Miracle

Brendan was still in front of the house updating Robby on our trip to Afghanistan before returning to his own family when the explosion rocked the whole neighborhood. Brendan and Robby circled the house in opposite directions. Brendan reached the back of the house at the same time that Jody ran from the trail through the woods wearing nothing but his underwear boxer shorts, half his face was still covered with shaving cream. His Sig Sauer pistol was in his right hand. Brendan heard Lacy shouting Jody's name as she tried unsuccessfully to keep up with him.

Lacy was restrained by Robby at the edge of the woods. Surveying the damage to the house, Lacy fell down on her knees praying for a miracle. The happiest day of her life turned into her darkest nightmare in mere minutes.

Jody and Brendan ran into the back of the house. Brendan cautiously entered the house from the back deck first, expecting the worst. "Oh my god." He stopped in his tracks.

Jody slid past Brendan and gasped while dreadful tears were rolling down from his angry eyes.

***

I had groggily risen to my feet from the grass, realizing that my house had just exploded. I saw a piece of the back door sticking through my left triceps. My eardrums were rebelling against all sound. I considered pulling the piercing wood out of my arm but didn't waste the time, because I was worried about Dale. I ran to find Dale, knowing in my aching heart that where we had parted in the kitchen that Dale could not have survived the blast. I knew that Jody and Brendan would have heard the blast, and that Robby was on guard somewhere up-front. When

I entered what was once the back door, the smoke was still thick in the room. I carefully took two steps into the room, testing each step carefully on the splintered floor. I saw Dale after a godly inspired breeze blew though the large gaping hole in the left side of the kitchen. Her body was crouched awkwardly on the floor, hunched over on the right side of kitchen, away from the large blast hole in the left side of the house. Most likely she had been blown to that position. Tears were streaming down my face.

As I carefully circled around to my right, I saw a huge gash on the side of Dale's head and the double compound fracture of her left forearm. One of the broken bones on her forearm was protruding from her skin.

As I got closer, I saw our limp and lifeless cocker spaniel, Shadow, in Dale's bloody lap. I slowed knowing that I wasn't prepared for this. I sighed a deep breath to gain control. She would be proud that she was able to hold Shadow in their deaths.

I grabbed a towel from the floor that must have been blown out of a kitchen cabinet, wiped tears from my eyes, and sat cross-legged in front of Dale. I jerked in surprise when she moved.

She slowly raised her head and looked up into my tear-filled eyes. Her face was covered with blood. We leaned into each other before both of our cries began to wail uncontrollably.

Dale managed between sobs. "I went to the bathroom."

I realized that she must have shut the bathroom door. Her weak bladder had saved her life. The bathroom door had been blown into the small bathroom and probably caused her injuries.

She screamed almost hysterically. **"They killed Shadow. I want you to kill the bastards**."

I screamed back, assuming her hearing was impaired like mine. **"I will. I promise."**

***

They had not heard Jody's approach: *ear damage from the blast.* Jody slowly knelt down beside them. He saw the blood running down his mother's face and onto her blouse. Through the smoke, he still wasn't sure if she was alive. He put a hand on both of his parent's shoulders.

When his mom looked up at him, he threw an arm around both of his parents' necks and pulled their heads against his bare shoulders while wailing some sentiments that were unintelligible to his deafened parents.

He grabbed the towel from his dad's hands and applied pressure to the gash in his mother's head and looked with concern at the board penetrating his dad's left arm.

Brendan tried to report the status, but his voice failed him. He swallowed several times, but got that strange squeaking sound in his throat and ears that always accompanies swallowing during emotional moments. He finally spat it out, "The King and Queen are nine-one-zero." The sirens were already approaching when he finished his report. Robby must have called nine-one-one immediately. He noticed all the blood as he walked past the three people on the floor whom he loved so much. He overcame the impulse to kneel down and gather the three of them into his protective arms, and he hurried to unlock and open the front door.

Paramedics were already approaching the door with large medical cases in their hands when he opened it. Paramedics could do more now to save a life than a doctor could decades ago with his little black bag.

Another ambulance arrived, and the paramedics brought two gurneys into the house as one paramedic put a large gauze pad on Dale's head and wrapped tape around it.

Dale looked at the gurneys and yelled, **"We don't need those."**

The head paramedic looked at me and insisted, "Your wife is not walking out of here. You shouldn't walk out either." Pat was able to read his lips.

I looked at Dale as she yelled, **"My husband and I are walking out of here together. You can take over after we are in the ambulance."**

"I can't allow that." The paramedic turned to one of his aides and told him to call the Sheriff.

Sheriff Bo Hannon entered the room saying in his usually calm voice, "Calling me won't be necessary." He looked at the blood covering Dale and Pat. He cursed under his breath and said loudly, **"Pat, you should follow their medical advice."**

I tilted my head toward Dale. Bo looked at her and saw the fiery determination in her eyes. She was determined to walk from the house. Any other option would be too confrontational and would probably be more detrimental to her health. Bo walked over and lifted Dale to her feet.

I stood, shaking off the paramedic that was tending my wounds, and joined my wife at Bo's side. I ordered, **"Bo, I want pictures of Dale and me walking from the front door of the house unassisted."**

Dale looked up at me questioningly.

Bo knew better than to argue with me, and he set up the scene and took the pictures.

The paramedics tried to separate us into the two ambulances. I explained forcefully that I was accompanying my wife. The head paramedic laid Dale on the gurney and started hooking up to plasma IV explaining, "She has lost a lot of blood. Her blood pressure is down and her pulse is too slow." There was no way that the paramedic could know that her pulse had always been slow like her dad's. After the paramedic finished hooking up the IV, he knocked on the front of the care compartment. The ambulance lurched forward, followed by the screech of its siren.

Dale turned her head on the pillow and looked at me. She saw my anguish, and smiled to comfort me—nonverbally telling me that she was going to be alright.

Chapter 47
Betrayal

After my biceps surgery, the doctor told me that the one-inch by half inch wide by ten-inch long splinter from the back door had severed a major artery in my triceps. If I had pulled it out, I would have bled to death in minutes. It also slightly cracked my humerus bone. They stitched three cuts on my back and one small one on the back of my head. They put a large bandage over my burnt right ear.

Our daughter, Mandy, had arrived at the hospital by the time I was stitched up and a plastic, removable cast applied to my left arm. Mandy told me, "Scott is on the way from California," She hugged me carefully, trying not to touch any of my wounds. She asked, "What happened?"

"Mandy, that is long story. I want to get down to Dale's recovery room."

The hospital would not allow me to walk down to Dale's recovery room, so Jody and Mandy pushed me down the hall to the elevator in a wheel chair.

Dale's head required fifteen stitches. An anesthesiologist put her to sleep before applying the stitches, and an orthopedic surgeon reset the two bones in her left forearm and stitched up the top of her forearm where the bone had broken through the skin.

My lifelong friend, Dr. Reymann, arrived and advised me to allow the hospital to keep Dale for observation overnight: that he was expecting that she had a concussion. I knew better based on her clarity during our conversations immediately following the blast. Jody's home would be safer.

Our son, Scott, arrived as we were pulling up to Jody's house. My family helped lay Dale on the guest bed. It was now 1:00 a.m.

I lay down next to her, draping my left arm, cast and all, across her abdomen. Jody turned off the light and left his guest room.

Dale croaked in a soft but upbeat voice, "I love you", before falling into a deep sleep.

Sleep didn't come so easily to me. Tears ran across the bridge of my nose and wet the pillow. My mind couldn't shake the image of finding her on the floor. *I almost lost her.*

Soon exhaustion overtook me, and I fell asleep.

I had a nightmare. *I approached Dale on the floor. She was covered with blood. I sat on the floor in front of her and reached to hug the dead love of my life as tears streamed down my face. When my dead wife's blood covered face looked up at me.* I startled awake. Feeling Dale next to me, I tried to remain calm, and as my mind cleared, I realized that the nightmare actually happened. I started to raise my head when Dale kissed me on the forehead. I tried to sit up too quickly, causing dizziness and nausea, while wondering what time it was.

As if reading my mind, she said, "It's almost ten in the morning. Lie back down with me awhile." Her voice was too calm and soothing. I barely heard her over the ringing in my ears. Somehow our roles were reversed.

I laid my head back down next to her and laid my left arm across her abdomen.

She said, "I lost Shadow" and added slight chuckle, "I was worried that I lost you too." Her voice was strong but wavering.

I admitted, "I was almost sure that I had lost you. I will miss Shadow." I tucked my cheek onto her soft breast for comfort, as a child does to his mother. "I love you, Dale."

"I know," she said supportively and squeezed me.

We held each other for another five minutes before I disengaged and slowly stood up next to the bed, verifying my stability with each move. I walked into Jody's guest bathroom still fully clothed from yesterday and relieved my bladder.

I looked away from the old, pitiful face looking back at me from the mirror. I removed the bandage from my right ear, wet my hair from the faucet and dried it with a towel. I opened a drawer and retrieved a comb, a toothbrush, and toothpaste: Lacy had done a good job stocking Jody's guest bathroom. I had little doubt that Jody had not accomplished the task. If it weren't for Dale, I knew I wouldn't have toothpaste, soap, or towels in an unused bathroom. After finishing my normal morning routine, I looked back into the mirror—not good but less pitiful. My mind was racing too fast to consider a shower or a shave.

I saw my suitcase in the bedroom and changed into shorts and a t-shirt, and threw my bloodied clothes into a wastebasket. I kissed Dale and asked her, "Do you need help getting to the bathroom before I leave the room?"

Dale said, "I'll be alright. I just need some more sleep." She added angrily, **"Find out who did this to us."**

When I entered Jody's computer room, Jody and my son, Scott, were typing on computer keyboards. Brendan noticed me entering the room, and he stood up and hugged me.

I shared hugs with Scott, who graduated from the Air Force Academy and now worked for a private military contractor in California. Scott positioned a chair where I could sit and have the best view of the evidence they had gathered so far.

A very tired Jody turned to me, looked me squarely in the eyes and said too softly, "You're not going to like what we are about to show you."

"What did you say?" I realized that my hearing had not totally recovered from the blast.

Jody nodded to Scott.

Scott said loud enough for me to hear, "This comes from the camera on the front of Jody's house." A picture of a vehicle came up on the screen. My son, Scott, hit the zoom button several times and two faces in the car came into focus.

Jody said, "We are not sure, but we think the one in the back is . . ."

I interrupted, "It's Gene Tanner in the front and CIA Deputy Director Bob Hill seated behind him in the back."

Jody nodded.

Scott advised as he retrieved a different video, "This is from the camera at Robby's house across the street from Jody's." He panned in, reset the angle, and zoomed in on the driver. Jody watched for my reaction.

It was Gene Kamper driving. I couldn't hide my shock.

Jody hesitated before proceeding, "Dad, I'm sorry but we have identified another man in the car that will upset you more than Kamper."

Scott said, "This is from the camera at Brendan's house, diagonally across from the end of the street leading to your cul-de-sac." Scott zoomed in making Gene Kamper's profile clear in the driver's seat and then Scott panned to the man in the back seat.

I exclaimed, "**No way!**"

Scott, the oldest of the O'Sheen children, knew and loved the man on the monitor. He was a long-time family friend. Scott was the only one who defended the man. "Dad this doesn't make sense. Pierre would never betray our family. Why was he even here in the United States?"

I shook my head. I didn't know. But I agreed with Scott that Pierre Boudreaux would never betray us. I said, "Maybe we should get Robby in here to see if he can clarify some of this last video?"

Scott responded, "Before we bring in anyone else, let me present the film to you frame-by-frame." Scott didn't understand how trusted Robby Clark was to our Alabama family and his computer skills.

I could tell that Jody was going to correct his older brother's misconception, so I put a hand on Jody's shoulder affectionately silencing him. I said, "Scott, please proceed from the view of Gene Kamper." I wanted to learn my oldest son's computer skills.

Scott rewound the video at 4x speed, saw what he was looking for and stopped the film. He then fast forwarded at 2x speed and stopped the screen. He looked back at me and asked, "What frame-per-second do you want?"

I was surprised at my son's computer skills and smiled, "Use your best judgment."

Scott hit a key. The video progressed at five frames per second (fps). Everyone in the room watched intently. I looked around the room and realized that no one in the room noticed what I saw.

I had never worked with Scott like this before. "Can you repeat that segment at half that last speed?"

Scott rewound the video and slowed it from five fps to two fps. I saw it more clearly on the slower replay. Brendan looked at me quizzically.

I put my hand on Scott and Jody's shoulders, "Scott, can you play images 1442 to 1482 as still shots one at a time?"

Everyone but Scott looked at me incredulously for providing the frame numbers. Scott cued the film as instructed, and slowed it down to stop frame and played it again, advancing one frame at a time.

Brendan finally saw what I wanted everyone to see.

Brendan turned to me to acknowledge his discovery. I raised my hand to silence him and said, "Play the 41 frames again, Scott. You and Jody have not yet captured the most important aspect of this segment of the video. Manipulate it any way you want, but without your independent confirmation of what I perceived, my analysis is questionable." I caught Brendan's eyes and tilted my head for a meeting outside the room.

When we were alone, I asked my genius friend, "You recognized what I saw in the video. Describe it to me."

"The angle is almost impossible, but Hill had a gun on his lap pointed at Inspector Boudreaux." Brendan added as a compliment, "Your oldest son would be a great asset to our organization. His computer skills are very impressive."

Pat smiled. "Scott and Jody don't know what to look for on the film. Help them see the gun. I need to check on Dale."

I stopped at the top of the stairs and called Kathie Boudreaux in Paris.

When I said hello, she said in French, "What was the emergency? Pierre hasn't called to tell me what's going on."

It took more conversation before I understood that they had received an urgent email from me that begged Pierre to come to Washington, D.C. and that a plane ticket would be waiting for Pierre at the airport in Paris. They tried to call but couldn't get through to Dale or me.

I didn't know what to tell her other than the truth: that I was not the one who sent the email or the ticket. I regretted informing her that I believed that Pierre was being held captive by my enemies to get to me. I promised Kathie that I would get Pierre back to her unharmed.

I asked her to give me all of Pierre's credit card numbers, his visa ID, and his arrival flight information to America.

I walked back to Jody's guest room where Dale was trying unsuccessfully to sleep. I told her about the video, the people in it, and my call to Kathie. "Can I get you a pain pill or help you to the bathroom: anything at all?"

Dale smiled, "I can tell you want to get back to the investigation. I've been to the bathroom. I'm okay . . . just pissed off."

I called Joe Cusimano at his NSA office and told him what had happened, what I wanted, gave him Pierre's credit card numbers, flight information, and returned to Jody's computer room.

Scott turned to me, "I knew that Inspector Boudreaux would never betray us."

Brendan had helped them see the gun. But Brendan wasn't in the room.

"Where is Brendan?"

Jody answered, "He went home to his family."

"Good. He has enough to attend to at home without always being here for me."

Jody asked, "Dad, are you alright? You don't look so good."

I nodded. "I called Joe Cusimano so he can help track down Pierre's credit cards and gave him other methods to track him. I gave him Gene Kamper and Gene Tanner's cell numbers to track. I think I know who I can trust to give me Bob Hill's cell number. With that knowledge we should find their route from here."

Scott voiced his concern, "Dad, that's probably why they brought Pierre here. If you survived the blast, they want you to follow him. It will be a trap."

Jody agreed, "Scott is right. He and I will gather the information, but we won't share it with you unless we are involved in the pursuit."

I smiled and said without arguing, "I understand." I stood up to leave.

Jody jumped to his feet, "Dad, are you sure you are alright?"

"I'm in pain, confused, and tired. Ask me again later."

Chapter 48
A new foe

I called Abdul's number when I left the room. I expected to leave a message when Abdul picked up, "Tell me quickly."

I relayed the bombing of my house; the players involved, and asked Abdul if he had assets near America that could give me backup. I explained that I didn't want to use my assets, because I was afraid that I was up against my own government.

Abdul and I agreed on his fee.

He said, "I'll need two days to set up." He explained that he would relay his status via email and told me what email name to set up.

Abdul volunteered that he didn't yet consider me a friend, but he was happy that I had requested his help. I found out in a later conversation that Abdul relished the thought of striking the forces in America who were plotting against Islam and attacking my family.

Scott and Jody were surprised when I reentered the computer room. I asked Jody if he would set up the email account for me so that Abdul could contact me.

Jody asked suspiciously, "Why Abdul?"

I hedged at first but admitted, "He helped us stop an international catastrophe. My government just blew up my house because I am becoming too much of a threat to expose the conspiracy. I don't want my friends and family assets going up against our government, so I want to have the option to use Abdul's mercenaries."

After Jody set up the email account, I went to the kitchen. Mandy had made turkey sandwiches. I grabbed two sandwiches, two plates and napkins. Dale and I ate leaning on the headboard of the bed. We both took a pain pill and slept most of the afternoon.

We got out of bed, ate dinner with the family, and went to bed early.

Very early the next morning, when I entered the kitchen, I smelled Scott's peculiar smelling coffee brewing. I opened the refrigerator and withdrew a bottle of orange juice, retrieved a small glass from a cabinet, and was pouring my juice when Scott entered the room.

Scott didn't exchange pleasantries. "Cusimano located Pierre. I assume you have a plan to deal with Pierre safely. If it's a trap, I'm sure that you will know what precautions to take. Jody will be furious at me for not telling him this first. But it has to be your decision how to proceed.

"Jody told me about his kidnapping, and about Brendan helping y'all stop a shipment of weapons into Afghanistan.

"Dad, your covert career is endangering our family. You need to handle this without risking Jody's life."

I nodded and could tell that Scott worried that he might be sacrificing my life for the wellbeing of the rest of the family. I thanked him for his good judgment in understanding that I had to do this alone.

Scott gave me the information that Joe Cusimano relayed knowing that Jody and his mom would chastise him. I started to leave the room, but I turned back and hugged him. He lovingly returned the hug.

The next afternoon, I entered the lobby of a Days Inn an hour north of Charlotte, NC, off an exit on I-77 close to the Virginia border. I walked up the stairs to the second floor. The site was remote: perfect for an attack against me. I walked down the hallway with my Glock 22 held close to my right thigh. I used the cast on my left arm to knock on the door of Room 201, which was at the end of the hallway and next to a door with outside stairs: *Easy entry and easy escape for the attackers. Smart!*

When the door opened, Pierre looked at my gun that was aimed between his eyes and waved me into the room. I did the usual gun-extended sweep of the room.

Pierre said too loudly, almost theatrically, "You should not have come here. Lower your weapon, I know you don't intend to shoot me."

At the same time, he was putting his index finger across his lips in a "be-quiet" sign, warning me that the room was bugged.

I grabbed the remote control from the console and turned on the TV. I announced, "Your friends are not going to hear this conversation." I wanted that little speech heard. Then I turned the TV up to full volume.

Pierre whispered, "Pat, I was hoping you wouldn't show. After you sent me the airplane ticket to meet you in Washington, your CIA man, Bob Hill, met me at the airport and told me there had been a change of plans, and we flew on a CIA jet to Birmingham to meet you at your house. You weren't there yet. Hill said that he didn't want to worry your wife, so we waited down the street. Minutes after you arrived your house exploded. Since then I've been a captive. They have threatened to kidnap my family in Paris if I tried to escape. They made me use my credit card to sign into this room. They used me as bait to draw you here." Pierre dropped dejectedly into a sitting position on the bed.

I withdrew a Glock 19 from the back of my pants and handed it to Pierre. "How much time do we have?"

"After your little speech and with the TV this loud, probably less than five minutes. These people are too much for you and me to handle. We don't have a chance. But I'll be proud to die with you. Let's get as many of them as we can."

I told him that I had a backup plan to turn the odds in our favor as we took up strategic positions in the small room and prepared for the attack. I turned off the TV so that we could hear their approach.

When we heard a lot of gunfire outside, Pierre looked over at me. I smiled. Abdul was becoming a very reliable friend.

The small town, which wasn't big enough to be visible from the interstate in daylight, erupted into violence. My adversaries were not expecting Abdul's forces. Ten men died. The action never got close to Pierre's second floor room.

After the police and Highway Patrol had control of the area, Pierre and I acted like curious citizens when we left the room to view the scene of the battle. After I took in the details of the melee, Pierre and I drove back toward Jody's home. Pierre called Kathie on my cell phone to tell her that I had rescued him. I called Dale, told her Pierre was safe, and that we would be home in six hours.

The networks and cable news had a field day. The story evolved into an American Homeland Security team bravely thwarting a terrorist plot. Two federal agents sacrificed their lives and two Arabs were killed. There was hardly any mention of the six other dead bodies. But, I had recognized two of those six dead men . . . *and I had good reason to fear their boss.*

Pierre pleaded after viewing the news report, "Pat, please tell me what this is all about." I had refused the same request on the drive from North Carolina.

I responded, "You and your family will be safer if you don't know. I want you to take my charter jet back to Paris. Have the plane take your family on a vacation holiday to an undisclosed location until I can diffuse this threat.

"Pierre, I am so sorry that your family got dragged into my horrific problems."

Chapter 49
In lethal hands

My return home got Scott out of the doghouse with Dale and Jody. I only shared the Italian connection with Brendan, and I swore him to secrecy. I knew no one on earth could ever drag something out of Brendan that I told him in confidence: not even Dale. He insisted that he go to New York with me. I didn't argue.

The second day after the action north of Charlotte, days filled with extensive research, Dale, Jody, Brendan, and Scott met in Jody's kitchen for breakfast. Brendan asked Dale, "Is Pat alright? Why isn't he out here for breakfast yet?"

Dale's eyebrows raised, "He left for New York early this morning." She saw the concern in Brendan's eyes. "**I thought you knew**." Dale was shocked that Pat hadn't told Brendan.

Brendan agonized over the realization that Pat was going to confront the danger alone, knew he didn't have Pat's ability to disguise his emotions, knew that Dale saw the concern in his eyes, and that she wasn't going to let it go.

She jumped to her feet. In an alarmed voice she screeched, "**Brendan, what is he doing now?**"

Brendan reigned in his emotions and shrugged, "Did he tell you why he was going to New York?"

"**No. I'm upset that he didn't tell you.**"

Brendan tried to calm her, "He is probably handling financial matters in New York that are none of my business."

***

I wore a three-piece, Brooks Brother's suit to a swanky office building on Park Place in New York. I surrendered most of my possessions, including my sat phone and Glock 22 to the guard in the lobby. I entered the elevator and punched the button for the penthouse suite. The elevator door closed, but it didn't rise. A mechanical, irritating female voice requested, "Please enter the code."

I waited, knowing what was coming next. The computer voice said, "Who do you wish to visit?"

I hit the talk button and stated, "Doug Benton."

The voice chimed in again, "Please state your full name."

I said loudly, "**Princess Diana**." Seconds later the elevator started up.

When the elevator door opened, four men reached into the elevator, physically pulled me out, and searched every part of my body.

I was ushered into a richly-decorated corner office. I didn't get to look around much, but I was pretty sure that the first painting I saw on the wall was an original Monet.

The goons still had me by the right arm and the cast on my left. They sat me forcefully down in an exquisite, black-leather chair, one of the goons kept his huge hands on my shoulders and pressed my butt into the chair. I was looking at the back of two leather chairs across an expensive, mahogany desk. The chairs spun around in unison. I recognized Doug Benton immediately; but more importantly, I recognized "Sonny" Gambito. His full name was Jildo Savatore Flaviana James Gambito, the Sicilian Godfather that controlled most of the world's godfathers.

Very effective. I was impressed.

Gambito was about my age, but his hair was jet black and slicked back the way he probably wore it when he was "made" after his first hit. His olive skin had aged pleasantly.

Doug recognized that their maneuver had the desired effect. "O'Sheen, it's been a long time. What? Twenty years?"

I looked him squarely in the eyes, scanned the room, and then looked back into his bemused eyes, "Good to see you too, Benton. Your surroundings scream success. Actually, it's been seventeen years."

Doug offered, "My lobbying office in DC isn't quite as nice as this." He continued with only a slight hesitation. "Pat, I have always admired you. I hate that you got involved with this . . ."

I interrupted insultingly, "Don Gambito, your men," *I almost said goons*, "took pictures from my breast pocket. Please look at them."

Gambito nodded to one of his goons who handed him the pictures. He looked at the pictures carefully and passed each one slowly to Benton. The last three pictures visibly raised Sonny's blood pressure. He didn't pass them to Benton. Instead, he looked with a steely edge into my eyes.

Before I could respond, Doug theorized on the pictures from the Pakistan border, "These pictures could have been staged anywhere. Are we supposed to assume that this is O'Sheen down by the road?"

I plodded forward, still addressing Gambito, "If we hadn't stopped that hologram shipment, thousands of American soldiers would be dying. My life is not worth the life of one of those brave soldiers."

"He is lying." Benton interjected, "Don't listen to him. He is a traitor. Remember the forces that killed your men in Carolina were Middle Eastern."

After listening to Benton's proclamation, Gambito glared at me.

Brendan and I had learned that Gambito still spent most of his winters in Sicily. I addressed him in Italian with a Sicilian accent. "Mr. Gambito, until I recognized some of your men at the aftermath of the conflict in North Carolina, I had no clue of your involvement in this matter. If I had been aware of that fact, I would have approached the conflict differently. The pictures you still hold in your hands are evidence **of an attack on my family at my home** three days before the incident in North Carolina."

My switch to the godfather's native language, and my forcefulness had the desired effect. The "at my home" was an affront to the Costa Nostra—innocent family members were off limit.

Doug Benton recognized the effect of my language change. He said, "Sonny, force him to speak English."

Instead, Sonny looked again at the pictures of O'Sheen's destroyed house: the pictures he hadn't passed to Benton. He was starting to understand O'Sheen's anger.

Gambito leaned back in his big, high-backed leather chair and crossed his legs. He rubbed the palms of his hands together a couple times and was ready to speak: *perhaps declaring my fate.* When I reached up the cast on my left arm, a gun barrel was pressed against the back of my head. I slowly pulled out three more pictures. Sonny waved his protection off and accepted the pictures.

The first picture showed what appeared to be a paramedic following Pat and a woman walking out the front door of a house. Pat and the woman were covered with blood. Sonny looked at the supporting pictures.

When Gambito looked up from the pictures at me, I could tell that his attitude had changed.

I said, "I assume you were not aware of this attack on my family. They almost killed my wife."

I knew the Sicilian code and I said, "I am fair game, but my family is off limits."

***

Gambito stared into O'Sheen's fearless eyes. He had learned of O'Sheen's background before he arrived for this meeting. He knew that O'Sheen could be a very dangerous adversary. Sonny's respect for the man sitting in front of him began when he was assured that O'Sheen arrived in New York alone as promised.

Sonny had set up the meeting that O'Sheen had requested and accepted Benton's advice to intimidate O'Sheen. O'Sheen was impressed by their theatric turn around, but Sonny never saw a hint of fear in O'Sheen's eyes.

Gambito again leaned back in his chair, entwined his fingers, and seconds later started twiddling his thumbs.

I knew to remain silent. Extremely powerful men have that dominating presence. That is why they are extremely powerful: *not so hard to figure.*

Benton interrupted, knowing that he was losing control. "Sonny, you're facing a very dangerous man."

Gambito turned his gaze to the right and looked at Benton with eyes that warned, *don't interrupt.* He verbally addressed me in English, "O'Sheen, tell me your side of this story."

I knew that Benton couldn't follow my story in the Sicilian dialect and started in Italian. Benton tried to object, but Sonny Gambito simply raised his right hand to silence him.

I explained the first encounter in Paris and explained that revenge from an old adversary got me involved. I continued into the next two attacks on me, the third while my wife was in the car. Gambito's blood pressure visibly increased on that story. Then I explained the kidnapping of my son, but I did not disclose the name of Abdul or Michelle. I explained the subsequent events at the Khyber Pass in Pakistan; and informed Gambito that my house exploded ten minutes after I returned home from that mission.

Sonny listened while leaning back in his chair with his fingertips steeped together and his eyes closed. I liked the thought that Sonny's three goons in the room could understand my story, and that Benton was totally in the dark. I paused, waiting for what I knew would be the final decision on my fate: *Live or Die.*

It was a long two minutes before Gambito leaned forward in his chair and spoke in English, "Mr. Benton is correct. Your story supported his claim that you are an extremely dangerous man."

Sonny paused for effect. "If I let you leave here alive, what will you do next, O'Sheen?"

I explained, "I have to do everything in my power to stop this threat against my family. The government I have served for so many years has turned against me. I'm sure that as a Sicilian you understand how difficult it is to deal with an ever-changing government."

I logically explained why I had approached the meeting in North Carolina with solicited outside help (the Arabs), and why I couldn't trust my own government. For centuries the Gambito family could rarely trust Italy's ever-changing government.

Several agonizing minutes later, Sonny leaned forward, his decision apparently made. Sonny spoke in English for Benton to understand. "I am going to allow you to leave unharmed, but you must never disclose Mr. Benton or my organization's involvement in this matter. I sense that I can trust you to follow my decree."

He pointed a thumb at Doug, "Mr. Benton is off limits. You must handle the rest of those responsible for the attack on your family without involving us, Capiche?"

I nodded, "Capiche."

Gambito stood up abruptly: meeting over.

Although Benton didn't understand what had just happened, he was reassured by Gambito's support for him, and he smiled at me like he had just beat me into submission.

I stood and risked another question to Gambito. "Is Inspector Boudreaux and his family safe?"

Gambito said, "They served their purpose. Once you showed up in North Carolina, they were of no further use."

I knew that Sonny purposely hinted at the worst case scenario to see my reaction.

I let my face show concern. He knew that I was a capable foe. He now knew that I cared deeply for my friends. I had shown sincere respect for him in arranging this meeting and by my demeanor during the meeting. The fact that I risked another question about my friends, despite my reprieve, drew a slight smile.

Gambito put out his hand for me to shake. I hesitated, a deep insult to a Sicilian.

Sonny noticed again that I had no fear in my eyes. He relieved my pain, "Boudreaux and his family are in no danger."

I shook his hand.

Sonny thought, *this fearless man has high level connections. One day I may need him on my side.*

Benton stood up as I turned toward the door, "Wait, O'Sheen, this meeting is not over yet."

I turned to my old acquaintance to see him for the last time. "It is for me, Jonathan Booth."

Benton was shocked. I explained, "I saw a picture of a man who called himself Jonathan Booth standing with Sheik Faisad. Your disguise was excellent. But the eyes gave you away. My seeing them again after so many years helped me identify you."

I advised Gambito, using the familiar address, "Sonny, too many people know about the hologram belt conspiracy. Whether I am alive or not, the hologram conspiracy will soon result in a train wreck, wounding or killing everyone aboard. I suggest you cut all of your ties to it."

I knew I was one of the major ties.

I said, "I have not told anyone of your involvement, and I never will."

When Gambito failed to respond, I shrugged, turned, and walked toward the door. I heard the poof from a silenced handgun. A bullet did not enter my head.

I believed that Gambito had already realized his mistake in getting involved in the hologram conspiracy before my arrival. Killing Benton was his first step in cleaning-up his mistake. *I might be next. But he wouldn't have me killed here. He had agreed to release me and would honor his agreement.*

Only one goon accompanied me down the elevator to the lobby. I retrieved my possessions that had been confiscated on my entry, including my Glock 22. I checked the magazine. It was empty. I didn't check the chamber. Most people who carry a Glock don't walk around with a bullet in the chamber because it doesn't have a trigger safety. I wasn't like most people. One bullet in the chamber was better than none.

Chapter 50
Getaway

My nerves were on edge as I left the building. I knew I had earned the Godfather's respect. I also knew that eliminating me like he did Benton would help clean up a government connected loose end for him.

I walked down to the New York subway, entered quickly into a timely arriving train car, and studied the passengers until I arrived at Penn Station. I caught a cab to Terminal A, the Marine Air Terminal at LaGuardia Airport. So far so good. But I suddenly wished I had brought back-up at least to this point. Gambito would have accepted that.

As I approached the inspection point at the private aircraft terminal, I noticed a man approaching me. I had seen the man at Penn Station, but even in my heightened awareness, I did not think he was tailing me. The small, effeminate man walked passed me without any threat, but said in passing, in a childishly high voice, "Mister Gambito wishes you a safe trip."

I turned quickly in his direction, but the man had already blended into the crowd.

I knew that I was outmatched by Sonny Gambito's organization. Sonny had just very effectively added the defining exclamation point to our meeting: simply said, *don't dare cross me.*

My private charter jet went airborne without another incident. Once we cleared New York airspace, I considered my two new "friends": Abdul, an international mercenary; and Sonny Gambito, the Sicilian Godfather.

I called home and assured Dale that I was safely on the plane leaving New York, and that I needed to talk to Brendan securely.

Dale asked, "Are you coming home? Or are you going to make your infamous 'one more stop'?" She already knew the answer.

"Hon, I need to stop in D.C."

She secured the phone, and connected me to Brendan.

Arranging a safe meeting with Deputy CIA Director Bob Hill in D.C. would take expert planning and exact timing. I had purchased a disposable phone at a Seven Eleven. After checking into my hotel, I sent an email to roberthill@gvmtsvs.gov and attached the incriminating photo of Hill leaving my neighborhood after the explosion. The email said that I was on the way to DC to confront him and included a phone number for Hill to call. I also explained in the email that whether or not he called me, a meeting would take place. I left the hotel and took a Metro train to Union Station in case Hill tried to triangulate my phone and dispatch hit men to my location.

***

Deputy CIA Director Bob Hill understood the threat: meet O'Sheen in public, or at a most inconvenient and compromising time and location of Pat's choosing. He made three quick phone calls and awaited answers before calling O'Sheen.

After receiving his instructions, he called O'Sheen. "I will meet you between the Washington Monument and the Lincoln Memorial. I'll call you tomorrow morning with the time." He hung up before Pat could respond.

***

I forwarded calls from the first Seven Eleven disposable phone to another. I knew a trace to the location of the second phone would give me enough time. I put the first phone in a trash container in Union Station and caught a cab back to my hotel.

I knew that Hill would be worried about the long-term consequences of meeting me. The real question was, would his conspirators try to hit me in a public place? *Maybe*! Hill had his high government position in his favor. He had already tried to paint me as a rogue agent.

The next morning, Hill called at 8:00 a.m. and said, "One hour, halfway between the Lincoln and Washington monuments, east side of the reflecting pool."

I jumped in before Hill could hang up, "I was sure that you would try to locate me in D.C. last night, and I wasn't going to take that risk. I am at least ninety minutes outside of D.C., maybe two hours if there is a traffic accident." The fictitious dilemma had the desired effect.

Hill ad-libbed, "I'll meet you at the Vietnam Veterans Memorial in two hours."

I arrived in a cab near the Lincoln Memorial two hours later. I began a leisurely walk toward the Vietnam Memorial in the open where I was easily identifiable. A man built like a stockyard, prize-winning bull exited from behind the Vietnam Memorial with Bob Hill and walked toward me.

I didn't wait for Hill to speak, "Bob, how do I get this yoke off my family's neck."

Hill smiled, sure that he had the advantage. He said, "Pat, I'm sorry to say, I think the only way for you to protect your family is for you to be taken into my custody."

I saw Bob Hill's confidence fade when I broke out into a wide smile and said, "That's not going to happen today, Bob."

Hill attempted to smile back, "If you surrender your weapons and accompany us to our vehicle, you may live to see another day."

"Bob, you are not in control here." I apprised Hill of the situation, "My men have already spotted your sniper. I have evidence that will disclose your betrayal of our armed forces. Your name will go down in history with John Wilkes Booth. But I can offer you a better alternative."

Listening to his earphone Hill said, "You are bluffing. My sniper is not compromised. He is targeting you now. Surrender to us and live."

I rubbed the back of my neck. "Hill, I repeat. You are not in control here. You might be good at politics, but you don't know how to compete in covert operations at my level. For your own salvation, you need to listen to me."

Hill had heard enough, "Tank, take this rogue agent down."

I smiled at Tank without fear, which unnerved him. Tank was a good name for him. I said "Tank, you have a very large man standing behind you." I looked back at Bob, who turned quickly to see Brendan large frame standing behind his bull.

Hill said, "Oh shit."

I noticed that the bull only slightly turned his head to locate Brendan in his peripheral vision: *Very experienced*. But I knew Brendan could handle him.

I volunteered, "Your sniper will be dead before you can finish your signal. Hill, we can still solve this without casualties."

Hill panicked at his loss of control and started to raise his arm while saying, "Die you bastard."

The bull turned and attempted a sidekick at Brendan. Brendan moved toward him, grabbed his thigh and ankle, and slammed the exposed knee down across a rising thrust from his own knee. The large leg bent in half sideways at the knee. ***Ouch!***

Simultaneously, I grabbed Hill by the lapels of his suit and thrust backward hoping to avoid the sniper fire. Two distant shots rang out almost simultaneously and echoed off the Lincoln Memorial, the Washington Monument, and throughout the most protected public arena in America. Hill's fat, three hundred pound, frame knocked the breath from my lungs as we landed hard on the ground with him on top of me. I quickly rolled over on top of Hill to regain the advantage, and I noticed the near fatal wound where the sniper's bullet passed through his neck. I built up the muscular control to recapture my breath by exhaling enough to allow me to inhale again.

Hill looked up at me knowing that he was dying and sorrow entered his eyes. He tried to speak despite the wound through his neck.

I knew Hill's Catholic affiliation and said, "Bob, now is a good time for a last confession. I don't think you will survive. Who is behind this?" I had to lean my ear toward Bob's mouth to hear his last words whispered before he passed out. I wasn't surprised to hear one of the names that Hill stated in his confession: the other name shocked me.

We were surrounded by D.C. police, all of their guns extended toward Brendan and me. We both remained motionless, following instructions with hands exposed. But I didn't remove my right hand from Hill's bleeding neck despite repeated police warnings. I yelled, **"I can't let go or he will bleed to death."** One of the officers approached aggressively with his gun aimed at my head. He saw the blood oozing between my fingers from the shot man's neck and recognized my effort to stem the flow. He then recognized that the wounded man was Deputy Director Bob Hill. He rammed his pistol into its holster and knelt down beside me in an effort to help.

Tank yelled an accusation that I shot Hill, and implicated Brendan. Brendan and I were handcuffed.

After the paramedics arrived and carried Hill off in their ambulance, another ambulance arrived to carry Tank to the hospital. Brendan and I were taken to the precinct with our wrists handcuffed behind us.

Chapter 51
Incarceration

Brendan and I demanded our phone call after being processed. My phone call was risky, but I knew that Brendan would call his father-in-law, Sheriff Hannon, who would cover both of us.

Six hours later, I was escorted to the prisoner-attorney room. Gene Tanner was sitting at a table, and I recognized the man with Gene. It was not legal to bug the room, but I knew that even though the recordings were not admissible in a court of law, a lot of serious crimes were solved by listening to this first conference. In my case, I assumed that many ears were listening.

Gene Tanner stood up and objected to the guard when he saw my chained wrists and ankles with a chain tying my arms down to the ankle chains. Gene said, **"This man is an American hero. Unchain him immediately."**

I said calmly, "Let it go, Gene. You know that I've been through a lot worse."

The guard ignored Gene's outburst and secured my chains to a large metal ring cemented into the floor, and he left the room.

I asked Tanner, "How is Hill?"

Gene shook his head, "DOA."

Gene introduced me to Petrie by first name only.

I looked at the effeminate man who had tailed me yesterday to the airport in New York. I noticed the castrato looked at me with admiration. I had met a eunuch once before, and I was amazed that wealthy Italian's would still castrate boys to preserve their beautiful soprano voices.

I addressed Petrie in Italian with a Sicilian accent, "Can you sing 'Ave Maria'?"

Petrie donned a big smile and started singing loudly in a beautiful soprano voice an octave above my singing range.

When Petrie was singing loud enough to thwart the room's listening devises, I leaned forward and whispered to Gene, "I can't believe you were involved in this conspiracy. Why would you let them attack my home and family? My god, Gene, we've been friends for over a decade. I've always trusted you."

Gene leaned back in shock and glared at me. He knew his career and maybe his life were in jeopardy. He tried to recover, leaned forward, and whispered, "There are forces at work here that you don't understand. I played along with the conspiracy to stop the big play. I'm sorry but in the big picture you were expendable."

My chuckle lacked levity. "I am fair game, but you almost killed Dale. You did kill her dog."

Gene said, "Pat, I swear that I didn't know about the bomb."

I didn't respond verbally. Instead, I smiled at Petrie, enraptured as his soprano voice finished the first Latin chorus of Ave Maria. Petrie acknowledged my appreciation.

I was hoping that my delay by listening to Petrie's angelic singing voice would give my old friend time to confess. Gene remained quiet.

Seconds before Petrie started the second chorus I said aloud, "Gene, what has happened to you?"

When Gene failed to defend himself, I continued softer when Petrie started singing the second verse. "Bob Hill knew that his death was eminent after being shot in the neck at the memorial. I knew he was Catholic and took his last confession. He exposed you as a conspirator before he passed out. I saw film of you, Hill, and Kamper driving away from my house after it exploded."

Tanner disclosed, "Gene Kamper was in the car that day, but he was duped. He was not involved in the conspiracy."

He hung his head, too ashamed to look me in the eyes. Gene's spirit fled his body during his last admission.

I motioned for the eunuch to pick up the volume and leaned across the table, "Gene, your life is in danger. You're an expendable loose end. If you can get me out of this jail and leave with me, you may have a chance. I will protect you."

Gene eyes warmed and got moist at my offer. "I'll try, Pat. But the political cards are stacked against you."

Gene failed to get my release. He disappeared that day and his body was never found. The eunuch that Gambito sent with Gene to my consultation in the jail was a message to me confirming that Sonny Gambito was severing all ties to the hologram conspiracy.

Despite my high-priced, expert council, bail was denied based on convincing evidence that I could easily disappear into almost any country in the world.

Brendan was allowed bail, but was charged as a possible accessory to Hill's death. He was released to Sheriff Bo Hannon's custody. But before Bo achieved Brendan's release, he tried to visit me and was shocked that all his efforts were blocked. He surmised that I was the federal government's target, the scapegoat for their failure to control the hologram leak, a project that he knew I would never acknowledge even under oath to protect myself: a top-secret project that Bo should never have heard of, and one that he could never acknowledge.

A week later, a grand jury issued an indictment. All of my attorney's motions were denied. The area where Hill was shot has more Government cameras than perhaps any place in the world. The judge did agree to subpoena the films. But for the day of the shooting, they all had mysteriously disappeared.

When my lawyer attempted to apologize for his ineffectiveness, I smiled, "I don't blame you, Jeff. The politics are stacked against us."

I had served America my whole adult life with sacrificial passion. I had no idea how to stop my country's degeneration. I knew at home, Dale and the family agonized over the governments' railroading of me. They knew what I had sacrificed to serve the country that had suddenly turned against me.

I was sent to the Federal Corrections Institute, Cumberland Prison. I was the biggest story on CNN. The other prisoners watched TV and knew that I was once a federal agent. My cell mate was an old man: a "lifer". He explained that I was a "fish": a new prisoner, and he warned me to not look directly into anyone's eyes. That was considered an insult and a challenge.

Only my cell mate sat at my table at breakfast the next morning. I had almost finished my breakfast when the whole cafeteria room grew eerily silent. A man walked up behind me and dumped the contents of his food tray on my head. The room broke out in raucous laughter. I was expecting something unpleasant based on the sudden silence and the concern I saw it in the eyes of my bunkmate sitting across from me.

I spun off my seat and jumped to my feet while grabbing the perpetrator's shirt. I pulled the short Latino man to where our noses were almost touching and glared into his eyes. I had noticed the Latino gang tattoo on his arm.

I slammed him down to the floor, grabbed my tray, and dumped it on him. I turned and walked at a fast pace toward the entrance to the cafeteria knowing that this was only the beginning of a potentially deadly confrontation.

I had made it to the end of the tables when the first man ran full speed at me from behind. At the last second, I squatted and moved to my left. He tripped over my extended right leg and went sprawling fifteen feet across the tile floor toward the exit. I straightened up and swung my tray as I rotated right, catching the next Latino above his right eye, sending him to the floor. Five more were approaching more cautiously between the tables from about ten feet away.

I threw the tray like a Frisbee. The closest man ducked but it hit the second one on his Adams apple knocking him down.

The tray momentarily stopped their approach. I looked for a defendable position. I saw an indent in the left wall, four foot deep by five foot wide containing three butler conveyors moving downward with shelves for dish trays.

Two gang members were circling around the tables near the wall indent: *no problem—only two.*

I walked in long fast strides straight at them. They both stopped with fear in their eyes. I didn't stop. I pivoted to my right and side kicked the closer man in his solar plexus. *He wouldn't be breathing for a while.* The other man took a fast step forward and sent a roundhouse right fist at my head. I stepped back from the punch and did a full clockwise pirouette and hit him with a backhanded fist on his jaw, breaking it and knocking him out.

I sensed the others were close and ran to the indent. I turned around and forced a big smile on my face. The two closest men stopped and stared at me. The six men following stopped behind them. They all had the same Hispanic gang tattoos. I assumed the two in front were the leaders. The one on my right had a cut on his cheek. I surmised that he was the first attacker who went sprawling to the floor over my extended right leg. More gang members were running to join the group.

I extended my left arm forward and waved my fingers to egg them to come forward while saying very loudly in Spanish with a Mexican accent, **"Come on. Don't quit now. I am just starting to enjoy myself.**

The two leaders looked at each other. The one on my right pointed his thumb at me and said, **"Loco!"** He pulled a toothbrush from his pocket: the plastic end was ground to a point.

They both approached cautiously. I knew that the one who came at me first would be the leader in this prison. I intended to put him in the hospital—or in the grave. In a smaller group, the followers in the group would retreat when their leader goes down. But the enemy number had increased to at least fifteen Latino gang members. I knew that some of them would be brave.

The one on my left came at me first. I executed a feint of a karate kick toward him slowing his progress. I was hoping the man with the tooth brush would keep coming.

He did, and he thrust the toothbrush underhanded at me toward my stomach with his left hand. I stepped to my right, grabbed his left hand with my left hand from underneath and chopped down hard on the crook of his elbow with the side of my right hand. I kept my left hand coming upward while gripping his hand tightly to keep it from dropping the toothbrush and sank the pointed shaft into the neck of the leader moving in from my left. I retracted my right arm and smashed my right elbow into the bridge of the nose of the toothbrush man, crushing it. He went down.

The leader backed away holding the toothbrush still stuck in his neck. The Latino gang was in shock at my effectiveness. I thought they might back off.

But a brave guy broke ranks, ran and dove over the leaders at my head. I dropped to a squat, grabbed him from underneath, lifted him up like a male cheerleader would raise his female partner, and used his momentum to stuff his head and shoulders down the center dumb waiter tray conveyer that stalled while trying to pull him down to the dishwashers in a level below.

I blindly thrust my right foot out and struck an approaching body and then spun in a circle to my left. A hard punch split the skin on my left eyebrow and blood rushed down into my eye. I continued my rotation and back fisted the man who hit me on his left eyebrow returning the favor. He went down.

A hard punch was approaching my nose. I tilted my head forward and took the blow on my forehead. I heard knuckles break . . . *or was that my skull*. I saw stars but was still conscious.

I tried to deflect another sharpened toothbrush, but it stuck into the side of my abdomen.

The group surged forward crushing me against the wall. My right hand was low, and I grabbed a set of nuts and squeezed as hard as I could. The man's loud scream backed the surge away from me. Another hard punch hit me above my left ear. I dropped to my knees. *I was getting too old for this.*

I was exhausted. From my knees on the floor, I grabbed another set of balls and squeezed hard while thrusting my left fist up into another set. Another hard punch hit me on the top of my head, probably from the guy whose balls I was destroying. I grabbed a leg to keep from falling all of the way to the floor, opened my mouth wide, and bit down hard on a thigh muscle intending to inflict as much damage as possible before I died.

I heard multiple guard whistles blowing as another blow hit my head. I went to my stomach on the floor—almost unconscious. I heard batons striking bodies and heads. I was struck on the head again. I heard a baton crack against a head close to me. *Perhaps it was my head.* I didn't care.

It seemed like a lot of time had passed when two guards had a hold of me from each side, hands under my armpits, and lifted me to my feet. I shook my head trying to clear the cobwebs. I was alive. My guardian angel was still with me. I staggered at first as the guards led me forward, and then I stopped and straightened up with dignity.

The ten or more guards had ordered all of the prisoners who weren't involved back to their tables. A large black man was standing at the end of one table with a look of concern for my condition written across his face. He reminded me of Big George from the Shelby County Jail in Alabama. I winked at him and smiled. A big smile spread across his face. He nodded his approval and admiration.

Chapter 52
Salvation

I spent the night in an isolation cell in the prison infirmary. The doctor put four stitches on my eyebrow. The stab to the side of my abdomen wasn't too deep and hadn't hit any vital organs. He gave me a pain pill for all my injuries. I was exhausted and slept like a baby.

The next morning two guards escorted me to the warden's office. The warden, Jeb Walker, was about my size and five to ten years older.

He looked up at me from his seat behind the desk and seemed surprised, "You don't look too bad."

I smiled and nodded as I was forced to take a seat.

The warden said, "O'Sheen, you put eight men in the infirmary and four more had to be rushed to a local hospital—two are still critical."

I didn't say anything.

"I was afraid someone would try to kill a Federal agent like you. I wanted to put you in isolation when you first arrived, but my superiors instructed me to treat you like any other prisoner."

I didn't say anything.

The warden told the two guards to leave. When the door closed behind them, he spun his chair around to his computer on a table behind him. *Turning his back to me without guards in the room showed a lot of trust.*

The monitor had a large screen. He clicked his curser on the play button on a video that was already cued and rolled his chair to the side to give me an unobstructed view of the screen.

I was watching the prisoners eating breakfast in the cafeteria. I was at the third table on the left, and I was facing the camera. I was easy to spot because I was sitting at the only table with just two people. I watched the events unfold until I tripped the man attacking me from behind, swung my tray knocking another man down, and threw my tray putting another man down. Then I ran out of camera range.

The warden rolled back to his computer and brought up another video showing the cafeteria from a different camera. He stood this time and walked to the end of his desk next to me and turned to watch the film saying, "This is where it really gets good."

I watched me put down two more Latinos and run to the indent in the wall where the lunch tray conveyors were.

The warden said, "Quite amazing for a guy your age."

The video showed me turning with a big smile on my face.

The warden paused the video while shaking his head. "You are fearless. You seemed to be enjoying this."

He started the video again, and I watched as I extended my hand beckoning the leaders to attack. I heard myself challenge the gang in Spanish. The video paused again.

The warden said, "I speak Spanish. You are one crazy motherfucker."

I laughed. I couldn't help myself. Watching the video made me realize that he might be right about me being crazy.

I said, "Only one."

The warden looked at me confused. "Only one?"

"I only fuck one mother. My wife—the mother of my children."

The warden chuckled, realizing I was referring to his curse word.

"You could have gotten yourself killed by retaliating against the Hispanic who poured his tray on you."

I shrugged, "I should have died with my friends in Nam over twenty years ago."

He stared at me for ten seconds and then restarted the video. He paused again after the gang leader turned sideways with a toothbrush stuck in his neck.

"If Juarez dies, this video proves that you acted in self-defense."

I said, "It only proves my innocence if this video doesn't disappear like all the videos from the cameras around the Vietnam Memorial on the day CIA Deputy Hill was shot."

The warden stared at me again, "You've got to be kidding me?"

I shook my head.

He sat down next to me. "So you didn't kill Hill?"

"Hill's sniper missed me and the bullet struck him."

"Who killed the sniper?"

I shrugged, "Apparently someone sent to protect me. Perhaps an **honest** CIA agent."

"You worked for the CIA?"

"I did many missions for the CIA on special assignment from the military, and a few times after I left the military. A short time ago, I was double crossed by the CIA and was almost assassinated in Paris. Then Deputy Hill blew up my house almost killing my wife. I met him in the public place with all the public cameras around in an attempt to reason with him."

Warden Walker stared at me. "What is this all about?"

I shook my head, "I can't say. It is classified top-secret by all of the government agencies."

Walker was quiet for a moment and then changed the subject. "There is no reason for you to recognize me, but I know who you are. I owe you and your team of volunteer snipers my life. I was a lieutenant in the Marines and was evacuated on one of the last helicopters from the Saigon while the NVA was overrunning the city. Man, you are a war hero. You should have gotten the Medal of Honor."

Walker was taken aback when I glared at him. "I am not a hero. The seventeen snipers who died that day should have been awarded the Medal of Honor."

I calmed and disclosed, "I turned down the Medal of Honor. I should have died with my men that day."

"You were offered Medal of Honor? Why have I never heard that?"

I shrugged. "It only makes news when a soldier accepts it."

Walker shook his head, moved to his own chair behind the desk, and sat down. "I am going to put you in isolated confinement until the trial. I . . ."

I interrupted, "I'd rather go back into the general prison population."

He chuckled. "I'm sure you would."

I said, "The Latino gang won't bother me again. I also earned the respect of most of the black men in there." I knew how the black gang members hated the Hispanic gangs and vice versa.

Walker nodded, "You earned the white gang's respect too. But, I'm sorry. Your presence could cause a gang war. And my superiors don't want you hurting any more of my prisoners." He laughed louder this time.

I nodded in understanding.

He said, "I'll make sure your guards in isolation know that they better treat you with the utmost respect, and you let them know if you want something—anything." The warden stood up: meeting over.

I befriended the guards who oversaw my solitary confinement unit. After three days in confinement, my disguise was ready. I had two escape plans. I knew that my escape would cause serious problems for my family and my defense attorney, but it wasn't in my nature to sit on my butt and not affect the outcome of a plot against me. And it wasn't in my nature to stay in a cage that I knew I could escape from.

I lay on my bunk in the isolation unit the night before my planned escape. I would try to minimize the injury to my friendly guard when he brought me back to my cell following my afternoon exercise hour. He was my size, and I needed to wear his prison-guard uniform to escape. I would give him a big enough lump on his head so that he would not be falsely accused of being complicit in my escape. My disguise would make me look enough like the picture on his badge for me to exit the prison. Exiting in uniform is a lot easier than entering in uniform.

The next morning, I was informed that my lawyer arranged a one o'clock meeting. That was okay. I was planning my escape during the five-o'clock guard shift change.

At the one o'clock meeting, my lawyer explained that a package arrived at Fox News Network office in D.C. The package contained government tapes showing Hill's death next to the Vietnam Memorial that proved my innocence. Fox news had shown it to my lawyer for his opinion. He encouraged the network to broadcast it. He was told that Fox News film analysts would have to authenticate that the film wasn't manipulated. My lawyer believed that I would be released very soon. I delayed my escape plan to learn the outcome of the tapes authenticity.

Chapter 53
The revelation

The best forensic experts in the FBI examined every inch of a package containing a film identical to the one Fox received that was sent to the U.S. Attorney General's office that proved O'Sheen's innocence. Whoever sent the packages was a professional. The only fingerprints were from personnel of the USPS delivery service, and there were no hairs, skin particles, or cloth fibers inside. The packaging was available from every Wal-Mart in the country. The package was dropped off at a USPS drop box in Baltimore, Maryland with correct postage attached.

A working man's wife received a third package addressed to her husband. When her husband arrived home, he put the tape on his home video system. He and his wife watched in awe as they saw the events unfold next to the Vietnam Memorial.

Officer Greg Pulaski knew that the video proved that O'Sheen never brandished a weapon and had pulled Hill toward him at the last minute in a protective move. The bullet that hit Hill came from O'Sheen's left where they found a body hanging in a tree with a sniper rifle still attached to his lifeless arms. The dead sniper was assumed to be O'Sheen's. But Greg didn't buy it. *If he was O'Sheen's man, who shot him?*

He watched as the film showed him and his fellow police officers enter the scene. The film stopped shortly after he had holstered his pistol and knelt down next to O'Sheen in an attempt to help save Bob Hill's life.

Greg had filed a written report to his captain, a man who had been like a father to him over the last ten years. His report concluded that O'Sheen was trying to save Hill's life when he arrived on the scene making the murder charge against O'Sheen nonsensical. He hadn't had a good night's sleep since O'Sheen's indictment. The negative news coverage about O'Sheen forced him to quit watching the news.

This video was proof that he was right. He also realized the implication. If this disclosure was going to foil the plans of high government officials, his career and the economic stability of his family could be in jeopardy. His wife saw his concern and turned off the video.

After he and his wife shared supper with their three kids and put them to bed, she queried, "Greg, the film has unnerved you. What are you going to do with it?"

They watched it again together, while Greg explained his part and the dire consequences that might result if he exposed the film. Greg's hands were visibly shaking. His wife grabbed his hands to calm him, and simply said, "You will do what is right. I'll support your decision, whatever the outcome." She retreated to their bedroom.

Pulaski sat bewildered alone in the living room. He considered his wife's advice, called his captain's home, and told him what he had.

His captain ran on foot from his home two blocks away. They watched the video in silence three times. They both knew that a high-level government fix was involved in O'Sheen's indictment.

Greg watched his mentor contemplate the risks with a better understanding of how to deal with the consequences of the film's revelation. The disappearance of the government videos was so inflammatory that careers could be crushed. For the past week, the biggest story on every alphabet news network (ABC, NBC, CBS, CNN, and all the other alphabets) had it wrong. They reported in unison that the decorated warrior, as O'Sheen was being billed, when they discovered his long-term service to the country, had turned against the hand that had fed him. How all these networks manage within hours to use the exact same terminology, even though that terminology was cloned differently in every crisis, is a mystery. When the first one brought on a psychiatrist that talked about "post-traumatic stress disorder", the other alphabet news channels picked up on it and conducted similar interviews. If O'Sheen had been a teenager, they would have blamed A.D.D or A.D.H.D.

After his captain's silence, Pulaski blurted out, "I was there. My report concluded that O'Sheen was innocent." He said angrily, **"My report was ignored."**

His captain made the right decision. He called the chief of police and told him what they had. At 10:00 p.m., most of the highest ranked officers in the department watched the video. No federal employees were invited.

Only the chief-of-police questioned the authenticity of the video. He decided to send the video to the FBI before taking any official action by his department: *CYA.*

The next day, the story broke on the Fox News Network when they showed their copy of the video on their morning news program, "Fox and friends". Two days later I was released on bail. I was warned by the prosecutor that my complicity in the death of the sniper in the tree had to be investigated. Their attempt to interrogate me about the sniper's death drew nothing but silence. Warden Walker and two of my favorite guards accompanied me to the gate of the prison and wished me well.

Fox News covered my release extensively at first, but when I refused an interview the story died. The other networks that had accused me of the atrocity of killing Deputy Hill barely mentioned my release.

It didn't take long for an intelligent, sympathetic reporter with the right connections to track down the knowledge that the government tapes that should have recorded the incident in front of the Memorial were all missing except for the one sent to Fox News. His article in the Birmingham News was reprinted across the country. But the TV media, embarrassed by their lack of investigation into the story, decided to play down the disclosure.

To my relief, the news stories about me were soon pushed aside to report other breaking news.

Chapter 54
Collaboration

My private charter jet carried six passengers on a flight to Montana: me, Dale, Jody, Mandy, Robby Clark, and Brendan Clary. Until the conspirators were totally exposed my family would not be safe in Alabama.

As our plane traversed the sunlit countryside, I regretted that too many Americans didn't know how far it is between Alabama and Montana, and how big and diversely beautiful the country appears from an airplane.

I left the small airport in Montana with Robby and Brendan in a rent-a-car. No one seemed to like my plan, but no one had a better idea that could override my decision to come to Montana.

After my first surveillance, I stationed Brendan and Robby at separate sniper positions with orders not to shoot unless I was attacked. After overriding their objections, I drove alone to the ranch house and straight up the driveway. I jumped out of the rented sedan and ran to the back of the house with my Glock 9 mm pistol in hand. Brendan had reported that the target was in a lounge chair on the back patio. I rounded the corner of the house, behind the house corner.

Gene lowered his weapon: *Déjà vu.* "Come on in, Pat."

When I walked across the concrete patio, Gene turned his weapon sideways, pistol butt facing up, and handed it to me. I smiled at him.

Gene said, "I've been expecting you. I saw one of your snipers setting up. It's hard to set up snipers in this territory with no trees to hide behind. Actually, you're blocking his view. He wasn't big enough to be Brendan, so I assume that he is also out there somewhere."

I moved a couple of steps to my right, believing Gene's claim that I was blocking Robby's view. I asked, "How did you know it was my sniper? Do you have friends at the airport?"

"Yes, I recently learned from a master the importance of making strategic friends." His smile was engaging.

"Why were you at my house when it exploded?" *Amenities were over.*

"Pat," Gene informed me, "Eileen and Junior are in the house. Let's take a walk. Your snipers have you covered."

He slowly walked toward the treeless horizon. At a good distance from the house he started to answer my question, "The reason I was at your house was that I was following orders. I was told to drive Gene Tanner and Bob Hill to your house, ostensibly because I knew where it was, and because they knew that you and I were friends. You weren't home yet, so we parked around the corner. I started the car when you arrived, but Hill told me to give you ten minutes alone with your wife before barging in. I liked that idea. I think that the explosion surprised Tanner. Hill was not surprised.

"However, I do think that Tanner is somehow involved with Hill in all of this. Tanner was the one who told me to 'drive the hell out of there', rather than drive to your house to help. I figured that I would be the next one who knew about the hologram belts to die. So at the first red light on a down slope, I waited for the light to turn green, pumped the accelerator, and jumped out my driver's door as the car careened down the road out of control. After I escaped, I was elated to find out that you and Dale survived."

Gene continued walking at a snail's pace down the treeless slope away from the house. He expelled a big sigh of relief. "I have been afraid that I might be killed before I could share my side of the story with you."

I was silent knowing that Gene had omitted a very important detail. Gene was used to this trait in my demeanor and forged ahead, "A Frenchman named Pierre Boudreaux was also in the car. I was told that you wanted him in the meeting."

Gene changed the subject, "How did you find me? I guess the CIA also knows where I am?"

I holstered my weapon in the back of my pants, handed Gene his Colt 45, and volunteered, "I doubt that they do."

Gene looked at me surprised, "Then how did you find me?"

I smiled, "Your CIA friend who helped us encounter the Sheik in Iraq had a Montana accent. I looked up his name on the Internet, found out he lived alone, found his address, and viola here we are. Your retreat to his house made sense."

"Damn, Pat. You recognized his Montana accent? How do you do that?"

I smiled, "Something I picked up as a kid and developed over the years."

I withdrew my sat phone and punched in a code and ventured, "Let's go back to the house. I'd like to meet Eileen and Junior. Although I must say that you should give your son a better handle than Junior: a name that gives him his own identity later in life. What is his real name?"

"Gene Kamper, Jr. I never was too happy with the name Gene. No one could call me by a decent nickname. I wanted to name him Joseph, but Eileen was adamant that he be named after me."

"What is your middle name?"

"Nicholas."

I dropped the subject.

Gene volunteered, "You do know that I would have come back to D.C. to testify on your behalf."

I stopped walking, "I believe you did a whole lot more than that."

Gene stopped and turned to me, "What do you think I did?"

I answered, "I can't think of anyone else who would take the risk and have the talent to find the missing government video tapes from the Vietnam Memorial, and then mail them to the appropriate people."

Gene smiled, "I overheard Hill talking on his sat phone when we didn't go directly to your house. I became suspicious. I got the number off his phone while he was taking a leak near your house. I tracked it after I got my family safely here. When I saw your arrest on the news, I followed up and confiscated the tapes from a house in Maryland."

I said, "Let me guess. It was Senator Dempsey's house."

Gene eyes widened in disbelief and was so confounded that he stuttered, "H…Ho…How could you possible know that?"

I chuckled, "Hill confessed to me before he passed out by the memorial that Senator Dempsey was a leader in the conspiracy."

I added with amazement, "You broke into the house of the Chairman of the Senate Armed Services Committee?"

Gene shrugged like it was no big deal. I realized the pieces were falling into place and that Gene knew more. "Who did the government contract to manufacture the belts?"

"Dynamic Industries." Gene answered without hesitation. He seemed as desperate as I was.

I knew the name. Jody and Scott had discovered the company name. It was one of the companies that Doug Benton lobbied for in D.C. I wondered if the Gambito family controlled it. If not, someone in the company had gone rogue.

"What are you going to do now, Gene? You can go back to your boss, Tom Kime, at the CIA and be rewarded for your effectiveness in saving my sorry ass."

"Pat, this is way too big for Tom Kime, and too big for you and me. I don't know who to trust. I would like to lay low for a while and raise my son here. We have grown very fond of Montana. People are much friendlier here."

I nodded. "Let's go back to the house so I can meet your son, Nicky."

Gene started to correct me and then smiled as he started retracing the hundred yards back toward the house.

Chapter 55
Montana

Jody got the code on his cell phone along with the rest of the team, and saw his dad's low security level for their approach to the house. He had argued against his dad's plan to move the family, and insisted on the sniper scenario at the Montana house. Jody wanted to be one of the snipers. He would love to pop a slug into the scull of an adversary who was present at the attempted assassination of his parents. Jody was still traumatized by seeing his exploded parents' house. But his dad insisted that Gene was innocent. His efforts to get his dad to provide a convincing explanation were thwarted by his dad's final declaration, ***"I'll know more when I talk to Gene."***

Since Dale and Mandy were flying with them, Pat ordered Jody to protect the women. His dad suggested that other adversaries may be located near the ranch house and the airport, so Jody could not turn down the assignment.

Jody was relieved when the code came through to proceed to the ranch under the lowest alert level. Dad had somehow worked his magic again. When he, his mom, and Mandy arrived at the house, his mother was relaxed when she rang the doorbell.

When a gorgeous woman opened the door, Dale explained, "I'm Dale O'Sheen . . ." and with the utmost courtesy added, ". . . and this is my son, Jody, and my daughter, Mandy."

Jody managed a proper hello, trying not to betray his attraction to the beautiful woman. The lady was gorgeous, comparable to Abdul's lover, Michelle Orleon. The small boy on her hip smiled at him.

"Hi. I'm Eileen Kamper. Please come in. I thought that might be your husband with Gene in the back. What a pleasant surprise! You all look just like Gene described you."

Jody was concerned with her calmness, considering that she should be paranoid at their unannounced arrival at their hide-away-home. She led them through the house to the kitchen while saying, "Gene told me to expect Pat to show up unannounced one day. Gene will be surprised that Pat brought his family."

Jody was suspicious of the beautiful lady's invitation into their safe house. He started to extract his Sig Sauer pistol from the back of his belt when the back door started to open.

***

Gene and I walked from the patio through the kitchen door.

Gene was shocked to see Dale. Junior squirmed in his mom's arms and reached his arms out to his father. Gene gathered him into a loving embrace.

Gene turned to me and saw the pleasure expressed in my eyes, "You s-o-b. You knew I was on your side all along: Why the charade?"

Brendan walked through the back door while I was answering, "I had to be sure that you weren't under surveillance. And I wanted to hear your side of the story before I had my family join us."

Gene reached out and pulled me into a hug. Even with his son in his arm, I felt the strength of a formidable man.

Gene withdrew from the embrace and turned to his wife and proudly handled the introduction, "Eileen, this is the infamous Pat O'Sheen."

Gene's lovely wife jumped forward and threw herself into my arms, surprising me and a slightly jealous Dale. "Thank you for saving him in Paris and sending him back home to me. Gene told me to expect you to arrive sooner or later. I am so happy that it is sooner. He has told me all he knows about you and your family. We are honored that you have trusted us by coming here."

I slowly disengaged from the embrace and looked at a grinning Gene with Junior on his hip. Junior smiled at me, and instead of a three-year-old's shyness, he held his arms out to me. I looked at Gene for approval, but Gene was already placing the three-year-old into my arms. The child put his arms around my neck and pressed his baby-soft cheek against mine. I realized that everyone in the room saw my surprise and noticed my emotional reaction to the child. I turned away while talking to the child, embarrassed that my emotions were so transparent.

Dale enlightened the Kampers, "Most children are drawn to him."

Mandy verbally agreed.

I realized that Gene had never met my daughter. I introduced them.

Although I suspected that he knew the answer, Gene asked me, "Why did you bring your family here?"

I answered, "I couldn't think of a safer place to leave my family while you help me straighten out this mess."

Now Dale fully understood the migration, and she agreed that this remote area of Montana was a safe retreat. She also knew that **retreat** wasn't in her husband's vocabulary. Her man would be leaving her and Mandy here very soon. Tension filled the room after Pat's disclosure.

Eileen was the first to break the poignant silence that followed, and she made a calming offer. "Does everyone like margaritas?" Everyone approved.

Dale volunteered to help make the drinks while Gene guided the men to the patio with his son back in his arms.

On the patio, I updated Gene on the events in North Carolina, including Abdul's involvement, the events in New York with Gambito (in strict confidence), and the events of my arrest in D.C., which Gene already knew about.

Brendan answered his vibrated phone. He relayed the message to me with two nods. *All clear,* and looked to me for approval. I nodded approval of the unasked question. Brendan spoke into the phone, "Robby, come on in."

Gene looked out into the open field where he had first seen whom he now knew was Robby setting up his snipers nest. He was surprised when Robby walked around the corner of the house rather than from the field. Pat's men were cleverly unpredictable in their protection.

Once Robby was seated, I forced Gene to describe to my group who all had witnessed the bombing of my house and saw him in the car retreating after the explosion.

Gene explained his role convincingly.

After Gene's explanation, he said that he had first called Eileen and had her take Junior from Maryland to a friend's house in Philadelphia. Then he sent an email to his boss, Tom Kime, describing the explosion that he had witnessed and the potential danger to his family. In the email he conveyed that he was taking a long overdue vacation, would be out of communication range for a while, and would check his email and voice messages periodically. He met his family in Denver where he "borrowed" an old car to prevent a paper trail, and drove them to Montana.

He explained that when he heard of Pat's arrest, he drove the "borrowed" car back to the Denver airport lot, parked it illegally hoping that the car would be returned to its rightful owner, and used a fake ID to fly to New York. Still afraid to use a traceable credit card, he "borrowed" another car at LaGuardia and drove to Maryland. He stated that I knew the rest of the story.

I encouraged him to continue.

Gene took a deep breath, not anxious to incriminate himself in front of more people about his illegal behavior, but he knew he could trust Pat's people. Gene explained about the phone number that he had retrieved off Hill's cell phone in Alabama that he later traced to Senator Dempsey. He knew that someone very powerful had prevented Pat's lawyer from obtaining the tapes from the government cameras stationed on the most filmed public arena in America. Gene explained that Senator Dempsey had been scandalously divorced a few years ago. Power entices greed and extramarital sex.

Gene was now preaching, so I pleaded, "Please continue your story."

"Congress was in session that night." Gene told them that he had no trouble breaking into the Senator's house where he found the missing tapes.

Everyone on the patio except Pat eyed him skeptically.

Gene recognized that he needed to explain. He looked at me for support, "Pat, you are a language expert. I am a security systems expert and a second story man."

"You're a thief?" Jody interrupted with fire building in his eyes. **"Dad's security system is one of the best in the world. Did you help Deputy Hill penetrate it?"**

Gene deflected Jody's biting question and continued. "I designed an almost impenetrable system in my early days at the CIA. I recognized my design soon after I arrived at Senator Dempsey house."

Jody repeated, not letting go, **"Did you help Hill penetrate my dad's security system."**

At Jody's outburst, Gene lowered his chin toward his chest. He looked back up at me instead of his accuser and said, "I didn't know the target at the time. Hill had the schematics of a complicated security system that included outside surveillance cameras. Pat, it may have been yours."

"How did Hill penetrate it?" Jody demanded.

Gene explained, still looking at me, "If it was your security system, one or two of your outside camera monitoring sensors can be occupied not allowing the other camera sensors to record. Dogs can easily be trained to occupy the cameras.

"Pat, when I detailed the method, I had no idea that it might be your house. Penetrating security is my specialty. I've analyzed hundreds of security systems for the CIA without knowing whose system was involved."

Jody started to relax, and he asked in a less demanding demeanor, "So the C4 explosives were set between the outside air conditioning condenser unit and the house, out of view of the security cameras while the cameras were scanning the movement of dogs on the other side of the house."

Gene shrugged, "That's a possibility."

Jody asked. "Who activated the trigger device on the explosives?"

I stood up and retrieved Junior from Gene's lap and walked toward the kitchen.

Gene was shocked at my sudden abandonment, hoping that I would help him recover from Jody's onslaught. "Pat?"

I ignored him and walked into the kitchen.

Gene looked back toward Jody and saw that he felt the same sense of abandonment. Gene had scanned Robby and Brendan on the way to looking back at Jody. It was obvious that these three men didn't trust him. Gene sensed that Pat trusted him but had left him with the chore of convincing a very emotional Jody, and a very intimidating Brendan. He looked at Robby. *No help there.* He looked Jody squarely in the eyes.

Jody saw pain enter Gene's eyes. It was obvious that Dad wanted him and Gene to work out their bad feelings. With his dad gone, Jody's demeanor softened. "You could have warned my dad when you followed orders to drive to his house."

Gene replied, "I tried to call him, but my sat phone wouldn't allow outgoing calls. In retrospect, I believe Hill may have blocked my phone."

Gene continued, "I was expecting a meeting. Bringing me along for a meeting with your dad made perfect sense. Hill told me that Director Collins prearranged the meeting.

"When we passed your dad's house the first time, your dad's charter jet had just recently landed, and I was ordered to stop down the street from Pat's house. I understood surveillance was prudent, similar to your groups approach to me today. After your dad arrived home, I was told to place a call into Langley to update our status. My phone would still not connect, not unlike my phone's failure in the safe-house in Paris, and the emergency call I made from your parents SUV during the chase that followed my arrival in Birmingham." Gene's voice got more animated while recalling each event.

"After your dad arrived home, Hill wanted to let your dad have ten minutes alone with his wife before we barged in."

He continued, "Hill got out of the car and made a short call. Afterward, he gave me a phone number to call to determine if my phone problem was corrected. Hill smiled while I dialed the number."

Gene Kamper stiffened, "When I punched the send button to make the call, Pat's house exploded." He choked up but managed to blurt out, "I think my call may have detonated the explosives."

Jody couldn't disagree with Gene's logic.

Brendan became a believer, but he watched warily as Jody jumped to his feet threateningly. Gene jumped up across the table from him.

Jody accused, "You have put my dad in jeopardy ever since he met you in Paris. With your CIA training, you should have known better. My dad would not have made your mistakes. I don't understand why he respects you. I almost lost my parents in that explosion. Damn the CIA and you with it."

To avoid more conflict, Jody turned and walked out into the treeless field.

Brendan saw the pain in Gene's eyes, stood up, and explained. "The explosion at his parent's is a very emotional subject. When I entered the back of the house with Jody after the explosion, I've never seen such anxiety mixed with rage in a man's face. Your recounting of the events brought back that trauma to Jody." Brendan followed Jody into the field.

Chapter 56
A plan

Brendan recalled Jody's reckless run down the mountain at the Pakistan border while he sat next to him holding on onto the ATV for dear life. When they started the protection business, Jody was inexperienced. But after the encounter in Paris, followed by the encounter in Australia, the encounter at the Pakistan boulder, and the encounter he just witnessed on the patio, Brendan had no reservations about following Jody if his dad retired. Jody had his dad's fire and guts. He didn't have Pat's relationship skills: *yet*.

Brendan was trying to frame his words as he caught up with Jody. He grabbed Jody's arm causing him to turn around threateningly with his fist cocked until he saw that it was Brendan.

Jody stood still in front of his big friend. Brendan's size and intelligence were humbling. He waited for Brendan's lecture. Instead he was enwrapped in a bear hug. Jody was determined not to be the first to release from the hug: Brendan's embrace was quelling his anger.

Brendan softly voiced into his ear, "The memory of the explosion at your parent's house still angers me, too. Don't wander too far or for too long. Your family needs your support. Kamper got your dad out of jail. He is not an enemy. Your dad brought us here believing that Gene can help your family get out of this crisis." Brendan released Jody and retreated back to the house.

Jody smiled as Brendan retreated. *What a great friend*: a great big friend.

When Brendan arrived back at the house, he assured everyone that Jody would be fine after some time alone.

Ten minutes later, while retreating further into the treeless field, Jody answered his ringing cell phone. He recognized the number and talked as he walked back toward the patio. When he entered the kitchen, he announced to his dad, "Jonny has rescheduled Keisha's European tour. They want to hire us again. We have three weeks to prepare."

Everyone noticed the prideful gleam in Jody's eyes. Jody looked directly into Gene's eyes, "You have experience in Europe. Our pay is much better than the CIA. Would you be interested in joining us?" His decision to accept Gene's explanation of his innocent involvement in the explosion of his parent's house was confirmed in the offer.

Dale objected, **"No way. Paris is where this whole nightmare began."**

I reached over and squeezed her hand, the squeeze reassuring her that we would talk about it later. I interrupted before Jody could respond. "Gene and I have more issues to deal with. But we may solve the problem in time for him to join you in Europe . . . if he is so inclined."

I stood and beckoned Gene to the patio. Brendan and Jody started to follow, but I shook my head, and they sat down at the dinette table after a small motion with my hand.

On the patio, I told Gene about Tanner's visit to me in prison, and that he had disappeared after that visit. I then told Gene, "You need to tell Tom Kime your roll in releasing the tapes to Fox News. You decide how to explain where you got them. It's the only way we can expose Senator Dempsey's involvement." I saw the discomfort in Gene's glare.

Gene said, "Pat, I know you care for my family. The senator probably assumes that whoever took the tapes from his house was the one who exposed them. He could make big trouble for my family and me. He probably reported the break-in, and I could be arrested and sent to prison."

I emphasized, "Gene, he's one of the top links. We have to expose him before our nightmare will be over . . . before the target will get off our backs. I need your help."

I understood the risk I was asking Gene to take. I did not want Jody and Brendan to be angry witnesses if Gene refused.

Gene glared at me, "Your nightmare might end, but my nightmare will continue and be much worse."

Gene walked away slowly and thought about the danger to his career and his family that Pat's request imposed. He noticed that Pat waited patiently on the patio. Pat had made his plea. He would not press the issue. Pat would accept Gene's decision and find another way without him. Gene was learning that Pat could always find another way. But if he didn't help, their friendship would be over.

Several minutes later an idea struck him like a thunderbolt from the sky. He hurried back to Pat, "There may be a better approach."

He shared his idea with Pat. Pat smiled and called Jody, Brendan, and Robby. An hour later they had agreed on a plan.

Chapter 57
Take the offense

Brendan called his father-in-law, the county sheriff, and told him to call back on a secure line.

Bo called back ten minutes later, "Brendan?"

Brendan replied, "Yes, Dad. If you are secure, I'm going to put you on speaker."

"My connection is secure. Go ahead."

Brendan disclosed all the parties who were listening on his end of the secure conversation and reintroduced Gene.

Brendan let Gene explain what he had and what we needed.

Bo responded, "I've got a dear friend in Atlanta's forensic unit who I trust totally. Their labs are very capable of lifting fingerprint off the most difficult surfaces. Let me get back to you."

Jody, Brendan, Gene, and I departed after hugs with the families. Robby stayed behind to guard the families. We entered the charter plane and flew to Denver where we dropped off Gene Kamper. The rest of us flew to Birmingham. I got off in Birmingham. Brendan and Jody flew to Atlanta, Georgia to the liaison with the sheriff's contact in Georgia's CSI unit.

Jody watched Brendan personally hand the evidence to Sherriff Hannon's friend in Atlanta's CSI office explaining that they hoped to identify all of the fingerprints on the tapes. Sherriff Hannon had downloaded a set of fingerprints from the FBI's database and sent them to his CSI friend in Atlanta without identifying the names connected to the fingerprints, he just numbered them.

Jody continued his flight on the charter jet from Atlanta to D.C.

Brendan accompanied the evidence to the forensic lab, videoing every step of the process and made sure that no one viewed the contents of the tapes recorded at the Vietnam Memorial.

Jody knew the whole exercise might be in vain. But if the Atlanta's forensic analyst found the proper fingerprints, the plan would be in motion. He needed to be in D.C. for the plan to work. He reported the progress to his dad who was eerily silent. Jody understood. Until the evidence, or lack thereof was revealed, there wasn't much he could say.

Jody was worried about fulfilling his vital role in the plan. He had covered every scenario in his mind's eye. He called Lacy and told her of his destination without a full explanation. Thankfully, she didn't interrogate him. Lacy and his mom were now becoming close friends, and his mother had apparently taught her to not dig too deeply into some of his operations. Jody called Robby in Montana. His mom appreciated the update.

Jody slept on the plane ride from Atlanta to D.C.

***

Sheriff Hannon picked me up at the Birmingham airport and drove to a remote double-trailer located on a private hunting camp in Shelby County, Alabama. He gave me keys to the old jeep parked by the hunting shack. I knew that the CIA would try to hunt me down if the fingerprints allowed me to put the threatening plan in motion.

Bo asked me, "Is Brendan going to be arrested if your plan fails?"

I looked into Bo's eyes. "I am the only one threatening our government. Jody is taking the biggest risk. Brendan is just an employee following orders."

Bo didn't doubt my love for Brendan. "What are you going to do if your plan backfires? You might be charged with treason."

"I will try to resolve this conspiracy from another country. If that happens, I hope that you will help Brendan protect my family until I resolve it?"

"What country?"

"I can't share that with you, Bo" Pat couldn't disclose that he would join his covert friends in the Mossad in Israel whom he had warned about the hologram conspiracy on his way back from destroying the hologram shipment at the Khyber Pass in Pakistan.

Jody left the plane through the large private terminal at Dulles Airport in D.C. The prearranged rent-a-car was ready and he drove to the Comfort Inn nearby as he watched for a tail. He asked the desk clerk if there were any faxes for Oliver Stone. The clerk eyed him curiously because of the famous movie director's name and handed him a small stack of papers that had come through on the hotel fax. Jody wondered if the clerk had read the faxes. If he had, he wouldn't have understood their meaning. Expediency outweighed secrecy at this point. Jody perused the faxes and drove toward Langley, Virginia.

Jody stopped a few miles down the road and studied the fax copies more carefully. He called me and told me what he had. "Dad, the faxes are incriminating, but I don't think it's enough."

I responded, "You've got enough for my threat to be taken seriously. Proceed according to the plan."

Gene Kamper had retrieved the tapes from Senator Dempsey's entertainment consol. Gene assumed that Dempsey had handled several of the tapes to watch them in his home video system. Once I learned that the senator's prints were on some of the missing memorial videocassettes, I called Gene Kamper who had arrived in Philadelphia. I simply stated, "Brilliant, Gene. We are proceeding as planned."

I was going to leave it at that when Gene said, "Jody will have a hard time selling this to the CIA. Let me make a call to help him."

"I know he can't sell it totally." I declared. "But he will raise all the red flags so that the CIA Director will take me seriously. That was our plan."

Gene was no longer afraid to challenge me, "I think that you are underestimating the danger to Jody. We may not have enough time to intercede. We need to preempt Jody's meeting, so he can get wheels turning while still assuring his safety."

"And how can we do that?" I asked, appreciating Gene's concern.

Gene said, "Are you starting to trust me now?"

He knew he had asked me a tough question. I still didn't trust anyone who worked for the government. Gene waited patiently for the answer.

Finally I replied, "Tell me what you're thinking."

After hearing it, I agreed. We both made several phone calls.

My last call was to Petrie, the right-hand man of Godfather Gambito. Petri answered in his childishly high voice as if he was glad to hear from me. I told him that I needed to talk to Gambito and that it was urgent.

Sonny got on the phone, "O'Sheen, my instincts warn me that I am not going to like what you are about to tell me."

I said, "No sir, you won't. Mr. Gambito, Senator Dempsey is about to go down with my government's help or against my government's wishes. If it's against their wishes, I am going to expose Dempsey's involvement in the Hologram Conspiracy from another country to the international community. I don't trust American politicians. After his exposure, Dempsey might take others involved in the hologram conspiracy down with him."

Sonny said, "Pat, what you're suggesting is against my wishes. Capiche?"

"I'm sorry, Sonny, but I have to protect my family. After Dempsey is exposed, I will go alone to anywhere in the world that you request. But this time I will be prepared to protect myself at the meeting place. Please take care of all the widows and children of your men that I will take to the grave with me." I disconnected.

Chapter 58
Blackmail

When Jody arrived at the gates at Langley, Schmitty asked him to step out of the car. Schmitty looked at him knowing that he looked familiar and after checking his ID. "Yes, I remember you. You're Pat O'Sheen's son."

Jody realized that it would have taken years to establish his individual identity in these covert surroundings. But for now, he was glad to be recognized as Pat O'Sheen's son. Schmitty called Tom Kime.

Jody entered the CIA headquarters and Tom Kime was awaiting him with a friendly smile.

Tom shook Jody's hand saying, "I regretted your resignation from the CIA. I was trying to get you into my group." He hesitated when Jody didn't respond, and he recognized the serious nature of this visit. Considering recent events surrounding the O'Sheens, the implication of Jody's silence unnerved him. Kime recovered, "At the gate, you said you had information from Gene Kamper?"

Jody corrected Kime's expectations, "Actually, it's not just from Gene. Can we meet somewhere in private that is not recorded?"

Tom looked at Jody suspiciously but led him to an empty meeting room off the lobby. Before Tom could pose a question, Jody handed him copies of the three faxes that he had received from Atlanta: fax copies that implicated one of the most powerful men in America.

Tom perused the papers, "Okay. Senator Dempsey's finger prints are on what."

When Jody told him, Tom immediately punched in a code on the phone on the table.

Jody knew the plan had just passed the point of no return.

When he and Tom were escorted to the most secure area, the director of the CIA and two men were seated at a conference table. Jody had never met her, but she was intimidating in a friendly sort of way. He wondered how his dad could so casually call her *Mary*.

Her demeanor softened while she watched him sit down. Tom Kime handed her the copies of the faxes. The others in the room, none of whom Jody knew, watched her intently. She read each one carefully. She didn't sit back and steep her fingers like his dad would have done, but she was obviously unnerved and went into deep thought.

She spoke aggressively, "Mr. O'Sheen, these analyses were performed in Atlanta. Are the original film cassettes still there now? Your implication is that Senator Dempsey was involved with the disappearance of the government tapes from the day Deputy Director Hill was killed next to the Vietnam Memorial."

"Yes, Ma'am. The CSI team in Atlanta has not seen the videos on the tapes. On your direction the CSI team in Atlanta will review the content of the recordings and give you a report."

Jody emphasized, "It will be obvious that they are the missing videos from government cameras surrounding the Vietnam Memorial. Those tapes would have exonerated my dad immediately following Hill's death. The faxes that lay before you are proof that Senator Dempsey's fingerprints are on some of the tapes, which proves that Dempsey was involved in their disappearance, and it also infers that the senator attempted to accuse my dad of killing Hill to keep a cover on the hologram conspiracy."

The director countered, "These tapes lost any credible chain-of-custody long ago." The director asked politely, "How did they get into your dad's hands?"

Jody didn't answer the question but boldly pronounced the crux of the issue using Abdul's British formal address for emphasis, "Madam Director, how can you explain Senator Dempsey's fingerprints on the tapes. His leadership involvement in the hologram conspiracy is now exposed. Dad asked me to inform you that a cover-up to protect Senator Dempsey will have dire consequences for the CIA and the Senate Armed Services Committee, and America's credibility around the world. And he asked me to convey a warning message to 'Mary' personally and privately."

The director understood the meaning of the familiar address: the technique that Pat had used in front of Mohammed during their communication from Jody's kidnapping. She was surprised that she was unable to read the handsome young man facing her. She was able to read the face of most people. Jody's poker face gave her no clue.

She understood that Jody was implying a specific threat from his dad who was very capable of creating international havoc if left unbridled. The fact that Pat O'Sheen's son was sitting in front of her testified to Pat's total commitment to fulfilling the threat. She pushed her chair back and stood up abruptly. "Stay seated, Jody." Every one stood and followed her from the room, leaving him alone.

Dad had instructed him how to proceed after this anticipated event. He sat calmly for twenty minutes, stood up and walked to the mirror, brushed his eyebrows, stuck out his tongue to examine it, and sat back down. Ten minutes later two guards entered the room and restrained his left wrist with a plastic cuff to the heavy chair where he sat. Jody didn't protest: if Dad was right, he knew what to expect next. He remained calm as the director entered the room with one of the security guards, made eye contact with Jody for several seconds, and ordered the security guard to leave them alone. She sat down across from Jody and waited without speaking. Jody knew the technique. He was not intimidated. He maintained eye contact with her.

The director recognized Pat O'Sheen in his son. Finally, she lowered her admiring eyes, "What is your dad's message?"

Jody stood up as much as he could under the restraints and removed a piece of paper from his crotch, placed it on the table, and sat back down.

Jody watched the director read the message without showing much reaction except a hint of anger. He suddenly worried that the plan was not going to work: Dad had misjudged the director. Perhaps she was not powerful enough in this vicious game of deadly politics: her position not quite high enough.

She grabbed a remote from the table and punched in a code. Jody feared the result.

He expected that the code she punched would bring guards in to incarcerate him. He informed her, "My lawyer is already outside the Attorney General's office. I was also followed to the gate by witnesses. You won't easily get away with my sudden disappearance."

Surprisingly, the director smiled at him. "Where is your dad?"

Jody answered honestly, "He would never send me here with knowledge of his location."

She knew enough about Pat O'Sheen to know the statement was true. "We can protect him."

Her offer seemed sincere. So sincere that Jody was wary, but he ventured, "The senator is a very powerful man. Dad would never trust the CIA to take his side against Senator Dempsey. Particularly after Deputy Director Hill bombed his house almost killing him and my mother, which happened after the CIA double-crossed him in Paris."

The director couldn't compete with Jody's logic. "I understand, Jody. The circumstances are regrettable. I'm sure your dad knows that what he is proposing in his threat could condemn him as a traitor. Your presence here makes you complicit in your dad's treason."

Jody shrugged, "I am just a messenger."

Collins stood up abruptly and left the room.

Two guards entered and informed Jody that he would be detained for the night. He was escorted to a small room. The door was locked behind him and bolted from the outside. The suite had a nice bathroom, a small, stocked refrigerator, a comfortable bed, and a 42" flat screen TV. There were no windows.

The next morning, Jody was shocked when the director walked into his room alone and unannounced. Jody had just finished his shower. She courteously averted her stare from his nakedness and turned away to allow him to wrap a towel around his waist. She sat down.

Jody walked across the room to the small refrigerator in an attempt to hide his embarrassment, grabbed a small bottle of orange juice, and sat down across from her with his knees held tightly together under the short towel like he imagined the nuns taught little girls to do under their skirts in grade school.

Collins started, "I'm sorry to barge in on you like this, but according to your dad's message time is running out. You need to contact him immediately to buy me more time." She looked at his muscular bare thighs.

Jody noticed. He sipped the orange juice before responding, "Time may have already run out. My dad is not a patient man. Not allowing me to contact him for so many hours may have been a mistake on your part."

Jody offered. "I can only contact him if you return my cell phone. Without it I can't reach him." Jody conjectured, "I assume you were unable to track him down overnight."

She failed to hide a slight smile at his correct assumption, but she didn't buy the phone story. She held up the cell phone. "You bought this phone at a convenience store thirty minutes before you arrived here. You can call your dad on any phone of your choice."

Jody countered, "Before I arrived at your headquarters, that phone was encoded from the other end and is the only one I can use to contact him. Any other attempt to contact him will result in an international full disclosure of the Hologram Conspiracy. My dad doesn't make mistakes . . . nor does he make idle threats."

He noticed her disappointment so he said, "I'm sure your people have tried to decode that phone. You are right to worry about the time constraints. You must agree to Dad's terms to expose Senator Dempsey or risk international exposure of America's top secret weapon security leak."

She handed the cheap cell phone to him, "Tell your dad that he has my total support."

Jody corrected her transparent ploy, "This phone only allows two responses: a number for yes that you will expose Dempsey and a different number for no."

Jody stood, knowing that the towel was too small to be modest while rising from his chair. "Time *is* short. You know what my dad is asking of you. I'll dress while you decide."

She watched his muscular back, tight hamstrings, and bulging calves as he grabbed his clothes from the bed and entered the bathroom. She took a deep breath reigning in her hormones and drew her mind back to the present crisis. She decided to leave the room knowing that Jody would never offer to help her gain control over his dad.

***

Brendan called me from Atlanta to see if I had heard from Jody. And he relayed the report he had received from Gene Kamper.

I listened to Brendan's report and asked, "Is Gene's extraction plan intact?"

Brendan answered, "Yes. Have you made your decision?"

I failed to hide my frustration, "No, I am still waiting for Jody's signal."

Brendan said, "Gene is in position. But will he be willing to stick out his neck for Jody?"

I answered the best I could, "I believe that he will."

My instincts told me that we were taking the best course of action. It was not in my nature to retreat and hide from a long term threat. Unexpected aggression from us was our only advantage against the U.S. Government's immense power.

***

Jody was alone when he exited the bathroom: the director had left. He tried the door and was not surprised that he was still a prisoner. Fortunately, he had kept the cheap cell phone with him when he retreated to the bathroom. Maybe Director Collins had forgotten about the phone. *Unlikely!*

He was in the CIA headquarters. Blocking or intercepting his outgoing signal would be child's play in this setting. Never the less, he punched in the numbers of the code to transmit and held his thumb over the # button, which was the "*No*" button, while positioning himself by the door. He knew the cameras had betrayed his intentions, and he expected a guard to enter quickly.

More quickly than he expected, the door opened. He put the phone in his pocket with his thumb still on the # button. To Jody's surprise, it was Tom Kime who opened the door.

They walked down the hallway together. Jody whispered to Kime, "Where are we going?"

331

"You are being released."

Jody pressed the # button on the cell phone—*NO*—and he spoke quietly, "Tom?"

Jody stopped walking and waited for eye contact. Tom turned toward him almost mournfully—his expression answered any and all questions except one—would Jody die inside the gates or be allowed to be the fox on the run outside the gates. He hoped the latter.

It seemed that they were walking interminably slow as they walked toward the front door. Gene Kamper burst through the front door and upon seeing Tom Kime exclaimed, "I'm back." He hugged an un-bewildered Tom Kime and whispered in his ear. Jody recognized that the exchange was not un-expected.

Tom answered audibly, "I've already arranged it."

Tom punched his cell phone and made a quick declaration into the phone. Less than a minute later, Gene, Tom, and Jody were escorted through the many checkpoints to the most secure room again.

Jody knew that Gene had just risked his career and perhaps his freedom. He couldn't look into Gene's eyes, afraid that his gratefulness would be transparent to the many cameras. When he finally built up his courage, his eyes met Gene's for a fleeting moment. Instead of the anxiety that he expected in Gene's eyes, he saw amusement. He got an eerie feeling that instead of looking at Gene, he was looking into his dad's confident eyes. *What were Gene and his dad planning now?*

While they were going through another interrogation, the director suddenly stormed into the room. The tone in her voice changed Gene's confident demeanor when she demanded. "Where is Pat O'Sheen?"

Gene responded, "I assume he is in Alabama with his family."

"No, he is not. Where is he?" Her anger was threatening.

Jody saw the concern in her face and asked, "What has happened?"

She explained, "Senator Dempsey was found dead in his home thirty minutes ago. Where were you last night?" She looked at Gene for the answer knowing Jody's location last night eliminated him as a suspect.

"I spent the night with friends in Philadelphia and drove straight here this morning. Why do you ask? Was the Senator murdered?"

The director was able to read innocence in Gene's face. "The initial coroner's report suggests his death was from natural causes. The police saw no evidence of foul play. But in this room, we know how sudden death can be inflicted and disguised as natural. There will be a complete autopsy performed immediately. You both are to remain here until it is completed."

She looked at Jody. "Your dad will be the main suspect if the autopsy suggests a possibility of foul play. In the interim, you will both have to answer many more questions." She started to leave the room.

Tom Kime interrupted her departure and told the director that Gene had convinced Pat to call her, and that Pat was waiting for Gene's signal.

"How will he contact me?" She demanded—her anger still on the surface.

Gene admitted, "He didn't tell me, but I am sure that he will find a way."

She said, "Let's do it. Follow me to my office."

When they were in her office, Gene signaled Pat with a code in his cell phone.

Collins knew Gene's expertise and asked, "Did you retrieve the video cassettes from Senator Dempsey's house?"

Gene got a slight gleam in his eyes, "Is this conversation being recorded?"

"Yes." She didn't press for an answer to her question. But she saw the answer in Gene's eyes.

The director told Gene, "You are taking a big risk by collaborating with the O'Sheens at this time. It might cost you your career and maybe your freedom."

Gene smiled, "My parents taught me that the righteous path was often the toughest path to follow."

Mary didn't manage to totally hide her approving smile.

Chapter 59
Surprise

I drove the old jeep to a pay phone near Sheriff Hannon's office and called CIA headquarters. I dialed an emergency code number into the phone and was surprised by the quick response. I identified myself with Gene's CIA code number using Gene's voice and accent.

I reflected on the quick response to the urgent code and the lack of response to the entries Gene had made during the critical encounters of the past few weeks. When a controller answered my call, I asked for Director Collins.

I was relieved when the director took my call. She didn't put me on a speakerphone, so I assumed she was in her office. I got straight to the point. "Director Collins, I assume that you were not convinced by the evidence that my son brought to you?"

A very tired voice came back to me. "Where are you, O'Sheen? And how did you get Kamper's code number?" She looked across the desk at Kamper.

I ignored her last question. "I am sure that you were informed that my call comes from Alabama."

"And I am sure you arranged for an Alabama number to show up on our system to give you cover for Senator Dempsey's death: a very transparent ploy."

The DCI heard a gasp and sat up straighter. The Senator's death had not been released to the media yet. She realized that Pat didn't know. She waited through his silence before finally asking, "What is the purpose of your call?"

The answer was totally out-of-character and subdued, "I am at a loss of how to proceed."

His inability to articulate the purpose of his call was convincing. Pat O'Sheen, who intrigued her from their first encounter and every following conversation, was not a man who would call unprepared. Her disclosure of the senator's death derailed him. She waited patiently to hear what his response would be.

I recovered from the shocking news, and said. "Apparently, my threat to make you disclose Senator's Dempsey's involvement in my imprisonment is a moot point." I asked, "Is Jody safe?"

"Yes, Jody is safe," she responded and disconnected, knowing that the call was being recorded.

She smiled at Gene, convinced that neither Pat O'Sheen nor Gene Kamper was involved in the senator's death.

Director Collins had never met anyone with the gonads or cunning to take on some of the most powerful people in the federal government like Pat O'Sheen and Agent Kamper had just done.

She hoped that she could utilize the incredible skills of Pat O'Sheen in the future. She would have to convince Pat of her loyalty first.

Later that day, when Jody was released after the results of the autopsy showed no evidence of foul play, Tom Kime again accompanied him to the CIA front door. This time he bade Jody farewell with a warm and admiring smile saying, "It seems that events have worked out well for your family."

His voice changed to a more formal business mode, "I would like you to consider rejoining the agency to work for me." He added, "The director has already given her approval."

Jody smiled, "Thank you, Tom. I'll consider your offer if these high seas buffeting my family ever calm down."

Tom's warmness encouraged Jody to ask, "Is Gene in trouble?"

Tom replied, "He has a lot of explaining to do. But he is like your dad. He'll come out smelling like a rose. He understands that honesty will eventually win the day."

Once Jody got outside the Langley gates, he called me.

I welcomed Jody's report, but didn't ask for details on Jody's unsecured phone. I told him that I would instruct the plane to pick him up at the Ronald Reagan Airport.

Sheriff Bo Hannon and I watched the report on the network news of Senator Dempsey's death from natural causes. I would never know whether the senator had died coincidently from natural causes at this critical moment in time as reported, or whether the CIA or the Gambito family acted to deflect the international disclosure that I had threatened. I didn't believe in coincidences. My threat was made clear to Director Collins when Jody presented my written message to her. I had also made my intentions crystal clear to Godfather Gambito.

I knew that the story of Senator Dempsey's involvement in a diabolical, worldwide conspiracy would never be told. The bigger question to me was troubling: was the senator's death the end of the nightmare? Who else was involved in the conspiracy? At least for now I sensed that I was free and clear and that my family was safe from the CIA and the Gambito organization.

Chapter 60
A month later

Keisha's concert tour in Europe was preceding incident free. Jody reported the normal, over-aggressive behavior of some fans in Frankfort, Germany, and in Paris, and the usual difficulty of handling "important" people trying to be recognized and photographed with the blossoming new international star.

Jody made a heartfelt prediction as Dale and I shared his enthusiasm on my cell phone's speaker, "She has a unique quality that supersedes her talent. Her music composition and her lyrics capture her audience's hearts. I become so engrossed in her performances that I have to fight the temptation to forget to scan for possible threats.

"Dad, she always asks about you. I am sure you will be asked to participate in her next tour. Jonny (Keisha's manager) is starting to believe that your presence no longer presents a danger to her. He always asks about you, too."

Dale looked up at me with eyes that expressed love and contentment. She offered, "Jody, maybe we can all get together at our house when y'all return to Alabama."

Pierre and Kathie smiled at us when Jody disconnected. The Boudreauxs had accompanied Dale and me as we covertly attended Keisha's concert in Paris the previous night. Dale enjoyed me disguising her, and she touched up my disguise and hers to her tastes.

We all agreed on Keisha's success possibilities over cocktails in the Boudreaux's kitchen as Dale helped Kathie prepare a gourmet meal.

Chapter 61
Celebration

After Keisha finished her successful European tour, we celebrated at our mostly rebuilt house. Only Dale worried about some imperfections caused by the explosion. The repairs were almost complete. Gene Kamper had suggested that I put up infrared security around my property and gave me the manufacturer and model numbers of the instruments he recommended. I bought the equipment, and earlier that day, Gene helped me install it. He had already upgraded the security system at Jody's house.

Keisha Steele jumped into my arms when she and Jonny arrived. She looked at Dale somewhat embarrassed until Dale quickly approached, hugged her, and expressed her heartfelt congratulations on her highly acclaimed European tour.

We all gathered around my Grosspoppi's large dining room table. Fortunately, the explosion only slightly damaged the heavy oak dining room suite. We squeezed eleven around the table designed for ten.

I was on cloud nine. Four generations of my family had celebrated special moments of my family's lives around this table. *Tonight was definitely high on the list of my special moments.*

I set up card tables in the adjoining living room for the overflow crowd.

Dale and I sat at opposite ends of the extended table as a king and his queen should. Our two sons, Scott and Jody sat next to me with Lacy sitting next to her fiancé. Keisha and Jonny sat across from each other. Mandy sat next to Dale with an empty chair next to her that was reserved for Robby. Brendan sat next to Jimmy Sue, who was holding their newborn son in her lap. Sherriff Bo "Papaw" Hannon and his wife Ruth sat on the overflow table with their other grandchildren. Gene and Eileen Kamper sat at the other overflow table with Nicky in Gene's arms.

Robby, who was outside instructing the sheriff's off-duty deputies on how to protect the perimeter, finally joined the gathering.

Once Robby sat down next to Mandy, we were ready to enjoy one of Dale's great dinners.

Gene Kamper and his wife Eileen proposed a toast.

Gene raised his glass. "Although this family is far from poetic, you all encompass the true essence of poetic altruistic vision. We are honored to be included in this gathering."

Jody laughed a bit too loudly, "Gene, you haven't yet experienced one of my mom's great meals. For god's sake sit down before it gets cold. As my granddad would have said, 'Good bread, good meat, good God, let's eat.'" He laughed again, looked at me, and then bowed his head for the formal blessing.

Keisha, Jonny, Bo Hannon and his wife, and Brendan's older kids stood around the table.

I smiled and slowly scanned the room, taking a second or two to look into each person's eyes. Every one of them looked at me expressing undeserved love and admiration.

Dale knew me and saw what was coming; so she stood-up, walked around the table, and put her left arm around my shoulders just as a big tear rolled down my cheek. Dale grabbed my hand as I lowered my head to pray the formal blessing. I coughed and swallowed three times attempting to clear the lump from my throat.

When Dale squeezed my shoulder, I managed to start, "Bless us oh Lord and these Thy gifts, which we are about to receive from Thy bounty . . .

The End

Please read the following preview of the second novel in the hologram trilogy

Hologram Deception
A Pat O'Sheen thriller

Chapter One
Place Unknown

I awoke with my bladder screaming urgently. The surroundings were totally unfamiliar. There was only one light in the area, and it guided me to a bathroom. Halfway through the bladder release I realized that my mind was muddled. I couldn't recall where I was.

After flushing the toilet, I lowered the seat by habit. I tried to make sense of that action. It came to me that there must be a woman in my life. But I couldn't make sense of that either—*what woman*? I turned the light on over the sink, turned on the water, and washed my hands: *another habit.* I looked in the mirror without forethought and gasped. I took two steps back defensively and instinctively reached for the Glock 22 pistol in the holster in the small of my back, which of course was not attached to my naked torso. I didn't recognize the fifty-year-old man with slightly graying hair looking over the sink at me. The man in the mirror mimicked my surprise and movements. I raised my left hand slowly turning my palm toward the mirror. The image in the mirror too perfectly mimicked my movements. I realized that I was the old man in the mirror. In my head I was in my 30's, but the guy in the mirror looked 50.

I exited the bathroom distraught, found my clothing, and dressed in the small amount of light trickling into the room from the bathroom. Then I closed the bathroom door to extinguish the light and allowed my eyes to adjust to the darkness before approaching the window. *Why? I had no clue.* I was operating on instinct and sensed a need to escape. *Escape from what? From where? From whom?*

Pulling back the edge of the curtains I saw a man leaning on the railing and smoking a cigarette directly in front of the door to my room. I went to the door and noticed it was held open with the bolt lock extended inside the doorframe to assure that the door would not close.

The doorknob was six inches from the wall with a light switch on the wall above it and two feet from the door. From where I stood in the room, I would be blocked from view by the opening door if the man entered the room. *What should I do?*

Still operating on instincts, I pulled the drawstring to open the curtains far enough to see the man on the balcony. Without a plan, I grabbed a lamp off the small table by the window, jerked the electric cord from the wall, and threw the cheap glass lamp across the small room smashing it against the wall near the door.

The man on the balcony ran to my door while pulling a pistol from his waist: *he was obviously not here to protect me.* As he reached through the door toward the light switch, I kicked my right heel against the opening door, and his head was slammed between the door and the door frame. The door recoiled back into the room, and the man fell unconsciously to the floor with the upper half of his body in the room.

After dragging him all the way into the room, I retracted the bolt and swung the door closed. I retrieved his pistol from the floor, searched him, and took his cell phone and a two-way radio. He had no wallet or other identification. I ran out the door and down the balcony of what I recognized as a cheap motel. I saw the high roof of a van parked below the balcony railing. I catapulted over the railing onto the roof of the old vehicle and slid off the cab to the tarmac below while looking for my next destination. I ran to the darkest area that was visible from my perspective.

Once I was in a small stand of trees, I released the clip on the absconded German Luger pistol. All of the bullets were still in the magazine. I slammed the magazine back into the grip as a warning to anyone nearby and ran as fast as I could manage through the wooded area toward the noise of trucks traveling on a nearby highway. When I reached the highway a quarter mile away, I was sweating. It must be summer. I noticed a bridge to my right and ran toward it, hoping to get under the bridge without being seen.

There was a very steep slope at the edge of the bridge. The highway lighting didn't illuminate the terrain below, so I sat down and slid down the steep slope on my butt. I knew the risk—if I failed to see a cliff drop-off, or even if I saw it and couldn't stop my slide, I could plunge to my death.

The terrain leveled twenty feet down and my semi-controlled slide slowed to a stop. I listened while waiting for my eyes to adjust to the darkness.

When the underside of the bridge came into focus, I ran underneath it. I stood motionless, listening while I caught my breath and wondering what to do next. Somehow I knew that I had never been in such bad physical shape in my life: albeit a life I couldn't recall. I discarded the cell phone and the radio that could be traced, and I tucked the gun under the back of my belt.

Without consciously making the decision, I scaled a vertical I-beam pier to an H-Beam girder 12 feet above me. From my higher vantage point, I could see a navigable river that ran under the bridge and the skyline of a city on the far side of the river.

I was probably safe for a while in my current position. But without forethought, I involuntarily slid underneath the H-beam. Hanging like a bug I used both hands and both feet on the bottom flange of the large H-beam and slowly traversed from the edge of the bridge to a point over the middle of the river. *Now what?*

I moved my left hand under the beam to a position next to the grip of my right hand. The pistol slipped from under my belt. I almost lost my grip in an instinctive move to grab the gun before it fell into the river below. I reestablished a firm grip and took a deep, shaky breath.

I released my feet one at a time from the beam, and slowly lowered them to hang vertically from the beam over the middle of the river below. I was exhausted and considered dropping into the river. Instead, I decided to try one time to climb up onto the beam, suspecting that my muscular exhaustion would not permit a second try. I hung straight down and pulled up with all my remaining strength in an attempted gymnastic kip to get my elbows above my hands. I managed to get my right elbow above my right hand, swung my right knee and foot onto the beam, and clambered onto the large steel flange. Tucked onto the beam, I paused to catch my breath. I was totally exhausted but felt safe: *no one would find me here.*

I was almost asleep, wedged comfortably on the H-beam, when I saw a high-powered light shine from the surface of the bridge directly above me. The light searched the waters and banks of the river below. After several minutes the searchlight was extinguished. I relaxed as best I could on the hard steel beam and fell asleep.

I was startled awake by a tugboat passing under the bridge. The sun was just starting to rise in the morning sky.

Where was I?

My instincts told me to recover my logic before moving, but my mind wouldn't think logically. I stared up at the bottom of the bridge above me and then peered over the edge of my perch and pulled my head back quickly when I realized how high I was above the river below. *How did I get here? Why was I here?*

Who am I?

I looked at the back of my hands without recognition and turned my hands over to look at the palms with the same result. The unanswered questions caused me to sit up abruptly. My sight started swimming in circles, mimicking the circular pattern of the thoughts running around in the whirlpool of my brain. The best my mind could reason was that I had been drugged and was trying to escape. I brought my feet up and untied my shoelaces, removed my tennis shoes, and tied my shoes around my belt with the shoelaces. I removed my socks and stuck them both into one shoe. *Why? I had no idea.*

I looked at the river below to make sure there were no motor craft on the water and frightfully realized what my instincts were about to make me do.

My mind screamed as I slid off the beam falling feet first toward the river forty feet below.

Hologram Deception: Coming soon

Made in the USA
Monee, IL
07 July 2026